M000195853

My Brother's
Best Friend

My Brother's Best Friend is published under Emerge, a sectionalized division
under Di Angelo Publications, Inc.

Emerge is an imprint of Di Angelo Publications.
Copyright 2022.
All rights reserved.
Printed in the United States of America.

This book is a work of fiction. Names, characters, places and incidents are either
the products of the author's imagination or used fictionally, and any resemblance
to actual persons, living or dead, business establishments, events, or locales is
entirely coincidental.

Di Angelo Publications
4265 San Felipe #1100
Houston, Texas 77027

Library of Congress
My Brother's Best Friend
First Edition
ISBN: 978-1-942549-84-0

Words: Karla De La Rosa
Cover Design: Savina Deianova
Interior Design: Kimberly James
Editors: Elizabeth Geeslin Zinn, Ashley Crantas

Downloadable via Kindle, iBooks, NOOK and Google Play.

No part of this publication may be reproduced, distributed, or transmitted in any
form or by any means without the prior written permission of the publisher except
in the case of brief quotations embodied in critical reviews and certain other
noncommercial uses permitted by copyright law. For permission requests, contact
info@diangelopublications.com.

For educational, business, and bulk orders, contact
sales@diangelopublications.com.

1. Young Adult Fiction --- Romance --- General
2, Young Adult Fiction --- Romance --- Contemporary
3. Young Adult Fiction --- Social Themes --- Dating & Sex

My Brother's Best Friend

KARLA DE LA ROSA

To my muses. My friends. And myself.

PROLOGUE

It was towards the end of my freshman year, and, as usual, I was scrolling through Instagram, watching as my feed filled with nearly identical photos. The girls in my grade, who had all changed their profile pictures countless times in the last hour, were all posting selfies with the same pose on the same local beach and the same cheesy song lyrics in the caption. I sighed. The boys in my grade weren't much better—an endless stream of boasting about how much money they were making and how frequently they were getting laid.

I rolled my eyes, scrolling continuously. I often contemplated deleting my account, but something about the site had me hooked. Then, the front door slammed, snapping me out of my mindless swiping. Footsteps stomped towards the hallway.

I got up from my bed, knowing it had to be my older brother,

Dylan, trudging up the stairs. My parents wanted the dishes done before they returned from some outing with their co-workers, and it was Dylan's turn. The second I opened my bedroom door, my brother stopped. But I was surprised to see he had a guest: another boy.

"Great, what do you want?" Dylan scoffed, his shaggy black hair falling messily over his eyes. He crossed his arms at me, eyes narrowed.

I dramatically ignored his attention, purposefully looking over the guy with him, whose curls fell about his face, before finally glancing back to Dylan.

"Nothing," I said, "I just wanted to tell you it's your turn to do the dishes."

"Bullshit, I did them last night."

"Actually, that was me; you haven't done them since Wednesday."

"Christ, Carter, I'll do them later." He sighed as he continued toward his bedroom. The boy slowly followed, offering me a slight smile.

After another hour of browsing YouTube and tragically returning to Instagram, I was bored out of my skull. As if presenting a cure for the monotony, my old LG phone vibrated. I snatched it as a slew of messages from my best friend buzzed across the screen.

Mitchell: carter

Mitchell: sos

Mitchell: my dad is marrying gabriella santos

Me: who's that?

Mitchell: it's elizabeth's mother

Mitchell: fucking elizabeth de leon

Mitchell: god out of all ppl my dad decided to marry the wicked witch of west's mother

Mitchell: now I have to consider her """family""" and refer to her as my """stepsister"""

Mitchell: I almost puked just spelling out those godawful words

Mitchell: pls kill me

Me: sorry to hear that

Mitchell: thnx I can almost feel ur sympathy over the phone

Me: I don't see why you don't like her

Me: elizabeth is really nice

Mitchell: carter r u serious

Mitchell: ugh it's just an act

Mitchell: she's a stuck-up bitch & I know it

Me: takes one to know one

Mitchell: wow rUde

I laughed, tossing my phone onto my bed. I made my way downstairs, stomach grumbling, to find that the kitchen was already occupied.

The countertop was cluttered with jars, bottles, random assortments of bread crackers, and a half-peeled banana. The fridge was being ransacked, the door shielding Dylan from my exasperation.

"You don't have time for dishes, but you have time to raid the fridge? You know that every plate you use is only gonna add on to what you have to clean."

My smirk morphed into a chagrined gape as the fridge door closed and I realized it wasn't my brother at all. The random boy I'd seen upstairs stood up, his olive eyes meeting mine. Suddenly self-conscious in his presence, I realized just how cute he was. A dimple-dented grin slyly appeared on his face, making my stomach flutter.

"Oh, I'm sorry, I thought you were my brother," I apologized with a sheepish smile.

The boy merely shrugged it off. "It's okay. You actually just missed him. He was down here, hence the mess."

"That explains a lot," I said. "So, you're a new friend of my brother's." I watched the boy lean against the counter and start brushing crumbs into a pile. "In fact, you might just be his *only* friend. You don't have to play nice out of pity. He's kind of a dick." I whispered the last part for effect.

He laughed. "You're cute. But actually, we've been friends for a while. This is the first time I've been to your guys' house, though."

"Really? Funny. Dylan never mentioned you."

"Yeah, you either." He smiled again, and my insides suddenly forgot their place in my stomach.

"Do you go to the same school as us?" I asked, somewhat in wonder of the effect he had on me. "Because I've never seen you around."

"Yeah. I didn't know you went there, either." He chuckled. "Freshman?"

"Sadly, yes. You?"

"Sophomore."

"Dude!" my brother called from upstairs. "Are you coming?"

The boy looked across the counter, then at me.

"I'm not even surprised; he treats everyone like his maid." I shrugged at the boy. "Go, it's fine."

"No way, I can't leave you to pick this up by yourself," he said with wide-eyed sincerity.

"Oh, I'm not cleaning this up," I said, shaking my head. "I'm leaving this for my mom to see. Dylan will be running down here the moment she pulls up to the house."

The boy laughed again, then regarded me with his head tilted to the side. "I guess I better get upstairs, then."

I nodded. A brief silence fell before I took a step towards him and held my hand out to properly introduce myself. "I'm Carter, by the way. Dylan's sister, obviously."

With a sweet smile on his lips, he gently placed his hand in mine. The warmth sent goosebumps up my arms.

"Nice to meet you, Carter. I'm Harry."

ONE

2 years later

"Carter!"

I growled from underneath the covers, knowing my brother would march in regardless of if I was napping. Right on cue, the door banged open. Dylan lived his entire life twelve decibels louder than everyone else.

"Hey, Carter, have you seen my Xbox controller?"

"No? Why would I have it?"

"Dude, I was just asking. I need it," he said. "Harry's coming over. Wanted to show him something cool. I finally have the newest COD and—"

"Okay, Dylan, that's great and all, but I really don't care—better yet—don't *know*—about that stuff."

"My old Xbox is wasted on you."

I looked over at the console, which I had hardly used since my sophomore year began. My parents had encouraged—or rather, forced—my brother to give it to me, along with some of his hand-me-down games, after he'd received the latest generation. But I didn't bother with any of the games; I only turned on the system to get to Netflix.

"I use it—not as much as you, obviously—but I also have a life compared to you."

Dylan threw himself across my bed, bouncing me out of my comfortable position.

"Seriously, Dyl? Can you like, *leave?*"

"Have you seen my controller?"

"I told you, *no.* God, just use mine!" I groaned in annoyance.

"No way." He shook his head with a disgusted expression. "Yours is white—it's too feminine for my liking."

I gave him a puzzled look. "That's the stupidest thing you've ever said. And you say a lot of stupid shit."

"No, it's not. It's literally girly." He scoffed.

"Dylan, you're *literally* refusing to use an inanimate object for its color, claiming it's too feminine. It's white. It's not like it's pink. Even if it were, you shouldn't have a fit about it. Because it's just a color—"

"All right!" He held his hands up in surrender. "Geez, *Mom.* I don't need a life lesson. I was just saying black makes me feel more masculine."

"Oh my god, Dylan, it's *just* a color—"

"Jeez, Carter, chill." Dylan laughed, only aggravating me more. "Look, I don't wanna use it, okay? Besides, I can't. I don't think I can use the old controller for the new system."

I shook my head, choosing to drop the subject before saying, "Okay, whatever. Shouldn't you be studying for your SATs, anyway? Mom and Dad said you really need to tighten up since you didn't take it last year."

Dylan scoffed. "I don't need to study for the SATs, Carter. It's like baby stuff, junk I already know."

"Dylan, you can't just Christmas tree your answers," I scolded him. "The school year is almost done, you're about to graduate. You really need to get your shit together." It was a miracle my brother had even made it this far in high school, considering his grades were always marked as "Nonproficient."

A scowl furrowed his eyebrows. "Well, what about you? I don't see you studying, and you're about to be a senior."

Dylan smirked, and the joy of being able to ruin his argument bubbled up inside me. "Sweet, sweet brother of mine. Your attempt at trying to turn this around on me is *so* cute. I already took my SATs in February."

Dylan's face dropped instantly. He grumbled nonsensically as he got up off my bed and made his way out of my bedroom.

Half an hour later, the doorbell rang, and within moments, my brother was running down the stairs to answer it. Just from that, I could already tell who was there. I stood up to lock my bedroom door before plopping back down on my bed, where I saw Mitchell had texted me.

Mitchell: carter

Mitchell: are you busy?

Mitchell: carterrr

Mitchell: why am I even asking I know ur reading some stupid book

Mitchell: can I come over

Mitchell: i rlly don't wanna be home, especially since elizabeth is locked in her bedroom blasting her shitty music

Mitchell: therefore I have no one else to bother

Mitchell: except you of course

Mitchell: but yet you aren't answering my messages

Mitchell: which proves your reading some lame fUCKING BOOK

Mitchell: screw it i'm coming over

I checked the time the texts had delivered and realized they'd been sent almost fifteen minutes ago; Mitchell would be here any second. He only lived a few blocks away, so I was sure he'd walk. Within minutes, the doorbell rang, and this time I was the one dashing down the stairs.

"I'm guessing you just read your messages, which does not surprise me at all," Mitchell remarked. He brushed past me and darted up the stairs to my bedroom. He practically lived here, so it was normal for him to barge in as if he owned the place.

My parents were okay with Mitchell's frequent presence, especially ever since he came out and they no longer had to hyper-analyze all the time we spent hidden up in my room. My brother had it in his head that Mitchell might find him attractive, so his general demeanor towards him was rooted in narcissism. Mitchell, for his part, had never changed over the years; he'd only flourished.

I walked in to find Mitchell lounging on my beanbag chair, his feet kicked up on my bed, typing away at his phone.

"Nice outfit," he commented without ever looking up from the screen.

I looked down at my tank top and old gym shorts, emblazoned with our middle school logo.

"What do you expect me to wear? A gown? It's just you, anyway," I muttered, making him shake his head with a smirk. "Who're you texting, anyway?" I laid down on my bed and propped my head up on my hand. "Is it a *secret lover* I don't know about?"

"*Ew*, as if. It's Elizabeth asking where I am." He sighed.

An aggressive, muffled shouting across the hall startled us, and we both jumped a little.

"*YES. Dude, I fucking knew they were going to score!*"

"Ryan owes me thirty dollars!"

"Who else is here?" Mitchell asked.

"The doofus and his partner in crime," I grumbled, ashamed they had made me jump like that.

"Should've known. He's always here. Not that I mind," Mitchell remarked, shrugging as he continued to text.

"Not even gonna bother to ask why, since I probably already know the answer," I said, flipping on the TV.

"As you should," Mitchell quipped.

Mitchell made it halfway through one of my favorite old movies before he broke.

"I can't believe you consider this funny; this is like, the worst cult movie ever!"

"What? It's hilarious! You just have no sense of humor," I retorted in defense of *Jay and Silent Bob Strike Back.*

Mitch grimaced, mocking a look of disgust. "The movie was so awful that I honestly don't feel the need to argue."

I shoved him playfully. "You're the worst."

"Yeah, I know. But anyway, can you, like, feed me now? I've been here for over an hour and your guest of honor is starving."

I groaned as I got up. "For as much time as you spend here, you'd think you'd make your own food by now. I'll be right back."

Nothing looked appealing in the fridge. Before too long, I heard footsteps enter the kitchen. "Mitch, I told you I was gonna be right back with snacks," I said, moving around a few containers as I searched the back for something edible.

"Cool, what're we having?" a not-so-soft voice asked.

I spun around, finding the one person I tried my best to avoid, leaning against the counter. He was smirking, as he always was.

Harry Evander.

Dylan's best friend. When I'd first met Harry, he was the sweetest. So sweet I wound up having a massive crush on him. He may or may not have felt the same way; it was hard to tell. We exchanged private smiles and flirty glances, the secret winks he'd send my way every now and then making my heart seize. He was hard to resist.

But then, summer came, and everything changed.

At the beginning of the school year, news broke that the former cheerleading captain, Stacy Kavanaugh, had been caught cheating on her longtime boyfriend, Danny Hughes. Danny and Stacy graduated as the most popular couple last year, and she'd been seen with some sophomore. And that sophomore had turned out to be Harry.

Harry denied it, but everyone knew how charming he was. It hurt knowing I wasn't the only one infatuated with him—but then again, how could I be?

When Danny found out, he'd tracked Harry down and beaten him so bad that his mother pressed assault and battery charges against Danny, who was lucky enough to only serve a couple months in juvie since he was still seventeen at the time. Harry's face was purple and black for weeks; apparently, he hadn't put up much of a fight. People found it strange. I wasn't there when it happened, but from what I heard, all Harry had done was deny everything while Danny pummeled him to the ground. Stacy went off to college shortly after.

For a while, Harry secluded himself and didn't speak to anyone. But, his stoic acceptance of his consequences and his following silence only attracted more attention. At the start of his junior year, Harry had, in my humble opinion, become an arrogant dick. Even with me. My crush turned to disgust, and our brief conversations outside of Dylan's earshot turned from genuine intrigue to terse, stinging commentary and harsh rebukes.

There was even a period of time in the middle of last year where I didn't see him around the house for a while; apparently, he'd made a risky remark about me to Dylan. My brother refused to tell me what he'd said, but I'd heard Harry had made a passing comment about me not being as easy as other girls. Naturally, he and Dylan had stopped hanging out for a while. I was offended, sure, but I couldn't help feeling a thrill at the knowledge he was thinking of me. Although, it also made me wonder just many girls he'd been with.

A few weeks later, he and Dylan evidently made up, and he hadn't been quite as big of an asshole since. But there were still constant rumors of who Harry might be sleeping around with, continuing to boost his ego and aggravate me more. Even when he'd started dating Jenna Montgomery last year, the whispers and gossip only lessened a tiny bit.

And here he was, leering at me in the kitchen, the very place I'd first developed a crush on him. "I thought you were Mitchell," I mumbled, pulling out a container of strawberries from the fridge. Before I could grab any, Harry snatched one and quickly devoured it before tossing the stem in the trash.

"You're such a pig."

"How? I didn't toss it on the floor."

"You also didn't wash the strawberry you just ate."

Harry rolled his eyes, attempting to pick at another one until I swatted his hand away. "Strawberries come from the farmers market," he protested. "They're already washed there."

"Yeah, but then they go through a process. They don't stay clean forever, Harry," I explained, finally plucking one and rinsing it before taking a bite.

"Dylan got boring. He started texting Lindsay and forgot I was even in the room."

I grabbed a package of popcorn from the cupboard and started microwaving it.

"Don't you do that to him when you text Jenna?"

Jenna Montgomery.

Harry's supposed girlfriend—though he always denied it. They had met around the time the whole rumor mill with Harry's flings started. For whatever reason, Jenna was mesmerized by how Harry was a bit of a playboy. They started going out at the end of their junior year.

I didn't really know Jenna all that well, given how I had never officially met her. I had only seen her from afar or passed by her once or twice in the halls. Admittedly, she was pretty, but there was something about her that had rubbed me the wrong way. If I'm being honest with myself, I probably only felt that way because she was dating Harry. Since then, I hardly thought about her or her relationship with him anymore.

I took the popcorn out of the microwave just before the timer went off.

Harry made a dismissive gesture with his hand. "Me and Jenna aren't even a thing."

"Liar. Aren't you guys, like, *majorly* in love with each other?"

Harry shook his head, watching my fingers move as I carefully pulled the seam apart and quickly took a steaming piece. "We're together, but it's nothing serious."

"Harry, you guys literally hold hands in the hallways, kiss each other hello and goodbye, drive home together... Need I go on?" I tossed a few more pieces of popcorn in my mouth. "If that doesn't sound like being in a relationship, then I don't know what does."

"Well, damn, Carter. If I didn't know any better, I'd say you're awfully invested in whatever it is I have going on with Jenna," he said with a smirk.

I wanted to gag, but I just replied, "I genuinely couldn't give less of a shit about what you two are. I'm just calling it how I see it. Besides, at least I'm not the one running around like a clueless monkey."

"She's not a clueless monkey." Harry attempted to defend her, but his expression revealed that even he didn't believe his own words.

"Who said I meant her?" I asked. He squinted a little and then paused before shaking his head. "Why are you wasting her time, then?" I questioned.

"Why do you care so much?" Harry asked harshly, trying to play it off with a subtle laugh.

I shook the bag of popcorn a little. "It's not that I care, it's just... Me being a girl, I'd be pretty hurt if I were in her shoes, especially with your history." I tipped the bag towards him. His move.

Harry was silent. He only stared blankly into the bag of popcorn before grabbing a handful.

Another question came into my mind, but before I could consider it, it had already spilled from my lips. "Did it ever get boring?"

"Did what get boring?" he asked, sucking the butter off his fingers, the sound forcing my head to turn in protest.

"I mean, I know you and Jenna are...*something* now, but weren't you ever bored with the whole rinse-and-repeat habit? Did you ever consider how people saw you when you jumped from one girl to another?"

Harry tensed briefly as he reached for another strawberry, and he exhaled heavily before replying. "I didn't care what people thought after the whole Stacy thing. And I definitely wasn't bored."

He laughed, but it felt forced. Before I could question it, though, he continued talking. "I mean, I liked someone at one point, but...I have no chance, even now."

"And that someone isn't Jenna?"

Harry simply shook his head in the negative, his gaze fixated on the floor.

"Yikes, how do you think she's gonna take it?"

Harry shrugged before answering, "I don't know; I haven't done anything about it yet."

"Double yikes." I feigned shock. "Who are you and what have you done with Harry?"

"Funny," Harry said, flashing me his best sarcastic smile before looking away again. If anything, he looked a little embarrassed. "It's whatever, though. Anyway, I'll see you later, Carter."

"Hey, wait!" I called out to him just as he started making his way over to the stairs. "Aren't you gonna tell me who it is?"

Harry snorted before replying, "You're a real jokester today, you know that? But, no."

"What, are you serious? Why not?"

"Nope, I'm not talking about this with you." He waggled his pointer finger back and forth at me.

"Harry!"

"See ya, Carter!"

And with that, Harry high-kneed it up the stairs, leaving me alone in the kitchen with a rapidly cooling bag of popcorn.

TWO

Mitchell wound up spending the night. We stayed up for a couple hours watching old movies and some show he'd been dying for me to get into for a while. Eventually, as the sky grew lighter, the laptop died, and he finally gave up on trying to get me hooked.

We somehow managed to wake up early that Saturday morning despite our meager hours of sleep. As we heading down the stairs, Mitchell's phone began violently buzzing with messages from Elizabeth, informing him that one of our classmates, Melissa Delgado, was hosting a party that night.

"How does someone throw a party out of nowhere?" I asked.

"Who cares? It's a party, and I'll be damned if I stay home and have to tell my future grandkids that I didn't live it up in my youth. You wanna go, right?" He looked to me hopefully.

"After that rousing speech? I can't tell you no."

"Hi, guys," my mother greeted us. She was on her laptop, sitting in one of the loveseats in the living room. "You two are up early. Morning plans?"

"No, just woke up kind of hungry," I said.

"Well, you guys can make yourselves some eggs, and there are frozen waffles in the freezer. Mitchell, you can help yourself to anything." She smiled sweetly at him.

"Thanks, Mrs. Matthews," he replied, smiling back.

After too much mixing, a little exploding, and a lot of cleaning, Mitchell and I scarfed down our food. We killed a couple hours before he went home to get ready. When he left, I showered, straightened my hair, and twisted my ends on my curling wand for a little wave. I threw on some makeup, my shitty mascara barely doing its job because I was too lazy and too broke to buy a new wand.

I traded my towel for an old robe my mother got me when I was in the seventh grade, which surprisingly still fit me. I went from hanger to hanger in my closet, indecisive. The humidity was awful, especially this time of year, but we'd be inside all night. My phone vibrated on my dresser, flashing Mitchell's name.

Mitchell: are you almost ready?

Mitchell: elizabeth is coming

Mitchell: when she texted me about the party i thought she was just informing us

Mitchell: also how are we getting there

Me: I haven't thought of that so idk

Mitchell: you're so stupid

Me: well why don't you get us a ride then???

Mitchell: well elizabeth doesn't want to drive

Me: tell her too bad

Group Convo // Mitchell, Elizabeth

Mitchell: why don't you tell her yourself

Me: mitchell what the fuck

Elizabeth: tell who what

Me: NOTHING

Elizabeth: and why did you guys include me in here

Elizabeth: mitchell you're two doors down from my bedroom

Mitchell: i told carter you didn't wanna drive us to melissa's and she said too bad aka you should

Mitchell: and i'm getting dressed liz pls

Elizabeth: carter what the fuck

Me: I don't recall

Mitchell: I have the texts to prove it dumbass

Me: MITCHELL SHUT UP

Elizabeth: so you have no way of getting there

Me: nope

Mitchell: why the fuck do you think we asked you to drive us

Mitchell: to be with you???

Mitchell: i already live with you which is bad enough

Me: she could be two seconds from giving us a ride and you're just ruining it

Elizabeth: I was…

Elizabeth: but now I'm just considering stuffing you in the trunk

Mitchell: fine by me

Mitchell: the more space between us, the better

Elizabeth: you are such an asshole. I'm definitely not taking you now screw you

Mitchell: omg okay wait

Mitchell: ugh i'm sorry, i just think it'd be better if you took us rather than spending money on multiple ubers to and from the place

Mitchell: think about it. we would spend much less on gas, especially if we all chipped in

Mitchell: you usually get, what, $20 regular?

Mitchell: that's like seven bucks each or so

Elizabeth: ……I hate that you're right

Elizabeth: fuck it, fine you guys have half an hour to be ready

Mitchell: sweet

Me: that's fine, i just have to get dressed

Mitchell: no one asked, just get ready carter

Mitchell: and thnx lizzie you're the best

I tossed my phone onto my bed in frustration as I looked over my wardrobe. I *really* needed to go shopping. The nicest thing I owned was a black dress I'd bought a while back, but it was too formal for a party like Melissa's.

I shuffled through my dresser and pulled out a spaghetti crop and faux leather leggings, then retrieved some three-inch, strappy heels from under my bed. I reached for a cream cardigan and threw it on before heading over to my full-length mirror. I twirled once or twice as I looked over my outfit choice, pursing my lips and debating on whether or not I should ditch the cardigan or leave it on.

I grabbed my phone and opened the camera app, then took a picture and sent it to Mitchell.

Me: thoughts on the cardigan?

Mitchell: ew take that off

Mitchell: the outfit is great it's just that cardigan makes you look like a 'oh im just gonna sit in a corner while i drink a pepsi' person

Mitchell: you should be wearing something that says 'im gonna booty pop while i drink my coke'

Me: you're so weird omg

Me: then what do I wear over the shirt

Mitchell: nothing just take the cardigan off

Me: but i don't like showing my arms idk i'm not comfortable like this

KARLA DE LA ROSA

Mitchell: god you pretentious bitch

Mitchell: I tell you every time that you don't have chubby arms

Mitchell: you look good

Mitchell: I wish you saw yourself the way others did

Mitchell: anyway don't you have a long-sleeved crop top in like burgundy or maroon

Me: omg yes thank you

Mitchell: yeah yeah you're welcome whatever just be ready

Mitchell: we'll be on our way soon

I tossed the crop on the floor and yanked the long-sleeved crop from its hanger in my closet. I looked at myself once more in the mirror, feeling completely satisfied with my outfit.

As I started to head out, I noticed in surprise that Dylan's door was open. I paused just outside his room. Harry was slowly spinning around in Dylan's computer chair, scrolling on his phone.

"You're *still* here?" I said rather loudly, and Harry stopped his scrolling as the chair turned him around. "Do you not have a home or something?"

"I'm waiting on Dylan—" He looked up, stopping mid-sentence. His eyes travelled over my body, and I felt rather...flattered? Harry cleared his throat and then carried on, "I'm waiting on Dylan; he's in the bathroom. Uh, where are you going?" He scratched the back of his neck awkwardly.

"Melissa's party."

Harry raised an eyebrow. "You're going?"

I nodded. "Why? Are you?"

"Yeah," he said, biting his lip and looking back to his phone.

"Cool," I said awkwardly. "I'll see you there, then, I guess."

I headed down the stairs and, thankfully, I recognized Elizabeth's car horn beeping at me. I didn't see either of my parents—probably at some volunteer event or work function—so I sent them both a quick text.

As I climbed in, Elizabeth complimented me, "You look nice, Carter."

"Yeah, thanks to me." Mitchell scoffed.

"Carter, you are so disgusting, that man is like, fifty years old," Elizabeth said, her face twisting up as if tasting something sour. Her eyes didn't leave the road, but I could see her expression in the rearview mirror.

"Oh my god!" I exclaimed. "I said he *was* hot. Emphasis on the '*was*.' Besides, Mitchell has a thing for Robert Downey Jr. and he's like the same age as Brendan, if not older, so that's not fair."

"Yeah, but that's the thing," Mitchell mused.

"Robert's *still* attractive for his age; however, Brendan Fraser is not."

"Men who are older than my father are not considered

attractive, whatsoever," Elizabeth opined. Mitchell and I stared at her, baffled.

"Um, you're one to talk," Mitchell retorted. "Pretty sure I saw Jeff Goldblum as your wallpaper on your phone not too long ago." Elizabeth gasped.

"What? Liz, he's *way* over fifty!" I shouted as Mitchell erupted into laughter. He snorted, then continued laughing with his hand over his mouth.

"Shut up, he doesn't count!"

"Oh, come on, Lizzie. Don't get so wound up because of your old man crush," said Mitchell.

"Okay, but for a man over fifty, he's not bad-looking," I said, offering an olive branch. "So I don't blame her."

"Right? Thank you. He's like another Leo, you know? Attractive when he was young and still handsome now." Elizabeth smiled proudly.

"Oh please, we all know young Leo was hands down the best Leo. He's still attractive, yes, but the only thing that was keeping him from being attractive was his lack of awards," Mitchell explained.

"Okay, well, now he has one, Mitchell, so shut up. Jeez, you'd think having a gay stepbrother would have its perks," Elizabeth went on mercilessly, "yet you just have a shitty attitude with an equally shitty taste in men."

Mitchell narrowed his eyes at Elizabeth, and I pressed myself further against the backseat.

"If we didn't get along before your mother married my father," Mitchell said, "what makes you think we would've gotten along now?"

"I would've thought we'd settle our differences by then. Besides, you're the one that doesn't like me," she said, pursing her lips.

"Well, you're the one who had two years to change that."

"*I* had to change? I've been nothing but nice to you, even *before* our parents got together."

Mitchell cackled. "You? Nice? *Ha!* That's a good joke, Liz. Seriously. *Love* that."

Elizabeth shook her head in astonishment before muttering, "You're mental. You really are mental, you know that? Why do I even bother anymore?"

The rest of the car ride was spent in silence.

We managed to park a few blocks down from the party and walked from there. The tension was a barricade between all three of us.

Eventually, I was relieved, and rather taken back, when Mitchell slung his arm around his stepsister.

"Lizzie, you know I love you, right? You're a bit of a stuck-up bitch, but that doesn't change the fact that you're family now."

Elizabeth kept her arms crossed tight against her chest as she spoke, "If this is your form of apology, you really suck at it." She shrugged Mitchell's arm off her shoulder and took long strides away from us as she made it to the lawn of Melissa's house. The sun had just started to set, and the party seemed pretty chill, at least from outside; a few Solo cups had been discarded in the grass, and flashing lights were lighting up the windows.

Mitchell stopped in his tracks and I caught up. "You were only saying that so we could get a ride back, weren't you?"

"Yeah, but I'll get her to lighten up at the party," Mitchell said nonchalantly. He cupped his hands around his mouth and shouted, "*Lizzie, I love you!*"

Elizabeth turned her head towards Mitchell, glaring in embarrassment as she entered the house. I laughed as Mitchell's hand grabbed mine, and he dragged me into the house as well.

After what felt like hours, I was beginning to grow weary. The smell of weed radiated strongly from the living room, invading my lungs even though I was trying to avoid inhaling it. I would have moved away, but the only thing keeping me guarded from the crowds was Mitchell, who was standing in-between my legs from where I was perched on a kitchen counter.

Being the social king himself, he chattered endlessly, capturing the attention in the room. I was content to just sit there, one arm resting on his shoulder, laughing at the occasional joke.

After two cups of whatever Mitchell had mixed for me, I whispered in his ear to move so I could find a restroom. He nodded and wiggled to the side, never once pausing his conversation.

I pushed and shoved to get through all the sweaty bodies

bumping and grinding to the beat of the music. I scurried up the stairs, shuffling past couples toppled on top of each other and making out on the steps. My stomach churned at the sight of mouths sloppily moving against each other.

I slammed the door of the bathroom behind me. While I was washing my hands, a fist pounded on the wooden door.

"One minute!" I shouted, rinsing off the soap from my hands. I unlocked the bathroom and slipped past whoever went inside.

"Whatever! We're through!" a voice boomed from one of the bedrooms. Curiosity wouldn't let me walk by, so I paused in the hall. Abruptly, Jenna pushed past me, nearly shoving me against the wall, and darted down the steps. I heard a frustrated grunt and glanced inside the bedroom, recognizing the head of curly locks bent towards the floor. Harry paced restlessly, his eyes burning into the ground with such intensity I was sure the carpet would catch fire. As I took a step towards him, his boot lashed out, and he kicked the wall. I gasped in spite of myself, and the low sound caused Harry to look my way. His hardened features softened.

"Carter." He sighed. "Hey, I didn't hear you come in."

"You don't look too happy," I said, not sure whether it was a good idea to point out the obvious.

"Yeah, it's just....Jenna. I just ended things with her," he said, his voice still breathy and tired.

"I thought you guys weren't a serious thing?"

"We weren't, but I...I don't know. Point is, it's over. I caught her downstairs with some junior and she was... Whatever." He cringed as he spoke.

"I'm sorry."

His lips parted and closed, and eventually he started nodding to himself.

"Whatever. I've been looking for an excuse to break up with her. I just... I didn't expect it to end *this* way, you know?"

There was a loud crash from downstairs. I took another step into the room, closed the door behind me, and leaned against it. I breathed a sigh of relief at the quiet.

Harry sat down on the edge of the half-made bed, legs spread apart, elbows on his knees, his head in his hands.

"Well, it's over now, isn't it? Didn't you like someone else, anyway?" Talking to Harry about a girl he liked felt weird, but I felt bad, seeing as how he'd just been cheated on.

Harry kept his gaze down, but I could see a small grin at the corners of his mouth. "Carter, that's the last thing I want to talk about."

"Okay, sorry. But I feel bad. Seeing you mope around over Jenna, your *nothing serious* girlfriend."

"So you're only here to pity me?" he asked, ignoring my comment.

"Well, no. Or yeah. I don't know, who cares! I'm here, aren't I? I'm *trying* to be here for you," I said with exasperation. He lifted his eyes from the floor.

"Why do you care?"

"Look, we may not be close or anything, but...you are my

brother's best friend. And I don't see him being here for you."

"Yeah, well, Dylan's had a little too much to drink tonight. I don't think he even noticed me leave the room, honestly. Not to mention Ryan—you know Ryan, right? Well, him and our other friend, AJ, brought some special treats, and, well—"

"Say no more," I interjected, waving my hand dismissively.

Harry chuckled and patted the empty space beside him. I obliged to his silent request and sat. "Besides, if I included him in my problems, then I couldn't forgive myself for ruining his fun tonight."

I nodded along. "That's very thoughtful of you. You know, you're a good friend to my brother. Which is weird because he's kind of the worst."

A smile played at his lips. "Thanks, Carter. But your brother is a pretty good friend himself." I couldn't stop myself from making a face, and he quickly added, "I'm serious. You might not be around for it, but Dylan's a good guy. He's had my back from the start."

"Well, it's gonna take a lot for you to convince me of that," I replied, but I kept my tone light. Harry didn't say anything in response; he just continued to look at me, his gaze piercing mine. I watched his chest rise as he inhaled.

A heartbeat later, he pulled a goofy face, crossing his eyes and sticking out his tongue. I cracked up, even though it wasn't really all that funny; it was the break in tension that had us both doubling over.

"Where the hell did that come from?" I said as I tried to stifle my laughter.

"I don't know, I just felt like it was getting way too serious."

"Makes sense. It's not like you can take anything seriously," I said, shaking my head at him.

He turned his body toward me, his expression unreadable as he responded, "Well, there are some things I can take seriously."

His face slowly leaned into mine. My insides drained to some depth near my feet, and my breathing quickened. His eyes fluttered closed, and his mouth angled towards mine.

Is this really happening? Am I really gonna let this happen?

Just as his lips were about to brush against my own, the door unlatched, and Harry turned away.

THREE

"Oh, sorry," a clearly intoxicated partygoer slurred, stumbling against the door. He shuffled backwards, making exaggerated apologetic gestures.

Harry and I locked eyes for just a moment before I turned and stood. He extended a hand out towards me, but I was already striding toward the door.

"Carter, wait—"

"I gotta go. Mitchell's probably looking for me." I slammed the door behind me and darted down the hall, where I nearly ran into my brother.

"Carter? What are you doing here?" His hands gently gripped my arms to steady me. "Have you seen Harry?" I just shook my head and pushed past him.

For the rest of the night, I stuck to Mitchell like glue. I spotted

Harry huddled up in a corner looking rather dazed and detached. We made eye contact a few times, unable to avoid the magnetic pull, but I always looked away. I kept a vice-like grip on Mitchell's arm as we roamed around the party, doing my best to distract myself with slurred conversation, my drinks, and my phone.

Finally, we decided to leave. I was the first one out the door. I practically dragged Elizabeth and Mitchell to the car, then sat in the back while they chattered on the drive home.

Mitchell turned around in his seat to ask, "Where'd you go, by the way? I know you went upstairs, but it took so long to come back down. Long line?"

I squirmed, biting my lip nervously. *Should I tell him?* Mitchell was my best friend. "I did. But then I ran into Harry. He was pissed off about something, so I stuck around to try and help him cheer up." The car went quiet. I watched Mitchell and Elizabeth share a look.

"That's...different," Elizabeth murmured.

"Yeah, since when did you start caring about Harry again? I thought you were over your crush on him," Mitchell commented with a little side-eye from the rearview mirror.

I fiddled with the hem of my sleeve.

"Who said I had to have feelings for him in order to comfort him?"

Mitchell only shrugged and continued staring at me in the mirror. He knew me too well.

Mitchell: hey carter i need to ask you something

Mitchell: carter

Mitchell: carter

Mitchell: carter

Mitchell: carterrrrr

Mitchell: carrrrrrterrrrrr

Mitchell: hellooooo

Mitchell: answer u ungrateful ho

Mitchell: ho

Mitchell: ho ho ho

Mitchell: cARTERRRRRR

Mitchell: I know you're not busy

Mitchell: it's not possible

Mitchell: what could you possibly be doing without me

Mitchell: carter

Mitchell: carter olivia fucking matthews

Mitchell: I swear if you're not texting me back bc you're fucking reading I'm gonna kill you

Mitchell: I bet you are

Mitchell: omfg

Mitchell: you're so lame carter i swear

Me: okay the whole "you're lame for reading" thing has to stop

Me: I recall you calling me in tears after you finished the percy jackson series

Mitchell: THAT'S NOT FAIR CARTER

Mitchell: THAT WAS THE ONLY BOOK SERIES THAT WAS WORTH MY TIME

Mitchell: UNLIKE YOURS

Mitchell: YOUR FAVE SERIES BEING FIFTY SHADES OF ALL SERIES LIKE SERIOUSLY CARTER

Mitchell: AND YOU FANTASIZED ABOUT ZAC EFRON THROUGHOUT THE ENTIRE THING

Me: LIKE YOU WOULDN'T

Mitchell: HE'S SO 2006 SO NO

Mitchell: HE DOESN'T REACH MY STANDARDS

Me: OF COURSE HE WOULDN'T

Me: I FORGOT YOU WERE INTO MEN THAT NEEDED VIAGRA TO FULFILL THE NEEDS OF THEIR TESTOSTERONE

Mitchell: YOU CANT EVEN SAY THERE AREN'T ATTRACTIVE PEOPLE WHO'RE OVER 50

Mitchell: DONT EVEN TALK JUST SHUT UP

Mitchell: BESIDES YOU WERE AND PROBABLY STILL ARE INTO BRENDAN FRASER

Me: NO I SAID HE WAS HOT IN THE MUMMY

Me: EMPHASIS ON THE "WAS"

Me: PAST TENSE BECAUSE HE WASN'T 50 AT THE TIME

Mitchell: YOU ARE SO ANNOYING, UGH

Mitchell: I STILL WIN CARTER

Mitchell: I KNOW I'M RIGHT

Mitchell: YOU'RE DONE BYE

Me: omfg whatever

Me: what did you have to ask me

Mitchell: oh yeah i almost forgot about that

Mitchell: anyway

Mitchell: elizabeth wanted to know if you wanted to come with us to the new café on the Square that just opened

Me: are you really asking me that

Me: of course i do

Mitchell: well we're going later so i'll let you know when we're on our way

Me: okay

I huffed, closing my book and getting up from my bed to stretch. I had, in fact, been reading since I woke up. My muscles ached and I had needed to use the bathroom for a while, but I'd been too lazy to move.

I was so beat. I'd hardly done anything aside from light drinking, but I'd spent the whole night tossing and turning anyway because of the stupid kiss that had almost happened.

My crush on Harry that had begun when I was a freshman, was torn to shreds in my sophomore year, and now was suddenly trying to make a comeback during the last quarter of my junior year. I didn't want those feelings for him again, especially not now, given his reputation.

I forced myself to start getting ready. *Nothing happened, and that's that. So why am I thinking about it so much?*

I left the bathroom, and there Harry was, standing in the hallway, wearing a Henley and torn-up jeans. I was used to seeing him around all the time, but now I suddenly felt underdressed in my flannel pajama bottoms and oversized T-shirt.

"Oh, hey, Carter," Harry said, his voice low and gentle.

"What are you doing here? Are you ever at home?"

"Look, I really need to talk to you. Dylan invited me over."

"About what? Where is Dylan, anyway?" I asked, crossing my arms.

"He's in his room getting ready to go out with Lindsay. She called and, like, begged him to take her out or something—whatever. That's not important. Can we go to your room?"

"Why? You can't just pretend it didn't happen? Nothing really did, anyway."

"Carter, I'm serious."

Against my better judgment, I led him to my room. As he moved to close the door, I said, "Don't. Just leave it open."

"Why?"

I arched a brow at him. "In case Dylan comes looking for you."

Harry nodded and left the door open. I leaned back on the headboard, and Harry slowly sat on the far corner of my bed, rubbing his hands on his knees.

"So?" I asked.

Harry sighed. "About last night…"

"What about it? Like I said, nothing happened."

"But something almost did, and you looked like you wanted it to! Until you walked out on me."

"What? Listen, dude, I was surprised. I wasn't expecting you to try to kiss me." I growled in frustration before sitting up. "Look, it didn't happen. And I'm glad it didn't. If someone had walked in on us kissing, they'd run and tell Dylan, and, let's be real here, Dylan has the worst temper. And the last thing you need is people trashing you for kissing his best friend's sister."

Harry just stared at me expectantly. I could hardly believe he didn't care about any of that, so I tried to change the subject. "Besides, now's your chance with that girl you were telling me about."

His brow furrowed. "Wait, what?"

"Remember? You were talking about some girl you said you have zero chance with? Well, look: now that you've dumped Jenna, you're single and ready to mingle. And what kind of guy would you be kissing someone that isn't her?"

Harry let out a little laugh and shoved a hand through his curls. "Carter, are you *serious*?"

"What?"

Harry scoffed. "The girl I like? I was clearly talking about *you*."

FOUR

There's no way. As of a few months ago, I was convinced he couldn't stand me.

"You like *me*?"

Harry nodded, his eyes frantically scanning my face. What was he looking for? Disgust? Joy? I didn't know what to feel. Back when I had been crushing on him, beyond his undeniable good looks, it was his genuine kindness and sense of humor that had really gotten me. I'd felt like we just clicked, that we talked as if we'd known each other our whole lives. But he'd changed, and I'd changed, especially after the Stacy incident.

"Look, I'm sorry. Please don't take this the wrong way, but...I just don't believe you," I whispered. His shoulders drooped. "This is just too sudden, you know? We barely talk anymore, and then you drop this bomb on me out of nowhere."

"I'm surprised you didn't know... I thought I made it obvious!"

"You really didn't. I mean, I just learned you liked someone; I'm not going to be cocky and automatically assume it's me. How big do you think my ego is?"

He slumped further, as if his chest was suddenly weighed down. "Are you serious, Carter? Why do you think I'm always coming over?"

I frowned. "You only came here...for me?"

"Yeah, for the most part." He saw my expression start to change and quickly added, "Look, I know how bad that sounds, okay? Dylan's my best friend and all, but besides coming over to hang out with him, a part of me always hoped I'd run into you."

"That's not really how friendships should work, Harry."

"Okay, look; yes, it's fucked up. I get that. But he's still my best friend, regardless. I'm not, like, using him to get to you, I swear. He's my best friend who happens to have a sister that I like. I like you, Carter. Bottom line." He huffed, making a funny gesture with his arm to make his point.

I couldn't lie to myself; no matter how long ago it was, I firmly believed that my feelings for Harry lingered, but I'd just chosen to ignore them. However, my mind was clouded in that moment. I couldn't tell whether he was being genuine or if I just wanted to believe him.

"Can I be honest?"

He snorted. "Weren't you already?"

My jaw tightened. "I did like you, a lot. But after that rumor with you and Stacy, it's like you changed and I just, you know...lost interest. Especially given your newfound reputation."

Harry scoffed, and I realized how bad that had sounded.

"And that's what you're worried about? You're worried about my *reputation*? Really?"

"I mean, the fact that you even have it, it's just—" I tossed my hands up in exasperation. "—unattractive to me. And, Harry, I don't wanna be *that* girl. I don't want to be another name on the list of girls you've hooked up with."

Harry opened his mouth, but Dylan barreled out of his room and straight into mine before he could speak.

"Carter, have you seen my wallet, I—" Dylan stopped when he noticed who was sitting on my bed. "Harry? What are you doing in *here*?"

Harry opened his mouth to speak, but I cut him off before he had the chance.

"He was just talking about Xbox, a bunch of shit I don't really care about." I crossed my arms, and Harry stood up.

My brother snorted and said to Harry, "Don't even bother. It's useless." He turned back to me. "Have you seen my wallet? I can't find it. I have to pick up Lindsay in a few, and she's probably already waiting. Like always. Have you seen it?"

"Have you checked on the shelf under your TV? You always leave it there."

"How do you know that?"

I shrugged. "Just a guess."

Dylan rolled his eyes and turned back to Harry. "I'm almost done getting ready to go. Are you gonna...?"

"I'll head out in a few."

Dylan nodded, then left my room. Harry followed, pausing at the doorframe to look at me with raised brows.

"Every once in a while, my parents give us some cash. Not always—we don't get allowances—but whenever it happens, I always notice that a couple bucks go missing. I found out he was taking some of my money, so I started taking back what's mine. It's not stealing if it belongs to me, ya know?"

My phone buzzed before Harry could reply. Messages from Mitchell began flooding my screen.

> **Mitchell:** hey start getting ready
> **Mitchell:** we're gonna come and get you soon
> **Mitchell:** and bring money
> **Mitchell:** i'm not paying for you again

I shook my head, not bothering to reply. Harry was still lingering in the doorway.

"I gotta go," I said, digging in my dresser for leggings.

"Where?"

"Mitch and Liz invited me out to eat," I replied simply. I found the pair I was looking for and reached into my closet for my favorite cropped hoodie. I pushed past Harry on my way to change in the bathroom. I was consciously aware of how strange it felt to leave him in my room. It was almost comforting to know he was there. When I returned, he was sitting in my desk chair, his legs tucked up as he spun around in circles. He grabbed the edge of the desk to stop himself when he noticed me standing there.

"Having fun?" I asked.

"Not really. Your brother's *still* getting ready, but that's okay, because we can finish our talk."

"I thought we already did that," I said as I put my hair up in a high ponytail and then pulled a few strands loose around my face.

"Carter, I *like* you." My heart leapt, but I refused to let my face give me away. "I was hoping maybe you'd feel the same."

I sighed, feeling an internal conflict brewing. I looked at his reflection in the mirror in front of me. Did he think it was that easy? Now that he was interested, I was supposed to just flip a switch and go back to how I'd felt two years ago?

"Okay, well, again, let me start out by saying that I did. I did like you. A lot, even. But Harry, *so* much has changed. And you know, just cause you're always here doesn't mean I know you that well. Because even though you said you come over for me, you're usually *with* my brother. So there's that. And then, you said you like me, right? My thing is: what exactly are you hoping to get out of it?"

"What do you mean?"

"You're telling me you like me. Okay, cool, but what do you want out of this? A relationship? One date? Are you just telling me you like me to mess with my head for shits and giggles? Like... what is it?" I sounded angrier than I really was. The truth was that I couldn't handle being made a fool of, not by him. I didn't want things to be too good to be true.

Harry blinked, and my phone's ringtone pulled my attention away.

"Shit. You know what, never mind. I'm sorry, Harry, I have to go." As I slipped on my old Converse and grabbed my shoulder bag, I texted Mitchell a reply, letting him know I'd be right out. I looked at Harry, whose green eyes seemed almost desperate. "I'll see you later?"

"Can I text you, at least?"

"Sure," I said with a shrug. "Do you have my number?"

"Yeah, I got it back in sophomore year. Has it changed?"

"Oh, right. No, it's the same." I awkwardly waved goodbye and ducked out to the stairs just as Dylan shouted that he was leaving.

I knew Harry was following me, but I didn't realize just how close he was until I turned to close the front door behind me and nearly hit him in the stomach with my bag.

"Whoa, sorry."

Harry just smiled, sliding his hands into his pockets as he waltzed out to the driveway. I closed the door and hurried to Mitchell's car, feeling Mitchell's gaze searing me with every step.

Elizabeth was blasting some indie band on the AUX, but they were both suspiciously quiet as we pulled out of the driveway.

FIVE

The line at the new café spilled out the door, wrapping around the side of the building. Apparently, everyone else had had the same idea. After what felt like forever, we finally placed our orders, and I went to search for a seat while Elizabeth and Mitchell waited for our food.

I wandered around, realizing how much I liked the new spot. The warm brown walls were cozy, decorated with black-and-white photos of cars, portraits of people I didn't recognize, Elvis in his "Jailhouse Rock" music video, and Marilyn Monroe infamously posed above the subway grate. There was exposed brick behind the counter, refurbished light fixtures, and a large menu hanging above written in colorful chalk.

A family at a small booth stood up, and I quickly snagged the table for us before gesturing for Mitchell and Elizabeth to join me.

A server wiped down the table.

"So, are you gonna tell us what happened back there or what?" Mitchell coaxed, sliding in across from me.

Elizabeth moved her side salad around with her fork, trying to fight back a smile. Apparently neither one of them could even enjoy their meal unless I told them my secrets.

"What do you mean? We were just leaving at the same time." I pulled out my phone and started scrolling through Instagram. I chuckled at Melissa's selfie of her pouting with her messy, party-trashed house in the background and decided to like it just for the hell of it.

"Are you sure?" said Mitchell. "It looked like something else from the way you both practically ran out the door together."

"We didn't run." I stopped and laughed. "Well, I did. But only because I knew you'd blow up my phone if I didn't hurry up."

I didn't want to tell them anything about what Harry had said until I was able to process the whole thing on my own. I still couldn't believe it.

I looked back at my phone, eating my panini and refreshing my feed. Melissa had just posted a new picture...with Austin.

Austin *fucking* Galloway.

"Austin was there last night?" I blurted out loud. My blood had already rushed to a full boil in my veins.

"Yeah, apparently he was the one who brought the weed and some other stuff last night. I don't know exactly what the 'other stuff' was, but I can only assume it was worse." Mitchell leaned in and whispered, "It was definitely pills. I didn't find out until I literally saw him pull the baggies out and start shamelessly charging everyone right there in the living room."

Elizabeth scrunched up her nose. "God, he's such a loser."

"Literally," Mitchell muttered, stuffing pasta into his mouth. "What kind of guy still goes to high school parties after graduating?"

I shook my head, unable to take my eyes off the picture. Austin's arms were wrapped around Melissa's waist, his chin resting on her shoulder and a cheesy smile on his face. I took in a sharp breath.

"I thought you were over him?" Mitchell asked, noticing my reaction.

"I am," I snapped back. "I'm just sick of him. He's annoying to look at."

"Obviously not. You're staring at that post like you could make it spontaneously combust."

"Why does it matter?" Elizabeth asked.

Before I could reply, Mitchell beat me to it. "They dated briefly, remember? And he was her first."

Kicking him hard in the shin, I growled, "Say it louder, will you?"

Austin had been my boyfriend in sophomore year for a short period of time. I'd been completely head over heels for him. He'd been super sweet, always saying all the right things.

Or so I'd thought.

No one had known about our relationship except for Mitchell, and I guess Elizabeth, but only the minor details.

Austin had told me it was best to keep our relationship hidden because his father didn't want him to lose focus on his football career. And me being a naive and vulnerable sophomore at the time, I'd agreed to keep it quiet.

Which is stupid because that's a basic line in every teen movie, and yet I still fell for it.

I gave Austin everything, but within a matter of weeks, I caught him cheating with a freshman. I'd confronted him about it, but instead of fighting back, he'd simply shrugged and then proceeded to tell everyone at school that I had been the worse lay of his life.

Luckily, he'd been playing so many girls besides me that he didn't even get my name right, so nobody really knew who the hell Catherine was.

But I did, so I cried for weeks. I'd even had to lie to my parents that I'd just been stressing over finals.

I purposefully locked my phone and set it on my lap, apparently so deliberate in my actions that Elizabeth stared at me.

"Don't worry about him," she said. "You'll find somebody worth your time."

"Or worth getting into your pants," Mitchell added. Both Elizabeth and I shot him a glare, but he merely cried, "It was a joke!"

"Real nice," I spat. "Whatever. Look, he's dead to me, and I could not care less about him and what he does, so can we just drop it?"

"Fine, sheesh," Mitchell snapped before attempting to change the subject but failing miserably.

My phone vibrated in my hands as a notification popped up at the top of the screen from an unknown number. I pulled the tab down and read the new message.

Unknown: hey carter
Unknown: it's harry

SIX

I thought I'd added his contact in the past, but maybe I'd deleted it when I'd gotten pissed at him last year.

Me: hi harry

Unknown: hi :)

Unknown: what are you doing?

Me: hanging out with with mitch & liz

Me: what about you?

Harry: starving

Harry: I just parked at my place but I want to eat and my parents aren't home so I know they didn't make anything

Harry: I'm also being super picky right now

Harry: hence my dilemma

Harry: so, any suggestions?

Me: oh, well I'm at this new café spot at Pembroke Square

Me: you're welcome to join

Harry: oh, wow

Harry: are you sure?

Harry: is that okay with Mitchell and Elizabeth? I don't want to impose

Me: I'm sure it wouldn't be an issue

Me: I'll let them know now

Harry: okay well then I'll just start heading over

Harry: I'll be there soon

"Hey guys, quick question," I started, watching their attention turn to me as I spoke. "So, what would you say if I invited Harry to eat here with us?"

They sat silently for a moment, then simultaneously looked at each other, then back to me. Both shrugged.

"What, like now?" Mitchell asked, and I nodded. "I mean, I don't see why not. But if he's going to come, he should make it quick; the line finally died down, and I'm not sure how long that's gonna last."

I quickly texted Harry the details. I vaguely rushed him, not because I was eager to see him, but because of what Mitchell had said. Who knew how long the short line would last?

A good half hour passed, and I couldn't help watching the cars go past the window. I recognized Harry's little sedan pull into the parking lot and rearranged my silverware.

From the corner of my eye, I noticed Mitchell give a little nod to Elizabeth, indicating Harry had arrived. When he realized I had caught it, the two of them tried to give me various signals and silent cues, but I had no idea what they meant. In all of the wordless conversation, Harry's green eyes met mine as he stepped up to the register. I gave him one long look, and when he smiled, I had to glance away, feeling my face heat up. I focused again on my silverware, pointedly ignoring the way Mitchell's eyebrows were rising halfway up his forehead.

How can a simple smile affect me so much? All I could do was forcefully tell myself, *I* don't *like him back!* But that didn't stop my heart from hammering against my ribs.

After Austin, I had developed trust issues. Like, an insane amount of them. Harry insisting that he liked me did little to ease my concerns. In fact, it felt safer to consider him untrustworthy. It felt safer to just assume he would hurt me, so that maybe I wouldn't be so wounded when the inevitable happened.

I didn't notice Harry approach until his arm brushed against mine as he slid in next to me with a tray full of food.

"Hey, you guys." He smiled politely. "Thanks for letting me join you."

Elizabeth gave a little wave and a small smile as Mitchell just stared. We had all been around Harry, but not like this. Not hanging out.

"Hey, Harry. What brings you here?" Elizabeth asked.

"Felt a little hungry. I heard about this new place, so I thought I'd give it a try." He turned to me, seeming to make a point of saying, "Hey, Carter."

I gave him a sidelong look, replying with an unintentionally half-assed "Hey."

His eyebrows knit together. "Are you okay? You look more disappointed than usual to see me."

"Don't worry about her; she's just down because she found out Austin was at the party," Mitchell stated bluntly. I kicked him under the table while Elizabeth elbowed his ribs at the same time.

"*Ow!*"

"Austin? Austin Galloway?" Harry asked.

I clenched my teeth together and nodded.

"Why are you down about *that*?"

I wanted to smack my head against the table. This was the first time Harry and I had truly spent time together, especially without my brother around, and of all things, *this* was the conversation we were having.

"He was my...boyfriend? I guess. Barely. I don't know. It's a complicated story."

"You guys were *together*?"

"Hardly. We weren't a real thing," I said, and a knowing smirk formed on his lips. I immediately realized it was the same line he'd used when he'd explained his relationship with Jenna. "Whatever. It doesn't matter anymore. Long story short, it was a fake relationship that started just as quickly as it ended, right before he graduated. He's gone now, or so I thought. That's that. Dylan doesn't know, and I want it to stay that way. So now that we've made that clear, can we please change the subject?"

"I never liked that guy. He talked shit about everyone, even some of the chicks he slept around with."

Oh god, you have got to be kidding me.

"I remember he was hooking up with someone and then out of nowhere, he completely trashed the poor girl, telling everyone she was terrible in bed. I think her name was Caitlin? Or maybe Catherine—"

Mitchell choked on his pasta, Elizabeth coughed, and I just wanted bury myself six feet into the ground and never resurface.

"Oh my god," I moaned, cradling my head in my hands.

"*Oh,*" was all Harry could say after noticing our reactions. "Carter, I—"

"I'm—I'll be back," I said. "I gotta go hang myself somewhere." I slid out the other side of the booth and walked out. I didn't give anyone time to interject; I just threw away my trash and left.

I couldn't believe he knew about that. I mean, everyone did, but it was just weird hearing it come out of his mouth, not even knowing it was me in the story.

The once-clear blue sky now looked dark and moody; the Florida weather was endlessly changing. The Square traffic had cleared up, and the quiet was soothing. Raindrops began to splatter, not swift or harsh, but just as an occasional drip. One plopped directly on my head, and I tilted my face up, breathing in the scent of rain.

"Carter." I didn't turn; I recognized Harry's voice and knew he wanted to pester me with questions I didn't feel like answering. But I was surprised to hear another pair of footsteps, and in my puzzlement, I was surprised to see that Elizabeth was with him. Mitchell knew well enough to give me space when I needed it.

"Look, I don't want to talk about it anymore," I told them. "It was a year ago. It's over. And it's none of your business, honestly."

"I'm sorry. I was overstepping," Harry said mournfully. "But I didn't do it to be nosy. I was just concerned."

"Mitchell should never have brought it up," Elizabeth added. "He knew better."

"It's fine. I don't care about him anymore." I looked directly at Harry. "Just promise me one thing, please. Don't tell Dylan, okay? It happened, but it's over now. So just forget about it. Please."

"Of course," he said.

They were silent for a moment before Harry added, "Can we go back in now? I haven't finished my sandwich, so..."

I laughed a little in spite of myself, and Elizabeth smiled, visibly breathing a sigh of relief.

"All right, fine," I said.

Elizabeth ducked back inside, and Harry held out his palm, offering a peacemaking handshake.

I looked down at his palm before glancing up at him and shaking my head no.

Harry gave a dramatic huff, then said, "Worth a try."

⊛

"So, how's senior year, Harry?" Elizabeth asked, her cheeks resting in her palms.

Harry wiped his mouth with a napkin before answering, "Well, despite stressing over college and everything, to me it's a hell of a lot better than junior year. Less assignments, exams, stress. Either that or I have a serious case of senioritis."

"Sounds deadly. Do you know what college you're going to?" Mitchell chirped. I could tell by his stillness and the keen glint in his eye that he was analyzing Harry.

And without missing a beat, Harry replied, "Most likely St. John's University."

My eyes widened. "Isn't that in New York?"

Harry nodded, setting his utensils on his now-empty plate.

"But isn't that school like, forty grand per semester?" Mitchell asked.

"My parents set up a college fund before they even planned on having me. They made one for my sister, too; she graduated not too long ago."

"So is St. John's your choice or theirs?" Mitchell quirked an eyebrow. I shook my head at him. It wasn't a question you just asked people, but Harry seemed unbothered.

"Mostly theirs," Harry explained, "but I've heard lots of good things about that school."

"What are you gonna major in?" Elizabeth asked before sipping the last of her Sprite Zero.

"I'm taking a double major, and one has to be in liberal arts. I'm still undecided on the other one."

"Why liberal arts?" I asked.

"My parents insisted my sister and I have double majors," he said, the words sounding worn. "One is their choice, and the other is ours. They'll probably have me go into finance or business, and then I'll figure out what I want to study."

If I was being completely honest with myself, I'd always thought Harry was just a stuck-up guy with wealthy parents who didn't plan on going to college because he claimed he didn't need to go. Kind of like my brother.

"No offense, but that really fucking sucks," Mitchell said.

"You think?" Harry asked with a raised brow.

"Well, yeah. I mean, isn't college the place where you make your own decisions and become independent?"

"Hey, I can't complain," Harry replied, unoffended by Mitchell's words. "I agree with you entirely, but my parents pulled a lot of strings for an opportunity as big as St. John's. I gotta give them that, at least."

Mitchell rolled his eyes. "Yeah, yeah, okay. Fair enough. I'm just saying, that seems like a little much—you're forced to have twice the workload, and half of it is something you might not even like."

"I think it's fair," I interjected. "It's not like his parents are making him choose one specific thing. At least he has a second option."

Elizabeth cut in, "Carter, where are you going for college?"

I spun my phone on the tabletop. "I'm not too sure yet. I mean, I wanna do a lot of things, but the one subject that stands out to me the most is psychology. I may try and find a university that has a good program for it, but I don't know yet. I've thought about The Art Institute, as well. I'll figure it out eventually. For now, I might just stick to community college."

"Where you'll see me!" Mitchell called out happily, putting a hand up for a high-five. I begrudgingly complied.

Elizabeth explained that she wanted to go to Nova—no questions asked—to study nursing, or something in the medical field. She wasn't entirely sure what major she wanted yet, but she was confident she'd have picked by senior year.

"We should get going; I feel like we've been here too long," Elizabeth said, watching some of the employees tidy up. She stood and brushed lint off her black skinny jeans.

"We have school tomorrow," Mitchell whined.

"I don't know why you're complaining. You always oversleep and come in late, anyway," I remarked.

Mitchell flashed a cheesy smile and pretended to flip his short hair. "Do you know how long it takes to look *this* good?"

"A *very* long time," Elizabeth shot back, Mitchell's jaw dropped while Harry and I laughed.

"Carter, do you want me to take you home?" Harry asked.

Elizabeth and Mitchell shared a look with each other and then a glance with me, each filled with a dozen different meanings I couldn't begin to interpret.

"I'm going over there anyway to meet up with Dylan," he carried on casually. "He just texted me to come by again for something."

I pressed my lips together to prevent a smirk from appearing. "Oh, you're hanging out with my brother? Again? Is that right?"

Harry couldn't help but grin.

I dared a look at Mitchell and Elizabeth, who merely wiggled their eyebrows and shrugged, respectively.

"I'll see you guys tomorrow," I said firmly.

I followed Harry to his car. He drove a little Toyota Corolla. "You know, this car is very small for someone who's pretty tall."

"This is only temporary!" Harry countered. "Anyway, you can put on the radio if you want, or slip in any CD; they're all in the glove compartment."

"You never heard of an AUX cord?" I eyed him skeptically.

Harry halted dramatically, his key only halfway in the ignition. "Well, *I'm sorry*. Am I not advanced enough for you?" Then he laughed and said, "The cord is wrapped up somewhere in there, too." I shook my head, biting back my massive smile.

SEVEN

Mitchell: you better tell me what goes down when you get home

Mitchell: i'm so serious carter

Mitchell: you better not leave out any details

Mitchell: i'll cut you

Mitchell: whore bag

Me: BYE

Mitchell: what even

Me: each time you text me my phone goes off like crazy

Me: like

Me: can you not

Mitchell: you love me

Me: negative

Mitchell: suck my ass

Me: I just barfed

"You ever listened to The 1975?" I asked Harry as we drove back to my house. The gray sky had faded into indigo, and the sun was peeking from behind a cluster of clouds.

"I've heard a couple of their songs, yeah."

I scrolled through my library and picked a random song of theirs. I looked out the window again, watching the plazas fade and palm trees begin to line the highway.

"So," Harry said, "why The Art Institute?"

I started putting my hair in a loose braid. "I mean, I really wanna major in psych, but graphic design has always been interesting. But at the same time, I'm interested in English literature, which is simple enough for me to take at community college."

"Why English?" Harry asked, one hand on the wheel as his other rested on his lap, fingers drumming on his thigh.

"I dunno, maybe to become a writer or something. Grammar and stuff, you know, it's fascinating."

"Really?" Harry raised an eyebrow. "Your texting style says otherwise."

I gently poked at his side, which made him laugh. He exited the highway, and we pulled up to a red light. I noticed that Harry's head was nodding along to almost every song that came on by The 1975.

Before long, we pulled into the driveway, where Dylan's car was already parked.

"What did Dylan want to give you?" I asked.

"Oh, a game. But he's going to want to hang—I mean, do you really think he'd want to spend *more* time with Lindsay?" He smirked.

Once we'd stepped inside the house, I locked the door and turned to find Harry smiling at me.

"I had a nice time, Carter."

I just laughed.

Harry frowned at my random outburst. "If this is your way of ending a date, you were supposed to say 'Goodbye' outside," I said.

Harry made a face. "Oh, so that was a date?"

My eyes widened. "Wait, no. What? I—Oh my god, I didn't—I just—"

"Carter, it's fine." Harry laughed. "That hardly counted as a date, but it will next time." He winked, then went up to my brother's room.

[HARRY]

"Yeah, yeah, yeah," Dylan murmured over the phone. "Lindsay, I know. Stop being such a control freak."

I suppressed a noise of exasperation, feeling the impending argument build.

I focused on the TV, continuing to kill random people on Grand Theft Auto Online, which Dylan was having me play for him. It was like this almost every time we hung out; Lindsay always seemed to call while I was here, and Dylan always picked up, apparently never realizing how rude it was. While I was annoyed, it also gave me an opportunity to mess with Carter when she wasn't locked up in her bedroom.

My crush on Carter had started out the same way most crushes do. And I was very much into her by the time I'd finished my sophomore year. We had nearly the same sense of humor, and I was obsessed with the way her eyes lit up whenever we talked about the things we had in common; I'm sure mine did the same. All the other girls I'd talk with, we didn't have the "spark" that I'd heard about. I'd finally gotten it when I'd talked to Carter. I'd come over every day last summer, and even when I'd hardly see her, I would always catch her eye before I left.

I had been considering asking her out on a date over the weekend. But only if Dylan didn't plan anything, which thankfully was pretty common, because when he *did* plan something, Lindsay always ended up inviting herself—and, in the past, Jenna.

I cringed at the thought of Jenna. I had liked her, at first. She'd been nice, attractive, funny at times, and clearly into me. We'd started dating within two weeks of getting to know each other. And though I hadn't had as big of a crush on her as I did on Carter, I'd given her a chance—partially to try and move on from Carter, honestly. But over time, she'd become someone else, and I no longer recognized her. It was like she'd cared more about the reputation I had and how it would've helped her popularity. Her attitude got worse and worse until she became stuck-up.

Towards the end of it, I'd realized I should've gotten to know Jenna better before jumping into anything serious with her. Although I hadn't expected our relationship to last nearly as long as it did.

"Aw, that's disgusting," Dylan muttered. He was watching me play, and I couldn't tell whether he meant the headshot I'd made, or whatever Lindsay had said. I huffed, pushing my overgrown hair back as I tried to focus.

But I couldn't focus.

I heard laughter across the hall and recognized it as Carter's. My head automatically snapped to the direction of her sweet voice, only to watch Dylan slam his bedroom door shut to block her out.

I would have made a remark, but I bit my tongue. If Dylan found out I had a thing for his sister, I knew he'd raise hell. With Dylan being my best friend, he knew just about everything I did. And given his knowledge of my previous relationships and such, I just knew he wouldn't be okay with me and his sister being together in any way. He had a horrible temper.

Dylan groaned, and it was then I noticed he had hung up the phone. He threw himself onto his stomach on top of his bed, hands sprawled out at his sides.

"Lindsay?" I asked, drifting in a souped-up Gauntlet.

"Yes," he roared into a pillow. "I know we're together, but we're not *together*-together."

I snorted. "What the hell does that mean?"

"Like, we hook up and everything. But she always expects more. Like, she'll try to get me to say '*I love you*—'" He gagged on the words and continued, "and she tries dropping hints on what I should do as a boyfriend. But that's not me at all."

I kept my attention on the TV.

"You know, I'm a little jealous of you," Dylan admitted, grabbing my attention.

"Why would you be jealous of me? You're the one with the girlfriend," I mumbled, but he heard me, anyway.

"Exactly," Dylan exclaimed, sitting up. "I can't tell you how much I miss having girls around me without worrying about Lindsay and her feelings. Ugh, it's like she has a leash on me. And for what? We never clarified anything. But she struts around like she has some sort of claim on me, when all I'm trying to do is get some ass—"

"Okay, hold on. Based on what you're telling me, it kind of sounds like you want a friends-with-benefits situation with her."

"Is that what it is?"

"Yes, that's what it is," I remarked, "but I wouldn't suggest it to her. It's too late now, anyway."

"Why would it be too late?" he asked, pulling out his phone.

I snatched the phone away from him because I knew he wouldn't hear a thing otherwise. "You're already in too deep.

You've been with her for a while, dude."

"A couple weeks is not a while," Dylan stated, reaching for his phone.

I stared at him blankly.

"Why are you looking at me like that?"

"Dylan, you and Lindsay have been going at it since October."

"So?"

"...It's April."

Dylan gaped at me. "Wait, are you serious? It's been that long?"

I rolled my eyes, tossing his phone onto his bed. "You have to stop smoking so much."

EIGHT

"Carter, I know you hate school, but the least you can do is dress presentably," Mitchell remarked, his nose scrunched up in disgust at my outfit choice as I jumped in Elizabeth's car.

I looked down at my leggings and oversized sweater. I didn't think I looked *that* bad. I never dressed up for school anymore, not the way I had freshman year. That was long before I'd realized how ridiculous it was to care about how I looked in class. Mitchell was another story. "It's Monday; who cares?"

"At least she did her hair," Elizabeth commented as we took off towards school.

"Seriously! And I'm not sure why my outfit choice is such a surprise. The only surprise here is how you're actually going to school early today," I retorted.

"*And* it's Monday," Elizabeth added, gasping for effect.

"Honestly, nothing has surprised me more than seeing Mitch be up and ready on time. Carter, it was amazing."

I laughed, and Mitchell jabbed at Elizabeth's arm.

We arrived at school, and I followed Mitchell towards our lockers. Elizabeth went her own way, tossing a wave over her shoulder.

As soon as Mitchell and I made it to the second floor, we were bombarded by the sight of couples kissing, half-hidden in corners to keep from getting caught by faculty for PDA. Mitchell was already gagging. I grabbed his hand and shouted, "Come on, Mitch, let's make out over here!"

One couple pulled away from each other to glare at my sarcastic comment, and the rest quickly dispersed. Mitchell and I snickered as we made it to our lockers.

"What do you have after homeroom again?" I asked, grabbing my textbooks for my first three classes.

"Horticulture." Mitchell pouted. His absolute least favorite class. "You?"

"Math," I said, scrunching my nose. "I can't stand my teacher. The only reason I'm passing is because of how much of an easy grader he is. Technically, everyone is passing for that exact reason."

"Well, at least you have me again right after."

Once Mitchell and I had made it to homeroom, we sat together near the back and talked.

"You have art with Harry fourth period, right?" Mitchell asked.

"Yeah, why?" Harry always sat near the back with a group of jocks or random people. He'd hardly acknowledged my existence in that class, so despite his recent sweetness, I still wasn't sure about this supposed crush on me.

"Just curious, considering how close you two seem to be getting."

"Don't start."

Mitchell actually changed the subject, and homeroom flew by.

It was a Monday and I was in no mood for anything, so I sat in the back of first period where no one would notice me.

Second period was health, and I felt as if it went by way too quickly, especially since it was with Elizabeth and Mitchell. Our teacher was very blunt when it came to talking about health, which meant Mitchell, Elizabeth, and I would make side comments and then laugh among ourselves.

In English IV, we just silently read a book that we had a term paper for, due by the end of the semester. Despite my love for reading, assigning it was a surefire way to ruin the pleasure of it for me. This was torture.

When I walked into art, I immediately scanned the back of the room, but Harry wasn't there. I sat alongside Andy and Sean who were considered the class clowns. They always played UNO every chance they got, and I often joined a few games here and there. We started up a game, and before too long we had a little crowd of onlookers and people who wanted in next. I dropped a +4 card and laughed as Sean lost his shit and started claiming I'd cheated.

I looked up and realized Harry had sat next to me.

"Hey," he said simply.

"Hey, you..." I replied with an awkward laugh, and Sean nudged me to take my turn. I put a card down and glanced back at Harry with a raised brow. "Fancy seeing you here."

"We have the same class."

"I know that. I mean it's weird to see you *here*. *Sitting* next to *me*."

"Do you not want me to sit next to you?" He frowned, his lips pouty. It took all of my strength to not look down at them, the memory of our near-kiss lingering in my mind.

"I never said that," I countered. "You just never do, so it's kind of weird. I guess I'm just used to seeing you always sit with Ryan over there."

Harry looked over to where Ryan was sitting, alone on his phone. "I don't know, it gets kind of boring over there. So I figured maybe I should start sitting with you." He made himself comfortable, or as comfortable as anyone could get in the plastic chairs.

Our teacher marched in and finally started class. We did an assignment defining color theory terminology, which was fine and all. I knew hues and tints, but not so much about CMYK.

It was hard to pay attention since I felt Harry's sneaky glances at me the whole time. I acted as if I didn't notice, when in reality, I was keeping count.

When the bell finally rang, Harry asked, "What do you have

right now?"

I slung my bag over my shoulder and walked out with him. "Lunch. You?"

"Gym, but I'm thinking of skipping. Mind having a lunch buddy?" I looked at him to see if he was being serious, and was surprised at the sincerity on his face, his dimple just beginning to show. My heart bounced off the walls of my chest.

"Uh, sure," I said hesitantly, tightening my grip on my bookbag. I tried to play it off as if his request didn't faze me at all.

"So, who do you usually sit with?" he asked, that small grin still on his face.

"Uh, most of the time I sit alone by the auditorium, since Mitchell and Elizabeth don't have the same lunch period as me."

Harry frowned. "You don't sit with anyone else?"

"Not really, but I don't mind. It's nice to just do my own thing, honestly."

We walked up to the line. I grabbed a cup of aggressively pink yogurt and a small pack of almonds, then skipped straight to the front to pay since everyone else was still deciding.

"That's all you eat?" Harry asked, eyeing me suspiciously.

I eyed him back skeptically. "The food here is pretty gross, in case you haven't noticed."

"I mean, yeah, but you should at least eat more than just that."

"Why do you think I empty out the fridge when I get home?"

"Oh, that's your fault? I always just blamed Dylan."

I shoved him playfully as we headed outside. The sun was

blazing, so I made a beeline for the shade cast by the auditorium.

"No one else comes out here?" he asked.

"Nope. Everyone has their group of friends out there, so I just sit here. Listen to music, read, try not to think about classes or homework."

Harry nodded.

"You know, I won't stop you if you choose to run. Not exactly thrilling out here. Now's your chance," I joked, pouring the toppings on the yogurt.

"You think you can get rid of me that easy? I don't plan on going anywhere." Harry smiled, and I couldn't help but grin in return.

NINE

Guy friendships were just as complex as girl ones, apparently. I hadn't realized how annoyed Harry was about his friendship with Dylan until he droned on and on about it, telling me how frustrated it made him, especially when there were days he actually *wanted* to hang out with my brother. And that's basically how we spent lunch, with Harry talking nonstop. It wasn't until the bell rang that he realized I had hardly replied.

But I didn't mind any of it. Sometimes it was easier for me to say things over text than in person. And frankly, watching Harry talk was just as interesting as what he had to say. I didn't mean to objectify him, but I couldn't help watching his lips move as he spoke. It was mesmerizing. For a guy who talked a lot, he sure spoke slow and soft. He laughed anxiously whenever he made a joke, waiting for my reaction.

Throughout that entire hour of watching him talk nonstop, I felt like a freshman again, my crush slowly reemerging, but now, on this new version of Harry. He was more critical now, more cutting, but I liked hearing his analysis of Dylan and Lindsay's relationship, and how deeply he thought about his friends. And we still loved the same shows and artists. I was getting to know him all over again, and falling just as deeply.

And although one small part of me was still screaming that I shouldn't let myself get close to him, that voice was growing quieter with every passing moment.

After lunch, he walked me to my next class. We ran into his friend, AJ, when we made it to the door of my biology lab room. AJ was a stocky guy, and I didn't know much about him besides the fact he had a rowdy, hyper energy both on and off the football field. He didn't acknowledge my existence; he just asked Harry, "Dude, are you coming over tonight? You and Dylan should swing by."

Harry hummed a little before saying, "I don't know, dude. I haven't really spoken to him today."

AJ raised a brow at Harry. "What happened? You two get in a little fight and break up or something?"

I tried to hold in my snort, I really did. But it came out, anyway, earning a weird look from AJ. I looked away immediately to hide my flushed cheeks.

"I'll see. Is Ryan going?" Harry asked. AJ nodded. I knew Ryan

KARLA DE LA ROSA

about as well as I did AJ—just a vague understanding that they were friends of my brother and Harry. Ryan and AJ were always together, causing a ruckus and making everyone laugh. "Then maybe. I won't lie, I'm a little tired, so I might just go home. I'll keep you posted, though."

"Sounds good. Let me know," AJ said, and he headed off. Harry finally looked back to me, and he gave me a little playful nudge and a small smile before going his own way. I could have just walked into class the moment he'd stopped to talk to AJ, but I was starting to crave every second with him.

I sat at my desk in the half-empty classroom, and Mitchell walked in, mouth gaping and his thumb pointed back at the hall. I tilted my head as he slid into the seat next to me.

"Do my eyes deceive me, or did I just see Harry walk you to class?"

I shrugged slyly, unable to hide my wide smile. Mitchell wasn't stupid. He knew something was up.

"Are you guys having a fling? Are you secretly dating? How long has this been going on, and more importantly, why the hell didn't you tell me?"

"Can we talk about this later?" I whispered, noticing the class begin to fill.

"Ugh, fine," he whispered back. "You better tell me in gym."

Biology was full of bookwork, and phys ed, as always, was a joke. Mitchell and I only participated in warm-ups before retreating to the bleachers.

"So are you gonna tell me why Harry walked you to class?" Mitchell asked, arching a perfectly waxed brow at me.

"When did you have time to do your eyebrows?" I asked in wonder, reaching up to touch them.

Mitchell swatted my hand away. "Don't change the subject. I'm obviously always flawless no matter what's going on. However, this isn't about me—for now. This is about whatever the hell is going on between you and Harry."

"Nothing *is* going on," I said, nearly in complete honesty. "He just skipped his class to sit at lunch with me."

"And you didn't bother to tell me?"

"Why does it matter? All we did was talk, anyway."

"Uh, Carter, this is my potential husband we're talking about," Mitchell joked. "What did you guys talk about?"

"Well, he did most of the talking, really."

"Okay, well, what did he say?"

"Uh, ya know, just stuff with his sister, and... Uh, okay, don't get mad...but I don't really remember."

Mitchell waved his hand dismissively. "You are so full of shit; how do you not remember? What, were you distracted by his *beauty*?"

I floundered, and it was then Mitchell realized he was right. His jaw dropped.

"No *fucking* way. Carter," he said, his grin widening as he gripped my shoulder. "You're crushing on him again, aren't you?"

"Wha—no, of course not."

"*Oh my god.* When did this start? Why didn't you tell me?!" He was practically shouting. Thankfully no one paid attention to us, because everybody shrieked in gym like middle-schoolers. "Does he like you back? Is that why you guys are hanging out more?"

"Well, first of all, lower your voice. Secondly, I'm not sure if I entirely like him. I mean, maybe, but I don't know yet."

"Why are you questioning it? If you like him, you like him."

"Yeah, but...so what? I mean, say he likes me back," I said, leaving out the part where Harry had actually admitted that he supposedly did, "then what? How do I know he's not gonna hurt me?"

Mitchell placed both his hands on my shoulders again, making me look him square in the eye. "You've been hurt before, and that sucked ass, but it was because Austin was a dickhead senior jock. You can't let that keep you from going out with other guys."

"Are you only saying that because you like Harry better?"

"That's beside the point! What I'm saying is: we all learn from our mistakes, Carter. You can't think that if one guy hurt you, then every guy is out to get you, too." Mitchell smiled sympathetically. "Plus, you always complain about not being in a relationship, yet every time you have the opportunity to be in one, you don't bother giving it a chance because you're scared."

"I didn't reject those guys in the past because I was scared; I rejected them because I was genuinely *not* interested," I retorted. "Like Tyler Frey, for example. He's asked me out nearly a thousand times in the past three years. Would you have been happy if I'd said yes?"

"I would have smacked the shit out of you for being stupid. When I said, 'Giving it a chance,' I meant to normal, nice guys, not *Tyler*," Mitchell said, cringing.

The bell rang, and Mitchell and I grabbed our things to get to our final class. We walked hand in hand, as per usual, and caught up with Elizabeth, who had class in the same area.

When we turned the corner to our hallway, I collided against something solid, my nose flattened by the impact, and Mitchell loosened his grip on my hand. "*Oww*, watch where you're going, will you?" I snapped, rubbing my face in annoyance.

When I looked up, I found Harry looking down at me with a smug look on his face, as if both amused and concerned by my crash.

"I'm sorry," he apologized casually, his eyes lingering on me as he walked away. I watched him as he turned his head and disappeared in the crowd.

Mitchell wouldn't stop gibbering about the incident, going on about how movie-magical it was. He swore he'd seen sparks fly between us, and I shook it off with a laugh. I had to stop running into Harry—literally—that way.

We made it to the staircase and did our usual routine of pretending to cry our eyes out at the sight of six flights of zigzagged stairs. We never made it on time, and although our history teacher had been annoyed with us about it in the beginning, he'd eventually stopped caring, as long as we arrived at some point.

The class dragged on, spent filling out worksheets. Mitchell and I finished first because we found the answer keys online on our phones. History wasn't my favorite subject, but it sure as hell beat math and biology. Our teacher was a social butterfly with the class, so he was always distracted. Mitchell and I would occasionally banter with him, but we tended to both doodle in our notebooks until we were free to leave.

It was ten minutes before the final bell and I was putting away my things, practically throwing them into my bag, when my phone vibrated twice.

Harry: sorry I couldn't stop staring at you
Harry: you look really pretty today

TEN

Me: is this some kind of sick joke

Harry: what

Me: I look terrible

Me: I'm wearing leggings and a sweater

Me: I'm positive I still have eye boogers from this morning

Harry: well I didn't wanna question why you chose to wear a sweater

Harry: in the middle of spring

Harry: when it's blazing hot out

Harry: you could get heatstroke

Harry: and die

Harry: but ima just sip my tea bc that ain't my business

Me: rolling my eyes

Me: the sun will do me no justice

Harry: okay batman

Harry: cALM DOWN

Me: rolling my eyes very hard at you right now, just so you know

Harry: did you know that if you roll your eyes a lot, they could strain

Harry: or you could get pink eye

Me: do you roll your eyes

Harry: barely

Harry: why

Me: you should start doing it often

Harry: HEY

Harry: THAT WASN'T VERY NICE

Harry: I came here to have a good time and I'm honestly feeling so attacked right now

Harry: I was literally just expecting a 'thank you'

Harry: and then this happened

Me: thank you for what

Harry: THE COMPLIMENT

Harry: CALLING YOU BEAUTIFUL

Me: oh

Me: no

Me: no thank you

Harry: what

Harry: why no

Me: because ur a liar

Harry: i wasn't lying

Harry: I really do think u look beautiful

Harry: even with eye boogers

I tried to stifle a laugh. Thankfully Mitchell was busy talking to a girl a few seats ahead of us. The bell finally rang and we took our time walking out. By the time we'd reached the second floor, the halls were cleared, and it was easy for us to exit the building. We went out through the doors behind the stairs on the first floor since everyone always bombarded the main entrance.

We ran through the parking lot and found Elizabeth already in the driver's seat of her car. Heat waves were shimmering off the pavement, and I was grateful for the blasting A/C. The entire ride home was just Mitchell going on about the whole Harry thing, and Elizabeth smirking at me each chance she got.

"I'm positive Harry likes her. You should have seen the way he was eyeing her. It was like the *I want you* kind of look," Mitchell practically squealed.

"It's funny how I didn't take it that way at all," I muttered. "And if you're this ecstatic for me, I can only imagine how you'd act if he was eyeing you in the halls."

"Oh, I'd be in cardiac arrest if that'd been meant for me. You'd see my underwear flying across the school." I mimed barfing, but I had to laugh. And then my phone started buzzing.

Harry: thanks for replying

Harry: means a lot

Harry: anyway

Harry: you're on your way home right?

Me: yeah

Me: why

Harry: see you there :)

When Elizabeth pulled over to drop me off at my house, Mitchell urged me to text him the minute anything happened. They both knew Harry was definitely going to come over, as per usual.

Once I made it in, I tossed my bag onto my bedroom floor before flopping on top of my covers and staring up at the ceiling. Feeling the cool cotton of my duvet against my warm skin, I inhaled, enjoying the solitude.

The sound of the front door slamming and feet running up the stairs made me jump. And then I heard giggling right before another door shut. My brother had a guest—a guest with a nasally laugh.

I groaned in disgust and made sure to lock my door. I grabbed my phone and started being nosy on Instagram and Twitter.

Moments after I liked a couple pictures from classmates, I began receiving countless texts.

Harry: are you home

Harry: I know dylan is because I see his car

Harry: and I keep texting him to open the door

Harry: but he won't answer

Harry: and now neither are you

Harry: which is odd

Harry: oh shit

Harry: are you guys fighting

Harry: should I come back later

Harry: bc I will

Harry: im always here anyway

Harry: my parents never question my absence anymore because of that

Harry: they're also probably happy im never home so they can have the house to themselves...

Harry: no but rly someone should let me in

Harry: like now

Harry: ....

Harry: Carter :(

Harry: so should I leave

Harry: no one is responding to me so

Harry: it's really hot out

Harry: im also very hungry

Harry: and thirsty

Harry: therefore your guest is dying

Harry: he's dying and he's not even inside yet

Harry: how does that make you feel

Harry: me

Harry: dead

Harry: on your porch

Harry: doesn't feel good does it

Harry: ....

Harry: didn't think so

Me: omg shut up already

Me: be right there

I tossed my phone back onto my bed and crept to my stairs, past my brother's bedroom, trying to ignore the sounds of heavy breathing coming from inside.

I opened the door to see Harry typing wildly on his phone. His head snapped up.

"Finally," he said loudly.

I put a finger to my lips and shushed him as he stepped inside.

"What's going on?" he asked.

I pointed my finger upstairs, and Harry remained motionless until the sound of a squeal and *"Oh my god, Dylan!"* bounced off the walls. He made a sour expression, and I chuckled at his reaction.

"If you want, you can wait down here until they're done," I said, strolling into the kitchen. My parents worked the majority of the day and sometimes well into night. And if they weren't working, they were going out with their co-workers, especially on weekends. So, it was up to me and Dylan to feed ourselves most of the time.

"I could do that, but I could also hang out with you," Harry suggested.

"And do what? All I do is eat and watch movies on Netflix," I responded, pulling out a box of macaroni and cheese to make. I filled a pot with water and started up the stove, feeling Harry's eyes watching me carefully as I maneuvered around the kitchen. "Are you enjoying the display?" I asked, trying to bite back my nervous grin.

"Sorry." He looked down at his hands, fiddling with his fingers. "Need any help?"

"Nope—not now, at least. But you can help when the macaroni is finished boiling if you want." I leaned up against the counter. I propped my elbow up and held my head in my hand. Harry sat on the stool across from me.

"So, eating and watching Netflix, huh?" Harry smiled again. "Sounds like a good second date. I'm not too picky, although it does sound better than yesterday—"

"That *wasn't* a date," I said, pointing an accusing finger at him.

"It could have been, if Mitchell and Elizabeth weren't there, but then again, I didn't mind them."

"Harry, you basically invited yourself, first off. Second, if that was a date, then that was the worst one I've ever been on." I poured everything into a strainer.

"*Ouch*," Harry said, mock-wounded. "How? Every other date you've been on was absolutely spectacular?"

I ignore his last comment as I prepped the noodles. "Because we started out talking about Austin, of all things, and you kept at it when I clearly didn't want to talk about him anymore."

"True. I apologize if I came off as pushy, Carter," he said tenderly. His change in tone made me catch his eye. "Honestly. I shouldn't have gotten into your business. And for the record, *Austin* is terrible in bed."

I snorted. "And how would you know?"

"Because every girl that he's been with said so."

"Said what, exactly?" I said, reaching over to the cabinets where the bowls were. "You want some?"

"Sure," he answered, getting up and grabbing the forks for us. "And let's just said he doesn't have the best...hip technique."

I gave him an odd look. "That sounds like something my grandpa would say."

"Why would you talk to your grandpa about sex?"

I sighed and said, "Anyway, I can't really agree or disagree, given my lack of comparison."

I filled the bowls, and Harry immediately went in for a bite.

"Hang on," I interrupted. "We're not eating here. Let's go to the living room and watch something. Unless you wanna go upstairs and—"

"Yes," Harry interjected.

"And watch Dylan and Lindsay have sex?"

Harry's eyes bulged out of his head. "Wait, no! I mean—*what?* Ew, Carter. I thought—"

"Chill, Harry. It was just a joke. Come on." I laughed, and we went into the living room. I turned on the TV and continued the last show I'd been watching.

ELEVEN

The heat was really taking its toll, especially after I'd turned on the stove, so the house felt like a giant oven. I turned on all the fans, then took a seat on the couch as Harry plopped down.

The minute the movie began, Harry asked with inquisitory glee, "*Jay and Silent Bob Strike Back*? What—wait, how do you know about this?"

"Am I not supposed to?" I said, my words muffled from a mouth full of food.

"It's not that, it's just surprising. I wouldn't have pegged you as cult-comedy type."

"Well, you look like you watch sappy romance films, but I'm not trying to watch that shit, so..."

Throughout the entire movie, all we did was laugh, talk over each other, and mock Jay after every insult directed at Silent Bob.

Halfway through, I put our empty bowls in the sink and stuck a popcorn bag into the microwave. Harry came back into the living room from the restroom, and I tossed him the bag.

"Dang, I haven't watched this movie in so long. I needed a good laugh," Harry said, wiping at his eyes.

"Tell me about it. I find this one so much funnier than *Clerks*."

"What?" Harry asked with wide eyes. "*Clerks* was equally hilarious."

I shook my head. "Not even close."

The sound of gunshots going off in the movie grabbed our attention again. I stuck my hand into the bag for more popcorn, then yanked it out when I felt his knuckles brush against mine. Harry smiled awkwardly before muttering a weak apology. I smiled in return, cautiously reaching for more popcorn, and Harry moved his hand to let me. I cleared my throat and shifted on the couch, and Harry did the same. I realized he had moved closer.

Is he...trying to make a move?

The sun was just starting to set, and the fans were still on full speed, so now it was a tiny bit chilly. I brought my knees up to my chest, trying to seem nonchalant as I watched Harry in my peripheral. He faked a long yawn and spread his arms out, resting one on the back of the couch just behind me. I felt all jittery, but I also was trying not to laugh.

I cleared my throat and asked, "Are you okay?" Harry bobbed his head, and I moved the popcorn bag to the coffee table in front of us. Harry placed his other hand on his leg. I could hear his breathing tighten as if he was trying hard to keep calm.

Is he nervous?

This was funny, and a little weird. I suddenly decided to help him out a bit.

"Hey, Harry?" I said softly, and he looked at me almost too quickly. "I'm cold."

"Oh! Uh, do you wanna borrow my sweater? I always carry one in my bag but almost never use it." Before I could even answer, he was tugging the sweater out of his backpack and handing it to me. I bit my lip, holding back a giddy grin, as I pulled it over my head.

But even though I was wearing his clothes and swathed in the scent of his cologne, it wasn't enough. I was filled with nerves, but I figured I ought to be decisive and take matters into my own hands if I wanted anything to happen. So, I slowly leaned into Harry. I knew he noticed because he tensed up a bit, and then moved closer to me as well. And after a little bit of awkward shuffling, I finally got comfortable as I leaned into his side.

My inner freshman-self was screaming like a girl at a Beatles concert, and I didn't blame her at all. Having Harry *this* close to me? I was mentally jumping in glee. I could feel my cheeks heating up.

From my side, I could feel Harry's gentle heartbeat against me. Mine was practically hammering against my ribs. I was positive he could hear it, as well.

The movie was almost done. I was surprised my brother was still up there with Lindsay, but I stopped myself before I gave *that* any more thought.

Harry's thumb began caressing my shoulder in slow circles. I froze on the spot. He slightly tightened his grip on me, then loosened it again. I could feel my heart crawling up my throat, threatening to burst out from my body.

Calm. Down.

But before I could embarrass myself in front of Harry, he said, "Carter?" I turned towards him as I watched his mouth open, close, then open once more to speak. "Are... Are you still watching?"

I was quiet for a moment, then let out a stupid giggle.

"What?"

"I'm sorry." I started to laugh harder. "Really, I'm sorry. I'm not laughing at you. You just sounded like Netflix after I after I binge six episodes straight."

"Oh, shut up." He laughed along with me, shaking his head at himself. "I actually wanna talk to you about something."

Oh, boy.

"Okay... About what?"

He fully turned to face me, arm still around my shoulder. "Well, we didn't get to finish that conversation the other day. You know, about me liking you."

"I remember. It's just... Why are you admitting it now? Honestly, Harry. If you've liked me this whole time, why did you wait so long to tell me?"

Harry hesitated. "Because, you know. It was hard for me to admit it, Carter. Especially because of your brother and—"

"What about him?"

Harry puffed out a breath. "You don't know how many times he's threatened me about ever making a move on you."

"So, my brother was the reason you hadn't told me?"

"Eh." Harry winced. "More or less. It was mainly because I felt like you sometimes hated me. But then, that night at the party where we almost kissed. Carter, I... I haven't stopped thinking about that night."

"Harry, look, I'll admit I really liked you two years ago, but ever since—"

He sighed heavily before cutting me off. "Ever since the whole Stacy thing, you lost respect for me, yeah, I get it. But Carter, I didn't—"

"No, no, I mean, aside from that, it's mainly because of the whole Austin thing. Don't get me wrong, I'm sure you mean well. But Harry, you have to understand that I'm scared of getting hurt, and even though Mitchell told me I should take a chance—"

"You told Mitchell?" he asked in surprise. I was surprised that *he* was surprised.

Was I not supposed to?

"...Yeah, I did," I said, narrowing my eyes at him. "Why?"

"Just asking."

"Right... Anyway, look, the point is, I was scared that you were going to, you know..." I was at a loss for words. *How do I say this without insulting him?*

"Hurt you the way Austin did?" He finished my sentence, and

I winced in embarrassment as I waited for him to get defensive. "Carter, Austin was an asshole. Okay, it's one thing to not trust me, but to compare me to *him*?"

"But how do I know you're not lying about liking me?"

"I'm not." Harry sighed tiredly. "I promise. Just give me a chance to prove it to you."

"How?"

It was silent, but his eyes poured into mine, roving from my lips to my eyes. Then I felt Harry tilt my chin up to face him, and he slowly began to lean in.

Is he about to...?

My body became more and more like Jell-O the closer he got. I could feel his lips brush against mine. But before I could respond, we immediately jumped apart at the sound of a door swinging open.

TWELVE

"Harry?"

Harry quickly stood from the couch, giving me an apologetic smile before answering, "Yeah, I'm down here." He pushed a hand through his hair as my brother plodded down the steps without a shirt.

Classy.

"Hey," Dylan greeted Harry, and they leaned in for that weird half-hug. "Sorry, dude. I only just saw your messages. Were you waiting long?"

"Not too long. I just wanted to swing by—" Harry stopped mid-sentence, both of us watching Lindsay as she emerged from the stairs in nothing but one of Dylan's T-shirts. The sight of her made me want to gag. Harry concentrated firmly on my brother and continued, "But...uh, looks like you were a little busy."

Dylan looked back at Lindsay, noting her presence before shooting a smirk back at Harry. "Yeah, my b. Um, maybe later we'll hit a few rounds of 2K?"

Harry nodded as he fished out his keys from his pocket. "All good. You enjoy yourself, yeah?" Dylan only laughed in response, looking towards the TV, and that's when he finally noticed I was there. His expression transformed from confused to annoyed in less than thirty seconds. But before he could say anything, Harry was already making his way towards the door. "See you, guys."

"Bye, Harry," Lindsay hummed sweetly before disappearing back upstairs, her cringe-worthy smirk making me uncomfortable.

Harry headed through the front door, and with his back turned to Dylan, he gave me a swift wink. My stomach exploded with butterflies—a feeling I hadn't realized I'd been missing since the ninth grade.

"Carter, *hello?*" Dylan called out, snapping me out of my little realization. "What the hell? Have you been down here this whole time? With *him?*"

"Sadly, yes, the *whole* time."

Dylan's nostrils flared like a raging bull's.

"Oh, please, as if we'd do anything." *Well, we almost did.* "I'd rather be here to keep *your* friend company than listen to the pig squeals going on upstairs."

"It's not my fault she's a screamer," he jeered, revoltingly smug.

"I was talking about *you.*"

"You're such a pain in my ass. Shouldn't you be at Miguel's or something?" He crossed his arms over his bare chest. "Having you here is a buzzkill, you know that?"

"Last time I checked, *I* lived here. Not her." I almost crossed my arms too, and then realized with irritation that we had the same habit. "Why should I have to go?"

"Because we haven't technically finished," he said, smirking.

"All that yodeling, and you didn't even let her finish? Why are you so bad at *everything*?"

"Fuck you, Carter," he spat, and he wheeled around to stomp up the stairs.

Since the whole "Stacy Kavanaugh" thing had involved parents, with Harry getting attacked and all, my mom and dad had eventually heard through the grapevine about Harry's drama and his constant rumored flings. That meant that not only was Dylan protective of me, but my parents also became that way, charging Dylan with looking after me. They were constantly busy at the hospital, and they trusted us enough to handle ourselves. Dylan was the oldest and, in their opinion, supposed to be my protector. They were fine with Harry being at our house and Dylan being friends with him, but they also knew he had a past. Dylan was already on guard with any potential boyfriend, but after that Monday, he didn't let Harry get anywhere close to me.

It was Thursday afternoon, and I had finally decided to go to

Mitchell and Elizabeth's place after school. As much as I hated to admit it, I was starting to miss Harry. I saw him at school, but only during our fourth period, and he'd been going to class instead of joining me for lunch. Seeing him at my house now only aggravated me, because I couldn't spend any time with him.

"Ooooooo," Mitchell exclaimed, "Melissa is having another party tomorrow night."

"Well, isn't that a surprise?" I asked sarcastically. Mitchell was sprawled across a reading chair, and I was lounging on Elizabeth's bedroom floor while she aggressively clicked away at a PC game.

"I'm going!" Mitchell announced. "It's my mission to be booty-bouncing at every opportunity." He hopped up so he could shake his butt in my face. I jabbed at the back of his knee, trying to make his leg give out, and he jumped away. Elizabeth glanced over her shoulder at us and laughed.

I stood up, stretched, and let them know I was going to grab a drink. Elizabeth requested a Yoo-Hoo. As I was jogging down their staircase, I checked my phone.

> **Harry:** you're not here? :(
> **Me:** nooo
> **Harry:** why?
> **Harry:** where are you?
> **Harry:** I wanted to see you
> **Harry:** that's why I even come to your house
> **Harry:** Dylan's up my ass lately

Harry: and I'm sick of him

Harry: I miss you

Harry: I miss "bothering" you

Harry: every time I try to go to you dylan makes me stay with him

Harry: he's talking to Lindsay right now and you're not here :(

Me: that's exactly why dylan is talking to Lindsay right now

Harry: what?

Me: ever since Monday he's been protective and doesn't want you around me

Me: so now that I'm not there, he can talk to her and not have to watch you

Harry: what a dick

Harry: where are you now?

Harry: I wanna see you carter, even if it's for 5 minutes

Me: I'm at mitchell's

Me: so I'll just see you later or something if you're still there when I get home

Harry: ugh doubt it :(

Me: are you going to melissa's party tomorrow night?

Harry: I didn't even know she was having a party lol

Harry: but idk maybe

Harry: why?

Me: I'll be there

Harry: so I'll see you?

Me: obviously

Harry: why there though?

Me: because dylan will get drunk or stoned and forget to care about us and

Me: well

Me: I kinda miss you too…

THIRTEEN

Friday rolled around, and school was a drag, as usual. Harry had been gone by the time I'd gotten home Thursday. He hadn't responded to me after I'd told him I missed him, which I found odd and, honestly, made me feel strange, like I'd done something wrong.

I was rather lazy for most of Friday, especially in my first three classes.

I got to art early and waited for the late bell to ring while everyone chattered out in the hall.

Harry came to art late and sat in the back by himself while I was with Andy and Sean, playing UNO. I laughed when Sean, as usual, claimed I was cheating each time I played a +4 card. It wasn't my fault they were absolutely shit at shuffling.

I looked over at Harry, who was looking down at his phone.

It was odd to see him by himself when he was usually with his friends. He hadn't even sat by me this week, and that bothered me twice as much as Dylan being a burden between us at home.

When class ended, I threw my bag over my shoulder and walked out with my jaw stiff. I scrolled through my Twitter feed and laughed at Mitchell's thread from when he'd live-Tweeted a debate between a physics teacher and a class clown.

I stopped by a water fountain, and I saw Harry slowly approaching me. He waited for a group of friends to go towards the lunchroom before he finally leaned on the wall beside me.

"Hey," he breathed, small smile playing at his lips.

"Hey to you," I said with crossed arms. "You alright? You seem pretty out of it."

Harry shrugged meekly. "Long day. Still going to the party?" he asked, sounding extra hopeful. I nodded, making him smile again.

He leaned in, surprising me with a swift peck on the cheek and a, "See you tonight."

"Uh, okay," I said in wonder, but he was already out of earshot as he jogged down the hall to his next class.

"So what're you going to wear tonight?" Mitchell's voice was tinny on my speaker.

"I'm thinking some graphic tee with a skirt. I'm leaning towards fancy-casual," I said as I shuffled through my closet. "What about you?"

"I'm thinking my dark blue jeans with my black jumper, but I can't decide on shoes," Mitchell whined.

"Picturing it now, I think you should go with your all-black Converse," I suggested. I pulled my button-down, corduroy black skirt from out of my drawer, along with a black band tee.

"You know, that's actually a good idea."

"I do have those on occasion," I said as I pulled the shirt over my head and then tucked it into the skirt.

"Sure, sure."

"Is Elizabeth taking us?"

"She doesn't want to go." Mitchell sighed. "She said she'd be willing to take us, though. She's just not gonna pick us up."

"Well, that's nice of her. Is there a reason she doesn't want to?"

"I asked her the same thing; she just isn't feeling it. We'll be there soon. I just saw some people's stories, and the party is already getting crowded."

"Okay, but really quick before you go..." I quickly changed the call to a FaceTime. I flipped the camera around so he could see my outfit in my full-length mirror. "What do you think?"

"Cute," he approved. "I think it'd look cuter with a denim jacket on top."

"Which one? I have, like, a bunch I bought from Rainbow last summer."

"The baggy light-blue one with the small rips. What are you going with for shoes?" He was touching up his hair in his own reflection.

"I think those black chunky boots from that website Lizzie showed me?"

"Sounds super cute," he said. "Leave your hair down and don't take too long to do your makeup. This is my nice way of saying, 'Hurry the hell up.'"

"All right, all right! I'll see you soon," I said. I put on my jacket and hung up.

As usual, Melissa's house was filled with countless people, possibly more than last week. Mitchell and I tried to convince Elizabeth to come with us, but she was set on staying in and didn't even put the car in park when she let us out.

Mitchell and I walked hand in hand through the front door and wandered into the kitchen. "Please tell me you're drinking tonight," he said. I pursed my lips as I hopped up on the counter.

"I don't know. To be honest, I sorta have a weird feeling about tonight."

"Come on, Carter," Mitchell whined, standing in front of me. "You drank last time and had fun, right? At least have a shot. For me?" He pleaded with puppy-dog eyes, blinking rapidly and folding his hands together.

"Ugh! Fine." I laughed. "Mix me something special."

Mitchell eagerly poured something into a couple plastic cups and shoved one in my hand.

"This is not a mix, this is a straight shot," I pointed out.

"As promised." He smiled as I rolled my eyes. I swirled the cup, and then closed my eyes and knocked back the drink. I winced as it burned all the way down, a rush of cinnamon disappearing with the aftertaste of straight alcohol. I felt the cup be pulled from my fingers; Mitchell was taking it from me and putting it on the counter.

"Jesus, Mitchell. What the hell did you give me?" I gagged, clutching my throat.

"That was Fireball."

"Ugh, so that's why it feels like I did the fucking cinnamon challenge."

"One is enough for you, I think. Looks like it hit you hard enough."

"I'm not *that* much of a lightweight." I rolled my eyes and pulled out my phone to check for notifications. Nothing.

As the party went on, I felt a little fuzzy. As I'd said, one shot was fine, but I started feeling it on my third. Or maybe my fourth. Mitchell, however, was probably on his eighth. He could down ten before he was gone.

We went from room to room, talking to every group we found, laughing and joking. I was, for once, being the social one while Mitchell watched, cackling at everything I said. I couldn't tell whether it was because I was actually being funny, he was buzzed, or I was slurring words.

KARLA DE LA ROSA

After what felt like hours, I pulled out my phone to find Harry's name flashing on my screen due to texts he had sent half an hour ago.

Shit.

Harry: are you at the party yet?

Harry: I'm on my way with dylan

Harry: and lindsay.....

Harry: blah

Harry: I'm here

Harry: Carter?

Harry: are you here?

Harry: I haven't seen you

Harry: have you got a ride?

Harry: I guess you're not coming...

Harry: unless you're on your way soon...or now?

Harry: if you are, I'll be in the kitchen

I locked my phone without replying. I leaned against Mitchell and whispered, "I'll be back. Don't move." Mitchell only nodded, swallowing yet another shot. I walked off, and the journey through the house felt endless. I had to shout *Excuse me* like fifty times to couples sloppily making out with one another. I made it to the last couple, who were leaned up against the doorway to the kitchen. They laughed when I politely asked them to move, then they continued their make-out session. I shoved them away. I didn't care that I was being rude or pissing them off.

I just wanted to see Harry.

I could already feel my stomach's fleet of butterflies taking flight. I was contemplating on going up to him and greeting him with a big kiss. It didn't matter what anyone else thought.

God, what is with me?

When I entered the room, I smiled lazily at the blurry vision of Harry. But I forced myself to blink a few times, and my grin vanished along with my happy, carefree mood. My buzz drained away at the sight of his lips roughly pressed against those of a familiar brunette's.

Lindsay.

FOURTEEN

Harry pulled away, and as if he could feel my gaze, looked right at me. With wide eyes, he said, "Wait, no."

My vision was still fuzzy, and it only got worse when tears of pained rage began to well. Out of pure instinct, I just turned and ran. I didn't even know where to go, so I stumbled up the stairs, tripping over people and not caring to apologize.

I knew Harry acting as if he liked me had been some sick joke. So why was I caught off guard? My emotions were everywhere. Was it the alcohol? I barged into a large bedroom, presumably Melissa's parents', screaming *Get out* to a couple toppled over each other on the bed.

They hurdled out the door, and I dropped to the floor, leaned against the bed.

What the literal fuck.

Harry and I weren't even together, but it felt like he'd stabbed me in the heart.

The door crashed open again. Harry. Of course.

"Carter," he gasped.

"Get out!" I shouted, grabbing the first thing I could get my hands on. I launched a hairbrush at him, and he ducked.

"Carter, wait!" he shouted. "Let me explain."

"What do you have to explain?" I asked him in disgust, stumbling to my feet. "I *saw* you. Harry, of all people, *her?*"

"I didn't kiss her," Harry protested.

I flung my arms out in exasperation, pacing now.

"*She* kissed *me.*"

"Oh, come on."

"Honestly, Carter, why would I kiss her? She's my best friend's *girlfriend*. And I didn't lie about liking you. I do. Why the fuck would I jeopardize that by kissing someone else? *Especially* Lindsay."

"I almost can't believe what I saw down there. And while I'm being honest, personally, I think that if you *really* liked me, you would've done something to show it a long time ago. Not wait an entire year."

His green eyes were chips of ice. He didn't respond. Instead, he strode toward me. I stumbled back, but I didn't have any time to react before his hands cupped my face and he pulled me forward for a searing kiss. I was stiff and tense, but my lips moved against his.

What the hell?

I was kissing Harry. Harry was kissing me. Harry's eyes were shut, and mine fluttering closed as I began to melt into the kiss. One hand went down to my waist and gripped the fabric of my shirt. The way he kissed me was indescribable. His mouth was surprisingly gentle, despite the ferocious moments before. I felt so moved. It was like a wave of euphoria. My hands made their way up to his neck and gently tugged on his curly hair; Harry groaned in response.

It felt like the whole world went mute and it was only us two. The heat pooling in my stomach gave me a warm, fuzzy feeling. I hoped it wouldn't end anytime soon. If I was given the opportunity to live in this moment forever, I absolutely would.

But, of course, nothing this good could last forever.

"What the fuck?"

FIFTEEN

My breath froze in my chest. Dylan was absolutely livid. "Dude, what the fuck!" he howled.

"Dylan, I—"

"That's my little sister!" Harry looked at me then back at Dylan. I was rigid, a deer in the headlights. I had no idea what to say.

Dylan moved between Harry and I, body-checking him out of the way. "I thought I told you to stay the *fuck* away from her!"

"Dylan, listen—!" Harry yelled desperately, but my brother cut him off.

"You're supposed to be my best friend! Jenny just told me you kissed my girlfriend, and now this?! What the hell is wrong with you?"

Harry gaped wordlessly, as if he didn't know where to begin. Hell, I didn't know what to say.

Dylan grunted as he snatched my wrist and began dragging me out of the room and down the stairs. No one gave us a second glance; everyone was drunk out of their mind, or dancing, or flirting. Dylan pulled me straight out the door.

"Dylan, stop!" I yelled. I struggled to release his grip on me, but he was too strong. "Dylan, let go of me!

"For what? So you can go crawling back to him?" he spat, turning to face me as we approached his car. "I don't ever wanna see him near you again. *Ever.*"

All I could say was, "That's not fair!"

"What do you mean 'not fair'?! Carter, you know the kind of person he is! Are you really that stupid?" He was raging, and he nearly shoved me in the passenger seat.

"Dylan, you don't get to control me! It was just a kiss!"

"Yeah? And I wonder what the fuck else would've happened if I hadn't walked in!" He threw himself into the driver's seat and muttered to himself as he started the engine. "First my girlfriend and then my sister, who the fuck does he think he is?"

The car ride was an all-out screaming match. He didn't even bother waiting for me when we parked; he just left me in the car.

I sat for a few minutes until I could stop hearing my own heartbeat in my ears. When I walked in, I saw my dad sitting at the kitchen table with a mug of tea. "Hi, sweetie," he said, a small frown on his face. "What's wrong with Dylan?"

"Bad night. Lindsay issues." I hurried to the stairs before he could smell the alcohol on my breath. "Anyway, I'm gonna head to bed, so...goodnight, Dad." I went up to the hallway.

"Dylan..." I called through his shut door. No response. "Dylan, please." Still no response. I pounded on his bedroom door, pleading, "Dylan, can you please just stop being such a baby and talk to me about this!"

Finally, he cracked the door open an inch.

"I have nothing to say to you."

"Then what the hell was the point of dragging me home?" I pushed my way in, and surprisingly, he let me enter. "Dylan, you're being so dramatic."

"Listen, Carter, he may be my best friend, or at least he was, but I've seen him go through chicks like they were nothing. He could've taken advantage of you."

"Dylan, if he'd tried to take advantage of me, I would've stopped him." He gave me a doubtful look. "It's just Harry! We made out, big deal. None of that is your business."

Dylan sat in his gaming chair, growling, "Shut up. You think you know him better than I do. Just stay away from him, Carter. That's an order."

I scoffed. "Since when are you allowed to tell me who I can and can't date?"

"I'll tell Mom and Dad, and you know they don't trust him. Especially for you." Dylan sneered. "Now, I won't tell them anything if you just promise to never see him again."

"You're being such a—"

"I don't care, Carter. Do you know what would happen if people found out about you and Harry? If you guys slept together and people found out, you'd be a slut. Without question."

I didn't know how to respond to that, so I just said, "That's stupid."

"That's high school." He pinched the bridge of his nose. "Carter, just promise me you'll stay away."

I shook my head and sighed. "Whatever." I left for my room where I fell onto my bed. I buried my face into my pillow and let out a high-pitched scream.

Mitchell: carter

Mitchell: what the fuck

Mitchell: where did you go

Mitchell: why the fuck did you ditch me

Mitchell: I had to hitch a ride to get home

Me: I went home early

Mitchell: why the fuck

Mitchell: you bitch

Mitchell: I hate you

Mitchell: die

Me: calm down

Me: I didn't want to go home

Mitchell: then why did you

Me: drama

Mitchell: ooooooh

Mitchell: brb getting popcorn

Mitchell: what happen boo

Me: first of all, ew

Me: don't ever, no ew

Me: second, it's harry drama

Mitchell: HARRY DRAMA!??!?!?!!!

Mitchell: YAAASSSSS

Me: but it's too much explain

Me: come over tmrw?

Mitchell: hell yes im coming over tomorrow

Mitchell: i cant wait wtf

Mitchell: i'm going to sleep early for this

Me: it's almost 2 am......

Mitchell: bitch

Mitchell: that's early for me

Mitchell: SEE YA

The night was awfully quiet. My parents had gone to their room once my mom had arrived home. I was lying on my bed, in my sweats, trying to read a book, although I'd been on the same page for what felt like an hour.

All I could think about was Harry and that kiss. That long-awaited, lustful kiss. The way his lips felt against mine. The way they moved. His hands holding me gently, pulling me in for more. The more I thought about the kiss, the more I wished I'd had the chance to lock the door before Dylan had come in and ruined it all. My phone buzzed against my nightstand. I picked it up warily, thinking it was Mitchell again, but grinned when I saw the name flashing on my phone screen.

Harry: hey

Harry: are you still up?

SIXTEEN

Me: maybe......

Me: you ok?

Harry: yeah I guess

Harry: but I wanna talk

Me: so talk lol

Harry: are u srs

Harry: not like this

Harry: god carter

Me: then how

Me: and that should be my new contact name in ur phone

Harry: i'm not putting you as "god carter"

Me: and why the fuck not

Me: it has a nice ring to it

KARLA DE LA ROSA

Harry: omg shut up

Me: how can I shut up if we're texting

Me: idiot

Harry: omfg

Harry: carter can you just

Harry: ugh

Harry: just look out your window

My heart leapt in my chest.

I gripped my phone and pressed it against my stomach as I quietly crept towards my window. I peered down, but I only saw our little yard and light pollution all over the sky. I furrowed my brows and brought my phone up just as another text came in.

Harry: look at the car across the street

Through the dim windshield, I saw a small hand wave in the darkness.

I scoffed, smiling to myself. *Seriously?* I didn't even bother texting back; I called him to make sure I wasn't dreaming.

"Hello?" he whispered.

"Why are you whispering? Aren't *I* the one under house arrest?"

I heard him chuckle. "Sorry, I just thought your brother would spaz out if he heard us talking."

"Oh, he would," I said as I sat at the edge of my bed. "So, you wanted talk to me?"

"Oh, yeah," he said, as if just remembering why he even came here.

"Are we gonna talk like this?"

"I was actually wondering if you could find a way to sneak out?"

I thought about it for a moment, looking over at my window and then the straight drop down to the ground. "Well, the climb from my window does look doable..."

"Really?" He sounded almost too surprised. "You'd climb out a window for me?"

"Hell no, does it look like I want to die?"

"I'd climb up to a window for you."

"Yeah, yeah, whatever, Prince Charming. Why don't I just sneak you in through the back?"

Harry hesitated before responding, "Are you insane? What if we get caught?"

"Got any other ideas?" I asked, opening my door a fraction to make sure Dylan's was still closed. When Harry finally agreed, I hung up and made my way downstairs to meet him by the back door.

The whole time I tried to get us in quietly, Harry kept trying to pull me back and give up on the whole plan. I'd never seen him so scared. And despite how cute it was, it was also annoying because he kept tugging on my arm, especially when he kept stepping on the stair that made the most noise. Thankfully that only happened twice. When we'd made it to my bedroom and I'd locked the door, Harry released the longest, most over-dramatic breath I had ever heard.

"We almost died," he exclaimed a little too loudly. I had to clamp my hand over his mouth and wait a couple seconds to make sure the house was silent.

"We could've made it no problem if you had just calmed down," I whispered with a glare.

"Well, *excuse me* for trying not to get caught," Harry mumbled against my palm.

"Yeah, well, you almost blew it," I muttered, removing my hand from his mouth. I turned on my little speaker, playing some music to hopefully tune both me and Harry out. I plopped onto my bed, and Harry gently sat next to me. He looked awkwardly around my room, the soft music filling the air. I could tell was nervous.

"Look, Carter, I'm sorry about tonight," he murmured. "I didn't mean to get you in trouble with your brother."

"He'll get over it. I'm sorry I ruined your friendship with Dylan," I replied. "He's really pissed at us. Well, he's disgusted by me, angry at you."

Harry just shrugged. "It wasn't working out, anyway."

"What do you mean?"

"I mean, Dylan has stuck by me more than anyone else, and I appreciate that, but we've both changed. The last few months, he talked to Lindsay the whole time I was here, and eventually he just became my excuse for being here so I could see you." He frowned deeply. "I knew the friendship would end eventually. I just didn't think it'd end like this."

"So, you were planning on breaking up with my brother?" I asked playfully. He anxiously rubbed the back of his neck, but his face cracked into a smile. "Anyway, since you brought her up, I have to ask: what happened back there with Lindsay?"

He heaved his shoulders in a sigh. "Your brother went upstairs to smoke with Ryan and AJ—you know them, right? He left me with Lindsay to watch her. Literally, he told me to watch *his* girlfriend like I was her babysitter." He shook his head in aggravation. "So, anyway, while I was waiting for you to reply to my messages, she came up to me and started getting all touchy-feely, and I don't know, I was getting uncomfortable. That's when she kissed me and then all that...happened."

"So you didn't initiate the kiss with Lindsay?" I questioned.

"Hell no. I never liked her from the moment Jenna introduced her to me and Dylan. That kiss meant nothing. I told you, I like *you*, Carter."

I smiled at him, unsure how to respond. But I was relieved.

"But anyway, look, I really wanted to talk to you about Stacy Kavanaugh."

What?

"What about her?"

"You know those rumors about me and her over the summer?"

I nodded, a little uncomfortable.

"It never happened."

"What? But if you didn't sleep with her, why did you admit to it?"

"I never said anything like that. Everyone said I owned up to it, but I didn't. I didn't even say anything when the rumor first started."

"Why not?"

Harry ruffled his hair. "I guess because at the time, I thought it made me look cool—a sophomore hooking up with a senior. I don't know, I was young, so I kind of just stuck with it. But now that I'm older, I kind of wish I had denied it."

"How come?"

"Because." Harry sighed, his eyes becoming glossy. "Now that I'm a senior, it's hard to want something serious when you have a reputation like mine."

I looked down at my feet. "But what about those weekly hookups everyone always talks about?"

Harry hesitated. "That's half-true," he confessed, "but it definitely wasn't weekly. They were just lame hookups that happened here and there. That stopped at the end of my junior year, though, I swear."

I only nodded in response, still keeping my gaze down.

"I really liked you when I first saw you," he insisted.

I looked up at him with a raised brow. "*Liked?* Past tense?"

Harry rolled his eyes. "I mean I *still* do. Meeting you towards the end of my sophomore year was probably my favorite moment in high school. I always thought you were cute and really fun to talk to. But you were also Dylan's sister, and then the whole Stacy thing... I had to—I dunno—grow up a little, get past all that. I'm not perfect, but I care about you. It's why I still came over every day to see you."

"I'm glad you did," I replied, my heart slowly beginning to race.

"Me too. It's hard for me to stay away from you, Carter."

SEVENTEEN

With the streetlights illuminating my room, I could see Harry pretty clearly. His hair was tousled, pushed back. His jaw looked more defined than usual with the contrast of light and shadow. I scooted closer to him, his body turning towards me. His gaze shifted from my eyes to my lips.

"It's hard for me to stay away from you, too," I murmured, my eyes wandering all over the beautiful features on his face. I placed a hand to his cheek.

A small grin appeared on his face, bringing out the dimple on his left cheek.

"You look cute like that," he whispered, "so focused on exploring my face." Embarrassed, I tried to remove my hand, but he gripped my wrist, stopping me.

"Don't," he murmured. "That felt nice."

He nuzzled his face against my fingers, resting his own palm on the back of my hand. Then he started to kiss my fingers. My stomach fluttered again; I was never going to get used to that feeling, and I didn't mind one bit. I leaned forward, and Harry took a sharp breath when our lips brushed together. Soon, our lips were parting and our tongues were dancing rhythmically with one another. I played with the ringlets of baby hairs on his neck and around his temples. I tugged softly when I felt Harry's teeth clamp down onto my bottom lip.

Harry's hand disappeared into my hair, his fingers twisting and pulling on the roots. My free hand rested on his waist, clenching around the fabric of his sweatshirt.

I got a weird fuzzy feeling at the pit of my stomach. Goosebumps were raising up on my arms and spine. Harry's hand pressed on my ribs just below my breast and moved to my back, pulling me closer. He removed his lips from mine and trailed kisses from my mouth to my cheek, my jaw, and then my neck. My breathing was erratic at the sudden contact, a whimper slipping past my lips.

Harry ran his tongue along my lips to my jaw till he reached behind my ear and bit down gently, his tongue lapping over the skin before sucking. My hand went from his waist down to the hem of his shirt. I couldn't help my wandering hands as I began to explore his torso with my fingers, his skin blazing hot. Harry's hands suddenly wrapped around my waist, hauling me over so I was straddling him, and our lips reconnected.

Our mouths hungrily moved against one another, aching and

urging for more.

Harry's hands grasped my hips. He pressed his hips into me, his prominent erection pressing onto my crotch. The feeling was new, but I liked it. His lips reattached to my neck; I felt my entire body weaken.

My mind was empty of all thoughts besides him, this, us. I was actually living in the moment.

But then he suddenly stopped. His eyes were watching me carefully, and I stared down at him, suddenly feeling embarrassed. *Did I do something wrong?*

"Carter, we don't have to do this. Not right now."

"But I—"

"I just don't want you to feel like I'm pressuring you—"

"No, no. I want to," I told him, my thumb running circles on the skin of his cheek. "Honestly, I do." The music continued playing softly, some low-key indie rock band Elizabeth had shown me. Our eyes raked over each other's lips, yearning to be touched by one another once again.

Finally, Harry leaned in, wasting no time as he pressed his lips to mine. And the trance we'd had just moments ago made its reappearance. Our hands were all over one another, trying to pull each other as close as possible. I felt the apex of my thighs beginning to dampen.

Harry bit gently on my lips, earning a moan from me, which only made him kiss me harder to prevent us from being heard.

He pulled away once more to ask, "Are you sure?"

I swallowed the lump in my throat and nodded. My blood was on fire.

Harry looked hesitant until I pressed my finger against his lips and said, "I'm ready. I promise."

He gave me another long kiss. His hands disappeared from my body and I heard his fingers fiddling with his belt and slowly unzipping his pants. I swung my leg off him so I could pull my sweats and underwear down my legs, moving quick so I didn't think about anything too much.

The rhythm of my heart increased immensely, and it skipped a few beats upon hearing the tearing of a foil packet in the background. That sound made it all too real. Once I pulled my sweats off my ankles, I was pushed down onto the bed as Harry rolled over on top of me, tugging a blanket over us. He pressed his entire body against mine as he trailed wet kisses along my neck. The pleasure coursing through me made my toes curl.

Harry kissed the skin below my ear, his fingers reaching down and rubbing me. I had to bite my lip harshly to keep myself from making noise.

"Ready?" he asked, and I nodded immediately with my lip still clamped between my teeth. Harry began to align himself against me. With his eyes locked on mine, he lowered himself down to press a hard kiss against my mouth as he began to push himself inside me. I gripped his sides harshly and hissed at the feeling.

"Are you okay?" he asked as he tried to keep his eyes open. He was in obvious bliss compared to what I was feeling.

"Y-Yeah," I croaked, trying to sound calm. "Just hurts a little."

"You want me to stop?"

I shook my head no.

"You tell me if you want me to stop, okay? I want you to enjoy this as much as me."

"Okay," I whispered, waiting for the part where this would start to feel really good.

Harry started off slow, focusing on me as I tried to relax. The pain disappeared as he steadily moved. Eventually, small moans slipped past my lips, watching as Harry enjoyed the view below him. We stayed like that for a while, the pain completely vanishing. I was surprised when Harry flipped us over with ease. I was now sat on top of him. I could feel him deeper inside me; the pit of my stomach burned ecstatically. Harry stayed still, breathing slowly with his eyes clenched shut and fingers clenching my hips. I took a moment to let myself fully adjust to his size.

Eventually, I slowly began to grind myself down onto his crotch, right where we connected, feeling him slide in and out of me. Harry's breath hitched in his throat. His hand went to my thighs, gripping my skin, and I bit my lip to suppress to groan of both arousal and pain. I made slow, steady movements. Harry opened his eyes, licked his lips, and watched between us. I spread my legs more, my body lowering down onto him further. I could feel him fully and I bit my lip harder, my hands reaching down and gripping his shoulders. I began moving again, afraid of going fast. I was nervous and rather worried that I looked foolish on top of him. I knew it'd take some time getting used to; I just hoped I had this right. I leaned back, one hand resting on his thigh while the other rested on his hard, toned stomach, trying to find a balance.

"*Shit*," Harry breathed. "Fuck, that feels *so* good."

"Am I doing okay?" I panted, letting out a laugh as I tried to catch my breath. It felt good on my part; I just hoped it did for him as well.

Harry chuckled and then rolled his head back against the pillow as I circled my hips.

"Yeah. Yeah, *fuck*, you're doing great," he muttered, his eyes rolling back a little.

I do the same movement again, earning a low moan from him. The sudden sound sent me into a pleasure-filled frenzy. Harry moved his hands to my waist, holding me still as he slowly began to thrust upwards, then picked up speed.

My breathing was harsh and rigid. I felt like the wind had been knocked out of me. Pleasure ripped through my insides. A fire had ignited inside the pit of my stomach and I could feeling it burn my insides.

Am I coming?

I felt my legs begin to shake as this amazing wave of pleasure hit me like a tidal wave. I collapsed into a heaving mess, coming undone on top of him.

"Shit. Shit, Carter," Harry panted. "I'm gonna—" I pressed my hand against his mouth again, feeling his muffled groans against my palm. Harry screwed his eyes shut, gripping at my waist and coming soon after. His body tensed and then relaxed.

After a few moments, I lay my chest against his and rested my head in the crook of his neck. My hair was sticky and sweaty against my forehead. Harry lay there, looking completely worn out as he pushed back my hair from my face. I wrapped my hand around the back of his neck, catching his attention, and pulled him in for another kiss.

"So, what happens now?" I asked with arms crossed as Harry ruffled his messy hair.

We were standing outside by his car, a pleasant nighttime wind blowing through.

"What do you mean?" Harry asked, his eyes sleepy.

"I mean, well..." I felt awkward asking this question. "What are we going to do now?"

"Hey. What just happened—it doesn't mean that's all I came for. Because it's not. I would never do that to you. I mean it." He pulled me closer and tilted my head up with his fingers so I would look at him. "I like you. I really do. It's just, well, you know, the only problem is—"

"My brother," I muttered, finishing the sentence for him.

My parents wouldn't have a problem with Harry and me being together if they didn't know about his stupid, unfair reputation. But Dylan was another matter; I was sure he'd rage war about me dating anyone, let alone his closest friend.

"So, what does that make us?"

Harry leaned against his car and wrapped his arms around me. He smiled lazily at me and said, "Well, you'll be my girlfriend. And I'll be your boyfriend." I traced my fingers on his shirt. "We will work something out. We just can't let your brother find out."

I backed up a step, really thinking about it. I really did like Harry. But he was asking me to be in a secret relationship with him. I understood why. But the thought of having to hide a relationship with someone who I had longed for even when I couldn't admit it? It didn't feel right. In all honesty, this reminded me too much of my ex. I wondered if Harry would stoop that low.

Starting a relationship with Harry would be a dream, but I wouldn't be able to fully enjoy it if I had to keep it hidden. I considered saying no, backing away. Harry could see the turmoil on my face, evidently, as he watched me anxiously and waited as patiently as he could, his knee bouncing.

But I could also hear Mitchell's voice screaming in my ear about taking a chance with someone who actually liked me and could potentially make me happy. Whether or not it worked out, at least I could learn from it.

So after a long moment of really thinking about it, I finally looked him right in the eye. "Okay, look," I said, "I'll be your girlfriend if, and *only if*, we are really careful."

"Wait, really?" A huge grin lit up his face. "Okay, yes, absolutely." He attacked me with a million little kisses all over my face, making me giggle. "I won't let you down, Carter. You have my word."

"I'm holding you to that," I laughed. "But seriously, Harry, as much as I hate it, we have to lie low. No matter what. I like you, and I want to make this work."

"I promise." He nodded and pressed his forehead against mine before pecking me once more, then pulling away. "It's almost five in the morning. You should head back, babe. I've kept you out too long now."

I melted at the sound of him calling me "*Babe.*" But then I looked at his car and pouted. "I don't want to go."

Harry chuckled and swatted my behind. "Go before it gets any later."

I gave him a grin and walked backwards so I could keep him in my sight. When the sidewalk gave way to road, I turned, glancing up at the moths fluttering around the streetlights.

"Carter?" he called, and I looked back. "Sweet dreams."

EIGHTEEN

"Bitch, wake up," a familiar voice shouted. I was too exhausted to acknowledge what was going on; I didn't even bother moving. "Wake the fuck up!" And then Mitchell jumped on my bed, bouncing me.

I groaned and glared at Mitchell, who was having far too much fun. I kicked at him from beneath the blankets, and his eyes went wide before he stumbled and nearly fell face-first onto the floor. I wheezed with laughter and cocooned myself further.

Mitchell stood up, ripping my duvet off, then the sheets. I was wrapped up in a ball, holding my legs up to my chest. I felt particularly exposed, even though I was still wearing the same clothes from last night. And then the memories of last night hit me like a ton of bricks.

"I get up bright and early to come see you, and you're *still asleep*," he said accusingly.

"I forgot you were coming," I mumbled, rubbing at my eyes.

Mitchell's jaw dropped. *"Ouch."*

I glanced at my clock on the wall. "And it's noon."

"Yes, bright and early! Now, you better dish on your Harry drama; I am not passing that up."

Accepting that I wasn't going to leave the bed any time soon, he made himself comfortable, stealing a pillow and curling up on his side.

I finally sat up and crossed my legs. Doing so made me realize I was a little sore, and I concentrated on collecting my thoughts so I wouldn't blush or otherwise give myself away. "All right. I didn't tell you this exactly when it happened because I wasn't sure if it was worth telling yet, but now I know you need to hear this."

Mitchell was a rapt audience.

"Harry had some sort of epiphany and confessed his feelings for me. However, I wasn't sure if he was bullshitting me or if I even liked him back. I definitely do now, even more than before, actually—"

"How so?"

"I'm getting to that," I informed him. "But yeah, that explains why he hung out with us when we went out to eat and the way he looked at me at school. Also, apparently one of the main reasons he ever came over my house every day was to see me. Anyway..." I paused, taking a breath before continuing, "So last night at the party, the reason why I left early was because... Well... I'm just gonna come out with it: Dylan walked in on us making out."

Mitchell's face was priceless. His mouth dropped open, and he gawked at me with owl eyes. "Are you fucking serious?!" He squealed, and I flailed my arms at him in the universal signal of *keep it down.*

"That's not all," I said. "After Dylan completely blew up on us, he dragged me home, and that's why it seemed like I ditched you."

"So, Dylan got angry at you for making out with his best friend, and made you go home? That's it?"

"He kinda forbid us from seeing each other until the end of time."

"Are you serious?" Mitchell asked again. "That's some Romeo-and-Juliet bullshit."

I traced over the designs of the bed sheets. "I mean, that didn't stop him from coming to see me last night..."

Mitchell grabbed my shoulder, forcing me to look back at him. "He came over!?"

I put both hands over his mouth. "Could you be any louder? Honestly. And yes, he came over."

Mitchell pushed my hands away. "So what happened? Did you guys make out some more or what?"

I hesitated. "Something like that."

Mitchell gasped, and now he was the one flailing his arms around. "What did you guys do? Holy shit, Carter. Holy shit." He was heaving dramatically, fanning himself with his hands.

"Do I really have to say it?" I winced. I wasn't ashamed of what

KARLA DE LA ROSA

I'd done, but I didn't feel like going into it, even with Mitchell.

"Yes! Did you...?"

I tried to hide my ridiculous, immature grin. "We did."

Mitchell whistled. "Wow. I mean, can't say I didn't see it coming, honestly, but still."

"Hey!" I smacked his arm. "Look, just don't ask for details, okay?"

"Aw, but details are my *favorite* part," he said teasingly. "Where was it?"

"*Mitch*," I groaned.

"All I'm asking is where you guys did it—it's not like I'm asking for all your favorite positions."

"Stop!" I laughed in embarrassment and shoved him. "I'm not telling you, it's weird." Plus, I was sure Mitchell would make a dramatic scene if he found out it happened where we were sitting. Mitchell just grinned deviously, and I couldn't help but ask, "Why are you looking at me like that?"

"I just didn't think you had it in you." Mitchell leaned back on his elbows, looking at the opposite wall. "You had sex with Harry. Carter, I'm so... I don't even know how to express how I feel right now."

"If you're proud of me for this, I'm gonna have to rethink our friendship," I remarked jokingly. "Look, just don't tell anyone."

"Well, *duh*." Mitchell rolled his eyes. "But, Carter, your brother can't keep you from seeing Harry."

"Yeah, but my parents can."

Mitchell sat up immediately. "He threatened to blackmail you?"

I nodded. I was a little overwhelmed. It still bothered me how it had all panned out. If things had been different, maybe Harry would be my boyfriend without an issue.

I continued on, "After me and Harry...*you know*...he asked me to be his girlfriend. I said yes. It's just...*ugh*. Mitchell, being in a relationship with him is amazing. But having to hide it? Just to keep my brother from finding out? It sucks."

"I see your point," Mitchell sighed. "I'd be conflicted, too."

"You know what would make me feel better, though?" I asked Mitchell with puppy-dog eyes.

Mitchell narrowed his eyes at me. "What...?"

"Some food..."

He rolled his eyes while laughing. "You're lucky I'm feeling nice today."

"Chicken soup, please!"

Mitchell scoffed. "You're getting Cup O' Noodles."

I launched a pillow at him, my aim failing miserably. He walked out and dramatically pulled the door shut while eyeballing me. I fell back onto my mattress and stared up at the ceiling, sighing, when my phone dinged, texts flying in from none other than Harry himself.

142

NINETEEN

Harry: gooooood morning beautiful :)

Harry: well afternoon*

Harry: I just woke up

Harry: and this is the latest I've woken up in ages

Harry: it's past noon

Harry: and I'm surprised nobody woke me up

Harry: aka you

Harry: then again you're probably still asleep

Harry: which honestly wouldn't surprise me

Harry: bc god knows you sleep like a bear hibernating in the winter

Harry: every time I went to your house you claimed you were always """"tired""""

Harry: that's gonna change tho

Harry: starting now

Harry: are you even asleep tho

Harry: bc if u aren't, a text back would be nice

"Carter!" Mitchell screamed from the kitchen.

"What?" I shouted back as I got up from my bed and moved over to my mirror. I wiped at the leftover mascara that had made its way to my under-eyes.

"I can't find that red pot you use; how am I supposed to boil this water for your dumb noodles?" I heard Mitchell rummaging through the kitchen. Then, I noticed the disastrous state of my room in the reflection. My mother would kill me if she saw my clothes on the floor right next to the hamper, and half my closet on the floor, and the shoes sprawled around like an obstacle course.

"Carter!"

"*Ugh*, did you check in the drawer under the stove?"

"What draw—oh!" I heard the awful screech of the drawer opening from upstairs and more clattering of pots and pans. "Got it!"

I stuffed my shoes under the bed, making a mental reminder to actually clean up later, or some other day. And then my phone continued buzzing, reminding me that I hadn't responded to Harry.

Harry: wow you must rly be out

144

Harry: like a light

Harry: HAHA

Harry: I know it wasn't even that funny

Harry: but it tickled my tummy

Harry: whoa

Harry: that rhymed

Harry: quick carter write this down

Harry: I think I just made a hit single

Harry: my road to stardom

Harry: my one-hit wonder

Harry: are you ready for this

Harry: I'm about to drop this sick verse

Harry: it wasn't even that funny

Harry: but it tickled my tummy

Harry: I'm dressed so bummy

Harry: my nose is runny

Harry: now here I am

Harry: playing chubby bunny

Harry: oOoOoOoOoOoOohhhhhhhhhh

Me: that sounds like a terrible song

Me: I wouldn't buy it on itunes

Harry: CARTER

Harry: YOUR AWAKE

Harry: HI BABY

Me: you're*

Harry: I MISSED YOU

Harry: wait

Harry: are you kidding me

Harry: I just woke up

Harry: buttering you up with my love

Harry: and you chose to correct my grammar

Harry: seriously carter, I'm offended

Me: calm down. let's start over ok?

Me: good afternoon harold, how did you sleep?

Harry: fine, thanks for asking, babe, you?

Me: swell

Me: i actually just woke up not too long ago

Me: I just chose to take a while to reply because I like when u babble

Harry: I'm sure you do

Harry: so what are you doing today :)

Me: I don't think anything really

Me: mitch is here

Me: he's making me soup right now

Me: because he's my slave

Me: my bitch

Me: what about you

Harry: laying in bed doing nothing as usual

Harry: I would've loved to make you soup btw

Me: you wouldn't make me soup, you can hardly rinse a damn strawberry

Harry: THAT WAS ONE TIME

Harry: and no really, I wanna be your bitch and make you soup

Me: HOW CUTE. But no

Harry: I'M SERIOUS. I'll come over right now

Harry: ya know now that we're a thing, it's kinda my job to do stuff like this for you

Me: yeah and it's my job to remind you that you're not allowed in my house anymore

Me: because I have security aka Dylan who will have no problem telling the parentals

Harry: well you could always come to my house

Harry: though I must warn you, my parents are strictly off limits to socialize with

Me: why omg

Me: are they evil?

Harry: no

Me: strict?

Harry: no

Me: judgmental?

Harry: no

Me: then what?

Harry: they're just really embarrassing

Harry: WHATEVER THEY SAY IS A LIE

Harry: so no socializing. I beg of you

Me: it's okay, it's too soon to meet your parents anyway

Harry: it was too soon to have sex but we did it anyway

ayy

Me: HARRY

Me: omg anyway, as I was saying

Me: if we're gonna want to hang out without getting caught, we should really discuss the game plan

Me: for starters, if I'm gonna be going over to your house, how am I getting there?

Me: because you know you can't pick me up, right?

Harry: duh carter, I'm not an idiot

Me: are you sure

Me: your grammar begs to differ

Harry: YOU KNOW WHAT

Harry: I'm starting to reconsider this whole "together" thing

Me: are you really?

Me: is it bad that although I know you're joking, it actually hurt my feelings for a sec

Harry: nah I'm kidding, I'd never reconsider you

Me: aw :')

Harry: ur too good in bed

Me: OH MY GOD

Me: harry wtf

Harry: ahahahahahahaha

Harry: I crack me up

Harry: no but really carter

Harry: I like you too much to just throw you away

Harry: I worked too hard to get this far

Me: you said nothing in the past 2 years

Harry: shut up I still said something eventually tho

Harry: now you're mine

Me: aw omg, harry

Me: you finally used "you're" correctly :')

Harry: carter

Harry: I hate you

Me: anyway can we go back to the game plan?

Me: when do you wanna hangout?

Harry: today if possible

Harry: miss you already :)

Me: how about I go to mitchell's & wait outside for you to pick me up?

Harry: oooh sounds like a plan

Me: k I'll text you when to come

Harry: oh I'll come tonight, if ur pickin up what I'm puttin down ;)

Me: ew stop bye

Harry: hahaha see you soon princess :-)

I rolled my eyes, trying not to giggle like an idiot. I stretched, knowing if I didn't get up soon, I'd fall asleep again. I was putting my hair up into a ponytail when Mitchell walked in.

"Okay, here's your—"

"Come on, let's go," I announced, slipping on my worn-out

TOMS.

"What?"

"We're leaving," I said.

"What the hell, you bitch? I just made you soup!" Mitchell shouted with wide eyes. "I put a lot of hard work into this. Fucking really?"

I narrowed my eyes at him. "All you did was boil water."

Mitchell scoffed. "It's not as easy as it sounds. God, Carter, you're so selfish."

"What do you—?" I stopped, knowing we'd just spiral. "I'll just take the cup with me."

"I hope it burns you," Mitchell muttered, holding it out. "Where are we going, anyway?"

"Your house. We're gonna hang out a while, and then Harry's picking me up from there," I said as I stuffed my keys and phone into my hoodie pocket. When I looked back at Mitchell, I found him smirking. "What?"

"Going for round two or what?"

I scrunched up my nose. "Ew, stop. Can we just go?"

"You're going like that?" he remarked, making me look down.

Shit.

Harry had already seen me in this outfit last night. I ran back to my drawer and rummaged for a white tank top and my favorite burgundy sweater. I grabbed a pair of leggings, a new pair of underwear, and a bra, then stuffed everything into a bag.

"Come on," I said, "I'll take a shower at your place and eat on the way there."

Mitchell sighed as we left my bedroom. I was feeling rather nervous about seeing Harry after last night—either that, or I was just nervous about getting caught with him. I shook the thoughts away as we started to head out. And just as we reached the door, my parents came in.

"Hey, where are you two running off to?" my mother asked. My dad moved sluggishly behind her, looking more exhausted than normal as he lugged his duffel bag inside. He gave me a pat on the head and Mitchell a nod.

"Heading to Mitchell's. Is Dad okay?" I asked my mom. My dad tossed his bag toward the stairs and flopped onto the couch. "Long day at work?"

She looked over to my dad, then back at me. "Overtime. He's really tired. Don't worry about it. Will you be back in time for dinner?"

"Um..." I looked at Mitchell, who only shrugged. "I'm not sure. I'll give you a call if I grab a bite to eat while I'm on my way home."

"I'll make you a plate anyway." My mom kissed my forehead before turning away and going to the couch as well. "Have fun, you two."

After bidding them both goodbye, we left and walked to Mitchell and Elizabeth's house.

TWENTY

"So when exactly does Harry come over?" Mitchell asked as I slurped the last of my Cup O' Noodles and prepared myself to shower.

"Well, to be honest, he was just gonna pick me up. But I can ask him if he wants to come in and hang out for a bit?" This was uncertain territory, Mitchell viewing Harry as a real person as opposed to his fantasy mock-husband in punch lines.

Mitchell rubbed his hands together in a plotting way that I didn't trust. I shot Harry a quick text about the offer and then gathered my stuff. "I'll be back. Do *not* text him anything stupid while I'm gone."

"No promises," Mitchell said with a wink.

After what felt like a glorious hour of scorching water, I went back to Mitchell's room.

"Well, it's about damn time," Mitchell remarked. "Your phone went off a few times."

I towel-dried my hair with one hand and then picked up my phone with the other. Mitchell was staring expectantly at me, so I said, "It was Harry. He just wanted me to let him know when I wanted him to come over."

"So, he's coming over right now?"

"I mean, yeah. Is that okay?" I asked, a little confused.

"Well, obviously; I don't mind." Mitchell shrugged and threw himself into a multicolored hammock hanging in the corner.

That's when I realized: "You're bored, aren't you?"

"Carter, I'm always bored when I'm home," Mitchell said as if I was supposed to know it.

"Where are your parents? Actually, where's Elizabeth?"

"My parents went out to buy groceries a couple hours ago; they should be back in a few. Elizabeth, however, went out. Not sure when or where, but whatever."

"Was it with someone?"

"Probably not." He waved his hand airily. "It's not like she has any friends. And if she does, they probably suck, anyway."

I glanced to the side and then at him for dramatic effect. "She hangs out with us, though."

"Yeah, but that's the thing: we're *cooler*," Mitchell emphasized.

"Your confidence is truly a marvel."

Mitchell ignored me as he changed the subject. "So, how's the relationship going?"

"The day-old relationship? Well, we haven't messed it up yet," I joked. "I don't think it'd feel real yet regardless, but with the circumstances, it definitely feels fake. Like, I know I should be happy, but I want my relationship with Harry to feel like an actual one, where I can go out on normal dates with him and not care what people have to say or think about us."

"First of all, fuck what people think. People talk a lot of shit because *hello*, welcome to high school. Secondly, just show him off. Who cares? He's your boyfriend now. You can do whatever the hell you want with him because he's yours."

"Mitchell, if I could show him off, I would. But it's my brother. He's such a dick. He'll tell my parents, and they'll *definitely* forbid me from seeing Harry. They dislike him because of the rumors. I wish they could know the kind of person he really is."

"Carter, if they don't know the kind of person Harry is, then tell them."

"You know they can be hardheaded. They aren't around a lot, so what they can control, they super-control. I love them to death and all, but they won't just be cool with Harry overnight. And I'm sure Dylan is dragging his name through the mud right this minute."

"Well, maybe if he comes around and proves what a good guy he is—"

"Mitchell, Dylan practically banned him from our house." I let out a harsh laugh. "I don't know, I'll see what I can do. Hopefully it'll blow over. I just don't want to think about it right now, you know? For now, I just want to enjoy it."

Mitchell smiled sympathetically. "That's good, Carter. I'm proud of you."

I smiled back as I reached for my phone to find a new text from Harry.

Harry: hiiiii, I'm here :)

"Harry's here," I said, and Mitchell practically ran out of his bedroom door before I could finish speaking. I could hear his feet stomping on every step.

I took my time following, and found Harry and Mitchell well into a conversation, laughing, in the living room. They both turned when I walked in.

"Hey," I greeted Harry, failing to hide my massive smile at the sight of him. For some reason, I felt so nervous. I felt like my heart was rising in my throat.

"Carter." Harry smiled just as wide, dimples and all. I felt my knees go weak;

it was hard for me to look away from him. Already, I could feel my fingers begging to reach out and run them through his hair.

My eyes helplessly skimmed over his body. He wore dark jeans with rips at the knees, an oversized white long-sleeve, and these chunky black shoes that should have been hideous, but he made look so good. His overgrown hair was thick and halfway down his neck. I looked away to hide my blush, and then back up to see him eyeing me carefully, his smile morphing into a smirk. Mitchell's voice snapped us back to reality.

"Hello?" Mitchell's voice rang. "Jesus, it's like you two were having eye-sex. And it wasn't as hot as I'd anticipated. If you want to kiss each other hello, then just do it, but don't stare at each other like freaks." Mitchell turned on his heel with a scoff of disgust and jogged back up the stairs to his bedroom.

I watched as he disappeared into the long hallway upstairs, then looked at Harry, who had taken two big steps closer to me. His hand was featherlight on the back of my neck as he pulled me in for a quick kiss. It was only a peck, but that peck was enough to relight the flame in my core.

"How are you feeling today?" Harry whispered to me, his dainty fingers lingering across my cheeks—so gentle, so delicate. I could hardly feel his touch.

"I'm good," I murmured in response, noticing the deep green and ocher flecks in his irises. "How about you?"

"Never been better," Harry replied, and he pecked me once more before linking our fingers together. "Come on. We don't wanna leave Mitchell alone. It's kinda rude." He smiled as he dragged me up the stairs.

After a bit of bantering, I thought the hangout was going well.

Mitchell, lying on the rug with his chin in hand, asked us, "Anyway, where are we going after this?"

Harry replied, "I mean, I think Carter is coming over to my place after?"

Mitchell grinned. "So you *are* going for round two? *Carter.* You total slut, I'm so proud of you."

Harry's eyes widened as he looked from Mitchell to me.

"Of course I know," Mitchell said, interpreting Harry's expression. "Look at her; she's glowing."

Harry laughed.

"Okay, well, I think we should go," I said, eager to leave before Mitchell could really get on a roll.

"Oh! Sure, if you want. Mitchell, do you mind if we...?

"Yeah, sure thing," Mitchell said. "Besides, my parents should be home soon from running errands, and they're not too keen on visitors. But if you want, we could grab lunch tomorrow."

"Sure!" I said, and I gave Mitchell a hug.

Harry offered Mitchell a fist bump, which Mitchell returned with an amused expression.

I grabbed Harry's hand and led him out. "Bye, Mitch."

"Text me!" Mitchell screamed before shutting his bedroom door, leaving me and Harry to walk out of his house on our own.

"Hey," I said, getting Harry's attention. "You're not mad, are you?"

Harry gave me a funny look before responding, "No, of course not. Why would I be mad?"

"I don't know, I just..." I shrugged. "I didn't know how you'd feel knowing I'd told Mitchell. It's not like I was dying to gossip to him or anything. But he is my best friend. He didn't know about any of this till just this morning."

"And I get that." He smiled kindly. "I'm not mad that you told him. You trust him to keep it quiet. At least you have someone to tell."

And at that, I closed my eyes, feeling stupid. Of course. Harry had lost his best friend because of me.

"I'm sorry."

Harry shook his head. "Don't be. It's not like I really told him much, anyway." I raised a curious brow at him, but pushed the thought away.

The car ride was silent, but thankfully it wasn't awkward. My eyes felt droopy and weary, slowly fluttering closed. I was still exhausted from the past few nights. Harry drove so smoothly that I was about ready to doze off. But then he parked, and I opened my eyes to see a cute little house.

Harry got out and walked ahead with me following close behind. I'd never been to Harry's house. Not once. He was at my house so much I'd forgotten he had a home of his own.

Upon entering, we were immediately greeted by a warm living room. The walls were painted a light brown and decorated with black-and-white portraits of people I could only assume were Harry's family. There was a sectional couch with one side facing a brick fireplace and a TV, and the other close to a coffee table holding home magazines and a vase with white calla lilies. My eyes were drawn to a large area rug below the table and couch. The design was a dark brown with white geometric shapes scattered along the sides. Otherwise, the room was simply decorated.

The smell of spiced gingerbread filled the air as we walked further down the hall; the kitchen looked like something off of Pinterest.

"I can't imagine what your parents must do for a living. Like seriously, Harry, this place is a dream," I said in amazement, looking at all the tasteful decor as he guided me along. On our way to the back of the house, I noticed photos of Harry as a child along with a girl that I assumed to be his sister.

Harry opened one of the doors, revealing his bedroom—different than how I'd expected it to look. The walls were painted a cool grey, one covered in vinyl records, another with some framed honor roll awards. His dresser was slightly cluttered with random little things and had a large TV balanced on top of it. Two small, wall-mounted lamps hovered above his bed. On his nightstand was a stack of books. His furniture was black, and the bedding white, with a plush gray blanket thrown carelessly over the covers. But still, the place looked like a stock photo.

The carefully folded clothes at the edge of his bed surprised me the most.

"I did not expect your room to be so neat."

"That's because it's usually not," he muttered, stuffing the pile into one of the drawers. "My mom is always cleaning up around here. Even though I'm capable of cleaning my room on my own, my mom does extra cleaning so it's *perfect*."

I stifled my laughter as he continued pushing clothes into an already full drawer. "Can I sit on your bed, then?" I jokingly asked.

"Go for it, although you may have to iron the creases out later."

"Well, it won't be as good of a job as your mom would probably do, but I'll try to make it respectable. Why aren't they here, by the way? Your parents, I mean."

"Today's Saturday, so..." Harry said to himself, cocking his head as he thought. "Oh, they're at a barbecue. Anyway, you want to watch a movie or something?" He was clearly changing the subject, but I didn't press him. He got up, turned on the TV, and asked, "What do you want to watch?"

"Anything that's funny would be great, please," I said, getting comfortable on his bed.

After a good hour and a half of *Bruce Almighty*, Harry and I gradually stopped paying attention as we got lost in our own little world, talking nonstop. It was cool, getting to know more about him and his childhood, his family, and his view of the world.

His family had moved a few times while he was young, and they'd settled in Florida while he was in middle school. Apparently, his stepdad worked in the appraisal business, whereas his mom had suffered an injury on the job during her career in mechanics, and now worked remotely from home to provide extra income. He wasn't close to his father and tensed subtly even when casually mentioning him.

The conversation drifted into a lull, and Harry's fingers traced circles over my legging-covered hips. "This sucks, you know?"

"What does?"

"This whole secret thing." Harry rubbed his fingers over his bottom lip, looking down at our entwined feet. "I mean, I get why we have to do it. I just think it sucks because I want to take you out, you know? Go on a normal date, like dinner and a movie or something. But then risk getting caught and having your parents keep me from seeing you?" He shook his head in annoyance. "It just sucks."

"No, I understand. And if it makes you feel any better, I feel the same. Harry, everything you just said is everything I want to do with you as your girlfriend," I said, the word feeling foreign on my tongue.

Harry smiled sadly. "Hanging out with you like this is great, but eventually I'm gonna want to take you *out* out."

"I'd love that, Harry. But for now, this is all we can do," I said with a frown I couldn't hide. But I felt a bit better knowing I wasn't the only one feeling this way. I was glad Harry wasn't one to hide what he was feeling.

He raised his hand to my face and caressed my cheek with the pad of his thumb, then tucked a loose strand behind my ear. I wasn't one for these corny moves, but something about the way

Harry did it had me swooning on the spot.

"Can I be honest, though?" I asked, and I received a nod from him. "I'm still a little iffy about this, I'll admit. Not about you, but this whole secret thing. I went through it once before, so I hope you don't feel offended if I lack trust in the whole scenario."

Harry kissed the tip of my nose before answering. "I understand. And I'll do whatever it to takes to make you feel like you can trust me. I promise."

I nodded, smiling when he placed a gentle kiss on my forehead before saying, "My parents might be home soon, though, and they kinda hate it when I invite guests without them knowing."

"Oh, okay. Then let's go," I said as I got up, grabbing my belongings.

"Want me to take you back to Mitchell's?"

I nodded, and Harry and I left hand in hand. He opened the passenger door for me before sliding into the driver's side. The car ride was silent; I was mulling over what we had discussed, and I imagined he was too.

We pulled up to the house, and I leaned in for a peck. However, before I could kiss him, Harry stopped me. "Hey, I know we didn't hang out much, but we will. I promise, all right?"

"Okay. Thank you. And I had fun, really."

"Same, although maybe next time we should actually watch the movie," he joked.

"Sounds good; your voice annoys me sometimes."

Harry's jaw dropped. "Well, then." But then he laughed and

finally gave me a kiss. "I'll text you later," he said.

"You better," I teased, and I hopped out of the car. I watched him drive away and then walked home, texting Mitchell to hold onto my bag of clothes for me.

TWENTY-ONE

Sunday flew by for me. I sat in bed all day, binge-watching *Friends* from the beginning. It wasn't until I reached the middle of Season Two when I realized the sun was already setting.

I lazily drifted downstairs just in time to see my parents setting up the table for dinner. I didn't say a word to Dylan as he came down, which wasn't uncommon, but there was an immediate tension that I did my best to pretend wasn't there.

We had spaghetti, and my dad, who still looked exhausted but at least had a sparkle back in his eyes, explained how there had been some complications in the surgery he'd been assisting with. I was intrigued, but by the time I'd finished with my salad and started on the pasta, he'd started complaining about administration to my mom, and I lost interest.

I started thinking about yesterday, and I missed Harry already.

It wasn't familiar, and that kind of scared me because maybe what I was feeling for Harry was *extremely* real. Maybe what I'd felt with Austin was just because of the attention he had briefly given me. I knew I shouldn't compare Harry to Austin, but it was the only source of experience I could draw from. But looking back on it, I realized the feelings I'd had for Austin couldn't hold a candle to what I was feeling for Harry. So, what was there to compare, really?

"So, Carter, where were you yesterday?" Dylan asked, snapping me back to reality.

I felt caught. It was like he could tell I was thinking about Harry. "Out with Mitchell," I replied nonchalantly, without looking at him. "Why do you ask?"

Dylan wolfed down noodles, splattering red sauce everywhere. "You guys woke me up this morning. But then you both left really quick."

I glanced over at him to raise an eyebrow. "What's your point?"

"Oh, nothing." My brother shook his head before continuing, "I just thought it was weird that he came here for you guys to leave again."

Our parents had paused to listen, but not intently. This felt like dangerous ground.

"And?" I asked.

"Well, I'm just asking. I can't know where my little sister went off to?"

"We went out for a bite to eat, but I don't see how that's any of your business."

Dylan gave me a hard look, and we went back to eating. I twisted my fork around in the noodles, chewing at the inside of my cheek and rapidly losing my appetite.

My dad was scrolling through the news on his tablet as my mom added more red pepper to her food. She asked Dylan, "You didn't do anything today, sweetie?" He simply shook his head, hardly paying her any mind. "I didn't hear Harry. Was he not over today?"

I couldn't help but stare at Dylan. His jaw locked before he finally responded, "Nope. In fact, he's not gonna be coming around here anymore, Mom."

"Oh," she replied, frowning slightly. "What happened?" Since both my parents were in the medical field—my dad a nurse and my mom a cardiothoracic surgeon—they were never really around much. They tried to make up for it by catching up during family meals, offering advice and attempting to get us to talk about our feelings. I appreciated that they cared, but it was times like this I wished she'd dismiss us with a *Well, that sucks, kiddo.*

"I caught him doing something I didn't like," Dylan said, the ice in his voice dropping the temperature of the whole room. My mouth felt dry.

"And what was that?" my mom asked, and the note of concern in her voice dragged my dad's attention away from his tablet.

"He betrayed me. Kissed someone *very* close to me." My dad

made a noise of disapproval. My grip tightened around the fork in my hand.

"Oh," my mother murmured nervously. "Do you mind me asking who?"

"It's pretty obvious, Mom."

I wanted to scream. I wanted to cry. I want to smash my plate over Dylan's head.

"It's why Lindsay hasn't been around, either. I broke up with her because of it."

I took a deep, shaky breath. Dylan turned to level an ominous gaze at me, and it took every ounce of control to keep my face neutral.

I had been stuck on the same page for far too long. I was nearly at the end of the novel, and I wanted to finish it so I could get to another book that had been on my waiting list for ages, but I was unable to move past the second-to-last chapter.

I couldn't shake off the uneasy feeling from dinner. Dylan had almost thrown me to the wolves. I had no doubt my parents would have had a meltdown if they'd known I had been seeing Harry in secret.

Just then, my phone buzzed.

Speak of the devil.

Harry: carter

Harry: I have a question

Me: what

Harry: why is carter ur name

Harry: like don't get me wrong I like it

Harry: but why

Harry: it's rly awkward for me to explain to ppl that you're a girl

Harry: bc every time ur name pops up on my notifications

Harry: it comes up like

Harry: carter ♡

Harry: and do you know how hard it is to explain to people

Harry: such as my parents

Harry: that you are in fact a girl

Harry: like did your parents want another boy

Harry: were u a mistake or???

Me: that's not why they named me carter you dumbass

Harry: my ass is not dumb

Me: a lot says otherwise

Harry: do u think it's cute tho

Me: eh 6/10

Harry: WOW

Harry: RUDE

Harry: are you joking you better be joking

Harry: i don't skip leg day

Me: yes of course I'm kidding. You're bootilicious

Harry: ;)

Me: Anyway

Me: with Dylan, they knew he was a boy pretty early. But with me, they didn't know until I was born, so they'd picked a unisex name

Harry: that's actually kinda cool

Me: liar, I know you think it's dumb

Harry: no really, I like that. props to your parents

Harry: we should do that when we have a kid

Me: whAt

Harry: anyway this convo went completely south

Harry: I wanted to discuss nicknames

Harry: so ppl can stop thinking I'm texting a guy

Harry: my mom has always questioned my sexuality

Harry: one of the reasons being i've never had a real girlfriend for her to meet

Harry: but mainly since she always thought your brother was gay

Harry: and I thought that was too funny to correct

Harry: ....for the past three and a half years

Me: I love how you completely changed the subject about giving our kid a unisex name

Harry: what the fuck

Harry: our kid???????

Harry: you want my kids already?¿

Harry: jesus carter

Harry: we only just started dating

Harry: we have yet to go out on a proper date

Harry: let alone get married

Harry: but here you are asking me to father your child
I just

Harry: I'm baffled

Me: ur a doofus. never mind

Me: the nicknames???

Harry: oh right

Harry: we should have nicknames :))))

Harry: something cute

Harry: something that reminds us of one another

Harry: liiiiike

Me: like jay and silent bob

Harry: uh

Harry: sure

Harry: that's a start.......

Me: yeah you could be silent bob

Me: I'll be jay

Harry: first of all jay is also a mALE NAME

Me: false. it's unisex

Harry: whatever

Harry: secondly why do I have to be silent bob

Me: bc ur my bitch obvi

Silent Bob: HEY NOW THAT WAS FOR GETTING YOU SOUP NOT THIS

Silent Bob: I'M NOT YOUR BITCH

Me: too late

Silent Bob: HOW RUDE

Silent Bob: WTF

Me: calm down lunchbox

Lunchbox: don't call me that

Me: too late

Lunchbox: too late????

Lunchbox: wait

Lunchbox: ....you changed my contact name didn't you

Me: :)

Lunchbox: I think we should break up

TWENTY-TWO

"Draw two, Carter!" Andy shouted. I huffed, pulling one skip and a red seven, then smirked.

"She's smiling, why is she smiling?" Sean said, pointing at me.

I tried holding back my laughter. "You guys are obviously shitty shufflers."

"You suck, you're never shuffling again!" Sean yelled at Andy, who looked taken back by the sudden accusation.

I broke out into a fit of laughter as they squabbled. I put my cards face down on the table and looked away, trying to sneak a peek at Harry, who sat only a few feet away from me. Our eyes met instantly, his dimpled smile already prominent.

I flushed, looking away. When the bell rang, I helped Andy pick up his cards. He thanked me, and Sean left with a playful scowl. "I'll figure out your tricks one day, Carter. You just wait," he called to me, then tripped on one of the chairs and proceeded to act as if nothing had happened. "You'll see! You'll all see!"

Andy and I just shook our heads at his dramatic flair. I noticed Harry give me a small nod as he left the room, the rest of the class emptying out behind him. Andy and I headed towards the door, and he turned to me to say, "He's not gonna figure out anything."

"Exactly." I laughed. "I honestly don't use any tricks. I'm just lucky, I guess."

"I don't believe that, either, but I don't mind you winning," Andy said with a one-shoulder shrug.

"Really? You look aggravated every time I do," I replied with a smile as we turned to the lunchroom.

"I only do that because Sean will accuse me of helping you otherwise. And seeing him lose his shit every time you put down a good card is hysterical."

"Honestly, he should join the drama club. He's made for the stage."

"I'd go to the shows if I was allowed to heckle." We laughed, and he adjusted the messenger bag on his shoulder. "Well, I'll see you tomorrow, Carter."

I nodded and slowly continued into the cafeteria, where I watched people crowd around the vending machines, argue at the tables, and scream and shriek for no reason at all. I felt a little sluggish today. Mitchell had said I looked pale this morning, but I was pretty sure it was just because I hadn't bothered to throw on any makeup.

My phone pinged, and I had to do an extreme search in my bag to find it. It had gotten wedged between my health workbook and math binder. I found a new message from Harry, the little bubbles appearing below, letting me know he was typing more.

Harry: keep walking

Harry: you're gonna stop to find your phone, really

Harry: jesus for a tiny bag how can you not find your phone

Harry: Anyway, I'm skipping class. Lunch date?

Me: sure

Harry: cool

Harry: now keep walking

Me: ***rolling my eyes***

Me: you're so lame

Me: let me at least get my yogurt first

Me: I'll meet you in the back

Harry: fiiiine

I stuffed my phone in my back pocket and bought my yogurt. I had to shimmy my way through the crowds to make it out the door of the cafeteria. This school was so overcrowded; I was eager to finally be free next year. I gave a quick look around as I headed outside, just to be sure no one was taking notice.

I found Harry seated at the doors of the auditorium on his

phone, nodding his head along to whatever he was listening to. At the sight of me, he pulled out his earphones and smiled.

"So, is this like our new secret meeting place?" I asked jokingly, shimmying my pink flannel off my shoulders and tossing it on the ground beside him. It was boiling today, the puffy little clouds doing nothing to block the sun.

Harry nodded with a smug grin, eyes flickering over my white tank. "Precisely. May as well have a place to call our own, yeah?"

"Yeah, but you can't skip class every day just to sit with me at lunch," I said, pulling off the lid of my yogurt.

"I never said I was going to skip every day. I was just missing you already."

"We saw each other Saturday," I said, even though I too had wished we had spent more time together.

"I know, but we missed out all of Sunday. The weekend is so long when you're crushing on someone, ya know?"

"It's not crushing if you're kind of with me."

"'Kind of'?" Harry repeated. "What do you mean 'kind of'? Who am I sharing you with?"

"Mitchell, obviously."

He laughed, then looked back at his phone. There were twenty-two unread notifications on his texts, and dozens more on Snapchat and Instagram.

"Someone's popular," I commented as he started to respond to some.

Harry chuckled. "It's no one special."

"Sure doesn't seem like it. You're two-timing me already?"

"Shut up; you know I wouldn't." He rolled his eyes, and then asked, "Babe, do you have plans Friday?"

"Yeah, I'm gonna be reading. Why?"

His mouth opened, closed, then opened again as he said, "It's so hard to tell when you're joking sometimes."

I laughed, and he continued, "Anyway, you want to do something?"

"Like what?"

Harry shrugged. "Maybe go to a movie or somewhere cliché."

"Define somewhere cliché," I requested.

"Okay." He stretched one leg out so he could slide his phone in his pocket. "How about watching the sunset on a hill or mountain or something?"

I narrowed my eyes at him and waved away a gnat that was intrigued with my nearly empty yogurt. "Where the hell are you going to find a hill or mountain in this state? It's nothing but flat land."

"What about watching the sunset from a hotel room on one of the top floors?" he suggested with a wink.

"What, does money actually grow on trees in your world?"

Harry laughed, shaking his head. "I was just throwing out some spontaneous suggestions. Spicing it up, you know? Trying something new."

"We've been dating for less than a week."

"And yet we've already been spicy," he said, wiggling his

eyebrows at me.

I whacked his arm and then finished my last bite of yogurt.

"How does the beach sound?" he suggested. "Ooh, you know what? Yes. I like that idea. Have you ever gone jet-skiing?" He picked at the leftover granola in the pouch.

"Hell no, and I don't plan on it. The ocean is terrifying. I'll go up to my ankles, but no more than that!"

"What? Why are you scared of the ocean? Haven't you lived in Florida your whole life?"

"Because once it's no longer shallow, you can't see what's down there. It could be anything."

"You realize shark attacks and whatnot are really rare, right?"

"So? You know my luck; it would totally happen to me. It could happen at any time. Haven't you ever seen *Deep Blue Sea*? That movie scarred me for life."

"Whatever. For your sake, fine—no water activities." He tugged at his shirt collar, probably because of the heat, and pushed his hair back from his forehead. "If you want, we could grab some pizza while walking on the boardwalk and stuff? Maybe ice cream?"

"You had me at pizza," I replied, and he grinned. "Why not just do this at your house, though? It's less of a hassle, you know, and we don't have to worry about anything that way."

He grunted softly before replying, "Carter, you're so difficult. It's like you live to rain on my parade."

"I wouldn't be doing my job as a girlfriend if I didn't, now would

I?"

Harry looked at me blankly, then said, "I wouldn't know. You're the first girl I've asked out that I actually *really like.*"

"Have you asked that many?" I questioned, a little scared to know the answer.

Harry gave a slightly awkward, coughing kind of laugh, and said, "I don't know, kinda."

"Right... Look, it's not that I don't like your ideas or anything. I appreciate it—how much you care. I even love them. I really do. But we can do simple things and I'd still enjoy them," I tried to reason with him, but he seemed reluctant.

Harry simply shrugged. "I know, but it's just that I don't want you to get bored of the same old cycle: my house, movie dates, and eating junk every weekend or whatever."

"Harry, that's literally my lifestyle," I pointed out jokingly, but he still didn't look happy. "Come on, I thought we said we'd be careful."

"I didn't think that meant we couldn't do *anything.*"

"It's too risky, Harry. I really appreciate you wanting to do something more, but everyone goes to the beach on the weekends," I told him matter-of-factly. He was quiet for a moment, his jaw noticeably clenching. He shoved both hands through his hair.

"So, what? All we'll ever do is hide out at my place? We'll get bored."

"Not if we make the best of it."

"But what's the harm in doing something spontaneous?" he

asked.

"It's not just spontaneous, it's dangerous," I said, trying to stay patient. "The chances of someone from school seeing us, telling my brother, who, by the way, happens to *know* almost everybody—"

"Just forget it," Harry cut me off, shaking his head. "I have to go before next period."

Watching him stand and walk away was like a slap to the face.

"Are you seriously getting mad over this?" I said, but he ignored me. "Harry!"

I felt like I had just caused a fight. It was only day three of us being together, and I had already started a fight—a rather ridiculous one, if I was being entirely honest. I stood up and slammed my empty cup into the trashcan. I quickly left before the courtyard could fill up.

Back inside the main building, I caught sight of Mitchell right as he turned the corner of the hallway. I ran up beside him and took his arm; he automatically hooked his elbow around mine.

He glanced down at me and then did a double take. "Whoa, what's up with you?"

[HARRY]

I sat in class, flipping my phone over in my hands. The teacher was lecturing, but I didn't hear a single word. The more I replayed my and Carter's conversation from lunch in my head, the worse I felt. I had gotten carried away, hadn't heard her when she'd tried to explain that she was scared of getting caught.

But I wanted to do this right. I'd never had a real relationship, one that I cared about. Not even with Jenna. And although I'd had the opportunity to do things properly, I'd just genuinely never wanted to do shit with her.

I was beginning to think the way I'd reacted towards Carter's hesitance was a little too childish. But I was also skeptical and frustrated because all she wanted to do was be at my place, apparently. And hell, having her alone in my room would be great, but that wasn't all I wanted. I wanted to build something real with her. But she was turning out more cautious and paranoid than I was.

I chewed at the inside of my cheek as I thought.

I decided what I should probably do was talk to her after school. Hopefully, she wouldn't have caught a ride with Mitchell. I didn't want to leave school with her still mad at me.

I had never argued with Jenna. Not because we hadn't disagreed or acted stupid, but because I had always fled when she tried to pick fights. I couldn't do the same to Carter. I knew relationships took work, but I guess in the moment, I had kinda forgotten that this wasn't some fling with some girl. This was the girl I'd had a crush on since I was fifteen, and there I was, finally with her and fucking it up.

Nice.

I looked around, and everyone's heads were either bowed to their phones or on their desks while the teacher droned on. I glanced at my phone, filled with messages from people I didn't want to talk to. I decided to wait to text Carter until I could find the right words.

[*CARTER*]

"And then after that, I guess he got annoyed, because he got up before lunch was over and took off." I huffed. "I feel like I fucked up."

"It's pretty obvious why you felt obligated to say no," Mitchell said, putting a dollar into the soda machine. People were swarming around us, rushing to their classes. I hadn't had the time or privacy to explain everything in biology, so I'd filled Mitchell in on the way to gym. "But you guys need to compromise. You still have Stockholm syndrome."

"What?"

Mitchell sighed as he opened his bottle of soda. Then he threw an arm around me and practically started dragging me to gym. "Carter, the only relationship you've ever been in was with Austin."

"Unfortunately, I'm aware. What's your point?"

Mitchell sighed. "You were never able to experience these types of thing with Austin. He always met with you in secret, he never bothered to take you out—it was literally the most discreet relationship ever."

"All right, *and?*" I pressed, still not sure where he was going with this. "It's the same thing with me and Harry. This is also a secret relationship."

"Oh my god, you're so stupid. Yes, it's also a secret

relationship. *However*, it's completely different from you and Austin," he said, stopping just outside the doors of the gym. "Carter, Harry is willing to take you out and do romantic things with you. Doing things Austin never bothered to offer. You're so convinced that the way Austin treated you was the way a relationship should be, but it's not. You just need to take a chance with him."

I didn't know how to respond. Mitchell was right. Austin had never been like that with me. With Austin, I'd gotten used to staying home on weekends from trying to have a chance to talk to him on the phone, pretending it didn't bother me. I'd always been introverted, but I realized then, looking back, that maybe my manipulative first relationship had been what had contributed to me becoming such a homebody. Once, I had suggested we go out somewhere quiet and isolated, and he'd flipped out. From there, I'd never asked again. I should've known at that moment he was lying about his reasons for us not being public. I still hadn't known how a relationship worked.

I could take that chance with Harry—I wanted to—but everything was so uncertain.

"Okay, I agree with you and all," I said, and Mitchell waved a hand as if to say *Duh*. "But my thing is, what if we get caught and it gets back to my brother? Or straight to my parents?"

Mitchell hummed as we walk towards the bleachers. "Okay, well, that's something Harry needs to understand. It's fine that he wants to be a good boyfriend to show you that he wants to keep this relationship and make it work. You gotta trust him, not shit all over his cutesy ideas. But you guys have to communicate. The way he handled a little spat was not right."

I sighed, nodding my head. "Yeah, I was surprised, honestly. But I see what you mean. I'll text him when I get home."

"Why not just text him now?" Mitchell pestered, and I couldn't tell whether it was because he wanted to know the outcome, or if he was truly looking out for me and encouraging me to fix things with Harry.

"Shouldn't I give him time to cool off?"

"You've waited a whole class period. You're his girlfriend. Take initiative."

I contemplated it for a moment. Mitchell took a pointed slurp of my soda. *It shouldn't bother Harry. And we both need to work on our communication a bit.* "Fine, fine. You're right." I sighed, reaching for my phone.

[HARRY]

A long breath escaped me as I mentally groaned in agony. I wanted to go home. History had always lasted forever, but today I couldn't bear it. Especially because the back of Dylan's head was looming two rows in front of me.

The truth was I did miss my best friend, especially who he used to be. He was pretty damn funny, and for all his obnoxious traits, he had been damn loyal. Which is why I understood how absolutely furious he was.

Lindsay was across the room, doodling on her desk and

blowing bubbles with her gum. And of course, Jenna sat next to her, twirling her hair and picking at her nails.

I couldn't believe I'd dated her.

My phone buzzed, and I was surprised, and relieved, to see that it was Carter. I felt my heart swell at the sight of her name. The effect this girl had on me was unfathomable.

Princess ♡ : harry

Me: hey carter

Princess ♡ : are you mad at me :(

Me: no not really

Me: why

Princess ♡ : really?

Princess ♡ bc you seemed pretty mad when you left

Me: I mean ok I was

Me: I guess it's bc I expected you to said yes

Me: but nvm, don't worry about it anymore

Me: I'm over it babe

Me: it was wrong of me to ask so much of you

Me: so I'm not mad

Princess ♡ : really?

Me: yes I promise

Me: we can do something else

Me: at least that's if you want

Princess ♡ : no, Harry, I want to do your beach plan

Princess ♡ : i really liked it

Princess ♡ : but I have to ask…aren't you scared of us getting caught?

Me: the only person I don't wanna get caught by is your brother

Me: otherwise, I don't care who sees us

Princess ♡ : but I thought we agreed something simple & more discreet at first :/

Me: …this really fucking sucks you know

Princess ♡ : I know, we talked about this

Me: no not that

Me: call me crazy but I feel like you don't wanna be seen with me

Me: like in public

Me: not just by your brother but by anyone

Princess ♡ : of course I do!!

Princess ♡ : how could you think that

Princess ♡ : It's just difficult right now

Princess ♡ : look I don't want to end what's barely started

Princess ♡ : but I also see your point of wanting to do relationships things. if it means so much to you, I'll make you a deal

Princess ♡ : we'll go to the beach and have pizza

Princess ♡ : saturday morning

Me: are u sure?

Princess ♡ : positive

Princess ♡ : im paranoid but we'll go

Me: you know you don't have to do this for me

Princess ♡ : I know but I want to

Princess ♡ : aaaaaand

Princess ♡ : it's mainly bc mitchell is calling me a wimp and saying that I should take risks.

Princess ♡ : especially if they're with you

Me: yaaaasssss

Me: give mitchell a kiss for me

Princess ♡ : IKNEW YOU WANT EFd ME PJDIEBIHAVT£)&!.*$)$2$"1

Me: whAt

Princess ♡ : omfg sorry

Princess ♡ : that was mitchell

Princess ♡ : but anyway

Princess ♡ : beach. saturday morning.

Princess ♡ : I like giant slices of pizza and I'll want a chocolate-vanilla ice cream swirl at that cute little ice cream shoppe by the bicycle stand

Me: haha all right

Me: so do you only ever agree to go on dates if they involve food?

Princess ♡ : most of the time

Me: so next time I ask you out on a date, I should just bribe you with food??

Princess ♡ : don't most dates involve food?

Princess ♡: but yes. yes you should

Me: …I'll keep that in mind

Me: hey carter

Princess ♡: yes?

Me: thank you

Me: I know you're scared but I can't tell you how much this means to me

Princess ♡: I want what you want, but most of all, I just want to be with you

TWENTY-THREE

[CARTER]

The week flew by quick. Harry skipped class twice just to sit with me at lunch.

On Friday, I sat with the sophomore girls during art and listened to all of them banter about the funniest things. They even asked me for advice on the next two years. However, I could only answer as a junior. I hadn't exactly figured out what I was going to do for my senior year, and school was a month and a half away from ending. The rest of the day was a drag.

Mitchell and I had a sub for gym that made us do physical activities. Mitchell ended up ditching me and hiding in the locker rooms until the period was over.

I waited for Harry after school, but I didn't see him anywhere and gave up on waiting after a while. Thankfully, Mitchell and

Elizabeth were bickering in the parking lot, so they hadn't left yet. The bickering continued after we drove off, though. We decided on a quick bite to eat and picked up some sub sandwiches from Publix, eating them in the car before heading home.

"I just think that if I'm going to learn to drive, I should at least start by using your car," Mitchell said with a shrug before taking a bite of his sub.

"Are you insane?!" she shrieked, startling Mitchell. He placed his hand on his chest before scowling at her. "Last time I let you practice in my car you nearly hit that incoming car."

"I had it under control. It's not like anything would've happened."

"Mitchell, it was a cop," Elizabeth snapped.

"Wait, you took him out to drive? By yourself?" I asked.

"No way," Elizabeth said, and took a sip of his soda. "His dad came with us."

"I don't see why we needed him around," Mitchell said, voice muffled by his stuffed mouth. "You have a license; you could've taken me yourself."

Elizabeth gave me a look before eyeing Mitchell. "I need to have my license for at least three years before I can teach you. If we got caught, we would be dead. My mom would snatch my license from me so quick, you could say bye-bye to all of our social lives."

"*Ugh*, you're so dramatic," Mitchell said, stuffing his trash in one of the bags. "Come on, let's go home already. I have so much homework to catch up on, I might actually cry myself to sleep tonight."

By the time they'd dropped me off, the bickering had died down. I waved goodbye, half of my sub in hand, as they pulled away. But as I approached the front door, I heard shouting. Screaming, even. I took a half-step forward, not even putting my hand on the doorknob. It was two male voices.

I jolted as the door wrenched open. Harry nearly walked right into me.

"Carter, hey," he said quietly, pulling me away from the door and windows. His eyes were wide and wild, and a little glazed.

"What are you doing here?" I whispered anxiously, moving to the side of the house.

"I got in a little scuffle with your brother, it's no big deal."

"Jesus, Harry—"

"I'm fine, it wasn't anything physical." I could smell beer on his breath. "Pretend you got here after I left, and that you didn't see me, okay?"

"Okay, yeah, sure. Are you sure you're okay? You've been drinking."

"I'm fine. I should go, though. I'll text you tonight and explain everything. And I'll see you tomorrow, yeah?"

I hesitated but then nodded. He quickly walked away. I wondered where he had parked his car.

I cautiously walked into the house and found the living room and kitchen empty, but I could hear music blaring from upstairs.

That's how I knew the "scuffle" was *really* serious. Whenever Dylan really lost his temper, he'd lock himself in his room and blast bad music to shut everything out; he'd done that since we were kids.

I sat on my bed and waited for Harry to text me. But, like earlier, nothing. *Friends* played from where I'd left off, but I wasn't really watching. My mind was spinning with questions. I made myself soup and took my time with it, trying not to check my phone every minute. I didn't want to text him first, not with how rattled he'd looked and how tense today had been—first a fight with me, then Dylan. I chatted with my parents when they came home, then went upstairs and lay in bed. Just as my eyes were beginning to flutter shut, my phone buzzed on the nightstand. I groaned against my pillow and grasped at my phone, getting a hold of everything except it for a minute or two.

Boyfriend: hi princess

Boyfriend: sorry for texting you so late

Boyfriend: I had a busy day

Boyfriend: how are you

Boyfriend: what're you doing rn

Me: I was about to fall asleep waiting for your text

Me: what took you so long

Boyfriend: sorry babe, I needed to chill out, and then I was running a few errands for my mom

Me: oh okay

Me: I was just wondering

Me: so. wanna tell me why you were here?

Boyfriend: ugh it got so messy so fast

Boyfriend: I skipped last period and went home bc i just wasn't feeling it

Boyfriend: we most likely weren't gonna do anything important as usual so whats the point, you know?

Boyfriend: clearly your brother felt the same because I ran into him in the parking lot

Boyfriend: and he actually stopped to talk to me, which was weird

Boyfriend: And it was awkward but he was acting like he wanted to make amends

Boyfriend: so I apologized, and he just telling me how he was still mad at me and everything but he also missed having me around

Boyfriend: not gonna lie, I do too

Boyfriend: so then, we may have gone and got some drinks and went back to your house

Boyfriend: and it was actually going great, really great. we were laughing and shit

Boyfriend: and then I mentioned you, and he just blew up

Me: .....what did you say

Boyfriend: well, I asked about you, if you were doing okay. I thought that'd be safe, not make it seem like we've been hanging out

Me: what why

Boyfriend: Well we couldn't keep dodging the topic forever. I thought he might come around to the idea of us actually being a couple

Idiot: that's when he got mad and asked me why I cared and idk he just started making accusations, slurring a whole bunch of shit and getting me angry too

Idiot: idk he was just being so fucking aggressive for no reason and saying the most terrible things like fuck man where the hell was it coming from

Idiot: but a drunk mouth is an honest mouth

Me: oh, Harry

Idiot: what??? it's true

Idiot: anyway your brother just went insane, and I was getting so fed up I started yelling back defending myself

Idiot: he kept going and then I was so angry I just left

Idiot: and that's when you saw me so yeah

Me: what was he saying?

Harold: eh, a bunch of stuff about how I betrayed his trust and that I was such a hypocrite for trying to give him relationship advice, etc. etc. That I was stuck-up and thought I was better than everyone. And how I was such a tool for sleeping around the school and then thinking I could just have you and Lindsay too.

And I was trying to explain how most of that wasn't even true, obviously, but I don't think he even heard me.

Harold: but you know what bothered me most??

Harold: in the middle of his temper tantrum, he was just about to say something but then he stopped himself, and it got me wondering you know like he was being so blunt just a few seconds ago. But then he just decided not to go on like.....?

Harold: isnt that weird????

Me: idk I mean I guess

Me: maybe something hit him like maybe he knew he was taking it too far. So he was just like whoa stop

Harold: idk maybe

Harold: still

Harold: it was fishy as fuck

Me: are you okay though? :/

Harold: yeah I'm fine, I'm over it now

Harold: tomorrow will be a much-needed distraction

Harold: have you got your things ready?

Me: holy shit I knew I was forgetting to do something! I'll set my bag up now

Harold: just bring a towel and extra clothes so you don't bring half the beach back with you

Me: lol okay

Harold: I'm being serious I hate when sand gets stuck

KARLA DE LA ROSA

all over me

Harold: especially in my ass

Me: I'm laughing omg I'll start packing a bag

Me: what time are you gonna pick me up?

Harold: is 9am all right?

Me: ugh no but the earlier the better so

Harold: all right. in front of mitchell's?

Me: sounds good. I'll text you when I'm done packing

Harold: okay :)

TWENTY-FOUR

It didn't take much convincing for my parents to let me go to the beach. I told them I was going with Mitchell and Elizabeth, and that I'd be home for dinner. My dad had barely heard my whole spiel before he dozed off on the couch.

The next morning, I threw my stuff in the backseat of Harry's car and then hopped in the passenger side. When I noticed what he was wearing, the stereotypical beachiness made me laugh. He had on these ridiculously bright yellow swim trunks and a white tank top that hugged his toned torso. His hair was curling out from under a black snapback, and black sunglasses hid the green of his eyes. I'd settled on washed-out jean shorts and a large black T-shirt I'd borrowed from Mitchell a while back, my bathing suit underneath.

I kicked off my shoes as we drove. My bet was that he was

taking us to Hollywood Beach since it was closest. Harry and I playfully argued over the radio. One station had on my favorite song and another had Harry's favorite. Eventually he gave in and let me put on my station; however, when I did, the song was just ending, and I ended up putting Harry's station back on. It wasn't until his I saw his smirk that I realized he'd bickered with me on purpose, knowing my song was about to end. In retaliation, I stole the cap off his head and put it on.

On the highway, the traffic wasn't as heavy as we'd feared it'd be. We started to pass the large houses and borderline-mansions by the barrier walls, boats and yachts and jet skis cruising along. We crossed a bridge and then began the long process of finding a parking spot.

Harry insisted on loading all my stuff in his bag. He took my hand as we strolled along the boardwalk, admiring the slow-rolling waves of the ocean, the bright hotels and inns, and the seagulls pestering one another. There were ambitious parents trying to get their young kids down to the water, and fitness addicts on bikes, rollerblades, and recumbent bikes.

Once we were down the stairs of the boardwalk, the smell of seawater coaxing us onward, we carried our sandals in our free hands. The sand was so hot that it nearly hurt, which wasn't a surprise seeing as it was already over 90 degrees. Little shells and stones were peppered throughout the yellow grains. Thankfully we didn't have to walk for too long before finding a spot. There was no one we recognized from school there, fortunately.

"So how long are we staying for?" I asked, fishing in Harry's bag for my towel before spreading it out.

"Maybe for an hour or two. We can relax and then go in the water for a bit—if you're okay with it. Up to you, really. We'll get your pizza and ice cream right after."

Harry pulled his tank top over his head, and I swore the world went in slow motion as he exposed his torso. His body was even more amazing in the sunlight, all broad shoulders and strong chest and a V-cut near his hips. He turned to me, and though I couldn't see his eyes behind his glasses, I blushed knowing that I'd been caught.

I tugged off my shorts, letting my shirt act as a cover. I folded my shorts, hesitant to remove my shirt. I felt a little self-conscious. After a couple of seconds, I finally gave in and tossed it over my head, then took the tie out of my hair. I replaced Harry's hat back on my head.

Harry sat on his towel, sunglasses discarded, leaning back on his hands and looking up at me in awe. I couldn't help but be a little nervous as he stared at my half-naked body. My bikini top was a baby pink bra with a lacy cloth hanging over the front. I'd thought it was so pretty when I'd seen it. The bottom was a plain black because I had refused to buy the matching piece.

I bit my lip as Harry's eyes caught mine. "What?"

Harry shook his head, grinning. "Nothing." Only his wandering eyes said otherwise. I couldn't read his expression.

As I slowly sat beside him, Harry grabbed my waist and pulled me close. He went back to his leaning position, and I put my head against his shoulder and hugged my knees against my chest.

My heart fluttered when Harry kissed my head and brought his lips to my ear to whisper, "You're so beautiful, Carter. I don't think I can keep my eyes off of you." His breath fanned my skin, sending shivers down my spine. Harry's lips hungrily nipped and kissed the skin on my neck, and the feeling was sensational. I gulped and jumped to my feet.

"Wanna go in the water?" I chirped, forcing a smile.

"We only just sat down, babe."

"I want to try. I'm terrified, but the only reason I'm going in is for you." Harry stifled his laughter, nodded, and pulled me to the shore.

As we edged closer to the water, I felt a little uncertain as I watched the endless expanse of ocean reach out to the horizon. But I wasn't nearly as uncomfortable as I usually was; Harry squeezed my hand, and I realized how safe I felt with him. Then, I stepped into a shallow wave and yelped at the iciness.

Harry didn't react, though. Instead, he just laughed as the ocean rushed around his ankles and then vanished.

"How is that not cold to you!?" I screeched, amazed at his nonchalance.

"Because it's not that cold," Harry said, still laughing.

"To you, maybe!" I stopped and shivered, waiting to adjust to the temperature. I looked at the view in front of me: Harry standing in the sun, the breeze ruffling his hair, and the sun scorching high in the cloudless sky.

The relaxing moment was cut short when Harry suddenly wrapped his arms around me and lifted me into the air. I shrieked as he carried me deeper, the water splashing against my stomach and goosebump-covered arms.

"No, no, no, *Harry!*"

He dropped me; my immediate reaction was to cling onto him like a koala to a tree.

"Carter, let go." Harry cackled while I clung onto him for dear life. "Baby, are you alright?"

I shook my head, gulping as I refused to look down at the shadowy, indigo water. He held me as I gripped his strong forearms.

"I don't want to touch the ground."

"Oh, Carter, nothing is going to bite you."

"You don't know that!" I shot back.

"Come on, nothing's gonna get you. There's nothing near us. Just put your feet down."

"No, no way. I *always* step on something!"

"No, you won't, I promise. Just let go."

I gulped, then reached one foot down and slowly set it on the ocean floor. I waited to feel something slimy or spiky, but there was just slick sand. I dropped my other foot down. Harry gave me a reassuring smile. "You good?"

"Yeah." I focused on getting my breath even, then swatted

his chest. "I can't believe you dropped me! Like I was a sack of potatoes!"

Harry's mouth gaped open. "I was helping you overcome your fears, my beautiful potato!" He could barely get the words out before he cracked up. And I had to laugh along.

Harry put his hands on my waist and pulled me closer.

"Seriously, though. Are you okay?"

"I'm fine. Still a little scared of getting eaten alive, but I'll be fine."

"Good. But if you get scared, you can cling onto me again."

"You'd like that," I commented.

"Mmmhmm." Harry pulled me even closer, and I put my arms around his shoulders. "You're so beautiful, Carter."

"You too," I mumbled, mesmerized by his lips. Harry grinned in an amused sort of way, and I realized that most boyfriends probably weren't called *beautiful*. We kissed, and Harry nibbled on my lip.

When Harry pulled away, he sunk himself lower into the water until just his head poked out of the surface. I squinted at him suspiciously, standing up on my tiptoes. Then he splashed a wall of water onto me; I was instantly soaked.

"Harry, I'm gonna kill you! It's freezing!"

Harry just laughed and dived deeper into the water, leaving me to go after him.

TWENTY-FIVE

After fooling around and splashing water at one another, we got out to look for a place to eat. Harry and I skipped the pizza and went straight to the ice cream shoppe, where we sat on the high chairs outside of the parlor and shared flavors.

When we got back to his car, we decided to go to Harry's place, seeing as it was only two in the afternoon. I pawed through the bag to get my dry clothes.

"Oh, great." I huffed.

"What's wrong?" Harry asked, turning down the music as he drove.

"I forgot to pack a bra. I wouldn't care if my top piece wasn't so damp."

"You want me to drop you off at home? If you're uncomfortable, I mean," Harry said, gently squeezing my thigh.

"No, it's fine. I'll manage. Are your parents home, by the way?"

"God, I hope not," Harry muttered as we pulled up. The driveway was empty, and when Harry opened the garage, that was empty, too.

We found a note from them on the table by the door; I thought it was sweet his mom had written him something instead of texting. We went straight downstairs and into his bedroom and threw ourselves onto his bed to relax from the day at the beach. I felt a little guilty about getting salt and sand on his comforter, but he didn't seem to mind. Harry flipped over and rested his head on my chest.

"What are you thinking about?" he asked. I started to play with his hair.

"Honestly? Right now, I'm thinking about how soft your hair is. Especially after being in the ocean."

"Wish I could say the same," he replied cheekily, running his fingers through my now-stiff hair and dramatically pretending to get stuck in it.

"Hey!" I giggled as he pressed a kiss on my nose. Harry pulled back a little, grinning, knowing I was watching. He bit his bottom lip, then licked it slowly.

Eventually I grew tired of the teasing and yanked him down onto me by his neck. Harry laughed against my mouth, his tongue slipping past my lips. I inhaled a sharp breath.

Harry's free hand gripped my hip, his fingers pressing into me, grabbing one leg with his other hand and hitching it up at his side. I rested one hand on his back, pressing him down onto me, and then mussed his hair. Harry lifted his head, and I quickly latched my lips onto his neck, nipping and sucking on the soft skin. I heard him whimper when I lightly bit down on his collarbone, and I traced my tongue up until I reached his jawline.

"Carter," Harry breathed, "you drive me crazy, you know that?" With my forehead pressed to his, I knew I was grinning like mad. I might drive him crazy, but if only he knew how he made me feel.

Just one look and I was his.

"Hey," he whispered, "I'm gonna change out of these shorts. I'm not very comfortable." I nodded and watched as he left the room, then returned just a few short minutes later.

He's so beautiful.

He tossed an old band sweatshirt towards me and proceeded to throw himself back onto the bed beside me. I gave him a look, and he noticed. "You said you were uncomfortable. This sweatshirt is pretty thick. So, bra or no bra, you wouldn't be able to tell."

I smiled gratefully, threw on the sweatshirt, and removed my top underneath. He was too sweet. Harry sat beside me again, nuzzling his head into my neck. He hummed, his lips leaving rough kisses all over my cheek.

"What time is it?" I asked. Harry craned his neck to his alarm clock.

"It's gonna be four soon. Why?"

I sighed. "I have to go soon. I promised my mom I'd be home for dinner."

Harry pouted, then nodded. "All right, let's get going, then. I'm surprised my parents haven't gotten home yet, anyway."

I knew it was risky coming home wearing a sweatshirt that wasn't mine, as Dylan might recognize it as Harry's. But I also doubted Dylan would notice, and if he did, I'd say it was Mitchell's. Plus, I didn't want *my* shirt to make my chest visible. I slipped on my sandals, straightened my ponytail, grabbed my things, and walked out with Harry to his car.

Instead of stopping in front of Mitchell's, we stopped a couple houses away from mine. I pressed a kiss to his lips then hopped out of the car.

"Bye, baby, I'll text you later," he called out to me.

I watched as Harry made a U-turn and disappeared down the street. And for what felt like the millionth time that day, I smiled to myself before walking back towards my house.

TWENTY-SIX

It had been five days since my beach date with Harry. And since then, we had only gotten closer than before.

The majority of the week consisted of us not being able to keep our hands off each other. Sneaking around in little hideouts outside of school. Flirty texting, back and forth, every second of the day. Late night calls until one of us fell asleep. Harry didn't skip class to sit with me at lunch that week, which was fine; I didn't want him to miss more than he already had.

By Thursday, I had decided to spend the afternoon at Mitchell's. I felt like I'd been neglecting him and Elizabeth since going out with Harry. And tonight was the night I was going to tell Elizabeth about our relationship. I felt bad that I hadn't told her yet. Even though Mitchell was my best friend, she had quickly become nearly as close to me as he was. We ended up going to Panda

Express right after school, trying to beat the crowd.

"Carter, can you pass the noodles?" Mitchell asked, actively stuffing more fried rice into his mouth.

"So, Carter," Elizabeth said. Her eyeshadow looked amazing—glittering blue swaths that made her eyes pop brilliantly. "Tell me, how are things with Harry?"

I darted a look at Mitchell, who was still casually eating his food. He peered up at me innocently.

"You told her?" I asked.

"I couldn't know?" Elizabeth said, a little bit of hurt evident on her face.

I looked at her, realizing it had come out wrong. "It's not that. I just wanted to tell you myself."

"Well, doesn't matter anymore," Mitchell stated, mixing his chow mein with his orange chicken. "She knows. I didn't mean to ruin the surprise, but we're together more than I'd like to be. I told her, because... Well, because it's her."

"What is that supposed to mean?" Elizabeth scowled at Mitchell.

He merely shrugged, focused on his food. "I know I can trust you?"

Elizabeth and I looked at each other, surprised by his compliment. We both turned to Mitchell, who was glaring back and forth at us.

"For the record, I wasn't trying to be *nice*. I was just being honest, so shove that sentimental shit up your ass." Elizabeth and I erupted in laughter. She didn't say anything for moment, just smirking as she quietly continued to eat.

"Carter, can I see your phone?" Mitchell asked—purposely changing the subject, I was sure. He held his hand out before I could even respond.

"Sure, why?" I asked. I checked the lock screen, found no notifications, then placed the phone in his palm.

"Mine is acting up. It's restarting, but I need to check something." He fiddled with the screen, then said, "You hardly post shit, yet you have a bunch of follower requests; what the hell?"

"What's so important on Instagram you had to check immediately?" I replied, but I knew he wouldn't answer. "And it's not like they're actual people. Most of them are probably bots or just random people that add just about anybody they come across."

"Want me to just accept them?" Mitchell asked, but I could already hear him tapping away on my phone.

"Pretty sure you already did."

Mitchell snickered. "You know me so well."

"Just don't follow anyone back. I'll do that myself when I get the chance."

"Which means never," Elizabeth quipped.

"Do you follow Harry?" Mitchell asked, and I tried to remember. Finally, I nodded.

"Yeah, I think I followed him around the end of our freshman year. Before all that drama happened."

"Can I spam him?"

I shook my head emphatically. "Absolutely not."

"*Why?*" Mitchell protested.

"Because no. I don't want Harry to know I'm stalking his page. That's so creepy; we only just started dating. And the last thing I need is him ending something that's hardly started. I draw the line on stalking—"

"Oh god, you're so dramatic, Carter. Shut up," Mitchell retorted, hitting me on the head with flimsy chopsticks. "Besides, girls probably spam him every day so I don't think he would even care, let alone notice."

"Yeah, thanks for that, Mitch. Because I just *love* knowing girls spam my boyfriend," I said. I shook my head as I sipped at my soda.

My phone buzzed, and I looked up.

"Uh, Carter? *Lunchbox* just texted you," he said with a puzzled look. I smiled at the nickname I'd given Harry. I liked to use it for discretion, and since not even Mitch guessed who it might be, I knew it worked well.

Mitch tossed the phone on my lap, and I read the new message from Harry.

Lunchbox: babe

Me: yes harold

Lunchbox: don't call me that

Lunchbox: do you wanna go get coffee with me tomorrow

Lunchbox: and perhaps maybe a tattoo afterwards

Me: what

Me: a tattoo???

Me: tattoo of what?????

Me: tattoo where???!

Me: since when did you decide on getting a tattoo?¿

Me: you can't even get a tattoo, you're not 18 yet

Lunchbox: I know a guy

Lunchbox: no but seriously, ryan just texted me that his brother is in town and he's a tattoo artist so maybe he can hook me up

Lunchbox: since i'm gonna be 18 in a few months, I may as well start planning now right?

Me: is that the only reason?

Lunchbox: uh yeah kind of...

Me: what's the other reason?

Lunchbox: idk I guess I just wasn't really sure what to get, I'm too picky

Me: well that answer is better than I expected

Lunchbox: why?

Lunchbox: what did you expect???

"Carter, can you pass the orange chicken?" Elizabeth asked, distracting me.

I slid the bowl over to her.

"Are you done eating?" Mitchell asked me. He was using Elizabeth's phone now.

"Yeah. I have twin food babies."

"Name one after me."

I snorted and looked back at my phone.

Me: I honestly thought you were gonna say you were afraid of needles

Harold: whAt no

Harold: I'm not afraid

Me: so what are you gonna get

Harold: maybe something tacky like "Mom" inside of a heart

Harold: on my arm

Harold: that way it's also a pun

Harold: "heart on my sleeve" haha. get it?

Me: you would seriously get a pun tattooed on you?

Harold: oh absolutely

Me: the worst part is that I believe you

Me: any other ideas

Momma's Boy: how about some lyrics? Maybe on my chest. Or my bicep

Me: what kind of lyrics? whose?

Momma's Boy: truthfully, I don't know yet

Momma's Boy: I just have this neat design in my head

but that's about it

Me: you don't have an artist in mind?

Momma's Boy: eh, I'm not sure yet. I don't want it to be just any artist

Momma's Boy: I want the lyrics to speak for themselves

:)

TWENTY-SEVEN

"So are you definitely going to stick to some lyrics on your arm?" I asked, swirling my iced chai. We'd driven out to the downtown area so that we could hang out with less fear of being caught. We were strolling through a maze of streets, wandering into small shops and boutiques, lingering in the A/C for as long as possible before returning to the heat outside.

"Sure, but not today. That part was a joke. Why?" Harry asked, churning his frappe with his straw.

"I don't know, maybe it's the way I'm imagining it that I'm not liking it. But hey, it's your body, your choice," I said. "Just remember it's going to be on your body forever. What happens in the long run if these lyrics that symbolize something to you now don't even relate to you later?"

Harry just looked at me oddly before conceding, "All right, well, what if I get a ship on my arm?"

"I'd rather you didn't."

Harry frowned. "Why? Do you have something against tattoos?"

"No, of course not. It's just, a ship? Really? I would've preferred the heart on your sleeve with 'Mom' written in the middle."

"Why not the ship, though?"

I tilted my head, thinking. "I don't know; it's just super random."

There was a brief pause after my reply, and my eyes landed on a little store with art inside. I grabbed Harry's arm and pulled him inside. I started exploring; the oil paintings were my favorite, but there were also watercolor paintings, statues, and mixed media pieces.

"Hey, Carter?" Harry whispered.

I hummed in response, looking at the layers of paint on a canvas.

A little shutter sound went off, and I turned to see Harry snapping a picture of me on his phone.

"Hey!" I grinned and whacked his shoulder in the same moment.

Harry held his free hand out in protection while his other gripped his phone as he looked at the picture he'd just taken. I pulled out my own phone and opened the camera app, then stuck it in front of his face. He squirmed away.

"Carter, stop!" Harry laughed. He blocked the camera with his hand, moving his head from side to side, trying to dodge me. "All right. All right! Want a picture? Here!" he shouted. He put a huge smile on, all dimples and wrinkles, eyes practically closed.

I snapped about ten pictures, giggling like mad. I flipped the camera and pressed a kiss to his cheek.

He opened his eyes, saw I was taking a selfie of us, and stuck his tongue out. We took dozens more like that, making faces and posing ridiculously, eventually wandering out into the street. After, I swiped through my album so that he could see.

"How can you make the most horrid faces ever and still look beautiful?" Harry asked.

"Are you serious? Look at this one, I have quadruple chins."

"And I love each and every one of them," Harry gushed, and I hit his shoulder again, my fist colliding with him. "*Hey*! Watch the muscles. I've been workout out."

"Aw, poor baby." I pouted. I planted a kiss on the spot I'd punched him. Then several more over his shoulder.

When I looked back up at him, there was heat in his green eyes. He reached for my hand and started pulling me down the street, into a quiet, shadowed side alley.

"Harry," I said, a note of wariness in my voice.

"I just need to kiss you," he whispered, and his hand cupped my jaw. I melted at his touch, and his lips collided onto mine with urgency. My breathing quickly became shallow. My hands went to his hair, and after raking my hands through it, I tugged on his head to expose his neck. I bit down on the soft skin by his ear, and he backed me up against a brick wall. It was unexpectedly cool against my skin. Both his hands went to my rear, his grip bordering pain and pleasure.

The sound of his phone going off made us jump. He reached into his back pocket and answered the call.

He stepped away, and I could tell by the "Yeah... Yeah, okay... Sure... Will do. Uh huh. Love you too," that it was his mom.

He hung up and said, "I gotta head back. Sorry. She wants me to help her set up for dinner, and it's kind of a drive. Some of my family from my stepdad's side are coming over."

"Sure, it's no problem. Thanks for driving all the time."

"Of course."

The trip back was quiet, Harry's hands traveling up and down my legs, making the hair on the back of my neck stand up. He dropped me off near my house.

Just as I stepped out of the car, Harry called out to me, "Hey, babe."

"Yeah?" I turned with a smile.

Harry smiled back, eyes roving up and down as if taking one last look at me before he said, "Send me those pictures, yeah?"

I nodded, my smile widening as Harry winked. Then he blew me a kiss and started his drive home.

TWENTY-EIGHT

[HARRY]

"Ah, I'm so glad you made it home on time," my mother squealed as I stepped through the door. She darted out from the kitchen, gripped my arm, and escorted me back with her.

"What's going on?" I asked. Mom took off and scampered frantically around the room as I stood in the kitchen doorway.

"I made dinner, and finished most of it, before we left to grab drinks—which is probably the smartest thing I've done because the family is coming sooner than expected." She paused to catch her breath. "All I have to do is make the salad and butter the bread, and I need you to set the table."

As I picked out my mom's nicest placemats, my stepdad, Ben, walked into the kitchen.

"Hey, bud," he said to me, and he gave my mom a kiss on the

cheek. He smelled like charcoal.

"Hey. What'd you grill?"

"Brisket. I need to show you how to make that sometime."

I nodded. I didn't really have an interest, but I figured it would probably be a good thing to learn how to cook at some point. "So who's coming, anyway?" I asked, grabbing the expensive drinking glasses to carry to the dining room table.

"Your uncle Max and his wife Johanna," Ben called. When I walked back in, he was chopping cucumber at the center island while my mom tore up lettuce.

"Max's kids aren't coming?" I asked.

My stepdad shook his head. "No, they decided to leave them behind."

"How come?"

"When you're a parent with young children that are as...uh..." Ben waved his hand around, as if in search for a good word to use to describe Max's kids. "...*destructive* as they are, you tend to leave them home so they don't cause...*destruction* somewhere else. That make sense?"

My mother rolled her eyes, shaking her head as if refusing to even correct him. Her hair was pinned back all fancy-like.

"So, you're saying...don't have kids?" I joked. Ben stifled his laugh until my mother glared at us. I hurried out to the dining room with the utensils.

"I want grandkids!" Mom scolded from the kitchen, and when I

218

looked through the doorway, I saw her cutting up tomatoes.

"*Now?*" I asked with wide eyes. "At least wait until Emma gets married, Mom. You do remember having another, much elder child, right?"

"Harry, don't be ridiculous," she laughed. "Obviously you'd have to graduate from both high school *and* college before you could even think of having a child."

"Take your mom's advice on this one, pal," Ben added. "Having a kid so young can keep you from great opportunities."

"Noted," I replied, hoping they wouldn't continue. But of course, they did anyway. I took my time in the dining room making sure the napkins were folded right, but my mom just continued half-shouting from the kitchen.

"I would hope so, Harry; you have a lot of growing up to do and a lot of responsibilities to deal with before you should bring a kid into your life. Kids are hard work."

"And expensive, too," Ben added

I wasn't sure how to reply.

Just as I turned to head back upstairs, knowing they wouldn't need my assistance anymore, my mother stepped out of the kitchen, holding a baguette.

"*Wait*, Harry!" I stopped on the first stair. "Question."

"Shoot."

"Speaking of kids—"

"Oh, god, please no."

"*Harry.* I have to ask, you know, as your mother... Is there, um, *someone* we should know about?" she asked with raised eyebrows. Ben swiftly grabbed the baguette from her and retreated into the kitchen.

"Uh, not sure what you mean."

"I would like to meet this girl at some point, that's all."

"*Mom,*" I whined.

"I'm just asking!"

I sighed. "How do you even know there's a girl in the picture?"

Her shoulders slumped, and she rolled her eyes. "Oh *please*, is it that hard to believe that I was your age once?" I felt unsure how to answer, knowing if I made an age joke, I'd be paving my own path to hell. "Harry, you laugh more than usual—you giggle, actually. You always go out in a rush, even though you and Dylan had that falling out. You smile every time you get a text during dinner, and you—"

"How do you know I text during dinner?" I asked, positive I'd been discreet this whole time.

"Oh please, Harry, no one looks down at their crotch and smiles."

I dramatically dropped my head back, groaning. I felt a stab of guilt for not being completely forthright about my issues with Dylan or my relationship with Carter, but I didn't need their lecturing right now. "Okay, I might be seeing someone... Might have been for a little while now, actually."

"Ah, I knew it! But why didn't you tell us?" she asked.

I opened my mouth, but couldn't string together the right

combination of words that would make sense to her. "I don't know, I guess telling you guys would've made it seem serious, and even though it is, to me at least, I just didn't wanna jinx it or anything. I really like her, so...yeah."

"Aw." Mom smiled, holding a hand over her heart. I was on the verge of making a run for it before she engulfed me in a massive hug. "I'm so happy for you, sweetie. Well, who is she? What's her name? And when is she coming over?"

"Uh..." I stammered for a bit, wracking my brain, trying to decide if I should make up a name. But this was my *mother*. I mean, she'd probably meet Carter eventually, and how would it look if I'd told my own parents a different name? Plus, Dylan and I weren't friends anymore and probably wouldn't ever be. It wasn't like my mom was going to ring him and tell him I had a girlfriend, especially since she had never really liked him. And our parents weren't best friends. They knew each other, but they weren't close; so why not?

"Well...her name is Carter. She's one grade lower, and I've known her since my sophomore year, only we just got together. And yeah, I just really like her, and we're taking things one step at a time."

If you don't count having sex before the relationship even started, my subconscious remarked, but I pushed that thought aside.

"What about meeting her?" my mom asked again. Ben stepped out for a half-second to give me a knowing look.

"Uh, meeting her? I mean, we're taking this one step at a time, and I don't think she—"

"Oh come on, Harry," she pleaded with excitement. "How about you invite her over for dinner?"

My eyes widened in alarm. "What, *now*?"

"No, obviously not *now*. How about...Sunday?"

"Uh." I scratched the back of my neck. "I mean, I could ask her... But I can't promise you anything. I have to see what she says first." *I'm sure she'd freak out as much as I am right now.*

"Well, okay, that's fine. Wait—Carter... You said her name was Carter?" my mother asked. I flushed at hearing her name, feeling suddenly anxious.

There's *no* way they knew her by name alone. I had never, ever talked about my crush on my best buddy's sister to anyone, especially to my parents. I'd kept all that on the down low ever since the Stacy debacle.

"Yeah..." I dragged out the word right before adding, "I don't think you know her... *Right?*"

"No." She shook her head. "Well... No. I mean, the name sounds familiar but, eh, I don't think I know a *Carter*. But anyway, ask her how she feels about dinner on Sunday. I'd love to meet her."

"I'll ask her." I leaned against the banister. "So," I changed the subject, "what time do Max and his wife get here?"

Ben stepped out into the dining room with a pitcher of water.

"Well..." He checked his watch, and the doorbell rang. "Right now."

Me: question

Me: why do ppl say 'suck my ass' now

Me: like it's so overused

Me: funny as hell

Me: but overused

Me: I just wanna know why

Baby: idk

Baby: I think bc 'suck my dick' is sexist, or some other word, on both parts

Me: how

Baby: bc for one obvious reason, not all girls have dicks

Baby: secondly, it's pretty messed up that we can use that term like it holds higher power whereas calling someone a pussy is an insult so it's like????

Baby: so yeah suck my ass is the phrase to use

Baby: since we all have one

Baby: unless you don't

Baby: whatever

Me: ....

Baby: what

Me: I was honestly expecting just

Me: "it's a new stupid trend harry ur so dumb"

Baby: I wouldn't call you dumb

Baby: you're a dumbass, but that's different

Baby: Also, aren't you at dinner with your family

Me: yeah

Me: but I'm bored

Me: bc they're all talking about adult stuff

Me: using big words and all that

Me: and I'm just sitting here thinking about trees and shit

Me: and you of course

Baby: soooo... you need entertainment?

Me: you could say that

Baby: hmm.......

Baby: interesting........

Me: why?

Baby: oh...

Baby: no reason......

Me: carter

Baby: it's nothing

Baby: so you're like sitting there

Baby: with everyone

Baby: right?

Me: ....I'm scared to say yes

Baby: brb

Me: okay.....??

I looked up from my phone, moving the leftover brisket around on my plate.

My family continued to talk amongst themselves, and I occasionally laughed, but most of the conversation was just *How's work? How's the business? How are the kids?*

The real question was: *how have I not stabbed myself with a fork yet?*

"So, Harry," Uncle Max suddenly asked, "tell me, have you decided where you're going for college?"

"Yeah, I'm working on a scholarship to St. John's University." I smiled a bit as he nodded approvingly. He and Ben looked nothing alike, despite being brothers.

Aunt Johanna gently swirled her wine glass with her dainty fingers, then asked, "What do you plan on studying?"

"I decided on taking a double major. One for liberal arts and the other is undecided. But I might just do both in liberal arts and choose English lit."

"That sounds wonderful," Johanna said, then she and my uncle turned back to my parents and discussed college plans for their own kids. That seemed a little ambitious, given they were still only in elementary or maybe middle school, but Uncle Max and Aunt Johanna were like that.

My phone vibrated in my hand as I reached for my glass of water, and I opened a new message from Carter. I inhaled my water and almost spit it all over the table as I stared at the picture on my screen.

"Holy shit," I choked out.

"Harry!" Mom gasped. "Are you alright?"

"Fine, just dying a little. Don't resuscitate me," I wheezed.

I got a few laughs for that, and after I was done coughing, they eventually went back to chatting.

Finally catching my breath, I looked back down at my phone. There she was. Carter. A selfie of her lying on her bed. Her long brown locks spread out on her bed sheets. Finger between her teeth and a hidden smirk, her eyes glinting with seduction.

Her chest was completely exposed, her breasts so full, round. I was immediately aching. I pulled at the fabric of my jeans, trying to create as much space as possible.

"Excuse me, I have to use the restroom," I announced, then immediately fled. I made it to the bathroom in less than ten steps. I quickly unbuttoned my jeans and pulled them down along with my boxers until my erection sprang free. I breathed out in relief.

I clenched my eyes and thought of Carter, wasting no time. I opened the picture once more. The second it appeared back on my screen, I bit my lip to keep from making a sound. I was internally groaning as I stared at the picture, thinking about our first night. The way she felt on top of me after I'd flipped us over. Her body lowering itself onto me with ease. How she'd leaned back, exposing her breasts to me in full view. The way her skin had felt below my fingertips when I'd gripped her hips and began to grind myself into her. The soft moans falling from her lips as she fell into her own climax. That was just enough to push me over the edge and come. My eyes fluttered shut in ecstasy, my breathing heavy.

After washing up, I waited a little longer until I didn't feel as flustered. Then I went back to the table, my family hardly giving me a glance as I sneakily sent a quick text to Carter.

Me: I'm so getting you back for that ;) x

TWENTY-NINE

[*CARTER*]

"You didn't mean it when you said you were getting me back, right?" I asked, tiptoeing on the shore as Harry held my hand.

We went to the beach again today. It was a Saturday, but the beach was practically empty because it was unusually cloudy outside.

"I did," Harry answered casually. "I haven't thought of how yet. But I will, and it's gonna be an even bigger tease."

I scoffed. "Is that so?"

Harry nodded, a mischievous glint in his eyes. "Absolutely. I'm thinking of it as a challenge."

"Fine. But if you can do better than what I did yesterday, I'll get you back ten times worse."

He came closer to me with an evil smirk. "We'll see."

Thinking I would be getting a kiss, I was disappointed when he pulled on the collar of my shirt to cover my shoulder.

"Why do you keep doing that?"

"Why do you wear it on one shoulder but not the other?"

"That's how it's supposed to be! It's an off-the-shoulder cut." I threw my hands up in frustration. We'd been at it all day with my shirt. It immediately settled back to being lopsided.

He stared at it. "That's so frustrating."

I shook my head and kept walking. The infuriating shirt covered my one-piece, and Harry wore white swim trunks, his snapback, and a graphic T-shirt.

"Can I ask you something?" he asked suddenly. "What made you want to send me that picture?"

"Um, I don't know really. I'd never done it before, and, I mean, I trust you. But mainly because I wanted to tease you. The timing just happened to be perfect."

He looked at me out of the corner of his eye. "I didn't know if you were a little frustrated at the interruption yesterday."

"Well, yeah, but I wasn't going to strip in an alley."

He laughed. "No, I know. I wouldn't ever ask you to do something that made you uncomfortable."

"I appreciate that." I turned to watch a seagull coast in the wind. "Hey, you wanna go eat? Grab some pizza?"

"Why not ice cream?"

"I'm only in the mood for pizza," I told him.

Harry pursed his lips, then shrugged. "Sure, why not? I'm getting kind of hungry, anyway."

We brought all our things back to his car. I put on my jeans, and Harry pulled on a sweatshirt, as it was starting to actually get chilly. When Harry wasn't looking, I reached up and pulled the hat off his head. He immediately turned to snatch it back from me, but I didn't let him.

"Come on, babe. I have hat hair," Harry whined, trying to reach around me and take it.

"Can I wear it? *Pleeeeeaaaaase.*" I held the hat behind my back. Forced to acquiesce, he threw his head back dramatically.

"Fine, whatever. I'll wear something else."

I placed the hat backwards on my head. Harry dug through his trunk and then found a blue beanie.

"Do you have a hat collection back there?" I asked, looking past him to see if he had any more.

"Shut up, let's go," Harry said, chuckling.

Harry and I spent a long time in the pizzeria. We probably stayed longer than we should've given how busy they were, but we kept ordering. We got a medium pie, and he was already full by his second slice, leaving the other four for me. However, even after I devoured those four slices, I wasn't full. Harry stared in a combination of horror and admiration when the waiter came back and I asked for another soda and a hot dog.

We were quiet while I finished eating, and I saw a flyer outside about an online college that sparked a question in my mind. "Hey, so, you said you were going to St. John's, right?"

I noticed his expression change.

"I'm just curious," I continued, "what happens to us when you have to leave for New York?" The question left a bitter taste in my mouth.

"Do you think we'll make it work?"

I shrugged. "I wouldn't know. I've never been in that type of situation."

"Situation?'

"I don't know what else to call it." I shrugged again. The atmosphere around us had already changed, becoming thick and tense.

Harry ignored my comment. "Look, we'll figure something out. I don't want to think or talk about that right now. I want to live in the moment and enjoy what we have going on here, so let's put that topic aside and cross that bridge when we come to it. Okay?"

Despite Harry's reassuring smile, I didn't want to drop it. Graduation was just a few short months away. I could see what he meant about living in the moment... It was, after all, the same reason I hadn't brought it up before. I just hoped that the conversation would come up again sooner rather than later.

The sun was beginning to set by the time we got in the car. On the ride home, I realized that Harry had gotten way into The 1975. He screamed lyrics of every song for the entire drive, making me laugh so hard my sides hurt. The ride was quicker that we'd both hoped.

When he parked, I took off his hat to hand it back to him, and he said, "Keep it."

I smiled at him. "As much as I'd love to, I can't."

"Why?"

"If Dylan sees me with it, he's going to know whose it is."

"Right. I get it." Harry sighed. "Still trying to grow accustomed to this sneaking-around thing, but it's for the best."

"But I guarantee it's going to be worth it."

"Absolutely." Harry pressed a kiss to my cheek, and I slid out of the car.

"Oh wait, Carter!" Harry called. "Wear something nice tomorrow, yeah?"

I raised an eyebrow at him. "Uh, for what?"

Harry pressed his lips together in a hard line. "Oh, uh. I forgot to mention something earlier..."

I narrowed my gaze at Harry, beginning to feel nervous. "Harry...?"

"Carter, I, well, I—"

"*Harry*... What did you do?" I asked sternly, my pulse getting faster.

"My mom invited you for dinner tomorrow." Harry said all the words in a rush, and before I could reply, let alone react, Harry shouted, "Bye!", blew me a kiss, and then took off down the street.

Wait... What?

THIRTY

I fidgeted with the hem of my dress, pulling it down every so often. My mom was running errands, and my dad was at a friend's house watching a game. Dylan had gone out to God knows where, thankfully, so I spent all morning darting back and forth across my room, trying to find something to wear. My stomach felt queasy from all the anxiety.

I ended up settling on a short-sleeve lavender dress that ended just above my knees. The neckline was round and gave me the opportunity to put on a small statement necklace my mother had given me for my sixteenth birthday. I was wearing my hair down, and today it was somewhere between being wavy and curly—the good kind of "in between" luckily, and not the ratty *just-woke-up* kind.

I rarely did my nails, so I left them natural. I hadn't been biting them lately, so they looked about semi-even. I chose not to wear too much makeup, just a mauve lip with curled eyelashes, and a coat of my dried-out mascara.

After slipping on my shoes—a pretty pair of white flats—I decided to wait for Harry outside. As I stood, pacing in the driveway, I felt my hand start to sweat from the death grip I had on my pocketbook.

I was about to meet Harry's parents.

Dear god.

Harry had met *my* parents, sure, but not like this. Was it normal to be this nervous? *Okay, you know what? It's fine. I just need to relax. It's no big deal. Just meeting my boyfriend's parents. No big deal, whatsoever...*

But wait—oh god—do they know he's my boyfriend? Should I introduce myself as his girlfriend? I shook my head to myself in response to my own question. *No, I'll just say I'm Carter. Yeah. They don't need a label. Just Carter. But what if they expect me to label myself? What if they recognize me as Dylan's sister? What if I have a panic attack and throw up on his mom's shoes? Or his dad's vest? Does his dad even wear a vest?*

My hands started trembling; I gripped the pocketbook even tighter. When Harry's little sedan pulled up, I tried to collect myself. Naturally, the soles of my flats skidded a couple of times as I walked to the car, almost tripping me. I could see Harry trying not to laugh, and ordinarily I would have laughed with him, but I was far too nervous. I was silent for a few moments as we just sat in the driveway, and then I heard Harry chuckle again.

"What's so funny?" I squeaked, suddenly feeling even more unsure of myself. He just grinned, shaking his head at me.

Was my dress too much? He'd said to wear something nice. Was this not nice enough?

"Do I look okay?" I asked. *If he says no, I'm climbing on my roof and throwing myself off.*

"You look beautiful, baby."

"Then why are you laughing?"

"Why do you look so scared? Honestly, Carter, you look like you've seen a ghost," he said, still laughing, and he finally put the car in drive.

"*Hello?* I'm about to meet your parents, Harry. I'm scared out of my mind right now." My voice was thick, and I had a knot in my throat, the kind that forms when you try not to cry. Harry put his hand on my thigh, squeezing it reassuringly as he drove.

"Don't worry about it. I'm nervous, too, but I promise, nothing will go wrong," Harry said softly. "Just don't stress yourself out too much. Be yourself; I'm sure my parents will love you. *Especially* my mom."

I took deep breaths through my mouth. Part of me knew I was overreacting, but the rest of me just didn't know how to cope. I knew, logically, I had every reason to react this way, but the knowing didn't help me feel any better.

"I just hope all goes well, and I don't make a fool out of myself,"

I muttered, grabbing Harry's hand for support.

Harry gave me another light squeeze, turning onto his street as we neared his house. As we parked in front of his house, he assured me, "Don't worry too much. My parents aren't ones to point out any flaws. And besides, they're just as nervous as you are."

"They are?"

"Of course." Harry shrugged. "Carter, you're the first girl I've ever brought home for them to meet. I'm sure they'll love you, and...uh, yeah," he stammered. "They'll love you."

I nodded, the knot in my throat disappearing. Harry stepped out of the car and then jogged to my side to open the door like a gentleman. He guided me out of the car and towards the front door.

"Wait." I grabbed Harry's hand, which was already grasping the doorknob. "Are you sure I look alright? No frizzy hairs or anything? Is this dress okay?"

Harry smiled, taking my chin between his thumb and forefinger and pulling me in for a smooth, lingering kiss. "You look perfect, baby." I smiled against his mouth. He pulled away, took a deep breath, and stepped into the house.

Immediately I was greeted by the smell of steak wafting through the air. Harry walked me to the kitchen, his grip growing tighter with every step. His mother was darting all around the center island, adding spices and whatnot to each pot and pan. Her dark brown hair was in a neat, high ponytail. She had on a pastel orange blouse and white pants. As she grabbed something from a cupboard, she noticed me and Harry. A huge grin broke out on her face, so much like Harry's, and she ran towards us like a kid running at presents.

"Hello! Oh, you must be Carter!" She took my hand in both of hers and shook it in pure delight.

"Hi, it's really nice to meet you." She only continued smiling at me, her eyes looking me over. I began to feel uneasy again until Harry cleared his throat.

"Oh! I'm sorry, I'm Amelia. Obviously, Harry's mom." I noticed Harry roll his eyes, clearly embarrassed by his mother's giddiness.

"It's really nice to meet you, Mrs. Amelia. You have such a lovely home."

"Oh, why thank you." She looked at Harry then towards me. "I'll be done with dinner soon. In the meantime, perhaps Harry can show you around?"

"Oh, that's okay, I've al—" I stopped mid-sentence, realizing what I was saying. "Uh, that's a great idea! Excuse me."

Harry pulled me up the stairs and into his bedroom.

"You almost got me killed down there." He laughed, closing his bedroom door.

"I'm so sorry! I completely forgot she didn't know I'd been here already." But Harry didn't seem phased by it. He leaned against his door, smiling. His blue shirt was unbuttoned at the neck, exposing some of his chest. He wore those tight black jeans *so* well. Instead of sneakers or loafers, he had on honey brown boots.

"Don't worry about it, baby."

I felt my cheeks growing pink at the pet name.

"Did I ever tell you how much of an effect you have on me when you call me that?"

He pushed himself off the door, and when his arms snaked their way around my waist, I took in a sharp breath.

"What kind of effect?" he whispered in my ear, his hot breath fanning against my neck, causing goosebumps to rise all over my skin. My eyes lazily trailed up his chest and face till they met his. I tilted my face to the side a bit, his fingers hovering over my mouth.

"I think you know what kind of effect," I whispered back. I placed my hands on his stomach, sliding down slowly and stopping just above the button of his jeans.

"Hmm," Harry hummed. "Is that so?" He lowered his head, his lips approaching mine. We were only an inch away from touching before he stopped. "Too bad I can't give you what you want. Especially after that stunt you pulled on Friday." He pulled away completely before turning on his heel and heading back towards the door.

I scoffed, a smirk forming on my lips.

Oh? That's how he wants to play? Fine by me. I took slow strides towards him, purposely swaying my hips before I stopped right at his side.

"You know, part of me knew you'd be a tease today specifically," I told him, and his eyebrow arched. I leaned into his ear, my lips brushing against them to add, "Which is why I'm not wearing any underwear."

Okay, maybe I was lying. But I couldn't help myself. I heard a gasp leave Harry's mouth as I walked ahead of him, stopping at the top of the stairs to glance back at him. His bottom lip was tucked between his teeth, his eyes trailing up and down my body in despair.

This was going to be *quite* an interesting dinner. I could already tell.

THIRTY-ONE

I met Ben, Harry's stepdad, when we returned to the dining area. He and Harry seemed pretty close, laughing and cracking jokes. I was a little surprised at how close Harry was with his parents, seeing as how he always seemed to be out of the house. They all had an easy, teasing manner that made me smile. I adored Harry even more in that moment, and it was then that he noticed me sitting on the barstool in silence, just observing.

"You okay?" he whispered to me, putting one arm around my waist as he kissed my head. I nodded, my smile only widening when I noticed Amelia glance at us with a half-hidden smirk before she turned back to prepping dinner.

Amelia and Ben made an amazing dinner: sirloin steak with mashed potatoes and broccoli. Harry sat beside me, while Amelia and his stepdad sat on each end of the table.

"So, Carter," said Ben, his deep brown eyes warm, "tell me about yourself."

I was unsure how to answer, and wiped at my mouth with my napkin to stall.

"Well...I'm not sure where to start, honestly."

"Tell us about how you two met."

I couldn't help but look at Harry. "Oh." I cleared my throat. "Harry and I met two years ago. Uh..."

If I mentioned my house, they might wonder if he had been going to Dylan's just to see me. They might not like it. Or what if it made me seem like I had just latched onto my brother's best friend like a clingy little sister? Or worse—much worse—what if they wanted to talk to my parents? They knew them. Then my parents would know... I fidgeted with the hem of my dress under the table, and Harry noticed my unease.

"It was at school," he announced calmly. "I bumped into her, and we hit it off from there."

"Oh," Amelia said, sounding rather underwhelmed but still smiling. "Well, when did you two start seeing each other?"

"A couple of weeks ago," I answered, finding my voice. "It's all pretty new."

His parents nodded until his mom asked, "You know, Carter, you look vaguely familiar. Do I happen to know your parents or anything, by any chance?"

"Ah, I'm not sure, honestly. I—my parents stay really busy..."

"Have you spoken to Emma?" Harry interrupted as he squeezed my hand under the table, saving me once again.

"Oh! Yes! She said she'll work out her schedule to visit," Amelia answered enthusiastically. "She's been extremely busy but cannot wait to come home!"

I knew Emma was Harry's sister, but he hadn't told me much about her. But I had never really gotten around to asking about her, either.

Apparently, she was older than Harry by a few years; in a way, that intimidated me. She seemed sweet from what I was hearing, but obviously it was her family talking, and they were not going to say anything negative about her personality—at least not in front of me. I knew how I felt about Dylan's girlfriend, so I could only imagine how a sister of Harry's might think of me. The thought made me shudder a little.

"Maybe you'll get to meet her, Carter!" Amelia said.

I smiled and tried to hide my hesitance in my tone. "Can't wait! She sounds lovely." We all continued eating, the conversation dying down a bit. I sighed in satisfaction when I finished my plate. "That was amazing, Mrs. Amelia. Best meal I've ever had."

"Thank you, Carter. I'm so glad you enjoyed it. I hope you all saved room for dessert!" She stood and started clearing the table with Ben's help.

"My dessert is right here," Harry whispered, his hand skimming my thigh. I sucked in a breath, batting Harry's hand away.

His parents headed into the kitchen with arms full of plates and cutlery.

Harry swiftly grabbed my face with both hands and pulled me in for a kiss. His tongue pushed past my lips, and I couldn't help the satisfied hum that was released. One of his hands remained on my cheek while the other went down my thigh; my fingers clenched around the edges of my seat. Harry's hand trailed up my thigh, and I let out a squeaky yelp when his fingers brushed against my aching center. He pulled back when he touched my underwear.

"I thought...?" Harry started, but then he noticed my sheepish grin. "You lied to me."

"I knew it would get you going," I mumbled against his lips, and in response I got a rough kiss. I nearly groaned in agony when his middle and forefinger pushed past the fabric and immediately slipped inside me.

My breathing quickened as his fingers worked like magic. I almost let out a moan, but Harry pressed his mouth harshly against mine to keep me quiet. I was on the verge of screaming in pleasure, seconds away from coming, just as footsteps were heard. Harry pulled away immediately and straightened his posture. I tried to collect myself.

Harry's parents walked in, all smiles, presenting an extremely chocolate-y cake and a pitcher of milk.

"Tell me how it is," Amelia pressed with a smile.

"I can't wait to try it," Harry said, angling towards me, his eyes lustful, hooded. I sucked in a breath and focused on grabbing a slice, knowing I'd come undone if I kept looking at his heated stare. *How am I going to survive tonight?*

After eating and conversing, Amelia excused Harry and me so she could tidy. And as much as I'd take advantage of that, I couldn't possibly leave her to clean up all by herself. I grabbed the dinnerware and took it to the sink. Ben un-sneakily ducked out to the living room to turn on the TV, making Amelia laugh.

She washed and I dried, putting dishes and utensils in the cabinets and drawers as she directed. We chatted throughout the entire time. Before too long, I noticed Harry in the corner of my eye, leaning up against the counter with arms crossed and a smile on his face as I spoke with his mother so comfortably. I was just glad it hadn't turned into one of those *bring-out-the-baby-pictures* type of meetings, as much fun as it would have been to tease Harry.

After we finished cleaning up, Harry and I bid our goodbyes and left hand in hand out the door.

"I kind of wish I'd had the chance to take you up to my room," Harry said as he backed out of the driveway. "After what we were doing back there, I'm pretty bummed."

"I'm glad we didn't do anything. Even though the teasing was fun, we have plenty of time for all of that... Do you think they liked me?"

"I'm sure they did." Harry nodded, taking my hand in his as he drove. We were quiet on the way back, and I watched the scenery through the window. Now that the evening was over, I wasn't as worried as I'd thought I'd be, but, in some ways, I felt like I should be. I hadn't expected to make a *perfect* impression, nor did I need them to absolutely fall in love with me, but I at least wanted them to genuinely like me. I thought it had gone well, but I also thought I wouldn't ever know their true opinions of me. I felt like they were too nice to tell me if they could barely tolerate me. Ultimately, I had been myself, and it was all I could be—

"Carter," Harry said, snapping me out of my reverie. "We're here."

We shared a smile, then a kiss.

"Hey, you'll tell me if they say they like me or not, right?" I asked, trying to hold a confident tone.

Harry chuckled before answering, "I'm telling you, they like you. But I promise, I will. See you tomorrow, baby."

THIRTY-TWO

In the middle of Monday night, I got a slew of texts from Harry.

Baaabe: I can't sleep

Baaabe: I am an insomniac

Baaabe: I have tossed and turned

Baaabe: I tried to watch a movie in my head

Baaabe: I was in Star Wars as C3PO

Baaabe: R2D2 was my little bitch

Baaabe: I killed luke and han solo bc you were leia

Baaabe: so I won you over ayyy

Baaabe: anyway that still didn't work bc I'm still fucking awake

Baaabe: I knocked back a bit of NyQuil

Baaabe: I binge-watched a couple episodes of

Supernatural

Baaabe: I did some pushups to tire myself out

Me: maybe you're nocturnal

Baaabe: omg you're up

Me: yeah

Baaabe: what are you doing up at 1 am. Are you nocturnal too?

Me: definitely not

Me: I was in the bathroom

Baaabe: are you okay?

Me: yeah just minor issues

Baaabe: what's wrong baby?

Me: I don't think you wanna know

Baaabe: are you sick?

Me: something like that

Baaabe: what's wrong babe, tell me

Me: I got my period :/

Me: it happened right after dinner

Me: literally fucking blood seeped through my sweats & I almost stained my bed

Me: I was so lucky I got up on time

Me: but I'm so mad bc I have to clean my sweats & my fave undies :(

Me: I'm also starving

Me: I'm craving chocolate-covered waffles with

powdered sugar & strawberries

Me: but then I also want pizza

Me: yeah I want pizza

Baaabe: jeez, no wonder you ate four slices of pizza and a hot dog that day at the beach

Me: this where you're supposed to be supportive & say "aw baby you'll be okay" n stuff bc I like when you call me that

Babe: aw baby

Me: there you go

Me: & now bring me food

Bruh: wow I swear you only use me for food

Me: duh what else are you useful for

Bruh: OUCH

Bruh: I SHOULDNT EVEN BRING YOU FOOD AFTER THAT

Bruh: rUDE

Me: AW BABY NO

Me: I'M SORRY

Me: THAT WAS MY PERIOD TALKING

Me: FORGIVE ME

Bruh: no

Me: come onnnn :(

Me: please obi-wan

Obi Wan: did you just

Me: please obi-wan. you're my only hope

Obi Wan: why, just why

Obi Wan: ugggghhhhh fine

Obi Wan: I'll find a way to go and bring you food

Me: YAAAAYYYYY!!!!!

Obi Wan: you know you should be thankful to have a bf like me

Me: I am

Obi Wan: you better be

Obi Wan: most guys wouldn't do this

Obi Wan: I go to great lengths for you

Obi Wan: I risk my life

Obi Wan: I go above and beyond

Obi Wan: and what do I get in return????

Me: sex

Obi Wan: ....fair enough

I put my phone down after Harry had told me he would be at my house in an hour. I groaned when I felt my cramps begin to attack my stomach. I continued shuffling through movies on Netflix. I thought I would finally decide on something, but I was still scrolling when my phone started dinging.

Unfortunately, my parents didn't have the night shift that night. I scurried down the back steps and did a mental prayer before slowly opening the door, only to hear it creak softly. I wanted to scream, despite how soft the noise was; my mood swings made me agitated and paranoid.

I managed to get Harry up to my room without having a total heart attack, a miracle unto itself. He tossed a shopping back onto the bed, which I eagerly dug into.

"*Aw*, babe," I cooed, taking out a bag of chips, "I haven't had jalapeño Cheetos in over a year."

"I was hoping you'd still like them," he said, looking through the books on my shelves.

"Kiwi strawberry AriZona; you know me so well," I said, sitting beside him.

"That was the last one. I knew that if they didn't have kiwi strawberry, then I'd bring you grape. You like grape, right?"

"Of course. It's my second favorite." I smiled before pulling out another item. "Sour Life Savers. Harry, I'm about to cry tears of joy right now."

"Is that fine? Or do you want more food? I could drive back to 7-Eleven if you want—"

"No, Harry, it's fine. Thank you. I'm good for now." I smiled, patting the spot beside me. "C'mere. Watch *Schitt's Creek* with me."

"You're watching *Schitt's Creek*? Ah, I love that show." Harry grinned, throwing his coat to the floor and kicking off his shoes before climbing on my bed.

"You've seen it?"

"Of course!" Harry exclaimed excitedly. I shushed him so he'd lower his voice, but I was smiling as he cuddled up beside me. "Well, come on, press play!"

I couldn't help but laugh as he wrapped his arms around me.

⊗

We were nearing Season Two before we finally turned off Netflix and just talked, slowly growing sleepy as the sky turned an indigo blue.

"You're so beautiful, baby," Harry whispered. My cheek was pressed against his chest as I traced circles over his magenta T-shirt.

"You're prettier." I yawned, my eyes never leaving my swirling finger. I could feel my eyelids growing droopy. Harry chuckled; the sound reverberated through his chest, and I could feel the vibration on the side of my face.

"You're too good for me, Carter. I—" Harry paused mid-sentence as if searching for the right word, then said, "I don't know how I got lucky enough to be with you."

I smiled lazily, trying to stay up, but he was so comfy, and I was so sleepy.

"Likewise," I responded. "I'm sorry, I'm really tired, so I can't—"

"It's all right, I understand." He laughed, playing with a strand of my hair.

"Are you going to school?"

Harry shrugged. "I don't want to. Are you?"

"I haven't had any sleep yet, so probably not," I said. "At least I'm hoping not. Got to find a good excuse not to go."

"Well, I should probably show up since I've been skipping classes now and again." He turned to look out the window. "I should leave soon."

I hugged him tighter. I didn't want him to go. I wanted him to spend the night with me.

"As much as I want to stay, I can't, baby. I don't want us to get caught, and I know you don't, either."

He slowly tried to free himself from my grip. I stayed sprawled over him, just pure dead weight, but didn't bother to put up an actual fight. He eventually shimmied away and then stood to throw his coat over his shoulder and slip on his shoes. He looked down at me, smiling before bending down and pressing a kiss to my cheek.

"I'll show myself out. I'll try to be quiet," he whispered.

"You don't want me to—?"

"No, you're way too tired, baby. Sleep. I'll go."

I pouted before nodding. "Okay. Be careful."

"Sweet dreams, babe. I, uh—I'll text you later," he said with a small smile, and he left.

THIRTY-THREE

[HARRY]

I ended up slogging through school, and when I made it home, I decided to wash my car. I was drying it off with a terry cloth when Ben arrived home.

"Lookin' good!" he called, hopping out of his truck.

"Thanks," I said, grinning down at the semi-old Corolla. "Oh, I think the oil needs changing again." I opened the door and popped the hood so he could take a look.

"We can get that done Wednesday, if you'd like. I have the day off," he said, grabbing some materials from the garage. "How are you and Carter?"

I smiled at the mention of her name, which I'm sure he noticed. "We're pretty good. Actually, more than good; we're great." I felt my heart swell when I said it out loud.

"Well, I'm happy for you. That girl seems to really have an effect on you. Your mother and I haven't seen you smile this much in a long time." I bit my lip so my smile wouldn't widen any further. Ben examined the oil on the dipstick, nodding to himself as much as me. "Although, there is something that I've been meaning to ask you that I noticed at dinner the other day," he said, his tone shifting. He closed the hood. "You wanna tell me why you didn't mention Carter was Evelyn and Owen Matthews' daughter?"

I could've sworn my entire body had gone numb. I think my heart dropped down to my stomach. *How does he know?*

"Well, I—" I stammered. I was at a loss for words. "I-I didn't—I just—"

"Why did you lie, Harry?" he asked with arms crossed.

"I-I didn't lie on purpose." I shook my head, trying to look anywhere but at him. But his stare was hard to avoid. "It's not like I genuinely wanted to keep this from you and Mom, but we were scared that if you knew who she was, somehow the news would get to her parents, and it'd jeopardize our relationship. I don't want to lose Carter."

"Why would you lose Carter?" he asked, leaning against the Corolla. "Why would her parents jeopardize your relationship? Harry, what's going on?"

I sighed, debating on whether I should just tell him the truth or lie again. But I couldn't lie. Not again. My relationship was important to me, but so was my family.

"Carter is Dylan's sister. He caught us kissing a couple weeks back and is angry with both of us, mainly me. He threatened Carter to stay away from me or he'd tell their parents," I said, watching his expression. It was mostly neutral, but his eyebrows were knit together. "Her parents have been against me getting too close to Carter ever since...ever since the Kavanaugh incident. So, if they find out about us being together, they could forbid her from seeing me."

He looked taken aback at that. He scratched his head, making his blonde hair stick up at the side.

"Why would they be against you for that?"

I looked down at my feet. "I don't think you want to know."

"Why? We dealt with this, Harry, all of us, as a family. That's behind us, behind you."

"I guess they think I'm not good enough for her or that I'm only with her for one thing," I said. "Don't overreact, please. I don't blame them for thinking that way, I—"

"What do you mean *you don't blame them*? Harry, that was nothing but a vile rumor that ended up in you getting seriously hurt. It was a terrible mistake."

"I know, but not everyone thought that it was a mistake. And, to be honest, last year, I sort of...played along at school. I thought there were some advantages to all the notoriety." Unexpectedly, I could feel my blood boiling in a sudden rage. I wanted to forget, to take it all back. "I hate that I did that. It was my fault. I should have kept denying it, not taken the praise."

"So why didn't you?!" he said, voice raising. "Your mother and I raised you better than that—"

"I was an idiot! I didn't think it'd matter! I'd gotten my face smashed in for no reason, and then when I went back, suddenly I was all everyone was talking about. It almost felt like, I don't know, a consolation prize or something. I didn't know anything bad could happen out of going along with it, 'cause I was a dumbass who couldn't even see a couple months ahead." All the bottled-up anger I had been holding in for the past year and a half was rushing out.

Ben didn't say anything for a long moment. It wouldn't have surprised me if he had looked at me differently after that. He and Mom had been nothing but supportive and sympathetic, if a bit defensive, when Stacy's claim had spiraled out of control. All they'd done to clear my name had been completely undone by my behavior.

"Look, I'm sorry for yelling at you," Ben said, not looking me in the eye. "I'm just appalled by all of this."

"Don't worry about it. It was my fault," I said. "But I promise, Carter and I will figure this out. We'll tell her parents someday, but please let us enjoy this while it lasts."

Ben stared up at the sky.

"You have to promise to keep this a secret for us," I begged. "I want to do right by Carter."

He grimaced at me, but nodded. "I promise. But it's not me you should be worried about; it's your mother. I don't know how she'll handle it."

"I'll tell her, but on my own time," I reassured him. "I just need to find the right words and the right moment."

He nodded, and a softness returned to his face. "That girl. She must mean a lot to you."

I let out a chuckle. "I'm crazy about her."

"I can tell." He reached over and smacked me playfully on the back. "We're going to finish this conversation another day. Right now, I'm going to let you finish up here. And your mother is also going to need help with dinner later; she's really tired."

I thanked him, saying I would help, and watched him walk inside. As he did, I heard my phone ring.

[CARTER]

"Some friend you are!" a voice shouted as someone barged into my room. It took me a few seconds to process who was yelling at me and why. I'd covered my face with a pillow to block the sun, and I lifted it by a centimeter to watch Mitchell march across my room and fling himself onto my beanbag.

"How was school?"

Something soft bounced off my blanket-covered hip. I suspected it was an old stuffed animal. I smirked, even though I knew he couldn't see me.

"I can't believe you ditched me."

"I can't believe you are yet again invading my room to wake me up against my will."

I forced myself to sit up and winced at the blinding sunlight. Mitchell had thrown a Build-A-Bear stuffed animal at me, and it was lying at my side. Mitchell was lying upside down on the beanbag, balancing his bookbag on the balls of his feet.

"This one kid tried me today in gym, Carter. This freshman got all pissy 'cause this soccer ball rolled by and I didn't do shit to get it, because why would I bother, and he just threw a complete fit."

"You should have wrecked his life."

"I am *trying* to be a better person."

I snorted.

"Oh, I wanted to ask you something," he said. He let his bookbag fall to the ground and sat up to look at me. "You don't have to answer if this is a touchy subject, but I personally want to know." Mitchell announced, "You and Harry have been dating for a while now, and—"

"Do you know how long Harry and I have been dating? Have you been keeping track?"

"Well, you obviously haven't." Mitchell rolled his eyes. "And I was just assuming. I don't know the exact day you guys got together."

"I know it was on a Saturday, at, like, five in the morning."

"Oh god, you really don't know. I may as well not even ask my question." Mitchell shook his head disappointedly. "I bet Harry knows the exact date and everything. That's so sad, like wow, Carter—"

"Okay, shut up. I do know; it was April 11. What did you want to know?"

"As I was *saying*, have you and Harry gotten to that point in the relationship where, you know, you exchange a certain *word*...? Y'know?"

"What?"

Mitchell rolled his eyes again. "You're such a dumbass, I swear. Have your feelings for Harry developed? Like, past crush? Past liking him? Are you comprehending now? Are you picking up what I'm putting down?"

"Are you asking me if I love Harry?" The words felt foreign rolling off my tongue.

Mitchell began to clap. "Wow, Carter. You are *so* smart. Literally, *wow*. *So* proud."

"Shut up," I said. "Is that what you meant?"

"Obviously," he quipped. "So, do you?"

I bit my lip in wonder, then shrugged. "I don't know. I've never really thought about it," I said. It was true. I had never gotten as far as thinking about whether I loved Harry or not. My feelings for him were strong and genuine. But was that love? I hadn't considered it yet. "I mean, we've only been dating a couple weeks, Mitch," I pointed out. "Don't you think that's a little too soon to throw some *I love you*s around?"

"For you, maybe," he muttered, then his voice became more focused. "No, but it's perfectly understandable. I'm not saying you have to love him. I'm just asking if you think you might."

"I love Harry," I said, making Mitchell's eyes light up. "But I'm not *in* love with him. At least not yet. I'm sure it'll happen at some point, though. You know?"

"Makes sense. Love him as a friend. Friend-zoning your boyfriend. Totally normal."

"Shut up." I laughed, tossing the Build-A-Bear toy back at him. It soared over his head and landed in the far corner. "Why do you ask, anyway?"

Mitchell shrugged. "I don't know. I guess I assumed one of you would have dropped the *L* bomb by now."

"What makes you think we're ready to say that?" I asked.

"I think Harry's about to say it to you."

"How do you know?" I asked, lifting my right brow in curiosity.

"*Come on*, Carter. The guy has had a crush on you since he was a sophomore. He goes out of his way to see you, talk to you, not giving a second thought nor giving a shit that he's risking getting caught." Mitchell smiled, and before I was given the chance to speak, he continued, "If that doesn't say he's in love with you, then I don't know what does."

"Have you spoken to him about this? Is this why you're asking?"

"*Me?* No. I wouldn't risk giving him my number."

"Why not?"

"Sweetie, if he had *my* number, he'd realize how much better I am and leave you for me."

I laughed, and considered chucking something else at him, like a pillow, but decided against it. "Whatever. So did I miss anything in class, besides annoying freshmen?"

"Carter, I don't even pay attention in class for my own benefit. Why would I pay attention for *yours*?"

"It's a miracle any of us are graduating."

Mitchell snorted, then said, "Oh, at lunch, I heard there's gonna be a big party on Saturday. Except it's not Melissa's."

"Really? Who's usurping her?"

"Some senior guy. I think he's friends with your brother and probably Harry, too."

"I'll ask him about it later." I kicked the blankets off and forced myself to get out of bed. "Want to order in food and watch some movies?"

THIRTY-FOUR

[*HARRY*]

Carter and I had barely spoken all day, which was rare. I couldn't really complain, though; she was probably still exhausted, as was I, and she seemed to have spent the whole day with Mitchell. I had nearly fallen asleep during several classes, but knew that if I did, I wouldn't sleep well that night. So, I stayed up, wearing myself out.

I went for a run after washing my car, then tried to immediately help with dinner, but my mom protested due to how badly I allegedly reeked of sweat. So I showered off before helping. After dinner, I did some homework, then tried to put on a horror film, but all of the "scary" movies looked terrible. I ended up messing around on my phone, going from app to app. When my eyes landed on the photo Carter had sent to me, I was immediately gripped by a frustrated aching.

God, I miss her. In so many ways.

My hand was already pressing on my sweats as I searched for her contact. I bit my lip anxiously, waiting as it rang. It was only half past seven; she had to be awake.

"Hello?" I heard her sweet voice from the other end of the line.

"Hi, baby."

"Hey, you," she replied, and I could almost hear her grin.

"What're you doing? I miss you."

"Just here, trying to watch *Charmed* because Mitchell practically forced me to. He just left, though."

"*Oh.* So you're alone?"

"Yeah." She laughed nervously. "Why?"

"I really miss you, baby," I breathed, my hand pushing past the waistband of my sweats and boxers.

"I miss you, too. Are you okay?"

"Yeah, I just really, *really* miss you, y'know?" I waited for Carter to understand my meaning, starting a slow rhythm.

There was a long pause until she finally spoke up. "Okay, I think I know what's going on. And as flattered as I am, right now is not a *good* time, Harry."

"What?" I whined. "C'mon, baby. *Please,*" I begged, my hand quickening.

"I'm not saying you shouldn't, you know, have a good time. You can. What I'm saying is that *I* can't do anything."

"Why not?" My hand stopped.

"Harry, I just got my period."

I sighed. "And there goes my boner." Carter only laughed.

"I'm sorry, Harry. I'd love to help, but I can't. For sanitary reasons," she joked.

"It's all right. It's only a few more days, right?" I asked, the tragedy slowly hitting me of how long of a wait that was. For me, at least.

"It depends," she explained. "Mine are usually kind of short, I'd say about five days or so. So it's going to end by Friday."

"Is that normal?"

"I mean, yeah. It just can't last more than eight days, and mine don't, so I'm good," she said confidently.

"Why can't it be more than eight days? I mean, I get it usually lasts a week, but why eight days, specifically?"

"Well," she began, "from what my mom has told me, it's a sign something's wrong. I just take her word for it. Just because she's my mom and she's always right."

"Do all girls get it, like, at the same time?" I asked. I wasn't an expert on women *stuff*, despite having a sister and a mother. "And I always wanted to know, is that why you all go to the bathroom together?"

Carter laughed again. "No, that's a different reason. But I don't do that as often as some other girls. Especially because Mitchell is a guy, and he can't come into the girls' bathroom. He did one time, though."

"How come?"

"It was freshman year, and we were by the gym doors. So, you know that corner where the bathrooms are? And how there's a water fountain right by the girls' restroom?"

"Yeah, what about it?"

"Well, while Mitchell was getting water and I was in the bathroom, I heard a commotion outside, and then out of nowhere Mitchell just flew into the room."

"Oh," is all I said. "He got pushed in?"

"Yep." She sighed. "It was this group of seniors. We were freshmen, maybe sophomores. But Mitchell was cool with it. It was actually super funny. I was washing my hands when it happened, and he just brushed himself off and looked around. He was so amazed." Carter laughed at the memory while I pictured it. "He had a little movie moment. He was all like, *Wow, our bathroom doesn't look like this. This is so clean. You have doors, we don't have these. Look at this, we don't have a candy machine in our bathroom, I'm—*"

"You guys have a candy machine?!"

"No, Harry," she retorted. "It's a dispenser with pads and tampons."

I sighed. "And now we're *back* to the period topic."

Carter laughed again before sighing. "Well, Harry, I don't know about you, but I'm still a little tired from earlier. And I can't miss school again. So, I'm gonna go to sleep. See you tomorrow?"

"Of course," I said, my heart suddenly aching a bit. "Goodnight, baby, I'll see you tomorrow. And, uh... I miss you. A lot. Night."

[*CARTER*]

After school, Mitchell and I took the bus to his house since Elizabeth had to stay for her student-council-treasurer thingy. On the ride back, I let him play an app game on my phone that he couldn't be bothered to pay for himself.

"What the literal hell?" Mitchell announced, and I raised an eyebrow at him. "I'm trying to play Emoji Blitz, and I can't when your Instagram notifications are blowing up like crazy."

"Really?" I asked, not really interested.

"Yeah, someone just spammed you, but I can't see who it is with their shitty-ass profile pic," he said, squinting at the screen. "They're on private."

"Don't follow them," I said.

"Ugh, you're so lame. Why don't you care about your Instagram aesthetics?"

"Because I don't post anything and all I do is judge people from afar on it."

"You don't need to be on social media to do that." He tossed my phone back to me. "Harry's been sending loads of texts to you, by the way." I quickly shuffled to the messaging app.

Baaabe: CARTER

Baaabe: CARTER I AM SO ANGRY

Baaabe: SO FUCKING ANGRY I CANT EVEN

Baaabe: IM ANGRY AF

Baaabe: LIKE AF

Baaabe: LIKE ASS FUCK

Baaabe: WAIT

Baaabe: NO

Baaabe: YOU KNOW WHAT I MEAN

Baaabe: CARTER IM ANGRY

Baaabe: AND YOU'RE NOT REPLYING

Baaabe: WHY ARENT YOU REPLYING

Baaabe: I CANT EVEN TELL IF YOU ARE READING THESE OR NOT

Baaabe: IM SO MAD

Baaabe: I WANNA BREAK SOMETHING

Baaabe: YOU NOT REPYING IS MAKING ME WANNA FUCK SHIT UP

Baaabe: CARTER

Baaabe: CARTER IM RIPPING PAPER

Baaabe: I JUST RIPPED ANOTHER ONE

Baaabe: FUCK

Baaabe: I THINK IT WAS MY HOMEWORK

Baaabe: NO

Baaabe: FALSE ALARM

Baaabe: IM OK

Baaabe: BUT IM STILL MAD AS FUCK

Baaabe: I JUST PUSHED MY CHAIR

Baaabe: IT DIDNT FALL

Baaabe: I JUST THREW MY PILLOW

Baaabe: IT'S ON THE FLOOR

"Carter, what the hell is up with your phone?" Mitchell asked, noticing the constant vibration from Harry sending one text after another.

"Harry's having a mild crisis, I guess." The bus grated to a halt near Mitchell's house, and we quickly got off, making sure to thank the driver. "What's up with you? Your phone isn't getting enough love?"

"Compared to yours?" Mitchell scoffed. "I wish. I don't know, I guess I'm just bored. To be honest, last night I decided to join, like, three different dating apps: Bumble, Tinder, even Grindr. But considering how two of those are just hookup apps, I wound up sticking to Bumble and deleting the others." A funny little smile was on his face.

"And?" I asked, trying to make him look at me. He wasn't taking the bait. "Well? Any luck, or what?"

"Any luck with what?" Mitchell tried to say it waspishly, but his smile gave him away.

"Oh, come on. I know you're hiding something from me. I'm your best friend, I know you better than you know yourself."

We went into his and Elizabeth's house and ran up to his room.

"Oh, all right, all right! If you must know, I started talking to this one guy. And it seems to be going okay, but that is all I am going to give you." Mitchell waved his hand as if he was buffeting me away. "I don't want to jinx it."

"Fine, fair enough." I thought about pushing him for more info, but I got yet another text before I could.

Baaabe: BUT NOT AS MAD AS I AM RN BC YOURE STILL NOT ANSWERING ME

Me: oh god, why are you so mad

Baaabe: WELL THEN

Baaabe: LOOK WHO FINALLY DECIDED TO REPLY

Baaabe: IM STILL MAD

Me: I'm aware

Me: what happened

Baaabe: CARTER

Baaabe: NEVER

Baaabe: AND I REPEAT NEVER

Baaabe: UNDER ANY CIRCUMSTANCES

Baaabe: DOWNLOAD THE GAME

Baaabe: FUN RUN

Baaabe: THAT GAME JUST RUINED MY LIFE IN UNDER A FUCKIN HOUR

Angry Bird: I HAVE NEVER WANTED TO THROW MY PHONE SO HARD AGAINST A WALL

Angry Bird: IM DONE

Me: you're mad bc of a stupid game

Angry Bird: IT'S NOT JUST A GAME CARTER

Angry Bird: IT'S HELL

Angry Bird: IT'S FUCKING AWFUL

Angry Bird: WHO MADE THIS SHIT

Angry Bird: IT LOOKS LIKE A CUTE GAME BUT ONCE YOU START PLAYING IT'S A BLOODBATH

Me: I love how you haven't bothered to stop writing in caps

Angry Bird: THERE ARE BIGGER CONCERNS HERE CARTER

Angry Bird: HOWEVER MY ANGER HAD SIMMERED DOWN SINCE YOU REPLIED

Angry Bird: I just need to breathe

Angry Bird: anyway

Angry Bird: hey baby

Angry Bird: babe

Psycho: angel

Psycho: princess

Psycho: beautiful

Psycho: my cinnamon apple

Psycho: babygirl

Psycho: fruitcake

Me: you're the fruitcake here bitch

Psycho: WHAT

Psycho: LMAO

Baby: what is that supposed to mean??

Me: I just wanted to make you laugh

Me: I miss you

Me: so so so so so so much

Baby: I miss you too baby

Baby: and right now I really fucking need you

Baby: get off your period already

Me: I wish lol

Me: I get super affectionate on my period

Me: I'm glad you're my boyfriend so I can be affectionate with u

Me: can I see you tomorrow? hangout at your place?

Baby: that wouldn't be a bad idea baby but I kind of already have plans :(

Baby: my friend AJ is coming over tomorrow after school

Me: oh :(well that's okay then

Baby: sorry princess, maybe thursday?

Me: maybe, depends on mitchell

Me: he wants to go shopping sometime this week & this guy could drag me to the mall at any given moment no matter what

Baby: ah fine we have the weekend if anything

Me: true

Me: but hey I'll text you later, yeah?

Me: my phone is dying & I'm gonna head home soon anyway

Baby: that's fine, just let me know when you're there

Me: sounds good, I'll talk to you later! :-)

THIRTY-FIVE

[HARRY]

Me: hey carter

Me: I'm kind of in a pickle rn

Babygirl: you're in a pickle?

Babygirl: how is that even humanly possible

Me: I'm not literally in a pickle carter

Me: it's a figure of speech

Me: so

Me: I'm debating on whether or not I should cut my hair

Babygirl: WHAT

Babygirl: NO

Babygirl: DONT

Babygirl: WHY WOULD YOU

Babygirl: NO

Me: it's past the point of being shaggy

Me: it's reaching my shoulders

Me: this is the longest it's ever been

Babygirl: pls don't cut your hair :(

Me: why notttt

Babygirl: because I like it exactly where it is right now

Babygirl: it's preeeetty

Babygirl: i likeeeee

Babygirl: so niceeeeeee

Babygirl: and preeeeettyyy

Me: aw baby :}

Babygirl: ew what the fuck harry

Babygirl: don't use that face

Babygirl: anyway

Babygirl: I like your hair long

Babygirl: honestly it suits you

Me: thank you baby

Babygirl: you look good with it long

Me: means a lot

Babygirl: more to tug on when we fuck

Me: ....

Me: is this rly carter....

Babygirl: yes... why

Me: bc you/carter wouldn't usually say stuff like that

Me: and

Me: as intriguing as it sounded

Me: I'm also unsure how to feel about it

Babygirl: how so

Me: bc shouldn't it be the other way around

Me: like shouldn't i be saying that

Me: to you

Babygirl: you know what

Babygirl: you're right

Babygirl: so tell me

Babygirl: why exactly aren't you saying that to me right now

Me: WOW

Me: OH FUCK

Me: THAT WAS SMOOTH

Me: DAMN BABY

Me: I AM SHOCKED

Babygirl: haha I know, thank you I try :)

Me: since you asked nicely, I will most certainly be doing that friday night

Babygirl: that sounds promising

Me: oh it is haha ;)

"So, who are you texting?"

I looked up, snapping out of focus on my conversation with Carter. My buddy AJ was messing on my Xbox, periodically

KARLA DE LA ROSA

typing away at his own phone. "It has to be someone special if you're smiling so much." I shook my head, finding it incredibly hard to get rid of my grin; I always did, when it came to Carter.

"It's, uh, just a friend of mine. The conversation, it's—it's funny, so yeah."

"Oh, yeah?" AJ said smugly, glancing down at one of his notifications.

"And who are you texting?"

"It's Galloway. He's telling me how he's trying to get back with his ex."

"Oh, yeah?"

"Yeah, he's trying to get her attention, but it's not working." AJ laughed again.

"Oh, really? That's a bummer." I shrugged, even though I had almost no clue what he was talking about.

"Well, he's an interesting guy. So, you heard about Ryan's party?"

"No. He's throwing something?"

"It's on Saturday, his place. Everyone is going." AJ grinned, tapping the controller against his leg as the game loaded. "It's going to be crazy, man! Ryan's had this shit planned out for weeks. Even Melissa is down."

"Cool, I'll think about going."

"Nice. Can you believe we have less than a month until we finish school? We are almost out of here."

I nodded, my mind wandering. How quickly time had flown by

these past four years never ceased to amaze me. And who knew that in my last I'd have finally gotten with the girl I'd been secretly crushing on since my sophomore year?

"It's crazy, man." I shook my head, still processing how little time we had left until we would finally step into the real world. "Who'd have ever thought we'd get this far?"

If I'm being entirely honest, I had absolutely hated high school in the beginning. From the moment I'd stepped foot into my first class and realized how much of my future depended on my work and effort, I'd dreaded the next four years of my life. But lately, I wished I could turn back time—not just because of the Kavanaugh incident, though if I hadn't kept my mouth shut about what'd really happened, I might have been in this relationship a long time ago—but just to try and appreciate my day-to-day life more. Yes, high school was hell, but this was my only time here.

I would have to become independent. The people I saw every day at school would soon become strangers. We'd all start a new chapter in our lives and everything would become a memory.

But then again, I was pretty happy with where I was. I had Carter, and I guess that's about as much happiness as I needed in my life.

"I don't know whether I'm going to miss it or not," AJ suddenly said, breaking me out of my mini trance. I found it funny how every thought I had would lead back to Carter somehow. I couldn't get her out of my mind, even if I tried.

"Do you know what college you're going to?" I asked.

"I've been thinking maybe Florida International or Florida State. Haven't really given it thought," AJ said, sounding quite unsure of himself. "If I'm being entirely honest, I'm kind of scared, man. It's a whole new world out there. I feel like I'm not mentally or physically prepared for all that."

"I get you." I sighed, mindlessly scratching at the back of my neck. "Makes me wish I'd stopped and smelled the roses a little more."

"I don't know, talking about college and my future stresses me out." The game loaded, and AJ went back to be playing. "So hey, I've been meaning to ask: what's up with you and Dylan?"

"What do you mean?" What I really meant was, *What have you heard?*

"Like, everyone's noticed you guys haven't spoken in a while. And if I'm being honest, you kinda fell off the face of the Earth within the past few weeks."

"How so?"

"Well, like, you still talk with me and Ryan, but you don't come to parties. You and Dylan clearly parted ways, and he told us you guys had a falling out," he confessed, and I could feel my heart begin to race.

"What do you mean by 'falling out'?" I asked in desperate curiosity.

"Well, we're guessing it's from you making out with Lindsay," AJ told me with a subtle smirk. "Jenna was the one who pointed it out and told Dylan. Then you disappeared."

I knew what happened after that. I guessed that was how Dylan had found me upstairs kissing his sister. It felt like ages ago, but in reality, it had just been a few weeks.

I knew I had to set the record straight immediately. "But I didn't kiss her; she kissed me. She told me she and Dylan were a hardly a couple and that she'd always had a thing for me. I don't have proof of her saying that, but I wouldn't lie about this."

"Wow. Yeah, I mean, I didn't know what to think, but I did have doubts you'd do that to Dylan."

"Thanks for the vote of confidence, man," I said, a little sour, but I shook it off. "Anyway, I hear they're broken up." I stretched in my desk chair.

"They were." AJ huffed. "They got back together for a little. Lindsay told him a completely different story compared to yours." And before I had the chance to ask what she could have possibly said, he carried on, "It doesn't matter now. Dylan doesn't believe her, and he couldn't care less about it anymore. Mind you, he's only been with her for sex since they first got together, so the only loser here is her."

I shook my head, chuckling. "I never liked her. But since Dylan was my best friend, I couldn't really find the strength or time to tell him that his girlfriend was the definition of 'awful.'"

AJ laughed.

"Guess it doesn't matter now, though," I added. I unlocked my phone and swiped through a couple notifications, none from Carter.

KARLA DE LA ROSA

"Harry!" my mother's voice rang downstairs.

I stood up, tossed my phone on the bed, and told A.J, "I'll be right back."

I found my mom chopping onions with a colorful knife, part of this fancy set Ben had bought her for Christmas two years ago.

"Is your friend staying, honey? I almost forgot he was here and, in all honesty, Harry, there's not enough for an extra person!" She whispered the last part as if AJ was listening in on us.

"I'm not sure if he's staying, but I can ask him. Plus, we stopped for pizza before we came, and he's probably still full."

"I don't want to just send him home. I can pop out and grab something else?" she continued, still whispering.

I only chuckled before responding, "Don't worry about it, Mom. I'll see what I can do."

"All right, just let me know. Oh, and see if Carter would like to come for dinner this Sunday. Your sister is coming over, and she'd really like to meet her."

I hesitantly smiled, remembering Carter being a nervous wreck last time. "I'll ask her once AJ heads out."

"I hope she says yes! Your sister is very excited to meet her." She smiled.

"I'm excited for Emma to meet her. I just hope Carter doesn't feel intimidated by her."

"Why would she?"

"I'd be intimidated if it were her brother," I said unthinkingly. Immediately, I regretted it, hoping she wouldn't ask about Carter's family.

"Well, I think you should assure her that your sister is not someone to feel intimidated by. This is Em we're talking about."

"But Emma has never met a girlfriend of mine," I remarked, feeling almost defensive of Carter and her understandable nerves. "I mean, I'm a little nervous about them meeting. This is the first time Em is meeting someone I care about. Oh, god... You know what—no. I'm not going to think about it. I'm sure it'll be fine."

"That's the spirit," my mom chirped, tossing the cut-up onions into a bowl. "Well go on, sweetie, I don't want to keep your guest waiting."

I nodded before turning and jogging up the steps. And just as my hand reached for the knob, the door swung open, and I was face to face with a wide-eyed AJ.

"Hey, what—?"

"I have to go," AJ breathed, trying to brush past me. I stepped to block him.

"Are you alright?" I asked in concern.

He looked bewildered, maybe shaken up. "I'm fine, Harry. I have to go." AJ exhaled deeply as he sidestepped me. "See you on Saturday."

Something felt off. But all I said was, "Sure, see you then."

I heard the front door close, and I went into my room, puzzled. I retrieved my phone from my nightstand, leaving me alone with a rattled mind.

THIRTY-SIX

When I walked into art, Andy and Sean were quietly setting up their standard UNO game.

"Hey guys," I said, pulling up a chair next to them. "No Carter today?"

Of course, I already knew she was at the dentist and her parents were letting her stay home on the condition she did homework all day, but they didn't have to know that.

The guys blinked at me in surprise and then shook their heads simultaneously.

"Well, mind if I join?"

We played for twenty minutes in silence, Sean constantly shoving his glasses up his nose. I was surprised by how listless they were, and it made me realize that Carter was what made them social. She was the tinderbox that caused all the sparks and banter.

I decided to take matters into my own hands and try once more to start a conversation. "So, you guys hear about the party Saturday?"

That grabbed their attention. Their cards hit the table.

"Yeah, dude. I heard half the seniors are bringing booze!" Sean exclaimed. "You're friends with the host, right?"

"Ryan, yeah."

"Is it invite only or open house?" His eyes were wide with hope.

"I think it's an open house. The invites would've been passed out by now," I noted, putting down my cards as well.

"I hope his house is big enough to fit the entire school," Andy remarked.

I snorted. "His house is pretty big, but it's not that big."

We kept chatting until the end of class. My next period was chemistry, which was a bore, so I texted Carter throughout the whole thing. She told me that Mitchell and Elizabeth were going to skip final period and go to the mall with her. I was a little surprised they were all willing to cut to do that, and as much as I wanted to see her after school, I didn't mind.

Throughout chemistry and English, I continued to hear all about Ryan's party. I just focused on getting through my periodic table assignments and reading *Hamlet*. Dylan didn't show for class, oddly, and I avoided both Jenna and Lindsay, as usual.

When school finally ended, I trudged towards my car, trying to avoid getting pushed and shoved by countless people. I was fishing for my keys when I heard someone call my name.

"Hey, Harry," Ryan said once I'd fully turned to look at him.

"Hey, man, what's up?" I asked lazily. I had presumed he was about to ask if I was going to his overhyped party on Saturday; I had starting having second thoughts.

"Hey, so, I need a favor. Are you busy tomorrow after school?"

"Nah, I don't think so," I answered truthfully. "Why?"

"You think you can come by tomorrow to help me set up for Saturday?" Ryan's eyes were pleading. "I asked Dylan and AJ, but I think we're going to need an extra hand."

"I don't think—"

"Look," Ryan interrupted me, probably guessing what I was going to say, "I know you and Dylan are having problems for whatever reason, but please—do this for me. There's so much to do before the party, and my dumb ass left it for last minute again. I need all the help I can get."

I nodded, feeling bad as I sighed in defeat. "Yeah, sure, I'll come by."

Ryan sighed in relief. "Thanks, man, it means a lot." He walked away with a satisfied smile, and I dragged my feet towards my car.

I just *really* wanted to go home.

[CARTER]

"You are literally so annoying and *so* picky." I huffed at Mitchell. He, Elizabeth, and I were at Revival, Mitchell's favorite store at the mall. He was finding a new outfit for the party.

"Okay, what about this, though?" Mitchell asked, pulling yet another shirt from the rack. It was a crisp, white, long-sleeved button-up.

I scrunched my nose. "You have hundreds of shirts like that."

Mitchell looked at the shirt again before frowning, realizing I was right, and then put it back to keep digging. Elizabeth had wandered off to find an outfit of her own; she'd asked me to come with her, but I'd refused. I knew that if I relented, I'd find clothes that I'd want, and then whine because I was pressed for cash.

I noticed Mitchell growing impatient as he ran from one rack to the other, grabbing at each and every hanger. I shook my head, stifling my laughter, and helped him look. Eventually I found a patterned, well-cut short-sleeve that looked good in my opinion.

"Mitch!" I called. "How's this?" I held up the shirt, wiggling my eyebrows for effect. His eyes lit up, and he rushed over to grab it from me. "I love the little flowers," I added, "and how the colors reverse on the cuffs and the inside of the collar."

He checked the tag, and his grin widened. "It's a medium and only seventeen bucks. Carter, this is perfect!" he told me graciously.

"And you can wear it with your favorite jeans and those cute Tommy shoes you're so obsessed with."

"Okay, perfect. Let's go find Liz and get out of here," he said, taking my hand before dragging me to the other side of the store.

When we spotted her, she was holding up a red blouse in one hand and a handful of clothes in the other. The moment she noticed us walking towards her, she smiled excitedly at me. She put the red shirt back on the rack and dug out a pretty black silk tank from her pile.

"Carter, look at this shirt! I saw it and thought of you; you *need* to buy it."

"Oh, wow. Liz, it's so cute," I said, admiring the soft material. "But I have no money." *I should have waited outside.*

"I know, silly." She snatched the shirt from me. "That's why I'm getting it for you. Mitchell has some exchange credit that I'm stealing."

He stuck his tongue out at her.

"Are you sure? Don't you want to use it?" I asked, eyeing the giant pile hanging over her arm.

"It's not like I'm going to buy all of this. I'll try these on and pick some favorites; I'm sure we'll have cash leftover."

I looked at the silk shirt, still unsure. "I dunno. Don't you guys think it's a little short?"

Mitchell eyeballed me. "Are you seriously making up an excuse not to buy it? Just let Elizabeth get it for you. God knows you need an outfit for Saturday, too."

"You can wear it with some high-waisted jeans and some cute heels," Elizabeth chimed in.

"I don't know if I have jeans that are high enough for that."

Mitchell rolled his head back and slumped his shoulders in exasperation. "Carter, you make it seem like you have a giant beer belly. So you have a little flab, so what? Don't we all? That's what makes you human. We're not models. You're beautiful no matter what, and I'm not just telling you that as your best friend; I'm telling you as a person who cares about you, and who, quite frankly, thinks you should get your head out of your ass and just let Liz buy the damn shirt."

"Okay, okaaaaay," I said, smiling. "Thank you, Liz. I'll pay you back or get your food in a couple weeks."

Elizabeth smiled, and we waited for her to try on her selections and put some back. As we headed to the cash register, Mitchell turned to me to add, "And if you're still uncomfy, you can put on that stupid cardigan you wanted to wear to Melissa's that one time. But seriously, you can't go wrong with high-rise jeans and a cute crop."

"You've been watching too much *Queer Eye,*" Elizabeth commented.

"As if you haven't." Mitchell scoffed.

"Thank you, guys," I said as I slid out the car with my bag.

"You're welcome, and don't forget, we'll pick you up tomorrow at eight!" Mitchell called as they slowly began to drive away. It was already sunset by the time I got home, and as I was dropping my stuff off in my room, I heard my parents downstairs. I headed back down to see them.

Yesterday, the texts between Harry and I had been pretty brief. He'd had his friend over, and I'd been busy studying. And then today, I hadn't spoken to him at all. I knew he was probably still busy helping Ryan set up for the party, so I decided to wait and text him after dinner.

Downstairs, I found my mom watching football in the living room, wearing a cute dress. Dad was nowhere to be found.

"Hey, Mom."

"Hey, sweetie. Dinner is almost ready. You can get some plates out when the timer goes off."

"Sure. Where is everyone?"

"Your dad is upstairs taking a shower, and Dylan's not here," she said, leaning forward as a throw was made, then flopping back dejectedly when the players missed the catch.

"Oh? Where is he?" I asked, making sure my tone was a little uninterested.

"I'm not sure. He got an oh-so-important call and rushed out."

"Oh," was all I could think to respond. "Hey, Mom? I've been meaning to ask: There's this party Saturday, and *everyone* is going to be there. Can I go? Mitch and Lizzie are going."

"Sure, just be safe."

I leaned on the back of the couch. "You know, not that I'm complaining, but most parents would be like, *No! Absolutely not! Your studies are more important! Partying is bad!*" I said it with a gruff, disciplinarian voice. My mom laughed.

"Well, for one, your grades are pretty good, so as long as those aren't slacking, I really don't mind." She turned to me, a bit of a sly smile on her face. "Your brother could certainly be trying more, but we've already discussed with him that he will be working through college to make up for his lack of scholarships. Two, you're such a homebody when you're not with Mitch, I'm not all that worried."

"Hey," I said in mock protest, but we were both smiling.

A commercial came on. She sat up straight and smoothened out her dress.

"You look nice," I commented.

"Thank you. Your father and I are celebrating our anniversary tonight. We're going somewhere *exquisite*, he claims." She rolled her eyes, amused. "So when your brother comes back, please try not to kill each other until we're home."

"Mom, it's a shocker we're even still alive to this day," I retorted. "But why are you making dinner if you're going out?" I nodded toward the kitchen to emphasize the question.

"It's for you and Dylan," she said as if it was obvious.

"Oh, thanks. If Dylan doesn't eat the whole thing, I'll put the leftovers up."

She nodded, then moved to grab her phone from where it was charging on the counter. The timer in the kitchen went off, and I eagerly went to go make a plate.

Boyfriend: so
Boyfriend: how was shopping day
Me: not as dreadful as I had expected if I'm being

entirely honest

Me: I helped mitch find a shirt and he stuck with it

Me: elizabeth bought two shirts using mitchell's leftover exchange credit or whatever

Me: one of them was for me ayyy

Boyfriend: oooooh what kinda shirt

Me: it's this silk tank with some lace at the neckline

Me: I'm wearing it for the party on saturday

Boyfriend: I didn't know you were going

Me: are you?

Boyfriend: I didn't want to buuut I guess I can go. I feel like I haven't seen you in forever so that gives me an excuse to finally spend time with you

Me: I know, last time we actually hung out was like almost a week ago

Me: that's the longest we've ever been apart harold

Me: omg

Me: the realization just hit me

Me: oh no

Me: I can feel us drifting

Me: my heart is breaking

Me: this is it

Me: this is the end

Boyfriend: out of everything that could cause us to break up, this is it? you didn't even give me a chance to hurt you

Boyfriend: not that I ever have or would

Me: what do you mean, yes you have

Boyfriend: what the hell, how and when

Me: didn't you kiss lindsay

Boyfriend: OH FOR THE LOVE OF GOD

Boyfriend: I DID NOT KISS HER

Puta: SHE KISSED ME

Me: same difference

Puta: SERIOUSLY CARTER

Puta: I THOUGHT WE WENT OVER WITH THIS

Me: we did

Me: but you're still a bitch for that

Puta: Carter please, I never wanted that to happen

Puta: you know how much I despise Lindsay

Puta: and that whole thing was another instance where it wasn't what it seemed, but I got a bad rap anyway :/

Puta: even though I've been telling anyone who will listen that I wanted no part of that

Me: Harry I was just kidding

Me: I didn't mean to upset you

Boyfriend: it's FINE everything is FINE

Me: it is, we're good

Boyfriend: good, I just have a lot of feelings

Me: well hey it's nice to see you don't buy into toxic masculinity

Boyfriend: wat do you mean?

Boyfriend: I am a BIG STRONG MAN WHO DON'T NEED NO LADY

Me: yea u got it, king

Boyfriend: really though do you think im sensitive or something

Boyfriend: too soft perhaps

Boyfriend: like 10-ply toilet paper

Me: lol no

Me: you do have a lot of emotions. and you can identify them and communicate them. that's a good thing

Boyfriend: aw

Boyfriend: you really do care about me :}

Me: ew

Me: what the FUCK

Boyfriend: :|

Boyfriend: way to ruin a moment

Me: YOU ruined it

Me: wtf

Me: :}

Me: ugly

Boyfriend: omg

Me: the disrespect

Boyfriend: you're lucky I love you too much to hate you

Wait... *What?*

THIRTY-SEVEN

[HARRY]

Okay, so maybe I had been planning on telling Carter I loved her for a while now... However, this was *not* how I'd planned it.

I shoved both hands through my hair and considered bashing my head into my steering wheel. I had been in my car for the whole conversation, parked outside my house and too lazy to go inside.

This past week, I had been wracking my brain about when and how to tell her. I was in too deep, *way* too deep. I'd known it the moment she'd met my parents. Maybe it was silly, but the way she'd bonded with them, especially my mother, had made me realize my feelings for her.

I knew many would have said it was too soon, but my feelings had evolved from a simple crush to a true love. I mean, it's not like I *meant* to fall in love with her. It had kind of just happened. I wanted to tell her. Not by making some grand gesture or anything, but in a way that wouldn't scare her off.

But here I was.

Now it was too late to take it back. I was an actual dumbass. I'd really just told my girlfriend I loved her...over *text*. That was it. I'd just dropped the *L* bomb on her, and not even in person. I was positive she was packing and getting ready to make a run for it. *She might've taken off by now, who knows?* She still hadn't said anything back.

I drummed my fingers on the dash, staring at the text I'd sent almost ten minutes ago.

Did I love her? Of course.

Was I ready to tell her? Absolutely not.

Not because I was scared. I mean, I was. But I was also scared of scaring *her*.

Without letting myself get second thoughts, I got a grip and called her. Ironically, before I had the chance to consider what I was going to say, she picked up on the first ring. I almost fainted.

"Carter?" I said warily, almost terrified to hear her speak. *What if she's angry?*

"Hey." Her voice was soft like velvet, to my surprise; my nerves slowly unraveled at the sound. She didn't sound unsure or scared, but there was a definite awkwardness.

I could feel my mouth going dry, my breath quickening. "I'm coming over," I blurted out. "If that's okay with you?" I corrected myself, softening my voice.

"Okay, cool," she breathed. I was so nervous that I mumbled a goodbye and then ended the call.

"*Shit.* Shit, shit." I white-knuckled the steering wheel, my feet tapping on the pedals in anxiety. I turned the car on and started down the street, debating whether I should speed to her house or take my time.

Wait, what time is it?

8:03 p.m. Shit, I hadn't even thought to even check the clock, and apparently neither had Carter. What if her parents were home and I ran into them? Or worse, ran into *Dylan*.

I shook my head and did my best to relax. First, I needed to figure out what I even wanted to say.

Of course, I couldn't even come up with a coherent sentence for the entire drive. I parked five houses down and turned my lights off. I paced back and forth, unable to sit still any longer.

What the hell should I say?

What did she want me to say?

Why do I suck at this?!

"Okay, so," I began muttering, "uh, hey, Carter. I just—I wanted to say that—I didn't mean it when I said I loved you. I mean—no. Wait, that came out wrong. I—I did mean it! I mean, unless you *don't* love me back, then I *don't* mean it! Even though I do. I do love you, but—" I groaned, running my fingers through my hair.

"Alright, um..." I hummed before shaking my head. "I didn't mean—no. I didn't *think* before I threw the *L* bomb on you. I—I did mean it. But I didn't mean to *say* it. I mean, I did. But not so soon. Un-unless, y'know, it's *not* too soon? Then, um—" I cursed to myself.

That was just awful. There was *no* way she was going to take me seriously with my shitty speech. She hadn't taken me seriously when I'd told her I liked her; why the hell would she take me seriously when I told her I *loved* her?

Maybe I just needed to relax. I was putting too much pressure on myself. All I needed was a little motivation. A push, a bit of a boost. *She's my girlfriend. Why am I freaking out so much?*

"Okay." I turned to my reflection in my car's window. "Carter, my feelings for you have been...growing, more and more since the moment I met you. And they only got stronger when I started dating you." My words weren't tumbling; I wasn't stammering. It was going well so far. I took a deep breath before continuing, "And it wasn't until you met my parents and actually *bonded* with them, that I realized I'd fallen for you. When I took you into a deeper part of my life, I knew I was head over heels for you." *So far, so good.* "Now, I understand if you don't feel the same. I get it. I told you I'd take things slow with you. But...I can't help it if my heart races when I see you. I melt at the sound of your voice. My insides explode when you smile or laugh—even more when I'm the reason why. Yes, I've fallen for you. But I'm not rushing you.

"I just thought I'd tell you how I feel..." I nearly choked, fear and nerves racing through my body. I shook away the thought before finishing, "Carter...I love you." I sighed, satisfied with my speech. *There*, that wasn't so hard. Now I just needed to memorize—

"That was beautiful."

"*Shit!*" I nearly jumped out of my own skin, clutching at my chest and jolting into the side of my car. "*Jesus*, you scared me!"

"Sorry." Carter giggled nervously, crossing her arms tightly across her chest. She was wearing an oversized hoodie and pajama shorts.

"Wha-What are you doing out here?"

"Well, I was getting worried, but I know you tend to park a couple houses down. And it didn't take long until I saw you pacing," she said, amused.

I felt a little embarrassed by that. I wondered how much she'd heard. Suddenly, I wasn't feeling so confident anymore.

"Carter, I—"

"Let's not talk here," she interrupted me, her tone flat and serious. She took my hand and led me back to her house. I noticed neither Dylan's nor her parents' cars were in the driveway.

I looked at her, and she answered my silent question. "My parents are at dinner. Dylan went out this afternoon and hasn't come back since," she explained. She opened the front door to her house and guided us in.

"Oh, weird. He was supposed to help me and the guys set up at Ryan's, but he never showed."

"My mom said he got some important call and ran out."

"Huh," was all I could say. I closed her bedroom door behind me. Carter took off her hoodie and tossed it on her bed. Underneath was a Bill Nye the Science Guy shirt; seeing it made me smile.

Carter sat at her desk chair, seeing my smile and matching it.

"So," she drawled. "You were saying?"

THIRTY-EIGHT

"Well." I swallowed nervously. "I mean, I'm guessing you heard everything?"

"I did. I just wanted to hear it again," she said, smiling.

I closed my eyes and just let the words flow right out of me, knowing it was now or never. "Carter, I'm in love with you."

I opened my eyes to see her ocean blue eyes were shining bright, but not because she was going to cry. I could see lingering surprise on her face, for sure. And in the following seconds, I realized she wasn't saying it back.

"I—" She stammered for a moment, her fingers moving nervously in her lap.

"You don't have to say anything," I muttered. I tried to keep my head held high, but it drooped down so I was staring at my feet.

"What?" I heard more than saw her stand up. "But I—"

"Carter, I can't say I didn't expect this. I didn't want to rush you or pressure you into saying it back, which is why I was waiting," I told her honestly.

"But Harry, I do—"

"And I'm sorry, but I just had to tell you how I feel." I felt frozen to the spot, studying the carpet under my Nikes.

"No, Harry, I—"

"And don't feel obligated to said it back just to make me happy, because I can handle you not saying it back, but I don't think I can handle you lying to me and—"

"Harry, I love you!"

Every muscle in my body stiffened. I looked up at her, my lips parting, my heart skipping a beat and then going double time.

"I love you," she said again, grinning.

"I-I thought you wouldn't, because... Well, because I thought it would be too soon."

She shrugged weakly, her eyes shifting from me to elsewhere. "I know. And it is soon. In fact, I never really thought about it until recently, and...I didn't think you loved me just yet. But now I know that I'm in love with you."

"But—"

"When you know, you know," she said, her smile never wavering.

"Carter," I said, taking a step towards her. My hand cupped her cheek, and I glanced between her lips and her eyes. "I love you. And I've wanted to tell you for a while. I was just too scared to."

"How do you think I felt?" She laughed as she placed my other hand against her chest so I could feel the thumping of her heart against my palm. I realized I was smiling bigger than I ever had. "But I'm glad you know now. I love you. I swear it." I cleared my throat, slowly pulling my hand away to take both of hers in mine.

"C'mere," I said, gently pulling her to the bed. I laid her down and climbed on with her. We spend the first couple minutes in silence. I admired her beauty more than ever before. Carter loved me. Her eyes were huge in the night, staring right at mine.

"What're you thinking about?" I whispered, my finger brushing over her soft, silky skin.

"You," she whispered, her fingers finding their way to my face before tracing lines against my skin. Trailing along my jaw, the bridge of my nose, then dragging through my brow bone down to my cheek until they stopped, just at the corner of my lips. Her light touch, as she slowly traced her finger along my lower lip, made me smile. Her eyes crinkled as she smiled back.

"What about me?" I asked, pressing a kiss to her fingertip.

"Just you, and the way I love you," she said, a sparkle in her eyes as she looked at me. I couldn't help myself as I leaned into her, pressing a gentle kiss to her lips. Her fingers found their way to my hair and tangled in the nape of my neck. The gentle tug made me groan, and Carter's breath hitched when I pressed a kiss on the base of her neck.

"Baby," I whispered, trailing kisses all over her neck. "I love you. Tell me you want me."

"I want you, Harry," she breathed, "I'll only ever want you. I love you. I love you so much." I groaned, feeling my body go all fuzzy at her words.

One hand went to her waist, circling my thumb against the exposed skin just above her shorts. I dipped my head to leave soft kisses along her collarbone. My lips moved down her chest, my finger pulling her neckline down. Carter's breath picked up as her fingers continued moving in my hair. I released the neckline of her shirt, and Carter quickly grabbed the hem and pulled it off, then proceeded to throw her bra across the room. I was breathless at the sight of her.

I slowly dragged her shorts down her legs, then hesitantly moved up again to kiss my way down her chest and belly until I reached her underwear. My fingers dug into the waistband before pulling it down. I could tell by her impatient squirming that it was too slow for Carter's liking.

But I didn't care.

I wanted to take my time with her and her body.

"Baby," I whispered as the cotton underwear smoothly slid down her legs. "Let me make you feel good." She bit her lip and nodded. She pushed herself up on her elbows as she watched my every move. I only grinned at her, nuzzling my face against the skin of her thighs.

Carter looked anxious, but the minute I pressed a kiss against her, a squeamish whimper slipped past her lips. I swirled my tongue around her. Her feet were pressed to my sides, and I could feel her toes curl up. Her hips rose with every lick, and I pulled away, teasingly, watching as she breathed erratically. I pressed my thumb against her, her back arching when I began to move it in slow circles.

"Oh my god," she moaned, and her mouth gaped as her fingers clenched her bed sheets.

"More?" I taunted. She nodded frantically as she tried to keep her eyes open. Her eyelids fluttered shut as my thumb moved at an even pace. But then I stopped abruptly, enjoying the view of her reaction far too much.

I was loving every minute of this and decided to kick it up a notch when I dipped down again. My tongue moved in figure eights. I slowly pressed two fingers inside of her. Carter's hands flailed around her bedspread, and I took it as my cue to guide her where her hands should be. With my free hand, I took one of hers and placed it on my head. She immediately grasped my hair.

She pulled gently as she began to grind herself against me. By that point, I felt as if I'd lost all sense of control I had left in me. Pleasure coursed through every inch of my body, and I was bulging against my jeans. I let out a throaty groan against her. I gently began to push my fingers in and out. Carter's hips lifted up on the mattress, and I had to use my free hand to gently push her back down again. I started to suck gently, flicking my tongue as she clamped a hand over her mouth, letting out a muffled yelp. I could tell she was in pure ecstasy as her fingers tugged on my hair, pulling me forward and burying my face deeper against her.

"Harry," she whined. I looked up at her, and she was back up on her elbows. Her eyes were scrunched, mouth gaped open; she looked as if in complete bliss. My fingers pumped faster, my tongue flicking relentlessly as she began to pant. I could tell she was just seconds from coming. But then she sat up completely and pushed my head back.

I was confused until she tugged my arms forward, pulling me on top of her as she fell back onto the mattress. Her fingers fumbled with the button of my jeans, and she practically ripped open the zipper.

"Why are you still wearing this?" She heaved my shirt over my head.

"Carter," I breathed.

She didn't respond; instead, she pushed her hand past the waistband and gripped my length. I groan at the contact. I held myself over her, relishing in the feeling as I left sloppy kisses along her neck. Her free hand reached between us and pushed my underwear out of the way to pull out my aching erection. I reached one hand around to my back pocket and pulled out a condom. I ripped open the packet and rolled it on.

As I slowly pushed myself inside her, I peppered Carter with kisses. My hips involuntarily rocked against hers, pleasure already taking over. I couldn't help closing my eyes as I savored in the feeling of satisfaction radiating throughout my body. The deeper I drove inside her, the more I could feel my entire body heat up. It felt better than any other time we'd done this. I know for a fact that the reason it was even better was because I knew she loved me.

And I loved her, too.

I continued my movements, the only sounds in the room coming from us, our heavy breathing and little whimpers. When I began to move faster, her nails clawed at my back.

"Carter," I called out, pressing my forehead against her shoulder as my motions became rough and a bit sloppy. "Carter... I love you, baby."

Carter pulled my lips to hers, and said, "I love you, too." I rolled my hips against hers, watching her eyes roll back into her head as she came. I felt her pulsating around me. And as she was in the middle of finishing, she let out a moan so vocal that the sound sent me into a euphoria. Knowing I was the one making her feel this good, it easily pushed me into an intense shockwave of pleasure. It was a feeling I had never experienced so intensely.

"Harry," Carter moaned again, "I love you so much. Come, baby."

Oh, *fuck*.

That was it. That was all it took to finish me off. I panted as I lay over her, trying to catch my breath. After a couple of moments coming down from my blissful high, I pulled out of her slowly and sat up. She lay back, pulling the blanket over to cover herself as I watched her. Her hair was sprawled out against the sheets as she looked at me, a weak smile playing at her lips.

"Fuck, that was amazing," I said breathily, making her giggle; her cheeks were crimson.

"There's a tissue box on my nightstand right there if you want to clean up," she said, weakly pointing. I got up and watched over my shoulder as she moved to her dresser and grabbed a new shirt and underwear. After I got dressed, I walked over to her and wrapped my arms tightly around her.

"Do you think I should go? I don't want to, but—"

"No, you probably should. I don't know when anyone is supposed to be back."

I kissed her. She smiled so sweetly, her eyes roving over my face.

"I'll see you tomorrow?"

"Definitely," she whispered, her eyes on my lips.

I leaned in for another kiss and enjoyed every bit of it. My fingers pushed into her hair, and our tongues danced with one another. And as much as we both enjoyed this moment, it didn't last as long as anticipated.

Both of us froze when we heard the door slam and footsteps stomp up the stairs. We both knew it was Dylan; there was no way I was going through the front door, as he could see the driveway from his room.

"I'll go through the window," I whispered, hearing Dylan's door open and close. Carter looked as if she wanted to protest, but from the fear in her eyes, I knew she couldn't say otherwise. If he heard me going out the back, I was screwed. She nodded, and I kissed her once more. "Bye, baby. I'll text you once I'm home."

"Okay," she whispered. Dylan's door opened again. "Harry, go. Now, before you get caught."

I nodded before moving as quickly and quietly as possible. I climbed out her window and took short, slow steps out onto the roof. I slid to the edge and looked for the best way to the ground. It really wasn't that high, but it felt far more intimidating being up there than looking up from the ground. And of course, there was nothing to help me down.

Great.

"Why does this feel like *Romeo and Juliet?*" I grunted to myself as I shimmied into a good position.

Oh, god. This is really what my life has come to.

I didn't want to rip the gutter off, so I just slid off rather gracelessly and made sure to bend my knees as I hit the ground. I stayed crouched to make my landing less audible. After a minute of silence, I took off to my car.

I jogged up the stairs to my room, eager to get in bed. As I was kicking off my shoes, I pulled out my phone to let Carter know I'd gotten home. I opened Instagram, and my first instinct was to jump on Carter's profile, since I hardly ever went on her page. I remembered being forced to go on the app every day, because Jenna would *beg* me to like her pictures. Ridiculous.

I easily found Carter's profile and put it on scroll view, then went through every one of her pictures slowly—not that she had a lot, anyway. She had a few pictures with Mitchell and Elizabeth, but they were mostly just of random stuff like music or book piles.

It kind of bummed me out to know that I wouldn't be able to post a picture of Carter for a long, long time. We had plenty of pictures together, but I couldn't even put one of them as my wallpaper.

I shook away the thought before it could bring my mood down. I continued going through Carter's pictures, laughing at her silly captions. Then, I noticed in all her recent ones that the same account was commenting, leaving compliments and flirty emojis.

What the hell? Who is this? The username looked strangely familiar: *thegreatgalloway,* along with a number—a birth year, I assumed.

Galloway.

Why does that sound so familiar? I swore I'd heard that name.

Galloway.

Galloway?

Wait... Galloway.

Immediately, I thought of AJ and our conversation, and felt a pang of both guilt and frustration for not paying more attention. *Shit,* what had he said again?

It's Galloway. He's telling me how he's trying to get back with his ex.

His ex. Wait, was Carter his ex?

I clicked on the username and realized I'd actually been following him. Most of the recent pictures were of stupid things, like memes, female celebrities, amusement parks, fishing trips.

I couldn't care less for this stuff. Then, I finally found a selfie. Instantly, a wave of anger washed over me.

Galloway.

Austin Galloway.

THIRTY-NINE

[HARRY]

Saturday morning rolled around. I had spent the majority of the night wide awake, my mind a whirlwind of Austin and Carter. I couldn't believe he'd been trying to get my girlfriend's attention.

I was aware that Austin didn't know about us. Nobody knew about us. Well, except for Carter's two friends...and my parents. But nobody else.

I hoped.

But I was not happy about the fact that the biggest asshole ever was trying to get *my* girlfriend's attention. Nor did I understand it. Didn't he trash her after about a week of dating? And now he expected her to give him the time of day. I also couldn't believe that I hadn't realized who AJ had been talking about.

And I should have.

Did Carter know who that profile belonged to? Had she even noticed?

I doubt it; she would have told me by now... Right? No, she definitely would have. Why wouldn't she? Perhaps she told Mitchell? No, because if she told Mitchell, that means she would have seen them, and if she had seen them, she would have deleted them. Right? Fuck.

My head was pounding. I felt like my brain was bound to burst from all this constant, ridiculous worrying. I started to feel nauseous. I pressed my palms against my face, groaning in frustration. My phone began to ding with notifications.

Grateful for the distraction, I opened a few messages from Ryan, asking what time I'd be able to come over. I huffed and stood up from my bed, then started to get dressed.

Carter's texts let me know she would be riding with Mitchell, and that she was going over to him and Elizabeth's that afternoon so they could all get ready. I had to push all these thoughts about Galloway aside, at least for the sake of my own sanity.

[CARTER]

"I thought I looked okay," I whined. Elizabeth was applying another layer of lipstick after putting about a pound of makeup on my face. She'd also done my hair, which I loved. She'd used this fancy wand to curl it. But I hadn't seen what the makeup looked like yet; Elizabeth was very talented, but she had a habit of going heavy.

310

"I didn't even put on a lot, and you do look *really* good," she said. She had me close my eyes so she could spritz my whole face with a finishing spray.

I heard the door open. "Who's your friend, Lizzie?" Mitchell's voice called. "Because that's *definitely* not Carter."

"Screw you."

"No, I mean, you look good. But really, I wouldn't recognize you for a second if we just ran into each other. It's just going to take some time to adjust, you know? I've never seen you with that much makeup." I heard the distinctive sound of him flopping onto Elizabeth's bed.

"Okay," Elizabeth said, brushing back a couple stray hairs from my face with her fingers. I opened my eyes. "Let's have a look."

When she spun me around in her makeup chair, I, like Mitchell, didn't recognize myself. The eyeshadow made the blue in my eyes look brighter. The eyeliner wing was far more defined than my past attempts. My eyelashes were so deeply coated in mascara, it almost looked like I had fake lashes pasted on. But I think what blew me away the most was how large my lips looked with the lip liner Elizabeth had put on me. The mauve pink blended in with my natural color so well.

I made a mental reminder to ask Elizabeth to do my makeup for my senior prom next year.

"Whoa," I whispered to myself. I definitely wouldn't wear this much makeup every day, but *holy shit*.

"I don't get how she looks better in *your* makeup, Lizzie. Tighten up your game," Mitchell commented, and I watched Elizabeth roll her eyes.

"I'll be right back," Elizabeth said. She gathered her chosen outfit and walked out to the hallway and into the bathroom.

"Remind me why you're still so rude to her?" I asked, getting up to grab my outfit. "She's been nothing but nice to you, even *before* your parents got together."

"I don't know." He shrugged. "I mean, we used to hate each other in middle school because I thought she was too prissy, which she still sometimes is. *Don't interrupt*—she *was* nice, but she also hated me because I was supposedly *loud* and *obnoxious*."

I honestly thought Elizabeth had loosened up since then. I wasn't going to go to Mitchell's defense about being loud and obnoxious, though.

"But she's grown since then, and she's your sister now."

"I'm not *that* mean to her. I'm just teasing, and you know it."

"Well, maybe she's more sensitive to your bluntness than I am."

"Well, then that's something *she* needs to work on."

I would *never* want Mitchell to change, but for Elizabeth's sake, I thought that maybe he ought to. I saw his point, but I knew the constant bickering wasn't fun for either of them, and something had to give.

Elizabeth came into the room wearing a drapey sweater-shirt combo and maroon pants.

"You don't know how hard it was to put on this shirt!" she said. "It was like *Mission: Impossible* trying not to smear lipstick on the neckline!"

"Probably because your big head is *Mission: Impossible* to fit through anything," Mitchell said automatically, and I shot him a dirty look.

At that, he sat up and said, "However, you look very pretty, Lizzie."

A small, confused smile appeared on her face.

"Uh, thanks, Mitch."

"Yeah, yeah. You're welcome," he muttered before clapping his hands together. "All right, anyway, let's go!"

FORTY

[HARRY]

"Where do you want me to put this?" I asked Ryan, nodding to the heavy amplifier I'd pushed into the room. It was an old one his father had gotten and then promptly stuffed in the garage.

"Oh, that," he acknowledged. "Put it in the corner of the living room by the TV."

I nodded before leaving him in the kitchen. More people shuffled in and out of the rooms, some putting out drinks and food, others just arriving early.

Ryan lived in one of the nicest houses in the state, and since his mother was an interior designer, also one of the most unique.

The living room was all white, featuring two white sofas full of white pillows, and a white coffee table. A single black stripe was painted around the entire living room, and at its height was where floating shelves and a wall-mounted TV hung.

Two men, one very large and one only large around the middle, approached me. "Are you the host?" the first man asked.

I shook my head. "No, sorry. Can I help you, though?"

"We brought the kegs," he responded. "We need to know where to put them."

"Oh, you can put those in the kitchen. The host is in there," I said, pointing them in the right direction. I pushed the amplifier up tight against the corner wall, unsure whether Ryan wanted it shoved in or sticking out.

As I turned around, I saw Dylan. He pulled two CD cases out of his pocket and then tossed his jacket on the couch. They were probably mixes of his own music.

I quickly went back to the kitchen, where I saw Ryan a little frazzled. It was already crowded, and he was setting out Solo cups.

"Need anything else?" I asked.

"Oh, yeah. Go into those liquor cabinets and take out Grey Goose, Everclear, Sierra Silver, and... *Oh*, I think my dad stuffed the absinthe in the back."

I looked into the hallway behind me and saw the cabinet, then began pulling out the bottles.

"Absinthe?" I repeated. "That 'Green Fairy' crap?"

"Yeah, so?"

"Don't you trip out on this?" I asked in amazement as I rotated the bottle in my hands.

"Some of it can give you hallucinations, I think. I've never tried it."

"Won't your dad get mad if he finds out all his liquor is missing?"

"Yeah, if it were missing from *his* liquor cabinet. No one ever looks in there; that's *my* stash."

"Oh, right. Anyway, count me out if you plan on drinking this," I admitted. I wouldn't mind trying most drinks, but the thought of hallucinations freaked me out a bit.

Ryan nodded. "Yeah, you're right. I think I'm going to put this back or save it for myself."

He looked at the gin as I put it on the marble counter. "This is more like it. You want to knock one back right now?" He eagerly pulled out two shot glasses and poured an equal amount in each. I lifted mine, and someone approached us, weaving through the crowd.

"Sorry about being late, Ry. I was busy setting up the projector. I have this crazy shit planned, and—*oh*."

AJ stopped when he finally spotted me; his smile dropped and his face went pale.

What the hell?

"*And?*" Ryan asked impatiently.

"Uh, nothing. It's just the senior year video montage," he replied, taking his eyes off me and finally looking back at Ryan. "Where's Dylan?"

"I saw him go upstairs," I answered for him. AJ only nodded and took off without looking at me.

"Anyway," Ryan said, shaking his head and raising his glass

once more as I did the same. "To the greatest night of our lives."

We knocked back the shots.

I hadn't ever *loved* drinking, but I had enjoyed the numbness, especially during my junior year. And then the appeal of it had lessened more and more up until Carter and I had started dating.

The crowd started whooping and shouting as more people flooded in. The party was starting in earnest. Ryan looked at me with a smug smile.

"This is going to be one hell of a night, I can already tell."

[CARTER]

"Okay, okay. Serious question now," Mitchell announced as Elizabeth and I groaned in aggravation. "Carter, if you had to choose between Harry or Zac Efron, who would it be?"

"I dunno. Harry's my boyfriend, and Zac is not only hot, but he's so, like, oh my god. Like, he's so, *ugh*. But then Harry is just, *ugh*."

"That's quite descriptive," Elizabeth sarcastically remarked. It was obviously easy for her to pick.

"What about you?" I turned the attention to Mitchell. "Between Harry and Zac, who would you pick?"

"*Well.*" Mitchell smirked. "As much as I truly believe I was *destined* to be with Harry, I'd have to choose Zac."

"Love that," Elizabeth remarked.

We had been driving for a solid half hour on our way to Ryan's place. Eventually, we found a massive house swarming with our classmates. Looking for parking was by far the most difficult part of getting in; we had to park at least three blocks away.

Thank god I had chosen to wear my flats, or else I would have been suffering the way Elizabeth was, trying not to wince in her strappy heels.

As we approached the front yard, we all locked hands, and Mitchell dragged us through the crowd. We finally made it in, and my first instinct was to find Harry.

There wasn't a lot of dancing going on, despite the music nearly shaking the walls. Everyone was mostly standing or sitting in groups, laughing and drinking.

Mitchell motioned to the kitchen, and our trio began moving that way. While I looked for Harry, I also wondered if my brother was there. I hardly saw him at home anymore—which was weird. I'd expected him to be home more often, trying to keep me on lockdown.

Mitchell and Elizabeth went to grab drinks, and I found Harry siting on the counter with a beer in one hand. Harry noticed me right away. He smiled and gestured for me to go upstairs. I stopped Mitchell to tell him I'd be back, then went up the stairs.

I opened a couple doors, finally finding the bathroom after a third try. I saw Harry as he reached the top of the stairs and made eye contact with him before going inside. After a few moments, probably making sure to give enough time so no one noticed, he followed. And before I was given the chance to greet him, he pushed me up against the bathroom wall, lips on mine.

Despite the foul alcoholic taste, I couldn't help the small moan that escaped my throat as he hungrily swirled his tongue against my own. He pulled away and leaned against the wall opposite with a satisfied grin on his face.

"Wow. You look beautiful, baby," he said, his smile brightening as he stared at me adoringly.

I laughed and looked him over. He wore jeans and a black long-sleeve shirt, and his hair was flopped forward, hanging over his eyes with beads of sweat glistening on his forehead beneath. Harry continued lazily grinning at me, and it was then that I noticed his glazed eyes.

"Are you drunk?" I couldn't help but ask.

Harry shrugged with a smug grin. "A little. Not really. I would say more like tipsy." He shook his head before speaking again. "But anyway... Hey, let's get out of here before someone catches us."

"We just got here—"

"Come on." Harry kissed me once more before swinging the bathroom door open and leaving me alone as he ran down the stairs.

"Did you find him?" Mitchell said in my ear, and I nodded in response. "Well, where is he?"

"He's right there." I pointed out Harry who was now back on the counter, knocking back a shot glass. I cringed at the sight of him downing another drink. "He's a little tipsy, or at least he was.

He looks like he's on the verge of getting drunk."

Mitchell probably noticed the disapproving look on my face before going to Harry's defense. "Oh, don't go all *Mom* on him. He's just having fun. Unlike *some* people, he's drinking to let loose. As you should, too."

I contemplated it for a moment. "I don't know. You know I don't mind drinking or anything, but...I have a bad feeling about this, Mitch. I guess I'm just scared of him getting *drunk*."

Mitchell nodded, glancing at Harry before looking elsewhere. I watched as Harry laughed really hard at whatever the group of people had said. His eyes crinkled and his nose scrunched up, his mouth was wide open with the biggest grin on his face. It was truly a sight to see. However, I couldn't help but feel uneasy. I didn't want to him to get into a state I couldn't handle, or that he would be embarrassed by later. And we had a secret to keep. But as Mitchell had said, maybe he was just having fun, and I should let him enjoy himself.

As the night went on, I followed my usual routine of clinging to Mitchell, while Elizabeth would rove around and do her own thing before meeting back up with us. But this time none of that was as comforting as it usually was for me, because I couldn't be with my boyfriend. We had to act like near-strangers. It felt so weird. I was already so used to being affectionate and attached to Harry from the past few weeks; I didn't like acting as if we didn't care about one another. It really sucked, in all honesty.

For me, at least.

What bothered me the most was seeing Harry have no problem handling it. I knew he was just getting drunk and having fun and all, but I was craving his affection more than ever. I also didn't want to be *that* girlfriend, controlling him and ruining his fun. So, I figured it was all I could do to just suck it up and try to have fun on my own.

I shook the sensitive thoughts away when I caught a glimpse of my brother, leaned back on a corner wall with one arm slung around Lindsay's shoulders.

Well, I guess they're back together.

Man, if only Dylan and Harry had never become friends. Maybe he would've become my boyfriend without the need for sneaking around and discreet hangouts. Then again, if Dylan had never met Harry, then I may not have met him, either.

I decided to move closer to Harry, even if we couldn't acknowledge each other, or if he was too drunk to notice me.

Harry was in the same spot in the kitchen I had seen him at before, so I made my way around the center island to pour myself a drink. With my back turned to the group, and the countless people surrounding Harry, I could listen inconspicuously to the conversation going on, smiling to myself as I heard him laugh and add commentary. For the most part, it was just banter and nonsense, but that didn't stop the small crowd from laughing immensely. I downed the soda I'd poured into my cup and cringed when I felt a tinge of alcohol in it.

God, they must have spiked everything.

I decided against tossing the rest of it down the drain and planned to give it to Mitchell once I got back to him.

"Harry," a girl said, "I don't get why you're single, you're *so* funny."

I waited for Harry to respond, but I only heard silence until she spoke up again.

"Trouble settling down?" She giggled, and I smiled to myself, remembering asking him almost the same thing and him telling me he liked a girl—at the time, not knowing it was me.

I waited for Harry to say those words again. But instead, I heard him say, "Nah, just haven't found the right girl yet."

Okay...

I knew we had to keep this secret, but deep down, I found myself hoping he would tell her exactly what he'd told me. I listened intently as she replied, "Well, I don't normally do this, but—" the crowd was boisterous, so I slowly moved closer, keeping my back to them so I wouldn't be noticed. "Here's my number."

I felt my heart pounding painfully against my rib cage as I awaited Harry's response, the seemingly endless pause giving me anxiety.

I heard him chuckle, and I winced. "I'll keep that in mind."

My heart thudded heavily once more, and I felt its weight plummet to the pit of my stomach. *Did he really just...?*

I didn't mean to be all sensitive, but my boyfriend had just told me he loved me. The words *I'll keep that in mind* sliced my heart in half. I felt a tear slide down my cheek, and I wiped it away immediately. How pathetic of me. *I shouldn't be crying about this... Right?*

No. No way. Why am *I crying?*

All I could think was, *is Harry really so willing to keep this a secret that he would text a girl behind my back?* No, I doubted that. I trusted him too much. Maybe he'd just said it to say it; it wasn't like he would actually do it, right?

I shook away the thought and took a swig of my drink, grateful I hadn't poured it down the drain.

After a couple moments of silence from both of them, I peeked over at where Harry was sitting—and regretted it instantly. With Harry sitting on the counter, the girl was standing between his legs, facing the crowd; he had one arm around her shoulders as he carelessly knocked back yet another beer.

I felt a second round of tears well in my eyes, threatening to spill. I had to fight them back with the very little strength I had left in me, but my heart was winning the battle so far. I poured another Jack & Coke.

I couldn't watch anymore, knowing I would probably break. I pushed and shoved my way back, looking down and hoping no one could see the glossiness in my eyes.

I felt someone bump shoulders with me, and I was relieved to see Mitchell slide in by my side. His smile immediately turned into a frown when he noticed my face.

"What's wrong?"

Everything, absolutely everything. I didn't know what to feel. My soul was telling me one thing while my head was saying another, but the sad part was, I couldn't hear either of them.

The only sound audible was the weakening beat of my breaking heart.

FORTY-ONE

[HARRY]

My blood was running wild, and my mind was hazy. I was feeling a bit exhausted, but still managing to have a good time. Despite the blurring lights and my lack of balance, I still felt like I was in control. It felt as though the room was being tilted from side to side, and nobody noticed but me.

Right then, I needed to lean on someone for support, my limbs and head too heavy. The only person available was the girl I'd just met, who'd noticed me nearly falling off the counter.

"Fuck, where's Carter?" I grumbled to myself. I needed to find her.

I nudged the girl to move away. She obliged, and I jumped down from the counter, slightly staggering and stumbling, but managing to stabilize myself within a couple seconds.

"You all right?" the girl asked with a hand on my shoulder. I nodded, politely removing her hand from me.

When she wasn't looking, I'd discreetly crumpled the piece of paper she'd given me with her number and put it in an empty used cup scattered with others on the counter beside me.

I lied, telling her I'd come back. I took that moment as my cue to avoid her at all costs from there on out. I moved away, although walking throughout the kitchen was a little more difficult than I had thought. The sound of music and overlapping voices was low and muffled. I held onto every bit of furniture and free section of wall, maneuvering my way through the room until I'd reached the fridge. I put the beer down and grabbed a water bottle. I felt a little nauseous as I continued walking, so I chugged the water; the chill of it woke me up a bit.

As I scanned the crowd, I caught sight of a face I recognized.

Austin.

Austin was here.

Austin *fucking* Galloway.

Already I could feel my blood boil and my fists clench. Even if Carter hadn't seen his attempts, I didn't like him. Not because he was trying to catch the attention of *my* girlfriend, but because he'd hurt her. He'd hurt Carter, and several other girls, and I didn't think I'd be able to stand looking at him without wanting to slam his head against concrete.

I began wandering the huge rooms in search of Carter.

When I turned the corner, heading towards the front door in the hopes she'd be outside, I almost passed right by the living room without looking. But then I saw a familiar head of long brown hair.

There she was, dancing in the middle of the room along with Mitchell. I smiled as I watched her from afar. She tilted her head back in laughter. She looked to be having the time of her life with a beer bottle in her hand.

And although it made me happy seeing her so carefree, I couldn't help the little part inside of me yearning to be with her and have her dance with me instead of Mitchell. I really wished I could just go up to her and kiss her and be by her side. I was suddenly aching for her touch. I turned away before anyone could catch me staring, looking down at my feet and smiling to myself at the thought of just Carter herself.

Without looking, as I headed to the table full of drinks, I bumped into someone. I looked up to apologize, when I stopped, noticing it was Dylan, about to do the same. I clenched my jaw, growing nervous. After a couple seconds of awkward staring, I turned and decided to go somewhere where neither Carter, Dylan, or even that girl who'd given me her number would be.

However, I felt a grip on my shoulder, forcing me to turn back and face Dylan. He had an unreadable look on his face.

"Wait," he said when I'd turned completely. "Hey, man. I just wanted to say that I'm sorry for blowing up on you that day after school. I'd had too much to drink, and I overreacted when you asked about my sister."

I shook my head. "Dylan, it's fine. I should have known you

were still angry about what happened at Melissa's—"

"No," Dylan interrupted, "I completely blew up. You've always asked how Carter's doing, even before that night. I just took it as you being really interested in her."

Uh...what? Is he messing with me, or does he not know?

"But seeing that you two have avoided each other since that night, and kept a distance since then, it goes to show that I have nothing to worry about." He smiled, and I felt a little uncomfortable and awkward.

Oh, god. He really didn't know.

I chuckled nervously, scratching the back of my neck as I nodded.

"I trust you, man. And I'm really glad you respected staying away from her. I mean, it was just a kiss. I'm glad nothing more happened." He laughed as if it were no big deal. I really wanted run away right then.

"No problem," I said weakly.

"But yeah. I'm sorry, and I hope we can get past this. I'll see you around." Dylan smiled once more and headed off to God knows where. I released a breath I hadn't known I was holding in.

I looked back at Carter, happy to see her happy. But my smile immediately dropped when I noticed someone making their way directly towards her. I couldn't really see who it was through the countless bodies covering them, but I could tell they were male. And I could only hope it wasn't who I thought it was.

I saw a hand land on Carter's waist. She was having far too

much fun to notice, one arm hung loosely around Mitchell's neck, who was dancing with her whilst struggling to also talk to some guy. A face came into view, and I tightened my jaw.

Austin had both hands on *my* girlfriend.

How *fucking* fantastic.

Carter was much too invested in her dancing to realize whose hands were on her. That was what angered me the most; I wasn't sure at first if he was aware that she wasn't in the right state of mind, but given how oblivious she was being, I became certain he knew perfectly well she was drunk. Watching his hands move lower and lower on her body, I began to make my way over to them. I watched as she looked up to Mitchell, whose back was facing her. She staggered slightly on her feet, clumsily regaining her balance as her face visibly went pale at the sight before her.

There was a bit of an awkward exchange between them as I struggled to make my through the many intoxicated, sweaty bodies around me. Carter's hands pushed at his chest to shove him off of her, and he continued to try and edge closer, invading her personal space. When she turned to look away from him, her eyes met mine as I reached them.

"Look." Austin tried to get her attention, not realizing that I was right behind him. "I just wanted to say that I'm sorry about everything. And if you could take me back, I—"

"Carter, let's go," I interrupted. Initially startled by my sudden appearance, Austin suddenly grinned, his expression changing to a deviant smile resembling the devil's himself.

"Excuse me?" Austin scoffed, his stupid smirk never leaving his lips. "I was kind of in the middle of talking to my girl here."

"She is *not* your girl," I growled at Austin before turning back to Carter. "Let's go. *Now.*"

"Well, it sure as hell took you long enough to remember *me*," Carter said lowly, glaring at me as if I were in the wrong here.

"What? What are you talking about? Never mind—just come on, Carter." I grabbed her arm and attempted to pull her with me and away from him. But Austin pulled at her other arm, yanking her towards him as if she were a rag doll.

"Now wait a minute," Austin said, still smugly watching me. "If I'm not mistaken, it looks as if I've intruded in *your* territory."

I tried not to show him any signs of guilt at Austin's words, but the way he smiled made me feel like he might know more than I'd thought. "What the hell do you know?"

"Whoa, man. Just a question, take it easy. You just seem a little... possessive, is all. What, are you her new boyfriend or something?" he asked, his smirk only growing at the sight of my reaction.

"Nothing's going on. You're just clearly being a douchebag."

"You know she used to be my girlfriend, right?"

Carter finally pulled herself out of Austin's grip, her growing anger evident. "*Excuuuuse me.*" She stumbled, trying to hold herself up as she staggered a bit. "But the last time *I* checked, you didn't even remember my *name.*"

Austin only laughed at her before looking back at me.

That only infuriated me more. I took a step closer. "Leave her alone. She's Dylan's little sister, and I'm looking after her for him. Like another big brother would do."

"*Ewww, gross.* You are *not* like a brother to me, *Harry*," Carter slurred. I looked to her with furrowed brows, but then focused my attention back on Austin, who was clearly amused by all of this.

"Just get away from her before I bring her brother into this," I threatened. I shoved Austin back to try and haul Carter away from him, but before I had the chance to reach out for her, he shoved Carter aside. She nearly fell to the ground before a set of arms grabbed her; Mitchell, who was now focused on what was unfolding, had caught her.

"Holy shit," he said just loud enough for me to hear.

"I don't think you want to do that, Harry," Austin said, smiling. My fists clenched.

"Try me," I said, thoughtlessly giving in as I shoved Austin harder this time. He only scoffed, rolling his eyes with a headshake and turning away. Carter was about to say something, but I grabbed her arm again and quickly dragged her across the room and up the stairs. I knew she was struggling, but I needed to get her as far away from Austin as I possibly could.

After several attempts of running into multiple rooms with half-dressed couples, we finally made it to an empty bedroom. I slammed the door shut and locked it, then turned to find Carter looking around the room. I snatched the bottle from her hands and tossed it into a little garbage can next to the door.

"Harry, what the hell?"

"First of all, you shouldn't be drinking. Especially given the fact that you had no idea who was clutching onto your waist until I stepped in. Which infuriates me, because of all people, it just *had* to be him. And you didn't even notice!" I shouted. I was trying to calm down, but the image of everything I'd seen kept replaying in my head.

"*Me?* You're angry with *me?*" Carter snorted. "What about *you*?!"

"What're you talking—?"

"You know exactly what the hell I'm talking about!" she yelled, surprising me with how aggressive she sounded. Could this be the alcohol, or had I actually missed something?

"What—?"

"You took a girl's number, and...and *then* you said you'd keep it in *mind* to call her or text her or...*whatever!*" she said, her breathing heavy and harsh.

Then it clicked.

"Carter," I breathed, making my voice much more relaxed. I wanted to explain to her what had happened, but I was so stunned by what she'd said, it worried me to think that she might've misunderstood what she saw. "That wasn't what—I wasn't really going to contact her. Baby, I promise you. I'm not interested in her, not even a little." Carter only shook her head, her eyes glossy and lip twitching as she held back obvious tears of hurt. Ones I never wanted to be the reason for.

"Why didn't you tell her you liked me when she asked if you

were struggling to settle down?" Carter asked, the memory of her asking me something very similar fresh in my mind like it had only just happened yesterday. "When I asked you, did you only tell me you liked me to mess with my head?"

"How would I have been messing with your head? Baby, you're my *girlfriend*," I tried to emphasize, my eyes wide, hopeful that she would believe me. "Do you really think I'd go this far just to mess with you? I love you. You know that."

"If you really loved me the way you said you did, then why were your arms around her, and why did you let her stand between your legs?" she asked. She nearly fell over, but I was quick to catch her.

"Baby, you're drunk," I said. *We can't fight about this. Not now, not while she's intoxicated.* "Come on, I can't have you like this. We have to—"

"Don't. Just forget it." She harshly pushed herself off of me. "I can do it myself."

"Carter, stop," I tried to reason with her. "Baby, you have to hold onto me. Let's go somewhere else to talk so you can at least let me explain. Come on, let's go before Dylan—"

"Who *carrrresss?*" Carter interrupted. "And for the record, *Harry,* I was pulling *away* from Austin! Do you really think I'd be stupid enough to be near him after what *he* did to *me*?"

[CARTER]

Just as Harry was about to make a remark, I turned on my heel and left the room, slamming the door behind me. I hurried down the steps. I didn't care anymore. If he wanted to talk about it later, fine! But I didn't want to fight with him right then, especially not at a party where I was *trying* to have fun.

I pushed my way through the crowd to get to Mitchell and Elizabeth, who were looking around the room, probably searching for me. From the corner of my eye, I could see Austin looking at me with a smug smile, but I ignored him. He walked out of the room once Harry entered. I huffed and continued walking towards my best friends.

And just as I made it to them and saw the relieved looks on their faces, the music stopped. The whole room was puzzled, until a figure stood up on one of the tables and a projector light illuminated most of the wall behind him; the figure turned out to be Ryan.

"All right, all right," Ryan said into a microphone, "I know most of you are wondering what is going on. And we'll get to that; I promise it'll be worth it. But can I just say, what a great turnout so far, am I right?" The room cheered wildly in response. "I just wanted to say wow. Just wow. The majority of our senior class is here, yeah?" Most of the people in the crowd shouted excitedly. "This was such a great year, honestly. Senior year was far greater than anticipated and, as much as I don't wanna get all sentimental..." Ryan paused with a hand on his heart before speaking once more. "I really am gonna miss most of you guys."

As Ryan continued to speak, reminiscing of high school and trying to lighten the mood with jokes, I tried to focus on him instead of Harry. I could feel Harry's eyes burning into me, but I went to Mitchell and hugged him.

When I eventually glanced back at him, the girl from earlier approached him and put her arms around his shoulders. Harry looked shocked at the contact, but didn't react quick enough to move her arms away. I tore my eyes away from the scene instantly, my lip trembling as I inhaled a sharp breath.

I'm not going to cry. I'm not going to cry. I'm not going to cry!

Struggling to keep calm, I stared down at my feet in silence. I could hardly pay attention to Ryan, but I tried to get my mind off any and everything having to do with Harry.

But just then, gasps filled the room. Catcalls, coughs, drinks being spit out, and shrieks of *Oh my god!* were heard, and Ryan suddenly stopped talking. Even Mitchell gasped, his grip on me tightening.

I looked up to see whatever could have made the whole room react that way.

FORTY-TWO

[CARTER]

For a moment, I was unaware of what was going on or what I was looking at, but when I saw my face on the projector screen behind Ryan, my heart dropped, and I felt as if my entire world had come crumbling down. The buzz of alcohol vanished.

There it was, in front of everyone on full display...the picture I had privately sent Harry not too long ago: the one with my breasts in full display.

I was frozen to the spot; I couldn't react or move. I started hyperventilating. Everyone in the room was all sorts of crazy. Dylan had spat his drink all over Lindsay, and Elizabeth had dropped the plate of food she'd had in her hands. All Mitchell could do was stare at me, a mixture of horror and pity on his face.

My vision went blurry as tears automatically began to flood

my eyes; however, I was still frozen, and still unable to process what was going on.

This is a nightmare.

"What the fuck is that?" I heard an angry growl in my ear. But I didn't respond until I was yanked back painfully by the shoulder. "Answer me, Carter!" The room went silent as everyone watched my brother scream at me. I didn't know how he'd gotten to me so fast when, only two seconds ago, he had been in the corner of the room. "Who the fuck was that for!?"

I finally met Dylan's eyes. Behind my infuriated brother stood a frightened Harry, looking at me in sorrow and helplessness as his eyes went from me to the picture. I felt entirely hollow as my brother glared at me, his hand on my shoulder tightening to the point I knew I would wake up with a bruise. "Where the fuck did this picture come from?!" he shouted out to everyone, looking around the room. "Who did this?!"

He shot murderous glares at Ryan, who was also frozen, and then AJ, who jolted to his feet and scrambled to unplug the projector. Dylan released his grip on me and rounded on AJ, shoving him onto the couch.

"Where did you get that picture?" he asked AJ. "Fucking answer me!"

He didn't respond, but the way he was clutching his phone was the only clue Dylan needed. "Gimme your phone," Dylan demanded, and AJ, terrified, obliged, giving him the cell unlocked.

Dylan looked through the device and, after a couple of moments, his eyes widened; whatever he saw only angered him even more. He shoved the phone back to AJ and began to scan the room like a madman. And when his eyes finally set on something behind me, I was too afraid to turn and look back. He marched through the crowd, and I dashed forward and snatched the phone from AJ. I saw my picture. In a text conversation with Harry.

I heard a shout and turned to see Dylan grab Harry by his shirt and push him against the wall, hard enough to dent the drywall.

"Dylan—" Harry coughed.

"I fucking knew it! I fucking knew you were a rat! Why the fuck would you do that to my sister?!" Dylan howled.

"Dylan, what are you talking about?!" Harry screamed, trying to pry him off. Without even realizing I was moving, I took long, determined strides right up to them, AJ's phone in my left hand. Harry looked relieved until I pulled my arm back and launched my fist straight into his jaw.

The room was still silent. My hands were trembling, and Harry was gaping at me. But my fist didn't hurt. Not in the way many had described it would or should. I was about to go for another swing when I was pulled back by two people—Mitchell and Dylan.

My tears and cries came out without missing a beat. My anger had been let out and I couldn't put the lid back on.

"How could you do this to me?!" I screamed, my breathing heavy as I tried in vain to release myself from Mitchell and Dylan.

"Carter, what—?"

338

"This!" I screamed, though it came out more like a painfully induced sob. I ripped my left arm free to throw the phone at his chest, which he clumsily caught. Mitchell gripped my arm again.

As Harry's eyes scanned the screen, they widened in ghastly bewilderment. "That's not possible. No. No! Carter, you know I would never—"

"Shut up!" Dylan growled at him, unable to let me go, knowing that if he didn't help Mitchell hold me back, I'd jump in again. My eyes were stinging as my tears flowed freely.

"I would never do this to you, baby, you know—"

"Don't call me that!" I screamed again, and when the crowd finally caught on to what was happening, I heard gasps all around us.

Dylan looked at me in shock, probably putting two and two together and realizing what the room had suddenly discovered as well. But he clenched his jaw and didn't question it as he looked back at Harry in anger. Harry's eyes were bloodshot, not focused on Dylan at all. I watched them fill with tears of his own, which only enraged me even more.

He took a step forward, rubbing at his jaw. "Carter, you have to believe me—"

I finally quit struggling from Mitchell's hold as I backed away, suddenly recoiling at the thought of being near him.

"Don't come near me," I said, and everyone backed away as if I was talking to them. "Stay away from me. Don't come near me ever again. *Ever.* I never want to see you again."

I tried to hold my composure and force myself to hold my ground as I spoke. But I couldn't. It was physically and emotionally impossible.

"Baby, I swear. I love you, I would never—"

As Harry tried to take another step, he was pushed back by Dylan, and I took it as my cue to make a run for it. I bolted out the door without a single glance back.

With hazy vision, I ran across the half-empty lawn and stopped when I made it to the sidewalk. I struggled to catch my breath as I looked down helplessly. All I wanted to do was curl up in my bed and just cry to no end, praying that my emotions would wither away. I hadn't felt an ache like this in my heart for so long, it was almost foreign to me then.

"Carter," a voice said, and I turned to find Austin. "Are you okay?"

I shook my head weakly before trying to find my voice. "I just want to go home," I squeaked. Austin only nodded as he put a hand on my back and guided me towards his familiar yellow Mustang.

"I'll take you home, babe," he said as he opened the door for me.

"No," I shook my head. "Austin, please, just—"

"Come on," he said, looping an arm around my waist. "I remember where you live." I could hardly hear myself think and just cried harder while I got in the car. I felt so weak and numb.

From a distance, looking out the window, I could see Harry running out the door with Mitchell and Dylan trailing behind. Only they couldn't see me as we drove away. At that point, I didn't

340

care; I just wanted to leave and get as far away from Harry as possible.

[HARRY]

"Goddammit!" Dylan shouted, sweating from running in circles around the neighborhood. Carter was nowhere to be found, and she wasn't answering her cell—to *any* of us. "This is all your fault," he growled, stomping up to me.

"How is it *my* fault?" I snapped back, getting up in his face, tears blurring my vision.

The last time we'd seen her, she'd been running out the door. I was scared, heartbroken, and worried for her. I wanted to see her, talk to her, and more importantly, I wanted to know she was okay and safe.

"I can't do this," Dylan said, panicking as Mitchell and Elizabeth approached. "I'm leaving to go look for her; you guys do the same. I don't trust her being out late at night all alone." Dylan stopped to catch a breath, pulling at his own hair before heading off to his car. I quickly followed.

"Wait, Dylan. Let me go with you," I said as he opened his door. "I can help look—"

"Fuck no," Dylan spat.

"Dylan, please," I pleaded, starting to cry hysterically. "You have to believe me, I would never do that to her. I promise you. Just let me go with you, I'll help you find her—"

"You've done enough," Dylan said through gritted teeth. "Harry,

I can't even stand to look at you right now. You better fucking hope, for your sake, that we find her."

He angrily slammed his door and sped off down the street. I stared at the car as it disappeared down the road, feeling helpless. I ran my fingers through my hair, frustrated, tears falling rapidly.

"We're outta here," Mitchell announced, taking Elizabeth by the hand as they headed to her car.

"Where are you guys going?" I asked in a panic.

"We're going to look for my best friend," Mitchell said. He didn't look me in the eye.

"Let me go with you guys. Please."

"Are you kidding me?" Mitchell glared at me. "Harry, I am so disgusted with you. You hurt my best friend; you broke her trust. You broke *all* of our trust with you."

Elizabeth nodded in agreement. "What you did was beyond fucked up, and you don't deserve to see Carter whatsoever."

"I didn't do it; you have to believe me! I—"

"Save your excuses, Harry. It's pretty clear you sent that picture to your friend. The proof is right there." Mitchell shook his head as he opened the passenger door. "I can't believe you'd do that to her. And more importantly, I can't believe we didn't see it coming."

I flinched like I'd been hit again.

"Mitchell, please—" I begged him to at least let me explain, but they both ignored me as they jumped in the car and started to pull away.

I couldn't believe this was happening. I felt like the world was spinning too fast around me; I might have puked. I looked up when I saw someone else come out of the house, head hung low.

I immediately seized AJ's shirt, then shoved him on the ground and pinned him down, my hands gripping his wrists.

"What the hell is wrong with you?! Why would you do that to her, AJ?! She didn't do anything to deserve that!"

"Harry," AJ choked out, squirming and struggling to pull me off. "Harry, stop. Listen to me!"

"No!" I yelled. "This is all your fucking fault! I lost my girlfriend because of you! You took her away from me! Because of what you did, she hates me, so fuck you! I thought you were my friend!"

"Harry, what the fuck are you doing?!" Ryan shouted as he ran towards me. He shoved me off of AJ, and before I could launch myself back at him, Ryan immediately held me back.

"Look, man..." AJ was struggling to talk. "I didn't know you guys were together, all right?"

"Nobody knew! And so that gave you the right to do that to some girl you didn't know? What the fuck is wrong with you?" I struggled in Ryan's bear-hug hold.

"Look, it wasn't my idea to do it!" AJ yelled angrily, looking at me with wide eyes. I didn't know if I could believe him.

"What the hell are you talking about? Why did you do it, then?"

"Just listen," AJ pleaded, speaking more calmly. Ryan's grip on me slowly began to ease. "The day I went to your house was when I saw the picture. I was on a call with Galloway while you were downstairs, and then your phone went off. You'd gotten a new message and I saw it was from some girl, but I had no idea who it was."

"So what? You decided to be fucking nosy?" I snarled, Ryan immediately grasping me again.

"It's not like that," he said, holding his hands up. "Look, I'll admit, I clicked on it. I just wanted to see who it was, cause you'd been smirking at your phone all day. I was just curious—"

"Jesus, AJ," Ryan muttered.

"I told you it wasn't my plan!" AJ carried on hurriedly, looking even more hurt that his best friend was reproaching him. "Listen to me! Austin heard my reaction and asked what happened. I told him you had a nude, and that it looked like Carter, Dylan's sister. Austin ordered me to send the picture to my phone and then send it to him. Harry, I *swear on my life* I tried to argue with him about it but—but he threatened me. I couldn't say no."

"Austin made you send the picture?"

AJ nodded before continuing, "I didn't want to do it, but he threatened to blackmail me with something extremely personal, Harry. I was scared."

"But that still doesn't explain why you put it up on the projector. Why did you bring it? Were you in on it? You looked guilty as shit when you got here and saw me, so this is all looking like bullshit so far."

"The projector wasn't meant for Carter's picture. I brought it because Dylan and I had made a video montage of senior year. I was scared because I couldn't tell you about Austin." AJ rubbed at his face. "Austin must have gone up and uploaded the picture to the projector. Harry, he set you up so he could win her back. I didn't even know he and Carter were together, that she was the ex he'd been telling me about."

I didn't know what to believe.

"Harry, you have to trust me. I wouldn't do that to you, or especially to *her*; I don't even know her! I'm *so* sorry. I didn't know that was gonna happen, and it's my fault. I swear to god I would take it all back if I could. I should've just said no and dealt with the consequences."

Every bit of my blood was on fire. AJ seemed to be telling the truth. It all made sense now; I just still couldn't believe it.

"Where the fuck is he?" I growled.

"Last time I saw him, he ran out the door just a couple moments after she did."

I started scanning all the cars parked around the block. "What kind of car does he drive?"

"Bright yellow Mustang."

I walked down to the end of the driveway so I could peer down the street. Of course it wasn't there.

"Fuck!" I shouted. "He probably took her! That motherfucking—"
I kicked the trashcan beside me and watched it topple and roll a couple feet away. I paced back and forth on the sidewalk. I couldn't fucking believe this. Of course it had all been Austin!

I quickly took out my phone and called Dylan a handful of times, but each call went straight to voicemail after a single ring.

He was clearly ignoring me.

"Call Dylan now! Tell him she's with Austin! Go!" I yelled at both Ryan and AJ, and they fumbled for their cellphones. I wondered briefly where AJ's phone ended up; I think I had dropped it somewhere inside after Carter had thrown it at me.

Everything about this felt wrong. I was angry and devastated, but more so, worried. Carter was with Austin; of all the people who could've taken her home, she'd chosen to go with Austin. I felt like vomiting. I wanted to jump in the car and take off, but I didn't have the slightest clue where to look. Where the fuck would Austin take her?

I turned to Ryan, who was leaving voicemails, and got Austin's address. Then I ran to my car and peeled off down the road. For the first time in forever, I had thought I had finally found my key to happiness. And in the blink of an eye, it had been taken away.

[CARTER]

Everything was a blur. It felt like I had been dreaming. But it had been a complete nightmare.

With my head propped up in my hand, I stared out the open window, watching the trees pass in the darkness. The wind blew my hair in such a relaxing manner and dried the tears on my cheeks. I was sure all the hard work Elizabeth had put into my makeup was now running down my chin.

Thankfully, the first couple of minutes on the ride home were spent in silence. I tried to recuperate and process everything. It was still unbelievable; I still couldn't put my finger on it.

I'd thought everything between me and Harry had been real. Everyone who knew we were together had believed him. I knew I shouldn't have given myself to him. I'd let him break down my walls; he'd torn them down with ease, and I let him do it. As my mind slowly began to catch up with my heart, and vice versa, I started to realize the gravity of my surroundings.

Seeing Austin in the driver's seat suddenly made me queasy. I regretted getting in the car with him then—him, of all people. My mind hadn't been in the right place when I'd first gotten in with him, and now I just wanted to jump out the window; I would've preferred to get hit by a car rather than be in one with him.

We pulled up to a red light, and Austin suddenly reached over and began stroking my cheek with his thumb and forefinger. I winced at the contact and struggled to press myself against the passenger door to increase the space between us.

"I wouldn't hurt you the way he did," he said.

I swatted his hand away, scoffing at him in disbelief. Yes, what Harry had done was beyond fucked up, and my heart was hurting immensely. But Austin was still no better.

"You shouldn't let a guy that fucked up or shallow get to your heart. You know I wouldn't do that," he said smoothly, and I could tell he was grinning without having to look at him. "You should've known better than to trust a piece of shit like Harry—"

"Look," I said through gritted teeth, "what Harry did was unforgivable. But don't think for one second that I'd ever give *you* a second chance."

"You wouldn't have gotten in my car if you wouldn't." He smirked, and I felt like launching myself at him and choking him with his seat belt.

"I got in the car with you for a ride home, not so I could be close to you." I was glaring intensely at Austin. "May I remind you that I still can't stand you after what you did to me?"

"Oh please, Carter." He laughed smugly, which only made me angrier. "If you hate me so much, then what are you still doing here?"

"You know what?" I forced a smile. "That's a *good* fucking question."

And with that, I opened the car door in the middle of the red light and walked out, looking back to watch his face drop. I continued across the empty street and to the sidewalk, ignoring his muscle car's incessant honking.

My house couldn't be that far; we'd already made it halfway there. I knew I was alone, out late at night, in flats, but that was better than being in a car alone with him.

FORTY-THREE

[HARRY]

I looked all over as I followed my GPS to Austin's house, hoping to see his stupid, ugly yellow car. My phone was clutched in my hand. After having called a million times, Carter had never answered. So I held it, in the hopes that she'd call me back. I knew it'd never happen, but all I could do was hope. My lips were trembling, my chest was aching, and I'm sure my eyes were twitching.

The sad music playing on the radio wasn't helping, either. It was irritating me how there were nothing but songs about love or heartbreak on, tonight of all nights.

Eventually, I had to shut it off and drive in silence, which only made me more miserable.

I knew Carter didn't want anything to do with me. But I didn't care. I was going to have to try. No matter how much she would want to avoid me, I wouldn't stop until she'd heard the truth. This was something she had to know, and she had to hear me out. I would spam her phone to no end until she listened. I wasn't going to sit back and do nothing about this. I couldn't let myself take the blame on something I didn't do. Fuck no, not this time. I had learned from my past. The sooner I told the truth, the better.

My phone began to ring, and without a glance, I answered it immediately.

"Hello? Carter?" I answered helplessly, but I was disappointed when I heard Ryan's voice instead.

"Hey, we told Dylan that Austin was with Carter," he said.

"Did you tell him about what happened? Does he know I had nothing to do with Carter's picture?" I asked.

"No," Ryan said grimly, and I heard shuffling on the other end before AJ started speaking.

"When Ry passed the phone to me, Dylan didn't even give me a chance to say a word before he hung up," he said, and I sighed in disappointment.

"We weren't sure whether he hung up because he set off to look for her more or because he genuinely didn't want to talk to AJ," Ryan said, and I believed them. Knowing Dylan, he was at least twice as stubborn as Carter.

"Look, don't worry about Dylan for now," I told them. "Eventually he'll have to listen to us. I just need Carter to know."

"The only way you'll get Carter to listen is if someone—who

isn't you—tells her," Ryan said, and it hurt to know he was right.

I groaned in agony. "I know, I know. *Fuck*, I'll see what I can do. I just want to fix this." I muttered the last part to myself and hung up before either of them could respond.

Still driving, I sat in wonder, knowing exactly who to call to help me, but also knowing the person I had in mind wouldn't even give me a single minute of their time.

[CARTER]

Naturally, it began to rain on my way home. It was only a drizzle, but it still made me shiver.

I'd shut my phone off, knowing my brother, Mitchell, Liz, and most likely Harry would be blowing up it like crazy. I needed time to be on my own.

I let myself cry on the way home, knowing it'd be better to let it out now than to randomly burst out in tears at home. The sound of a car's engine revving noisily made me jump, and I picked up the pace, nearly jogging. Every gust of wind through the trees or trashcan falling made me burst into a short sprint.

There were a couple of times when I turned corners onto streets I wasn't familiar with. At one point, I nearly ended up in Torrenhill, which wasn't the most pleasant area. I was just glad it wasn't that far from where I lived. There were more people lingering on street corners and leaning against buildings here, and it was making me uneasy, even though they weren't doing anything threatening or approaching me.

Eventually, I reached my neighborhood, and I slowed down again, catching my breath as I passed by the familiar streets. I felt like I was finally able to relax for a few moments until the memory of everything that'd happened began to replay in my head. I couldn't even begin to think about returning to school, going through another year after everyone had seen that photo, had seen that meltdown between me, Harry, AJ, and Dylan.

The moment I made it inside, I noticed my parents asleep on the couch together. It was nice to finally see them home at night rather than only in the morning.

I softly shut the door and tiptoed through the foyer. But of course, with my shitty luck and bit of leftover haziness from earlier, I bumped into a small table just as I turned the corner to make my way up the stairs. I thought it'd went by unnoticed when I heard a yawn from my mother.

"Carter? Dylan?" I heard her murmur in her sleepy state. I quickly went up a few steps so she wouldn't see my face. The last thing I wanted was my mother wondering why I looked like a mess. I had yet to see myself, but I was certain I looked frightening.

"It's just me, Mom. Dylan's not here yet," I called out with a forced neutral voice. I jogged up the steps and said, "I'm heading up to shower, then I'm going to sleep."

I didn't wait for my mother to reply; the minute I stepped inside my room, I sat down heavily right on the floor. I felt like shit, not only mentally, but physically. My face felt like it had melted off, my body trembled, and I was a little sweaty from running despite the rain. My mop of wet hair felt foreign and filthy, and I just wanted to wash it all away along with my emotions and exhaustion. I crawled across the floor to my dresser and pulled out a massive graphic T-shirt and my cheap biker shorts. After kicking off my shoes, I made myself trudge toward the bathroom. It was extremely difficult for me to not look in the mirror, but based on a quick side-eyed glance, I looked as bad as I'd expected.

I showered for what must have been at least an hour. I just stood under the running water, blanked out like a total zombie. As the water cascaded down my bare body, all I did was remain motionless, hoping it'd release the tension in me. Unfortunately, it didn't do much as I had hoped. I couldn't say I was surprised, though.

I stepped out of my shower with my old robe wrapped around me just as I heard Dylan coming up the stairs.

"Carter," Dylan breathed out with wide eyes as he looked me up and down. "Thank fuck you're alive."

"Shit, I'm sorry. I know I must have scared you," I murmured, squinting at him. My eyes felt heavy and stung like hell.

"It's fine. I'm just glad you're okay and home safe. Where were you? When did you get here? Why did Austin take you home? In fact, how do you even know him—?"

"Dyl, please. One at a time." I held my hands up to pause his mini rant, feeling as if each question had come in through one ear and flown out the other. "I turned off my phone on my way here. Austin offered me a ride, but it didn't last long; I jumped out of the car in the middle of a red light and walked from there. I just needed to be by myself. I'm fine now." That was all I could tell my brother, honestly. Because I knew that if I told him I'd known Austin from dating him, he'd ask even more questions—questions I wasn't ready to answer.

"Is that all? I'd really like to go to bed," I said, and watched as he hesitated.

"Carter, I have to ask..." he began, and I felt a sudden wave of nervousness consume me. "Although I think I know the answer to this question, I just need to know...were you and Harry in a relationship behind my back?"

My eyes shifted to the ground, knowing whatever answer I gave him wouldn't matter because he already knew the truth, anyway. I looked back up at him morosely and nodded weakly. Dylan nodded in disappointment.

"Something told me you guys were secretly together, but... But I didn't want to believe it. I want to say that I'm so angry and betrayed, but Carter—" He let out an exasperated breath. He looked as if he were about to cry as he pulled me into a hug. "I'm just glad you're safe."

It was another push over the edge. Tears automatically fell; I had hoped that I had already cried as much as I could, but apparently not. I sobbed against my brother's shoulder as I hugged him back.

"Hey, listen, look at me—" he said, trying to pry me off him to see my face. But I refused to let him go. My grip only tightened. Eventually, he gave up on pushing me off, and he softly wrapped his arms around my shoulders.

"I loved him," I cried out. My brother tensed at my confession but then released his muscles with a long breath.

"You should've listened to me when I told you to stay away," he mumbled against me. For once, I actually regretted not listening to Dylan. Of course, Harry had had a way with words; he had me swooning with everything he'd said to me.

"Give me your phone," Dylan suddenly requested, finally pulling away from me.

"You can't take it away. I need to talk to Mitchell, at least."

"I'm not taking it away," Dylan said, the sincerity in his eyes letting me know he was telling the truth. So I unlocked my phone and handed it to him. He fiddled with it for just a few moments before handing it back.

"What did you do?" I asked, looking to see what he'd messed with. But he had been smart and cleared out all of my recently used apps.

"Just trust me, Carter," he said with weary eyes. "Get some sleep. We both need it." With that, he gently left me to go to my room.

I knew I wasn't going to sleep well, though, and the moment my face hit my pillow, I was instantly shedding countless tears.

FORTY-FOUR

For a moment, I felt like everything that had happened within the last twelve hours had all just been a nightmare—a game someone had been playing on me just to scare me.

But seeing all of my used tissues scattered all over my bed and on the floor sobered me. I felt weak, like I didn't have the least bit of strength to sit up or even move. All I could do was lie there while I stared up at my ceiling, watching the fan spin rapidly, thinking that that was my life now—spinning endlessly. It wasn't until my door creaked open that I moved, turning my head to see who it was.

"Good morning, Carter," Mitchell said with a small, sympathetic smile. His head was poking in through the door, and I wanted to laugh at how that made it seem like his skull was floating. But I couldn't even do that.

"Hi," was all I could manage to say. My arms eventually obeyed to lift me a little.

Mitchell walked into the room, holding a bag from a local supermarket. "Can I ask how you're feeling?"

I shrugged, my eyes stinging as I fought to keep them open. "I've been better," I muttered, rubbing my eyes tiredly.

"Well, I hope this makes you feel better," he said, placing the bag in front of me gently. I opened it and saw a fruit salad and a few other snacks.

"I know that stuff is like crack to you," he joked, clearly trying to make me laugh. But nothing came out. I felt dead inside. "Carter, seriously, how are you feeling?"

Suddenly, the rush of raw emotions I thought I must have surely cried out came flooding back in. I didn't know how to answer. How *was* I feeling?

"I don't know," I mumbled, shrugging as I shoved three spoonfuls of Nutella and then two slices of green apple in my mouth. "Can we not talk about it? Like, I think it would be better for me if we pretended like it didn't happen."

Mitchell shook his head at me. "Carter, don't do this to yourself. We have to talk about it eventually—"

"Yeah, well, I don't want to."

"You can't go through this alone, not again. I won't let you—"

"I don't want to talk about it, and that's final," I snapped. There was a heat in my throat like I might cry yet again.

Mitchell sighed, shifting uncomfortably on my bed before

nodding and looking elsewhere.

"I'm sorry," I told him, my fingers fidgeting with the spoon dug into my Nutella. "It still feels unreal to me. But anyway, tell me about your night. What happened on your end? Did you meet anyone?"

Mitchell grinned at me, then looked down at his fingers, tracing my duvet patterns as crimson shaded his cheeks.

I gasped, happy for the distraction. "You *did!* Oh my god, tell me about him, who was he?"

"No one important," he said smugly.

I tried to smile—I forced it, actually. "*Come on*, tell me. Who?"

"Well, he's this guy."

"Obviously," I remarked, rolling my eyes playfully.

"Shut up," he said, shoving my shoulder lightly. "Anyway, we didn't talk much. I mean, we did, but I don't know; it's complicated."

"How come?" I asked.

"Because..." Mitchell trailed off, pausing and leaving me on the edge of my seat. I wanted to push him, but I could tell he was struggling, not drumming up excitement on purpose. "The thing is, he's not out yet."

"Oh..." was all I said. Mitchell nodded with a sad smile on his face.

"It's not like it's a huge deal-breaker or anything, but I don't know, like, it's new for me. I can't say anything about it because we kinda only just met, so I'm gonna get to know him some more and see where it goes from there. He's pretty cool so far, though.

Really good-looking, too."

"Oh?" I wiggled my brows. "Do tell. In what way?

Mitchell clicked his tongue against the roof of his mouth as he looked off in wonder. "It's hard to describe, but okay. So, if it were up to me, I'd say he's like a mix of Jesse Williams and Michael B. Jordan. Like, if they had a lovechild, it would be him."

I started to laugh, really laugh, my head thrown back as I tried, and I mean *really* tried, to get a mental image of this guy. "No way."

"I'm serious!" Mitchell smiled excitedly. "And the best part is, he's not clingy or into that lovey-dovey bullshit."

"And that's a good thing?"

"Oh, come on. Anyway, that's basically it—like, that's about as much as I know about him right now. Although," he said before grunting, rolling his eyes dramatically, "I would've known more if it hadn't been for Michael Garcia. Carter, do you remember him?"

Michael was this guy we'd met back in sophomore year who Mitchell didn't hate, but definitely didn't like, either. He was the iffy kind with a big ego. Mitchell had also said that apparently, he was the type to point out your flaws. Mitchell's reasons for disliking him were because of his suspiciousness and backhanded compliments.

"What did he do?" I asked, bringing my knees up to my chest.

"Well, when you disappeared, he gave me a backhanded compliment—*as per usual*—and legit compared himself to me, trying to be subtle, but clearly not trying hard enough. And then he had the nerve to even diss my outfit, saying it looked like hand-me-downs. I was about to fight a bitch. Carter, I swear, he was begging for me to snap." I laughed again as Mitchell went on with his tirade. "I might've popped off if not for—well, anyway," he ended awkwardly. I winced. After a couple moments of tense silence, he spoke up again, "Has he tried contacting you?"

I slowly looked for my phone before finally finding it under my pillow. One part of me hoped my notifications were clear, while another was begging to find something from him.

But there was nothing from Harry—just the calls and texts from Dylan, Mitchell, Elizabeth, even Ryan and A.J. I looked up at Mitchell, shaking my head sadly before tossing my phone behind me.

Mitchell tried to smile in order to lighten the mood. "Well... It's for the best."

FORTY-FIVE

[HARRY]

I'd made it to Galloway's house last night, but Austin either hadn't been there or had done a damn good job of ignoring the way I'd pounded on his front door. I'd tried to look inside his garage to see if his car was there, but the windows were too high. After I'd finally given that up, I was out until almost three in the morning driving around looking for Carter. At last, Ryan texted me that Dylan had found Carter and she was home safe. I'd sighed in relief, and before I knew it, I'd driven to her house. With the utmost confidence, I was seconds from knocking on the front door when it swung open. Dylan had come out and gripped me by the arm before dragging me away.

We'd practically had a screaming match on the front lawn, and it was surprising that Carter hadn't heard a thing. The argument went on for a while, till nearly four in the morning. After my countless attempts of trying to push past him to get in the house to see her, not caring about their parents, Dylan was aggressive, more than I'd ever seen him be, to the point where he pinned me to the ground. After that, I'd left, not wanting to get in a fight with him.

I'd driven back to my house and gone straight to bed, where I'd tossed and turned in my damp, grassy clothes. By five, I had cooled down but was unable to sleep. I relentlessly scrolled through my old conversations with Carter.

I went through my other texts and realized that AJ must have deleted our conversation to clear the evidence.

I went back to my messages with Carter. I could not imagine what she was feeling or would have to face on Monday. The things people might say to her and how they could affect her mentally— it scared me.

The thought was beginning to make me feel sick.

Okay, relax, Harry. Focus on fixing the problem with Carter. That's your main priority right now. You need to do this.

Me: Carter, we need to talk. I don't care what you say or do, you're gonna hear me out. You have to know that I'm innocent, and I didn't do what you think I did. Please let me explain. I'm glad you got home safe. I love you.

I noticed that the little "Delivered" notification beneath my message was nowhere to be seen.

> **Me:** is your phone dead

Still nothing.

> **Me:** or did you block me?

6:41 AM
> **Me:** baby…
> **Me:** baby please
> **Me:** I love you
> **Me:** I hope you're okay

At one point I even tried messaging her on Instagram, but that's when I realized I'd definitely been blocked, because I couldn't find her on it or any other app.

7:39 AM
> **Me:** you should be waking up soon unless you haven't gone to sleep yet
> **Me:** but then that would mean you're awake and your phone is on
> **Me:** but that's also if it isn't definitely dead of course

7:57 AM

Me: Carter, please.

8:04 AM

Me: I need to talk to you

Me: this is driving me insane

Me: hopefully you wake up, charge your phone, and get all of these messages

8:16 AM

Me: I'm not giving up on us

Me: and I can only hope you won't either...

I felt a little unstable. I couldn't let myself register the fact that Carter had blocked me. I wasn't going to let it stop me, though. No. No way. Absolutely not. I decided I would go to her right then; God knows I couldn't wait. I needed her. I loved her too much to let her go. She had to know what had really happened. I had to go see her.

I stood up abruptly and started slipping on my shoes as the door cracked open. But I didn't pay attention as I searched for my keys.

"Hey, you're up. Your sister should be here any second," my mother chirped, poking her head in my bedroom door as I continued to search from drawer to drawer. "When is Carter coming?"

At the mention of her name, I glanced over at my mother, who was looking at me expectantly.

"Wait, what?" I asked.

Fuck. That's right. She was supposed to come for dinner to meet Emma.

My mother sighed, rolling her eyes before repeating herself. "Your sister is coming, and I'm asking when Carter is going to arrive."

I bit my lip, looking down at my feet. I sighed before finally answering her, "Carter's not coming."

My mother's face dropped at my words. She frowned with furrowed brows. "What do you mean she's not coming? Why? Is she still intimidated by Emma? Harry, I told you to tell her that she—"

"No, Em has nothing to do with it," I breathed out helplessly, sitting back on the edge of my bed. She noticed my weary expression and sat beside me, one hand on my back.

"Then what is it? Is everything all right?"

"No, everything's just... I don't know, it's a mess," I told her honestly, and before she could ask further questions, I cut her off. "But I don't want to talk about me and Carter's...uh, relationship. Not while Emma's here."

"But that's the only reason she's so excited to visit, Harry—"

"Well, there's plenty of other things we can talk about," I snapped. I watched as she pursed her lips and nodded silently. I hadn't meant to come off as rude or anything; I just genuinely didn't want the attention on me and Carter's problems throughout dinner.

It was silent for a moment. Her expression was sad as she sat there, probably waiting for me to open up to her and tell her what was going on. I fell back onto my bed and closed my eyes.

"Do I have to stay?" I asked, and I could already feel the disapproval.

"Of course you have to stay. Harry, your sister came a long way to see us. You haven't seen her for a whole semester."

"Okay, what if I hang out with Emma, then go out? And I'll be back for dinner?"

She pressed her lips into a thin line. "I'll consider it." And with that, she stood and walked out.

I awoke to the sound of loud greetings and laughter in the main hallway downstairs. I hadn't even realized I'd fallen asleep; seeing as I had been awake for twenty-hour hours, I certainly needed it.

I tried to compose myself, trudging down the stairs. As much as I wanted to look presentable for my sister, I knew I looked like total shit. And knowing her, she'd pester me about my appearance throughout the entire dinner. Then my mom would tell her what had happened, and my sister would probably tease me about not being able to keep a girlfriend. Then I'd say she was right and continue hating myself for losing Carter. My mom would try to reassure me and tell me positive things I probably wouldn't even need to hear, and my stepdad would awkwardly pat my shoulder. The cliché-ness of my family was on a whole other level.

The second I made it to the foyer, my sister turned to me with a bright smile, arms open as she walked towards me gleefully. I wished I could feel the same.

"Harry!" she squealed, hugging me in a tight embrace. She was wearing a nice blouse and a skirt, and I was painfully aware of the fact I still hadn't changed.

"Hi, Em." I chuckled against her, trying to sound as neutral as possible, though I was sure my groggy voice had thrown her off.

"What's with the voice? Did you finally hit puberty?" she said before turning back to my mother. "Hey Mom, from which side of the family did Harry get the late bloomer gene from again?" I playfully shoved her away, earning a punch to my shoulder.

My mother stepped in between us with a stern look on her face. "Emma's been here for three minutes, and you two are already about to kill each other. It's not even noon."

My sister put a hand on her chest, pretending to be wholehearted as she crowed, "Just like old times."

"Just let them be, Amelia," Ben chuckled, sending us a wink. Emma and I went to the living room, trying to trip and shove each other the whole way, while Ben went to get the grill started and my mom dipped into the kitchen.

"So, are you excited to finish high school?" Emma asked as she sat in the loveseat.

I forced a bright smile and nodded. "Yeah. But, I'm a little scared to start a new life once I'm out of here."

"Ah, you'll be fine." She grinned. "I mean, it's scary at first, like it should be. But you get the hang of it after a while. As long as you have the right kind of support, you'll be good."

I nodded once more, unsure what to say. And in all honesty, I couldn't care less about what my future held if it didn't have Carter in it.

"So, who's this 'Carly' Mom keeps blabbering about?"

I sighed before speaking, "It's Carter. And she... She was my girlfriend."

"*Was?*" my sister asked with a raised brow.

"Was," I repeated before going on. "We had a... I guess you could say a falling out." Based on the way my sister's facial expression twisted in amusement, I knew she was going to make a remark I couldn't handle. So I cut her off. "Em, please don't. I was, and still am, in love with her."

Emma's face softened at my words, and she even looked a little guilty. "Well, I was wondering why you looked so awful. Why'd she break up with you?"

This was something I had wanted to avoid throughout this whole visit. But I would rather my sister know than my own mother; it was a sibling thing, and I was grateful to be able to share that kind of bond with her.

Especially now.

"Truthfully? It was basically another Stacy Kavanaugh moment."

Emma's dark eyebrows furrowed. "You were accused of sleeping with her? But wasn't she your girlfriend? Did she have another boyfriend? I don't get it."

"No." I shook my head. "I was just accused, in general, of doing something I would never do to her."

"Like what?" she asked softly.

I sucked in a breath, knowing this was something I definitely couldn't tell her. Who knew what she'd think of Carter before even getting to meet her. "Let's just say something extremely personal of hers got out that was only meant for me," I said.

Emma shifted in her seat uncomfortably before going on, "Okay, I think I have an idea of what it could be. Do you mind me asking how exactly it got out, though?"

"Someone took my phone when I wasn't looking."

My sister frowned, and before she could say anything, my mother walked in with a bright smile, holding a plate of snacks, with Ben behind her.

"We'll talk later," Emma whispered.

The day dragged on, and I felt like I could sense every minute slide by. Eventually, Ben asked me to go out with him to the grill.

It was a beautiful day, and I resented how nice the weather was when I felt so horrible. But Ben didn't even open the grill, which was lightly smoking.

"So. I heard about you and Carter. What happened?"

I just stood there for a moment, exhaustion overwhelming me. "Everyone found out," I muttered.

"Everyone including her parents?"

"That, I'm not sure of," I told him honestly. Though I was sure if they'd known, they'd have been outside with torches and pitchforks by now.

"Basically the whole school found out, but in the worst way possible," I said, mentally begging for him to not make me further explain how and why, or ask for details. "I got accused of something I didn't do. Just like the Stacy thing. Carter hates me now."

Ben patted my shoulder, as expected. "I'm sorry... Listen, I've got this. Why don't you go upstairs and take a nap? Your mother didn't want to say anything, but you look like you'd been doing meth with those bags under your eyes."

I laughed, and gratefully nodded. "Thanks, I appreciate it," I said, and he gave me a small smile of reassurance.

Just as I made it to the stairs, he called to me, "Harry."

"Yes?"

"Do us both a favor, and get her back. Don't sit back and let her believe you did something you wouldn't." He looked pained while speaking. "I saw how much damage that last rumor did to you. Your mother would hate to see you go down that path again."

"Of course," I told him.

"Good." He smiled. "I'll be waiting for the day you both come through that door, together."

"Yeah," I whispered as I turned back towards the house. "Me too."

"Well, did she love you, too?" Emma asked.

I popped my head up from the pillow, startled and feeling a little delirious. Emma was sitting on the edge of my bed.

I sat up and slumped against the headboard. "She told me she did. And I believed her when she said it," I admitted.

"Well, I'm gonna tell you something that, though I know I shouldn't have to, I will anyway."

"Which is?"

"Win her back."

I gave her a look. "No shit."

"Shut up, let me finish." I nodded as she went on. "Look, I can tell this girl means something to you. And based on how shit you look, this whole thing clearly destroyed you."

"Wow, thanks, Em," I muttered.

"Harry, I'm serious," Emma retorted, and I looked up at her. "Fight for her. Fight for her until you get her back. And if she really loves you like she said she did, or does, I'm sure she'll come back."

I sat in awe at my sister's words. Eventually she stood, ruffled my greasy, gross hair, made a face at how disgusting it was, then walked away.

As silence took over the room again, I thought about getting up and going to Carter's house, regardless of what my mom wanted. But my head was starting to ache, and my limbs were so heavy. I wasn't in the right state of mind, honestly, and I was worried Dylan would actually physically fight me.

I lay down on the bed again, slowly succumbing to sleep. I thought, *I'd run circles around the world for Carter. I'll tell her tomorrow, at school, where she can't hide from me. Hell, I'll even tell the whole school. Fuck it. There's nothing to hide anymore. I'm in love with her, and it's something I'd want everyone to know.*

Especially her.

FORTY-SIX

I searched for Carter all day on Monday, but I couldn't find her. Her usual spot in the morning, empty. Her normal route to classes, no show. I was starting to worry. *Did she skip out today?* It wouldn't have surprised me, honestly, but the anxiety of being unable to reach her was ruining my stomach.

Yesterday, when I'd woken up right before dinner, I'd texted Carter in hopes I'd been unblocked. I'd even tried calling. But my calls had gone straight to voicemail after a single ring, and my messages stayed undelivered. I thought about DMing Mitchell or Elizabeth, but I didn't want them to be my messengers. I needed to talk to Carter directly.

I stood dumbly in the hallway, just praying Carter would show. I got multiple stares, smirks, and, as expected, disgusted looks from everyone who passed by. But I didn't pay much mind. They didn't know the truth, and though I was determined to set the record straight, at the moment, my main focus was Carter.

Of course, each class before fourth period dragged on. I had to sit impatiently throughout each lesson, helplessly staring at the clock. It felt like death.

Finally, after what felt like years of waiting, the bell rang, and I stumbled over a few tables as I rushed towards the door. I practically flew out, pushing past people and accidentally shoving them, muttering *Sorry* left and right. They were whispering about me now.

"That's him."

"That's the guy that fucked over Carter Matthews?"

"That Harry guy took advantage of Dylan's little sister. His own best friend!" "Why would he do that to them both?"

"What an asshole."

I did the only thing I could, and stopped in the middle of the hall.

"Hey!" I called out, grabbing everyone's attention. "Maybe you should know both sides of the story. I would never have hurt Carter like that. I had nothing to do with what happened at the party." I considered saying more, but decided to leave it at that.

I turned back and continued towards the art department, hearing mutters and mumbled insults the whole way. But I didn't care.

When the late bell rang, I ran in. As I stepped into the room, my eyes were all over the place in search of long brown hair and ocean blue eyes. And as I saw the room was filled with my usual fourth period classmates, I realized my suspicions were confirmed: she hadn't shown up at all.

The next day, Carter skipped again. When I got home that Tuesday, I thought of calling her again, but through my house phone. There was no way she'd blocked that number. So after I dialed, I waited for her to answer. I waited, and waited, and waited, and *still* waited. The tone rang one final time until I heard a click... I held my breath, but then the line disconnected. My hopes of hearing her voice were crushed in an instant. I grunted as I slammed the phone back against the wall.

My desperation and anger were spiraling out of control more than ever as I paced throughout the house. I spent a good couple of hours working on my car in the garage, making minor tweaks, and believe me, I tried to find as many as I could to work on just to keep myself occupied. My phone was set on "Do Not Disturb." I wouldn't be bothered unless there was a notification or call from my favorites list, and my only favorite was Carter. I had to hear from her eventually. It wasn't until I looked up from my car that I realized it was dark out. And despite how long I'd been in there, I felt as if I hadn't done much at all.

On Wednesday, unable to focus on any of my work, I skipped my last period to sit in the courtyard as various students passed back and forth from building to building. Five minutes before the bell rang, I went to the parking lot and waited.

School let out and the lot flooded with students. I looked for the only people who would have seen Carter and *might* talk to me.

Finally, Mitchell waltzed out the doors.

"Mitchell," I called, watching as he walked faster. I jogged to meet him. "Mitch, where's Carter?" Still no response. "Has she been missing school? Is she okay?" I asked, stepping in front of him so he had to stop. "Mitch. Please."

"She's been absent," Mitchell grumbled, attempting to push past me, but I didn't let him.

"After what happened at Ryan's party," he said, staring right at me, his hazel eyes piercing, "I don't blame her for not showing her face here."

"Mitch, I—"

"Do you know how many times I've had to hear people call my best friend awful names for taking a picture? I had to use every inch of my very little patience to keep from going off on them. And I have no problem using all my held-in anger and energy on *you*."

"Mitchell, I didn't do it. I told you I was in love with her, I still am!" I shouted frantically, not caring that people could hear us. I needed to at least get *him* to listen to me. "I promise you, I would *never* do that to her."

"Yeah, *right*." He scoffed, taking a step away, but I stopped him again.

"What makes you think I would? You know me!"

"Apparently not well enough," he spat.

"I would never do that to her, come on. I'm innocent!" I was enraged, my blood beginning to boil.

"Harry, chill," Mitchell told me, suddenly calm, but I was far too angry to *chill*.

"No! Not until you believe me," I said. "I love her too much to hurt her. I swear, I didn't fucking do it!"

He crossed his arms. "Then who did?"

"Austin!"

I could see something flicker in his face.

By now, most people had cleared out, wanting to go home more than listen to the drama.

"What does Austin have to do with any of this?"

"*Everything*. He did it. He did *all* of this. It wasn't me. I was accused of this because of him, I promise you." My voice was cracked and strangled. "AJ confessed it all to me after you, Carter, Elizabeth, and Dylan left. He told me *everything*."

It was silent at first, as Mitchell thought it over. "You better not be lying," he warned with an icy glare.

"I swear. I'll tell you everything if you just give me a chance to explain."

I watched as Mitchell tightened his jaw, his nostrils flaring before he finally said, "Okay. Tell me everything."

FORTY-SEVEN

[CARTER]

Mitchell: carter

Mitchell: carter pick up

Mitchell: carter

Mitchell: carter I've called you like a bajillion times

Mitchell: CARTER

Mitchell: omfg you need to answer NOW!!!!

Mitchell: IT'S IMPORTANT

Mitchell: BRUH

Me: what omfg

Me: it's so hard to read when you're blowing up my phone fuck

Me: this better be worth it

Mitchell: it is, I promise

Mitchell: so something came up

Mitchell: you're never gonna believe this

Mitchell: but you're gonna have to. I can't call bc I actually need to pass this class.

Me: what is it?

Me: everything okay?

Me: did I miss something at school?

Mitchell: hell yeah you did

Me: well????

Me: what is it

Me: am I missing a project

Me: omg are we starting one in biology

Mitchell: no no it's nothing to do with school academically

Mitchell: carter

Mitchell: it's about harry

Me: .....what about him?

Me: actually

Me: no

Me: don't answer that

Me: I don't wanna know

Me: nor do I care

Me: the last person I wanna talk about is him and you know that

Mitchell: carter what I'm about to tell you is gonna

make you think otherwise ok

Mitchell: that boy is innocent

Me: wow seriously

Me: that's bullshit ok no he's not

Mitchell: yes he is you dumbass just listen to me

Me: no

Me: mitchell the proof was literally right there

Me: HE SENT THAT PICTURE TO HIS FRIEND

Me: I can't believe you'd take his side knowing that

Mitchell: yeah I'm aware but it didn't go down like that

Me: I don't care

Me: I don't care about him anymore

Me: so just stop

Mitchell: oh please

Mitchell: you and I both know that's complete bullshit

Mitchell: if you didn't care about him, you wouldn't be avoiding him

Mitchell: friendly reminder tho, you're gonna have to see him eventually when you come back

Mitchell: so tighten the fuck up

Mitchell: and listen

Me: you know damn well I'm not missing school because of him. he fucking humiliated me, so fuck him AND you

Mitchell: me??? for what, being a friend?? looking out for you, telling you that you're poor, heartbroken,

INNOCENT boyfriend is legitimately crying over your ass??

Mitchell: he's still fucking in love with you

Me: whatever

Me: he's not my boyfriend anymore

Me: and if he really so-called "loved" me, he'd have done something about it

Me: but he hasn't called or texted me ONCE

Me: so again, BULLSHIT

Me: whatever you have to say I don't give a single fuck

Me: bc it's bullshit

Me: you're supposed to be MY best friend

Mitchell: you're such a dumbass

Mitchell: I AM being a best friend which is more than I can say for you

Me: whatever mitch

Mitchell: you're the wrong one here

Mitchell: you're just too fucking hardheaded to realize that

Mitchell: so get your head out of your ass and fucking listen to me

Me: you know what

Me: bye

I didn't bother letting Mitchell finish once I saw he had begun typing. What else could there be for him to say? I didn't care enough to find out. It wasn't worth it anymore. I was trying to move on, and this wouldn't be doing me any service, so I hit the block button before he could send his last message. Some things were just better left unsaid.

[HARRY]

My mind was all over the place as I paced my room anxiously. Mitchell had told me he would talk to Carter for me, and get her to be willing to hear me out. I had never been so thankful, but the wait was killing me.

Then, my mom stepped into my room, practically singing.

"Okay, the executive from the St. John's University college board will be here on Friday!"

I balked at her. "When did we talk about that?"

My mother's cheery grin, bright with shiny lipstick, fell with frustration. "We talked about it during dinner when your Uncle Max was here. We even discussed it with your sister. Harry, were you not paying attention?"

I shrugged weakly. "I'm afraid not."

"Harry, we've been going on about this all week, prepping for your future. How could you have not—?"

"Mom, I have a lot of things on my plate," I told her, trying to refrain from sounding harsh, but my mixed emotions getting the better of me. "I couldn't care less about some ridiculous interview for some stupid school—"

"Harry!" My mother gasped at my words, eyes wide and clearly taken aback.

I breathed heavily, pushing my hair back.

"Listen, young man, I understand you're having a hard time with whatever is going on between you and Carter, but that should be the *least* of your worries right now."

"Well, I'm sorry if the only thing I can think about lately is my girlfriend and what she's going through. She means a lot to me—"

"And your education means nothing to you?!" my mother shouted, crossing her arms.

"Of course it does." I looked away, then back at her. "That's not my point, though—"

"Harry, you need to step back into reality. You two have only been together a few short weeks. Don't you think you're overreacting just a bit? You're going to college in New York, so regardless, you'd be too far from her to even keep a stable relationship," she said. Her voice softened. "Maybe what happened between you two was for the better."

"What makes you think she's the reason I don't wanna go anymore?" I shook my head in disbelief at her words. "I'm not saying I'm refusing college completely; I just don't want to go St. John's."

My mother looked at me in disapproval. But I didn't care. St. John's was never even my first option; it was just a school my parents had driven me into believing I was meant to go to.

Now, I didn't want it. And I couldn't believe it had taken me this long to realize that. I could study English at any college. So right then, I didn't care if I was ruining my chances of getting into St. John's University. It was the least of my worries, honestly.

"Harry, this school is your future," she finally said.

"To you, maybe. But maybe it's time I thought for myself and *my* future."

I needed to get away. With my mind crowded by too many thoughts to count, the best I could do was get away from my house, and especially from my parents. I couldn't handle the thought of them constantly pushing my life in the direction they wanted. It was my life, and I had every right to do what I wanted with it. Whether I ended up screwing it up entirely or becoming successful, my life depended on me and what I did. I had just been going after what my parents had wanted me to, and that was wrong. I couldn't think of what I really wanted to do in life when I'd had the idea of being led in another direction screwed so deep into my head.

I walked to the closest park, which was still half an hour away. But I didn't mind. I tried messaging Mitchell to ask for an update, but he never answered.

My mind wandered off to thoughts of Carter. It was both physically and mentally impossible to not think about her. Feeling like I'd lost her was an excruciating pain. I felt like I had pins and needles shoved so deep through my skin, they were poking at my heart, which was threatening to explode in my chest.

After finally making it to the park, I walked over to a bench by a large oak tree. Despite the loneliness, I still felt surrounded. I didn't know what to do. My best bet was to go over to Carter's place now. But her parents were most likely aware of what had happened, as I felt pretty sure Dylan had already told them. And I knew Carter probably needed time; everything that had happened had affected her far more than me. I didn't care about the extra weight in my shoulders—the weight being *another* rumor giving me *another* bad rep. As sad as it was, having gone through it once already made going through this mess look like nothing.

With my head hung low, my fingers tracing over my torn-up jeans, I felt a presence. And though I wanted to scream at this stranger to leave me alone, I decided to just stay on the bench quietly.

"Is this seat taken?" The voice was familiar. I looked up and saw a young woman. It took me a moment to realize who was standing before me. When I did, I felt my throat go dry.

"Stacy?" I nearly choked out. She smiled and took a seat next to me.

"I thought I recognized you," she said, her smile still as bright as I'd remembered. I was never all that close to Stacy, but I had considered her a friend before she'd roped me into her drama. We'd had two classes together, and we'd made each other laugh.

"What are you doing here?" I asked.

"Well, I'm in town visiting family since I just finished the spring term," she said. "I brought my nephews to the park, and I saw you here—looking a little bummed, I might add," she tried to joke, and I had to force an amused smile.

"Well, congrats on finishing out this year." I didn't want to hold a grudge against someone I hardly knew.

She smiled once again and said rather proudly, "Thanks. It was tough when I first started, but eventually you get the hang of it."

"So I've heard." I chuckled, remembering Emma's words. "What's tough about it?"

"Basically, in college, it's like...not as easygoing, per se, the way high school was," she said, stammering slightly. "It's stressful, if I'm being entirely honest. You have to change the way you view your classes."

"That makes me less excited for college," I said. To be honest, I never was excited for college; I just wanted to get away—or at least, back when I'd decided on St. John's, I'd been excited to get away. Not so much anymore. And besides, the thought alone of leaving and starting over somewhere scared me. Though I'd never admit it, I was scared of leaving a place I'd grown up in with a lot of people, to live in a different state where I didn't know a single person.

That, and Mitchell's words, which had been ringing in my head from the moment he'd said them: "*Isn't college the place where you make your own decisions and become independent?*" Yes, it is.

"But it's not all bad," Stacy continued. "You just have to be flexible, I guess."

"You guess?" I asked with a smirk.

"Look, I've only finished my second year. I don't have proper advice, and I won't have any until I graduate. Cut me some slack, I'm still struggling." She laughed, and I laughed along with her—a genuine laugh—which made me feel kind of good. "So, how are you? If you don't mind me asking."

"I'm currently going through a rough patch," I admitted.

"Trouble in paradise?" she asked sincerely.

"It's, uh...history repeating itself, I guess you could say."

"What does that mean?" she asked. I stammered for a moment, not wanting to bring back any unwanted memories, but unsure how else to break down the issue to her. And who knew? Given the fact that Stacy had gone through something similar to this, maybe she could give me some advice—only if she wanted to, of course.

"Well, I don't know how else to put this, and I definitely hate having to bring this up, but..." I shrugged before going on, Stacy's stare on me making me a little nervous and fidgety. "Basically, I was accused of something bad, and...my girlfriend, or should I say ex—I...I don't know what we are right now—she was humiliated, and—"

"Say no more," she said, sighing with sad eyes. "I know what you're referring to..."

I hadn't meant to make Stacy uncomfortable, but that was what it felt like I had done.

"Harry?" she suddenly said, and I looked up, meeting her blue eyes. Carter's were lighter, and warmer. "I just wanna say I'm sorry."

I shook my head, knowing what she meant. "You don't have to apologize. It was just—

"I just feel so bad."

"It doesn't matter anymore—"

"Yes, it does. I ruined someone's reputation along with my own, and, god, it was so awful having to suffer through all of that drama with Danny, and I can't believe you were in the middle of it. The way he hurt you and—" She shuddered at the memory. "Can you just do me a favor?"

"Stacy, just forget about it," I told her. "It's all over and done with—"

"Can you just—?"

"Don't worry about it—"

"Apologize to Dylan for me."

I furrowed my eyebrows, taken aback by her request. Dylan? Apologize to Dylan? For *what?*

"Uh..." I said, unsure what she meant or why she wanted me to do such a thing. "Apologize to Dylan for what?"

She looked confused but answered, nonetheless, "For ruining his reputation..."

An awkward silence followed until I chuckled nervously. "I think you're mistaken."

"No, I ruined it. When I cheated on Danny with him, everyone found out and started to hate him, and I just feel so bad. And then when you defended him, and Danny attacked you for it—it was just awful."

"Wait," I stopped her, my heart beating wildly at this newfound information. "You really cheated on Danny? With Dylan?" Stacy nodded, looking confused, and I suddenly felt nauseous. I wanted to throw up. *What the hell? So Dylan slept with Stacy? Her cheating on Danny wasn't just a rumor? But how did I become the target?*

"But...if you did it with Dylan...then how did...?" And suddenly, realization hit me, and I balled my fists and abruptly stood up in anger, startling Stacy.

"Are you okay?" she asked, and I nodded, turning to her once more.

"Yeah. For the record, I didn't defend Dylan. Everyone thought that I was the one you slept with. But, honestly, Stacy, I'm so over that."

She stared at me in shock.

"I need to go," I announced. "I have something to deal with."

FORTY-EIGHT

[CARTER]

This was the third day I had skipped school. To my surprise, I had yet to get caught; I had been calling in pretending to be my parents and excusing my absences.

Dylan had promised not to rat me out the first two days, considering he'd do anything to keep me and Harry a safe distance away from each other. Not that I minded; it was sweet, really. He'd come straight home and check on me instead of locking himself in his bedroom till dinner like usual.

This morning, Dylan had tried to finally get me to go to school. I'd begged him to just let me miss one more day, and he'd relented. So I decided to actually ask my parents if I could stay home, since they had the night shift, and I knew that if they saw that I was still in bed when they got up, I'd be caught.

As Dylan was getting his stuff together, I walked to my parents' dark room and asked to stay, claiming I was sick. When my dad turned on the lamp on the bedside table, I flinched from the light. That's when my mom started sounding worried, talking about the heavy circles under my eyes and my pale skin. I just nodded and went back to bed.

Every time I thought about going to school, my nerves got the best of me, and I got incredibly anxious. Cooped up in my bed with my duvet clenched in my fists, I continued sobbing to no end, hoping and even praying this was going to end. Each time I thought I was doing better, a tidal wave of emotions washed over me like one big *Fuck that, keep crying.* It was endless, and my chest just hurt nonstop.

On top of all of that, the fact that my own best friend had been brainwashed by Harry and convinced that he was innocent was really it for me. I was sure Elizabeth had taken his side, too. Despite now having Dylan, it wasn't the same; I needed my best friends.

I heard my door creak open, and I tried to blink back any tears. Why now? I'd been doing so well hiding my emotions.

"Carter?" my dad asked. I didn't want to turn around, but I knew that if I didn't, it would only make the situation seem worse than it already did. "Sweetie, what's wrong?"

I felt my dad sit on the edge of the bed, the mattress dipping. I wiped at my eyes with the sleeves of my sweatshirt so it didn't look obvious that I'd been full-on sobbing.

"Nothing," I croaked, shaking my head and forcing a smile at him. He didn't look convinced.

"Something's wrong. Tell me, sweetie." I almost weakened at his compassion, only wanting to cry more. But how could I tell him that the boy I'd fallen in love with, the boy neither he nor my mother trusted, had broken my heart into pieces? Harry had exposed me. That's one of the few things a father never wants to hear of his child.

"It's... It's just finals, Dad," I lied once again, using the same line I'd used the last time I'd had my heart broken. "The tests are only getting harder, and it's just freaking me out."

My father clicked his tongue against his teeth. "Aw, Car-Car." He scooted closer and pulled me into his strong arms. "Don't stress yourself out about it too much," he said, patting my head. "You can make it through this. You're much stronger than you think. Hell, you're stronger than me." He kissed my forehead, his mustache tickling me.

"I've seen you get through this before, and you only came out stronger. This time, you might even double your strength," he went on. "Don't let anything make you think otherwise."

Somehow, I felt like he wasn't talking about finals anymore. Still, I refused to question it as I nodded against his chest. After a moment, he let me go.

"Listen, your mother and I are going to go out and get some groceries. Why don't you come with us? It could get your mind off things for a while." He smiled, full of sympathy.

"I'll let you know in a bit."

He nodded, then stood and walked out of the room, leaving me with my thoughts once again.

[HARRY]

I sped off to Carter's. Not only did I need to see her, but now I hoped Dylan was there so I could confront him and get him to admit the truth.

This is it. It all makes sense now. Everything became clear to me. The memories flooded back of all the taunting and awful things said *to* or *about* me.

That was why Dylan had stuck by me, pitying me. I'd taken the praise, sure, but also the beatings and rumors and harsh treatment. He'd just stood back and watched me accept it.

For the past two years, I'd taken all of the bullshit he'd deserved, yet he hadn't said a thing. I should have known. How the fuck did I not realize it? How had I been so blind? There I'd been, thinking people had just decided to accuse me, when in reality, it was my so-called *best friend* who had targeted me in the very beginning. I felt like a fucking idiot.

I tried calling Mitchell a few times, but he didn't answer. Finally, I made it to Carter and Dylan's. I drove slowly as I eyed the house. It felt like I hadn't been there in forever. The atmosphere seemed suddenly eerie.

I shook off the sudden jitters and parked up front by the sidewalk, then jumped out of the car and ran to the door. I hesitated for a moment as I faced the mahogany before me, but, deciding to go with my gut, I pounded my fist against the door. There was no answer at first, so I pounded again. After the third try, I hit harder and much faster, growing impatient, until the door swung open.

At first, my heart leapt out of my chest, and I tried to smile in case it was her. But it was Dylan.

"What are you doing here?" he snarled the moment he realized it was me. I glared back at him, and with full force, I shoved past him and took long strides towards the stairs. The minute I reached the first step, I was pulled back by my wrist and pushed roughly against a wall.

"What the hell are you doing here?" he repeated.

"Where's Carter?" I asked. "Carter! Carter, talk to me!" I called out up the stairs.

"She's not here—"

"Carter!" I screamed again, pushing Dylan off me and attempting to go up the stairs once more. "Please talk to me!"

"She's not here!" Dylan shouted again, pushing me once more as he looked at me with a clenched jaw. "She went out. She doesn't wanna see you; nobody does!"

"You're a fucking asshole!"

"*Me?* Who was the one who betrayed my sister?"

"Who was the one that betrayed their *best* friend and let them get accused of something they didn't do?!" I screamed back. Dylan went silent, eyebrows furrowed as he shook his head in confusion. *Fucking typical.*

394

"What are you—?"

"You know *exactly* what the fuck I'm talking about," I growled, stepping forward as I glared at him, my voice lowering. "I wasn't the one who slept with Stacy."

Suddenly, Dylan's face went pale. "I don't know what you're talking about—"

"Why the fuck did you do that to me?" I yelled, shoving him hard enough that he stumbled away, not fighting back. "You ruined my life. You backstabbed me and kept it from me for the past two years. Why?"

Slowly, barely meeting my eyes, he said, "I don't know what you're talking about, Harry, I—"

"*Don't fucking deny it!*" I'd never been this loud before, and I sounded intimidating to my own ears. "I know. I know everything. And I just can't seem to figure out why you'd do that."

"Harry, get out—"

"Why did you do it, Dylan?"

"Harry, my parents are gonna be home soon, and Carter is not gonna be happy when she sees you—"

"Tell me why you did it!"

"Get out!" Dylan shouted, finally pushing me back; my head slammed hard against the solid wall. I felt Dylan grab ahold of my shirt as I was slowly regaining my balance. He marched me to the door, and I was suddenly thrown out of the house. I stumbled as I stood, and he immediately shut the door; I heard the deadbolt lock. I pounded on the door until my hand heart.

"Fuck!" I screamed, pacing for a moment before my phone began to ring. I walked to my car and took several deep breaths. "Hey, Mitchell, what happened? Did you tell her?"

"Sorry I didn't pick up the first time. And no, the stupid bitch didn't even let me explain." Mitchell grunted.

"Don't call her that. How come?" I asked as I opened my car door and got in.

"Long story; I'd have to show you the texts. Let's meet up tomorrow so I can tell you. School is closed for last minute teacher planning, anyway."

"I can't tomorrow, I have to pick up some things for my sister before she leaves this weekend," I said.

"Why are you breathing so hard? Did I just interrupt something—?"

"No." I shook my head, though he couldn't see me. "I just had an argument with Dylan."

"Whoa." Mitchell gasped. "What happened?"

I huffed before responding, "It's complicated. I'll talk to you later, all right? I have to go."

"Sure. Later."

[CARTER]
I had never felt so relaxed, even if it was just for a couple hours.

I felt tired, in a satisfying way, without having to think about *him*.

All in all, I was kind of starting to miss Mitchell more than I missed Harry. I really wanted to talk to my best friend, but I thought I'd put our friendship on really bad terms. And knowing Mitchell and how petty he could be at times, I knew he wouldn't give me the time of day, and that frightened me even more. I could only hope he'd forgive me for being so bitter and ignorant to him. I just couldn't stand to think or talk about Harry after trying so hard to get over him; hell, I was *still* trying. And today I had actually managed to not think of him for a little while.

Perhaps I would hang out with Elizabeth over the weekend if she wasn't busy.

I helped my parents unload groceries, and when I went upstairs, I found Dylan in his room, the door actually open for once.

"Oh, shit. You're back. Hi," he breathed.

"Hi?" I replied questioningly. "Are you okay?"

"Yeah." He nodded frantically. "Are you? Where were you?"

I shrugged, heading to my room with Dylan following behind. "I'm okay. I went out with Mom and Dad. We did some chores, I guess. Then we went out for shakes at Steak 'n Shake."

Dylan only nodded, a bored look plastered on his face as if completely uninterested in what I was saying. I wasn't offended; it wasn't that interesting of an answer. Plus, I noticed how pale his face was now that I was getting a better look at him.

"Dyl?" I asked, and he hummed in response. "Are you sure you're okay? You look like you've seen a ghost."

Dylan's breath hitched in his throat. "I'm fine... I just..." He hesitated before speaking again, his breathing now harsh, "Carter,

I need to... I have a... I..."

He was at a loss for words, which was rare for him, and his entire demeanor seemed completely off. He didn't look like himself, and it was starting to scare me.

"Dylan." I went up to him and put my hands on his shoulders, then shook him a little. "What's wrong? You're worrying me."

He turned away. "Nothing... Nothing. I just had a..." Dylan huffed before finally answering, "A weird dream, is all." He left my room almost immediately. Knowing Dyl, if I questioned him too much, he would only shut me out even more. I just hoped it was nothing too concerning.

FORTY-NINE

[HARRY]

"So, she didn't even let you explain?"

"Literally, Harry, the second I texted her *everything*, she had already blocked me. Like, what the fuck?" Mitchell shook his head as we drove around. Mitchell had asked me for a ride since his stepsister was busy. I'd debated on it at first, but it wasn't like I had anything else to do.

"What about Instagram?" I asked.

Mitchell clicked his tongue against his teeth before answering, "The bitch never even goes on there..."

"She's just being stubborn. You're her best friend; she'll come around and unblock you. I mean, it's you," I told him. "You probably know her better than I do."

"The only difference is *you're* madly in love with her," he said quietly, looking out his window.

"I don't think I could ever stop."

"Harry," Mitchell said, turning to me. I was too focused on the road to look back at him. "If you love her *so* much, why aren't you doing anything right now?"

"Look, despite the fact that she's been missing school, she's almost never home when I go to her place. Every time I *try*, something or someone stops me. I even tried calling her from a different phone, but that clearly didn't work out."

"She doesn't talk to unknown numbers," he said, still eyeing me sorrowfully. It was quiet for a while, until Mitchell finally spoke up again, "Harry?"

"Hm?"

"What if she never gives you another chance?"

"Don't say that." I shook my head. "I'm hopeful. She just has the wrong idea about me. I can change that."

"I'm only thinking of the *what if*s," he said much more seriously. "Regardless, aren't you going to that fancy-shmancy school in New York? I have nothing but faith in you two working things out, but I'm just speaking the truth when I say that long-distance relationships *never*—"

"We'd make it work," I cut in. "However, that would only be if I *was* leaving."

"What do you mean by that?" Mitchell asked curiously.

I took a while to respond before finally saying, "I'm not going to St. John's." I heard nothing from him, but from the corner of my eye I could see his jaw had dropped dramatically. "I passed it up to stay. I only needed two seconds to consider it, and I realized I couldn't go... You know, you were right about everything. I should be more independent for *myself* and about what *I* want. Not my parents, not even Carter. Not anyone else. *Me*."

After a couple moments of silence, Mitchell finally spoke, "Wow. I'm happy for you, Harry. Really. That's good." I merely nodded and pulled into the Square.

"What are you gonna do here, anyway?"

"I'm meeting someone," Mitchell said shyly as he got out of the car. Before he closed the door, he turned to me once more with a small smile. "Anyway, look, I know my best friend is being stupid right now. But just know I'm still holding out hope for you both... I'm the fucking captain of this Harter ship."

"Harter?" I asked, smiling at the funny word.

"Harry and Carter meshed together. God, Harry, get with the program!" Mitchell huffed, shutting the passenger door, and stalked off to one of the stores. I laughed as I took off, the ride to my house thankfully being a short one. I had to blare music and sing along just so my mind could revolve around anything but Carter.

Once I'd made it to my house, I walked up to my door, my head slowly pounding. I could feel a slight headache coming on as I opened the door and walked in; I was ready to just be in my bed and sleep the weekend away.

[*CARTER*]

My eyes had been squinty and tired all week, and the bright lights in the coffee shop weren't helping. Yawning again, I checked the time on my phone. I considered that I had become accustomed to the dark throughout this week, as morbid as that thought was.

My fingers drummed on the screen of my phone as I waited at a two-seater table. Eventually, the bell above the door chimed, and I was relieved to see Elizabeth.

"Hey, Carter!"

"Lizzie." I forced a smile as I stood up and pulled her into a hug. "How are you?"

"I should ask you the same thing," she said as we took our seats.

"I'm holding up." I chuckled, or at least *tried* to chuckle. I probably sounded like a dying mule.

"Well, I'm glad you called." Elizabeth smiled warmly at me. "I was starting to get worried about you."

"I think a lot of people were," I tried to joke, but Elizabeth didn't find it funny. "So, um. How is everything?"

"Everything's fine." She shrugged. "School's a drag, per usual. You haven't missed much."

"No one has asked about why I've been MIA?" I asked, hopeful that no one had noticed whatsoever.

"I mean, the truth?" she asked, and I nodded. "Well, at first people were talking. I heard rumors flying back and forth, though I tried to ignore them. But by the third day you missed school, no one seemed to care anymore."

"What were they saying?"

Elizabeth sighed, reaching over and placing her hands over mine. "It's best I don't repeat it."

I nodded feebly. "So how are you?"

"You already asked me that. But I assume you mean 'How's Mitchell?'" She smirked. "He's fine, just so you know. A little pissed off with you, but he's fine."

"What's he been up to?" I asked, swirling my finger around the table mindlessly.

"He's fine, he's just been hanging out with a friend." She shook her head, refusing to look me in the eye.

"Oh," was all I said at first. "What friend? Do I know them?"

Elizabeth shifted in her seat with an uncomfortable look on her face. "I'm not trying to play sides or get anyone in trouble, but I'm not going to lie, either: he's been with Harry."

It was quiet, as if all the noise around me had diminished.

"You know, it really wasn't Harry's fault."

I scoffed before replying, "Great, you too." I grabbed my things and stood up, but she gripped my wrist, stopping me.

"Carter, you're being *way* too stubborn. I understand you didn't wanna listen to Harry, but quite frankly, you were being unfair to Mitchell. But you're not gonna ignore me."

"Listen to Harry? What are you talking about? For someone who's trying so hard to prove his innocence, he seems to be doing it to everyone except me." I huffed, sitting back down with a scowl. "So? What do you need to tell me?"

"Harry's innocent," she said, and I wanted to bolt out the door.

"Lizzie, *everyone* literally saw—"

"Carter," Elizabeth warned with a glare. "There's more to the story than what you know. I'll tell you *everything*. And I think you should see Harry in person when I'm done."

⊚

My mind was rotating. I felt like I was trapped in a spinning teacup, going in circles for hours until I felt nauseous. My insides felt like they were floating, my throat constricting the more I thought about throwing up. But I wasn't going to puke in Elizabeth's car.

What Elizabeth had told me was making me rethink everything. From the party, to Harry and Dylan's friendship, to Harry trying to tell me he was innocent. And Mitchell, my own best friend, trying to tell me the truth, and me being an idiot and ignoring him.

The whole time I'd thought Harry didn't care about me enough to try and really talk to me, when in reality, it had to go from Harry to Mitchell to Elizabeth to tell me that he'd been blocked. It didn't take much for me to realize it was my brother who had done it the same night everything had blown up in my face.

I couldn't say I should have known it was Austin. I'd been too blinded and hurt to think it could have been anyone other than Harry. I'd had the thought of Harry playing with my feelings screwed so deep into my head since the beginning that I'd immediately blamed him without giving him a chance to explain. I felt like an idiot and an overall bitch. If it hadn't been for Elizabeth, I would probably still have been clueless and blaming Harry for something he hadn't done. God, I couldn't imagine how he must have felt—being blamed for something he'd had nothing to do with all over again. I hated myself at that point.

My stomach churned within every turn, and the closer I got to facing reality, the sicker I felt. But I didn't know if it was because I was excited, happy, scared, or flat-out nervous as hell. Perhaps all of them all at once. Maybe that's why I was feeling so sick; I didn't know what to feel. All I wanted to do was throw up.

"Lizzie," I breathed out, my insides twisting, "do you mind slowing down a bit?"

Elizabeth looked at me with a raised brow and an amused smile as she said, "Carter, I'm driving below the speed limit. Calm down."

I shook my head, swallowing the big lump in my throat. "I can't." My chest was starting to hurt. "I feel like I might fly out this car and puke like crazy, like my dad at every New Year's party."

"*Ooh.*" Elizabeth scrunched up her nose and cringed as she focused on the road. "That's a little dramatic. I remember how shocked my and Mitchell's parents were at that thing. Your dad vomited like he was in *The Exorcist.* Carter, I doubt that'll happen to you—that's if you do vomit, anyway. But if you do feel like you need to, please tell me the minute you feel it so I can pull over."

"That means a lot."

"I meant so you don't puke all over my car," she said. She rubbed the dashboard. "It's my baby." Elizabeth flashed me an amused grin to indicate she was joking.

My breath hitched in my throat when we turned the corner onto Harry's street.

"I'm glad he's here," Elizabeth said softly, referring to his parked, and very clean, car.

I didn't wait for her to say anything else as I slowly got out of the car and began to nervously walk towards the house. To say that I was scared would be a complete understatement. What made it that much worse, was that it would all come down to this.

After the picture incident had happened that night at Ryan's, never did I think that *I* would be the one at Harry's front door to ask for his forgiveness. The thought of how stupid I'd been angered me once more. But now was not the time to be so hard on myself, though I completely deserved it; right now, all I could do was hope and pray Harry would forgive me for being so unfair to him.

My hand shook as I raised my fist towards the door. I held it up for a solid few seconds until I got a grip, swallowed my pride, and knocked.

My heart was racing as I waited for the door to swing open. I stopped breathing when I heard the knob wriggle from the other side.

However, when the door finally opened, I was welcomed by a surprised and completely confused Amelia standing before me.

"Carter," she said, her voice slightly high-pitched. From the

KARLA DE LA ROSA

surprise in her tone, I was almost certain she already knew Harry and I hadn't been on the best of terms throughout the past week. "This is...*quite* the surprise. What are you doing here?"

"Hi, um—" I croaked. I cleared my throat. Compared to how I felt about seeing Harry, I wasn't even jittery at the sight of her anymore. "I'm so sorry to show up uninvited and all. But I just came here because..."

I felt my emotions kick in. The feeling of being both anxious and overwhelmed caused my lip to quiver.

Amelia looked me over, completely puzzled. I couldn't blame her. I would probably feel just as confused to see the girl my son had dated at my doorstep after being told who-knows-what.

I sucked it up and forced myself not to cry. I couldn't break down, especially not in front of Harry's mother. She would either pity me or kick me out, and I didn't know which one I would prefer in that moment.

"I came here because..." *I made a mistake. I'm an idiot. I blamed your son for something he didn't do.* "Because I need to see Harry, please."

Okay, that works, too.

"Oh." Amelia looked away. She finally glanced back at me with a small smile and stepped to the side. "He's upstairs in his room. If you want to...?"

I nodded, mumbling a thank you to her as I made my way inside and towards the staircase.

"Carter?"

I looked back to her.

"Please don't hurt him, if that's what you're here to do. He's tortured himself enough this past week. I've never seen him that way, and I don't ever want to see it again."

She looked completely sorrowful for her son. And I took the full blame for it.

"The last thing I want to do is hurt him any longer," I said, my voice merely above a whisper. "I promise."

And with that, I made my way up the steps slowly. The stairs seemed to stretch farther up ahead of me with every step I took, and my heart stopped when I made it up the final step and saw Harry's bedroom door closed just a few feet ahead of me.

I sucked in a breath, wanting to burst with every emotion I was feeling—happy, sad, scared, angry...but I composed myself and knocked lightly on his door three times. Nothing. Twice more, and still nothing. I leaned in closer, hearing muffled sounds. As I pressed my ear against the door, I could hear a deep hum.

Harry; it had to be Harry. He was humming along to a familiar song. I guessed he had his earbuds in the more I listened, hence why he probably hadn't heard me knocking. My fingers, frail from anticipation, grasped the cold knob and turned it slowly. I mentally thanked God he hadn't thought to lock the door. I cracked it and peered my head in to see him.

My breath caught, causing a small hiccup to erupt from my throat at the sight. Harry stood in front of me, back facing me as he rummaged through his dresser wearing only a set of boxers. His hair was drenched, hanging and flopping around as little droplets flung all over the carpet beneath his feet.

A song by My Chemical Romance was audible from his earbuds, sounding tinny and hollow. I felt like an idiot, completely dumbfounded, standing in the doorframe and watching as he looked for clothes while half-naked. I was being a total creep.

Does he even want me here? Would he even want to see me? What if he turns around and sees me and asks me to leave? What if he's gotten over me because I've been avoiding him? I wouldn't blame him for kicking me out, if that was the case.

No, no way. I can't think so negatively. I'm sure he wants to talk to me about this just as much as I do. But I just can't stand here and gawk at him until he realizes I'm here.

I didn't know whether I should just stay outside until he came out and saw me or maybe just knock louder until he let me in. He'd think I'd just barged in if I waited any longer.

And as if on cue, before my body could catch up with my mind, I was a stumbling mess when he turned to face me, shirt in hand. Our eyes met and his expression changed from one of utter confusion to complete astonishment. "Carter," he said breathlessly.

"Hi," I croaked. I was at a loss for words.

Harry's face looked frail. His eyes were a little droopy and not as bright as usual.

"This can't be real," he whimpered softly, as if talking to himself. He was looking me up and down, blinking multiple times, and nearly stumbled as he took a step back. I matched him by taking a step forward.

"Harry, say something," I requested, my heart racing. His silence only fueled my anxiety.

Before I could take another step forward, Harry moved first, his hands cupping my cheeks as he pushed me back against the door and wasted no time pressing his lips to mine. I had grown all too familiar to his touch in the little time we'd been dating. His lips felt like home, and I'd only just realized how homesick I'd been.

My cheeks felt hot, the warmth of his touch radiating against my skin as it raised goosebumps on the back of my neck. His kiss was so needy, full of love and want. My face grew wet from the way his tears washed over my cheeks. And it didn't take much time for me to realize that I had started to cry, too, in the middle of our kiss.

Our lips parted briefly as I let out a shiver, causing Harry to pull away completely. I looked up at him through blurry eyes and saw him backing away slowly.

"I'm sorry," he said, wiping his eyes with the backs of his hands quickly. "I know you probably hate me. I didn't mean to kiss you. I mean I did, but it was a reflex, or a reaction, or—" Harry hiccupped, taking more steps back from me. "I'm sorry."

I sniffled and took a deep breath to keep from crying anymore, my back pressed firmly against the door. I wasn't as shocked as I thought I would be when he'd kissed me. I'd missed it just as much as he had.

"You have nothing to apologize for," I told him honestly. "I know."

Harry quirked an eyebrow, but I knew he knew what I was talking about. There was no way he couldn't.

"I know everything. I know it wasn't you who did...*that* to me at Ryan's. And I know Austin framed you."

He looked somewhat relieved, his eyes wide and face expressionless.

"I'm so sorry, Harry. I shouldn't have ignored you when you were telling me the truth. I should have listened to you the moment you said you didn't do it. I should have known you wouldn't do this to me. I'm such an idiot—"

"Carter," he whispered, approaching me once more. His hands cupped my cheeks again, and his thumbs wiped away the leftover tears smeared on my face. "I don't care. I don't. I really, *really* don't. All that shit with Austin and the party and the picture and you blaming me—just fuck it. I don't care."

"But you—"

"Listen." He leaned in closer, our noses brushing as he hushed me. "All I care about right now is having you here. With me. Knowing the truth. And I hope you can forgive me—"

"There's nothing to forgive," I said, and from the way his face changed to fear, I rephrased to what I'd really meant to say. "*I* should be the one asking for *your* forgiveness. You didn't do anything. I did. *I'm* the sorry one, Harry."

He held me, and I leaned into him. It felt like a dream.

"Carter," Harry breathed above me, and I looked up at him. His green eyes had gone brighter.

"Yes?" I whispered meekly.

"I—" His lip trembled. My heart wrenched, and I tried to hold myself together as I anticipated the words I knew he was dying to say, just as much as I was dying to hear them. "I just—I wanted to tell you..."

Why can't he just say it? Is it because he thinks I'm not ready to hear it? Does he think I still haven't fully "forgiven" him? I had desperately missed those glorious, heart-fulfilling three words for what felt like forever.

"I-I need to change into some clothes."

I swallowed the lump in my throat, feeling my chest grow hollow and my stomach turn queasy. I looked down again and nodded, trying to restrain from showing any sadness. But I just couldn't let it go. I didn't want to just keep quiet. I couldn't just bite my tongue or wait for him until he could say it. Not when I knew that he felt it. I felt it. I knew I would always feel it.

As he turned to find his clothes, my nimble fingers reached out to him and grabbed his hands, only to slip away from the grip since they were still kind of wet from his shower. He turned to me, confused, but I ignored his expression as I stepped towards him. I raised a hand to his jaw and roughly pulled him forward. I wrapped my arms around his neck, feeling him relax into the kiss. I felt his large hands grip the sides of my waist as he pushed me back, nearly stumbling, until my back hit the door once more. He easily lifted me up, my legs wrapped around his waist as his

KARLA DE LA ROSA

hands held me up by my legs.

Harry was the one to break the kiss, leaning his forehead against mine as he caught his breath and said, "Carter, what—?"

"I love you," I told him, right then. I couldn't hold it in; I needed him to hear me say it.

A huge smile took over his whole face. He pressed multiple kisses all over my cheeks, chin, and corners of my mouth, making me laugh as he did.

"Carter." He laughed as well, his hands releasing my legs so that my feet could touch the ground. He held my face once more. "Carter, I love you so much. You have no idea."

"I think I do."

"I missed you so much," he exclaimed between kisses.

"It's okay. I missed you, too." I smiled slightly. "I just still can't believe this is real... I also wanted to apologize for not texting you back, if you have texted or called or anything. I didn't block you, if that's what you thought. I would never have blocked you. I honestly thought you were avoiding speaking to me. It wasn't until Elizabeth told me that I had supposedly blocked you that I realized what had happened. I checked, and it was true. The night of the party, after I got home, my brother took my phone and blocked you *for* me. So, I apologize for that."

His expression immediately darkened at the mention of my brother.

"Look, I don't know about you, but I wanna keep this thing going. I still love you, Harry, and I know my brother isn't all that happy with you, thinking you did this to me, but I'm sure he can look past it." Harry's lips parted, but I finished what I was saying before he could speak. "And my parents—we can just tell them that we're gonna be together whether they like it or not. Who cares what they think of you or—or the thing with the rumor! It shouldn't matter."

"Carter, the rumor wasn't true—" Harry cut in, but I stopped him.

"And I know that, but they won't believe us unless we tell them—"

"But Carter, your brother—"

"*I know*, he clearly shouldn't have opened his mouth and told them about it. At the time he was just looking out for me, but they don't know the truth, and if we just—"

"*Carter*," Harry interrupted once again, his voice much sterner than the previous time as he shook my shoulders for my attention. "Listen to me, the rumor *isn't* true. And I know you know that, but what you don't know is that Stacy actually *did* cheat on Danny. But it wasn't with me."

What was he getting at? He'd made the false-rumor thing clear a good fifty times already. "Yeah, I know. I just *said* that I know. What's your—?"

"Carter, it was with your *brother*."

"What?"

My brother? Stacy slept with my brother? My brother slept with Stacy Kavanaugh? How is that possible? And more importantly, how does Harry know that?

Could it be true? I paced by the door of his bedroom as I thought about it all. I had just started actually being friends with Dylan again.

"Look," Harry said behind me, "I know you're probably confused and...thrown off by what I just said, but—*ugh*, shit." I turned to find him struggling to pull up his pants. "But you're gonna have to hear me out so I can explain to you how I know this."

I nodded as I took a seat at the edge of his bed. Harry finally buttoned his pants, but forgot his shirt on the ground. He took a seat beside me, one hand on my knee as he looked at me with a very serious stare.

"A few days back, maybe like two or three, I went to your house after running into Stacy at a park nearby." He hushed me once again when I tried to interject. "I didn't know she'd be there. I ran into her, and we started talking. Casual conversation, just bantering, or whatever. She started apologizing about everything that had happened with the whole cheating-rumor thing. I tried to get her to forget about it until she asked me to apologize to *Dylan* for her."

I raised a rather curious eyebrow at him, and he nodded as if understanding what I wanted to ask.

"I know, same. Anyway, when I asked her why, she confessed to having slept with Dylan, hence she *actually* cheated on Danny." Harry sighed, but I knew he wasn't done. "So that same afternoon,

I went to your house to try and get you to listen to me. Dylan was there, and he said you weren't home, which I didn't believe at first, but since you never came down and apparently didn't hear the commotion, I guess it was true. Anyway," he shook his head, almost losing his train of thought, "we got into a verbal argument that turned physical, but it wasn't too bad because eventually I was kicked out before it could turn into some sick bloodbath. I now know your brother is completely psychotic—no offense. I took off and—"

"That's what Dylan tried to tell me," I whispered in realization. *Oh, the irony*; the day I had chosen to leave my house, what do you know? Harry showed up. The entire situation could've been over with sooner.

"What do you mean?" Harry asked.

"I mean..." I paused for a moment, remembering Dylan standing in front of me, paler than a ghost. "That same day, when I came home, I think Dylan was trying to tell me something. Only he said he'd had some bad dream and just left to go to his room or something. His whole atmosphere was off, and I knew he was lying or hiding something. I guess *that's* what he was trying to me tell me. But why didn't he?" I asked the last part as if to myself.

"Why would he?" Harry asked casually, and I looked up at him, completely puzzled. "I mean, think about it, Carter; it makes sense. If he'd told you, don't you think it would've made things a little clearer between us? If he'd told you about it, he probably knew you'd hate him for it. Then you'd tell your parents and make

416

it easier for us to see each other, even be together, and you and I both know he doesn't want that."

"But why would he do that to you?" The answer must've been obvious based on the way Harry was looking at me.

"It was so people wouldn't give him shit for it. Carter, he put the blame on me so he'd have a clean slate."

"And he just sat back and watched." I huffed in disappointment towards my own brother.

"Yeah. Basically...I'm surprised at how well you're taking this."

"What do you mean?"

"In truth? I expected you to defend your brother and angrily throw my own lamp at me." He laughed, and I shook my head with a small but amused smile.

"Well, last time you told me to hear you out, I didn't, and it wasn't pretty," I responded.

"Let's put that behind us. Honestly, I'm just glad you know the truth now and you're here with me." He smiled sweetly, a sight that still made my heart swell.

"So while I was in mourning, and by mourning I mean missing you—"

"I get it, because same." Harry smiled, and I laughed at his choice of words.

"You've clearly been hanging out with Mitchell *way* too much," I joked. "Anyway, so this whole time you've actually been trying to get my attention, but I wasn't getting anything because you were blocked?"

"It's not only that you didn't get anything," Harry answered. "No offense, Carter, but you're stubborn as hell. That's the only thing you and Dylan have in common. I mean, he's awful, but you were *really* tough to get through to."

"*What?* What makes you say that?" I asked, but even I knew I was stubborn.

"Seriously?" he asked. "You didn't even listen to your own best friend."

I sighed in slight annoyance. "I know, I know. God, he must hate me."

"He doesn't exactly hate you; he's just waiting for you to come to your senses."

"Really?" I asked. That didn't sound like something Mitchell would say.

"Well," Harry started with a wince, "he didn't *exactly* say it like that. I just cleaned up the language a bit. But yeah, basically."

I sighed, deciding to change the topic. I promised myself I'd deal with it later—later being after I'd seen my brother. "So what now?"

"I mean, do you really want to try this again?"

"Of course. Do you?"

"Definitely. I just wanted to ask to make sure you really want it. This whole thing was like a living hell. It felt like an eternity without you," he said with terrified, wide eyes.

I placed my palm to his cheek with a pout. "There's nothing for us to go through. Our relationship was going perfectly until *that*

418

happened. And, mind you, it was all a setup." There was a silence between us, my hand moving higher and running through his soft hair. He sighed comfortably, continuing to let me play with his hair between my fingers.

"Let's make a promise to each other," I told him softly. His eyes filled with curiosity. "The next time we...fight, or something, let's promise we'll try to communicate like adults. I don't want to run away from my problems if it means losing you."

"Carter," Harry whispered softly. "How did I get so lucky with you, baby?"

My heart stuttered at the pet name I had so longed to hear. "I should be asking you that myself," I told him. He grinned as his cheeks turned crimson. The way he was looking at me made me want to melt.

I tore my eyes away from him, trying to stay serious, and looked towards his nightstand, still smiling—that is, until my eye caught sight of a small, half-crumpled pamphlet. The bold words on the front were large enough for me to read, diminishing all the happy thoughts in my head.

So I sighed, looking down at my feet again. Harry must have noticed my quick change of mood because he pulled my chin up with his thumb and forefinger, face full of concern.

"What's wrong?" he asked sadly.

"It's just..." I shrugged before fully answering, "Regardless of us getting back together, it'd be impossible for us to *stay* together."

"Why do you say that?"

"Because," I said, and nodded towards the pamphlet.

When Harry turned, he froze momentarily before turning back to me with a small, morose smile. "St. John's is, and should be, the least of our worries."

"How?"

I was a believer in love, whether I showed it or not. But my hopes in long-distance relationships were almost nonexistent. I always knew they were less likely to work out, and my attachment to Harry was a perfect example as to why one wouldn't work for us, either. How I'd lasted a week without seeing him, I didn't know; it'd felt like years. Not seeing him for months, then given only a few days to be with him, I would definitely lose it.

"Because," Harry said, snapping me out of my thoughts, "I'm not even going to that school anymore."

My jaw dropped immediately. *When did this happen? How?*

"Wha—why? I just—how? Did they change their minds?" I asked. This had been Harry's dream school and now, he wasn't going. And... And he wasn't even worried about it?

"No one changed their mind except me."

"What? Why? What happened?" I furrowed my brows, even more concerned. And suddenly, something hit me, and I mentally *prayed* I was wrong. "Oh god, Harry. Please, *please* don't tell me it was because of me. Oh god..." I gasped as I stood and began to pace in front of him. "Do your parents know you're not going?"

"Yeah, I told them the exact day—"

"*Oh god!*" I whined. "Your parents must hate me. They probably think I'm the reason you chose to stay. I just—"

"*Carter*, it wasn't because of you," Harry said.

I shook my head and took a seat back on his bed before asking, "So what really made you change your mind, then?"

Harry simply shrugged. "I never really wanted to go. It was all my parents. They screwed the idea of me attending an Ivy League school so deep into my head, I believed that I was destined to go there. But I wasn't. I didn't want to."

"When did this happen?"

"Um..." He hummed in thought before answering, "I think Wednesday."

"And your parents are okay with it?" I asked, probably knowing the answer to the question.

"I mean," Harry winced, "they were pretty pissed, but by the time I start at BC, I'm sure they'll get over it."

"You're going to BC?" I asked, shocked at his choice of school. "Like, here in Broward BC?"

"Mhm." Harry nodded proudly. "It's closer to home and closer to you. And the best part is, they offer the same majors I was going to take anyway. I think it's only fair I choose a liberal arts major just so I don't piss off my parents even more."

Before I could think of a response, my phone vibrated in my bag.

"It's Dylan," I muttered, checking it. "He said Mom wants me home for dinner." I felt sick and disgusted by my brother. I turned to Harry with a frown. "I really don't wanna face him. I don't even know how to feel, if I'm being entirely honest."

Harry pursed his lips for moment. It was quiet, and he looked deep in thought. He then looked at me, smiled cheerfully, stood up, and, rather suspiciously, said, "I'm going to put on a shirt and shoes."

"Why'd you just look at me like that?" I laughed nervously, watching as he silently slipped on some shoes and pulled on some old graphic T-shirt. "Harry?" I asked. He ignored me as he walked to his desk on the other side of his room.

I heard keys jingle behind me, and after a couple seconds, Harry suddenly came back and opened the door of his bedroom, looking at me quizzically. "Well?"

I looked at him, completely confused and unsure what he was expecting me to do.

"Well, come on, baby," he said with a sly smile, reaching his hand out for me. I anxiously took it. "We're going to be late for dinner."

FIFTY

"Harry..." I tugged back at his hand as he nearly dragged me down the hall and towards the stairs. "Harry, wait."

"Babe." He stopped and turned to look at me. "We may as well come out with our relationship. What have we got to lose? We know the truth, and we wanna make this work." Harry's voice was confident and clear as he spoke. He gently took my face in his hands. "Our secret relationship was bound to come to light. Maybe this isn't the way we had hoped, but we can take this opportunity to fight for what we want. Right?"

The way Harry looked at me with wide, hopeful eyes tugged at my heart. How could I say no? I would be a complete fool to say no. So, I nodded, my head still being held in the warmth of his large hands. He smiled widely and gave me multiple pecks on and around my mouth.

"So, let's go," he said, and he yanked on my wrist to pull me towards and down the stairs.

"Harry?" We stopped at the front door and turned to see his mother with a confused look on her face. "Uh... Where are you two off to?"

The way she said *two* made it clear she hadn't expected us to be together after nearly a week of pure hell and only fifteen minutes of being upstairs and talking it out.

I looked at Harry who had a blank look on his face before he said, in complete seriousness, "We're going to get married in Vegas, Mom. You want to come?"

Her eyes widened as well as mine, and I had to force myself not to swat at his chest as a reaction, especially because his mom was right in front of me.

"Obviously, I'm kidding." Harry laughed, but the room was still awkwardly silent. "We're going to Carter's really quick. We, uh... have some things to settle."

And just as Harry almost pulled me out the door, his mother's voice stopped us again. "Settle what kinds of things?"

Harry sighed, not turning to her yet, with a painful expression that read, *God, how am I gonna break this down to her?* Clearly, he hadn't told her about our relationship being kept a secret. And in truth, I wouldn't have wanted her to know, either.

"Don't worry about it, Mom. I'll tell you later, I promise," he said with a small smile before heading out the door with me right behind him.

We got to my place a little faster than I had hoped. My insides were vanishing, like my body had gone completely. I was extremely terrified for what was to come.

My heart leapt in my chest when Harry opened the door for me; I hadn't realized he had already climbed out the car. He reached his hand out for me, and when I placed my palm in his, I felt like a spark had gone off—like I'd been brought to life again just by the touch of his skin against mine.

"You ready?" he asked softly before releasing my hand and closing the passenger door behind me.

I nodded meekly, crossing my arms and biting my lip to suppress the anxiety that was coursing through my entire body all over again. We walked up to the house together.

When we got there, Harry looked at me expectantly, trying to smile at me. Clearly, he wasn't expecting me to open the door right away. The look on his face read how patient he was.

"I'm not rushing you, baby," he said quietly, locking our fingers together tightly. "You know that, right? Because I completely understand how much harder this must be on you."

"What if, even after we tell them the truth, they still don't let us be together?" I asked nervously, my heart crumbling at the thought of no longer being with Harry.

"Together or not, Carter, that's not going to stop me from loving you," he said. He cupped his free hand against my cheek and leaned in slowly to press a soft, chaste kiss to my lips. He pulled away and looked at me with a smile, then nodded towards the door and said, "Whenever you're ready."

"I am," I said as I struggled to pull my keys out of my pocket. When I got the door open, I could hear my parents chattering from the kitchen.

"Let me do the talking," I whispered to him as we edged closer.

I hid our intertwined hands as we turned the corner of the room. My dad was at the dinner table, reading off his tablet, and my mom was prepping some plates.

My dad glanced up at us briefly before looking back down at his tablet. It took him less than two seconds to look back up, eyes switching from Harry to me, back and forth.

"Honey, do you want the mashed potatoes on the side or—?" my mother asked, looking towards my dad. She followed his gaze until she spotted us in the entryway, and her eyes widened for a moment in surprise.

"Harry," she said, a slight edge to her voice as she put down everything she'd been holding. She wiped her hands on her jeans and walked towards us with arms crossed. "What a pleasant surprise. What are you doing here with...? Why...? Are you—are you looking for Dylan? Because he's upstairs and—" she stammered uncomfortably. "And he didn't tell us you'd be joining us for dinner. Quite frankly, I didn't know you boys were friends again."

"Mom," I breathed out nervously. Her attention turned towards me, and I tore my eyes away from her expectant stare to look towards my father. "Dad?"

My dad slowly rose from his chair and walked towards us. He

426

stood right next to my mother with a matching look of discomfort.

"Harry and I are... We're together." Immediately, I pulled our locked fingers forward, making the statement somewhat clearer.

My mother let out a small gasp while my dad stared down at our hands, his calm complexion slowly growing cold.

"Harry and I have been dating for a while now, actually."

Harry remained still, his thumb drawing circles over my shaky hand to try and keep me calm.

"You have been dating this boy behind our backs?" my mom asked.

"For how long?" My dad looked at me with wild eyes, and it was clear he was already infuriated.

I bit my lip to suppress any potential outbursts. "For a little over a month—"

"A month!?" my parents yelled in unison. It was silent for a moment or two, my parents noticeably ready to blow.

My mom looked at Harry. "Harry, I think you should go—"

"What? No, he shouldn't have to go," I retorted, stepping in front of Harry. My parents let out an exasperated sigh. "You guys don't know him. You don't like him for the wrong reasons—"

"Carter, please," my mother begged. "I don't feel comfortable talking about this right now. Let's do this in private."

"For what? So you guys can try and convince me that he's bad for me? He's done nothing wrong," I said as my parents shared a look.

"Carter, please. Try to understand that we are only trying to protect you—"

"Protect me from what? You're only basing everything off of some rumor that's not even true!"

My mom inhaled deeply. "I understand people have to learn lessons on their own, but Carter, I draw the line here. I'm not letting him ruin you. It's *not* happening."

Harry tensed up, and I could hear him suck in a breath of his own. I was outraged. The fact that they would insult him right in front of his face as if he weren't even here, saying that he would *ruin* me?

"I'm so disappointed in you," my dad said. I only grew more agitated. The worst words a parent could say to their kid.

"I'm disappointed in *you*," I snapped back. "You don't even know him. That's not who he is. I actually took the time to get to know him. Everything you know about him is false. He's innocent—in fact, he's more innocent than your own son!" I finally yelled, my hand tightening around Harry's as he quietly listened to the heated argument.

My father inhaled and exhaled sharply, almost whistling through his nose. Mom asked, "What are you talking about—?"

"Dylan is the one to blame here. He framed Harry; he did *all* of this. If it hadn't been for him, you guys might actually *like* Harry."

"Carter, what on Earth are you—?"

"Hey, guys," we heard a loud voice say from behind us, and we all turned to find Dylan descending the stairs with his phone in hand and his headphones on. "When is dinner ready? I'm—"

The moment Dylan looked up, he stopped mid-sentence at the sight of me, Harry, and my parents all together. Immediately his entire demeanor changed, and he took long, quick strides towards Harry.

"What the *hell* is he doing here!?" he shouted.

"Don't!" I screamed at him, shoving him back harshly. "Don't you dare, Dylan!"

"The hell are you talking about, Carter?"

"Don't you dare try to play the victim; I know everything! You sick, twisted, lying bastard!" I shoved him again.

Just as I raised my hand up towards Dylan, Harry grabbed both of my arms and pulled me back and away from my brother. My parents stood back in horror, trying to understand what was happening.

"Tell them!" I screamed at him. "Dylan, tell them what you did! There's no point in lying, tell them!"

"Dylan, what's going on? What is she talking about?" our mother asked, voice filled with concern.

"Dylan, tell them!" I glared. "Tell them Harry's innocent. Tell them you accused your so-called *best* friend of doing something he didn't do. Tell them how you ruined his life with your lie—"

"All right! Cut it out, Carter, I'll tell them!" Dylan roared. He looked towards our parents in both shame and anger. "Mom, Dad... I... *I* was the one who hooked up with Stacy Kavanaugh... And then I blamed it on Harry. I didn't want to suffer the consequences, but I also didn't mean to blame Harry—"

"Then why did you?" Harry asked, his grip on my arms slowly releasing.

"Look, at the time, people knew I was close to Stacy, in a way. So when they found out she had slept with some sophomore, I was immediately the first one people decided to go after. Danny confronted me, and so I panicked and blamed you," Dylan confessed, my parents' expression unreadable. "I get blaming you was a mistake, but eventually you took it as an excuse to sleep around, so this doesn't clean up your rep as much as you'd like to think, Harry—"

"Dylan, are you serious? Yeah, I did things I'm not proud of, but I didn't ask for any of it. Everything I went through was because of you. This was *your* doing," Harry said, his voice making it clear that he was hurt. "Despite what had happened, it never meant that I didn't want something serious. I dealt the hand that was given to me, I suffered the consequences, and you didn't do a damn thing."

My parents stood back, watching as the truth unfolded before them, and I still wasn't sure how to feel about it all. I could only hope there would be a positive outcome to this. But from the looks of it, I doubted it.

"You know what's funny, though?" Harry asked rhetorically. "I can't decide if I'm angry because you blamed me, then sat back and watched me take all the beatings and insults that were meant for *you*. Or that I actually thought you were my best friend."

My brother looked away from Harry, clearly guilty of everything he'd done, but refusing to show it.

"Dylan," our mother whispered in disappointment, a hand on her chest. But he still refused to look at any of us.

"Mr. and Mrs. Matthews?" Harry suddenly turned to my parents, who looked a little embarrassed. "I know you both think poorly of me. But I hope now that the truth has come to light, you'll see that I'm not a bad person. And I can only hope that you'll believe me when I say—" Harry paused and turned back to me, then reached for my hand and pulled me next to him before finishing his sentence— "I care about Carter. I... I have deep feelings for her. I'd *never* do anything to hurt her."

I smiled softly as I squeezed Harry's hand, then added, "Mom, Dad... He makes me happy. I just want you guys to get to know the person he really is."

My parents sighed, glancing at each other, then gave us a small smile. "Look," my mom said, "I'm not saying we don't approve of you two—"

"Evelyn—" my dad tried to cut her off, but she hushed him before he could speak.

"I'm not finished," she stated before continuing. "But this is a lot to process, and...well, Harry, we don't know you that well. Despite having you in our house for the past three years."

Harry looked down at his feet sadly. "I understand that, Mrs. Matthews. I—"

"So how about we start over?" my mother said, shocking all of us.

"Wait, what?" I asked, unsure if I'd heard correctly.

"*What?*" Dylan echoed. "Mom, you can't be serious."

"Of course I am," she replied, shooting a glare at him before looking back at us. "Now, look you two, before you get all *excited* about this, there are still some ground rules."

"For instance," my dad began on her behalf, "I'm sure Evelyn and I would like it if we got to know you better, Harry. I mean, I know I would. Since we clearly got misinformation from Dylan."

Harry smiled. "I'd really like that, Mr. Matthews."

"Wait, so that's it?" Dylan took another step forward, his expression angry and bewildered. "You're just going to let them see each other? That was way too easy. This is a joke, right? That's all you guys are going to do?"

In the midst of a short, awkward silence, my parents glanced at each other before my mom spoke up, "No, that's not it. Dylan... you're grounded."

My brother's jaw dropped. "Are you serious!? Why am *I* the one getting in trouble? Carter's the one who lied and snuck around with Harry behind our backs. Why is *she* getting the easy way out?"

"Carter will be grounded also," my mother declared, prompting Dylan to smirk, but it wasn't until my mother finished what she was saying that his deviant smile quickly fell. "But you're grounded for a month. We'll figure out what privileges we'll be taking away from you later—"

"*What?*"

"Dylan, you put the blame on someone for something he didn't do and lied about it for two years." Our mother couldn't look more disappointed.

"You're lucky your mother isn't grounding you for that long," my dad commented.

"Don't tempt me. I have half a mind." She scowled at Dylan.

Dylan huffed, turned on his heel, and headed off to his room after sending us both a harsh glare.

"I'm sorry about that, Harry," my mother said sincerely. "For everything. I really wish things would have been different for us. I look forward to starting over with you."

"Dinner will be ready soon," my dad said. "Harry, would you like to stay?"

"Of course I'll stay. I'm just going to give my parents a call to let them know."

My mother smiled and nodded, and Harry stepped out of the room to call his parents. My mom turned to me to say, "Sweetie, go get your brother."

"But he's still mad."

"The quicker he can accept this, as well as his consequences, the easier it will be for everyone."

"But what if he ignores me?"

"If he doesn't open the door, I'll go up and get him myself," my dad said. "But right now, just go."

I jogged up the stairs, then knocked on Dylan's door, hoping for a response that didn't end up with us screaming at one another.

"Dylan?"

"Go away," he shouted from the other side of the door, but I ignored him as I knocked harder. The door swung open a few moments later. "I don't know what you're doing here, but whatever it is you wanna say, I don't care. Go. Away." Before Dylan could slam the door in my face, I put my hand out to stop it. "Seriously, Carter? What part of 'Go away' is difficult for you to understand?"

"I don't want drama with you."

"Neither do I, but you're the one who chose to go off and date my best friend behind my back."

"Dylan, we didn't date to piss you off. We have genuine feelings for one another; I really like him, and I know he likes me, too."

"I just didn't want him to hurt you," Dylan mumbled. He made his way over to his bed and sat at the edge. I followed behind and sat on his gaming chair. "You're my little sister, Carter. And he's my best friend. I know him too well. And even though I pinned what I did on him, that doesn't change the fact that he took advantage of it by going around with plenty of girls. Knowing that about him and then hearing he's been sneaking around with my sister? How do you think that makes me feel?"

"I understand that. But you also knew the guy he was before that. He's still there. He was there the whole time. You were just too focused on that one bad part of him that didn't even last long. But he's good to me. He always has been."

"That doesn't excuse what he did," Dylan reminded me.

"I'm not excusing it. That one year he wasn't himself was because that rumor kind of ruined his life."

Dylan rolled his eyes before replying, "Did you come here to hash shit out or lecture me?"

"I came here to assure you that I'm okay, and me and Harry want to be together. We just want you to be okay, too."

Dylan didn't say anything. He just sat there silently for a moment, contemplating his next words, and he let out an exasperated huff. "I'm not gonna be okay. At least not for a while. But as long as he doesn't hurt you, I think I should be fine."

I reached forward for a hug before he stopped me.

"Hell no." He shook his head. "I'm still upset that you guys did this behind my back."

I rolled my eyes. "It's not like we had a choice. But, I also wanted to say thank you for being there for me when I needed you."

He nodded, a little stiffly, but there was a softness in his eyes.

I gave him a reassuring smile. "Now let's go down before Mom or Dad have to come up and drag us down for dinner."

FIFTY-ONE

[HARRY]

Carter and Dylan took so long to come down that I was surprised to see them descend the stairs unbloodied and not kicking and screaming.

Dinner went by smoothly. Or so I thought. Their parents asked questions about my life, my relationships with my parents and my academics, the college I planned to get into. Typical get-to-know-you questions. We talked about me applying to the community college nearby. I didn't mention the whole St. John's thing because I didn't feel like explaining the situation. Still, they seemed rather pleased to know I would even be attending a college and already had most of my future planned out. *Most.* Not all.

However, despite how well *I* thought it was going, it was also hard to have a decent conversation when, from the corner of my eye, I could easily see Dylan's harsh glare. It was like his eyes were throwing fire-ignited daggers at me. It was difficult to ignore.

But, having Carter's hand held in mine under the table kind of made it all better.

Eventually, dinner was over, and Carter went to help her mom with the dishes. Dylan stomped off upstairs, and after a quick nod from Carter's dad, I followed him.

He huffed on the upstairs landing, hearing me behind him. "What do you want?"

"Dylan, can we talk?"

"About? What, have you decided to date my mom, too?" he growled. I followed him into his bedroom, where he went over to his Xbox and turned it on.

"*Dude,*" I whined, my agitation slowly growing. "I don't get it. Why? Just *why* do you hate me so much? Why is me dating your sister such an issue for you?"

He paused his game and turned to me with an icy glare. "Look, you're fucking lucky I didn't tell them about that stunt you pulled on her," he spat.

"Wha—?" I said, completely lost. "What are you—?"

"Don't play innocent." He pointed an accusing finger at me. "You might have my family fooled, especially my stupid sister, but I swear to god, Harry—"

"Dylan, what are you talking about? What stunt?"

"Are you really going to pretend like it never happened? You taking advantage of my sister and then throwing her under the bus like that at Ryan's? Seriously?"

"Whoa, whoa, whoa." I was suddenly hit with realization. "Wait, you can't possibly still think that was me, right? Dylan, I didn't—"

"Yeah, yeah, yeah, Harry," he mocked, "I fucking get it. You *didn't* do it. I don't know how you got my sister to believe you, but I'm not as gullible as her—"

"Dylan, I really didn't do it," I said louder, suddenly feeling my blood pressure rise.

"Oh, yeah? Then who did—?"

"Austin!"

"Austin? Austin Galloway? The guy who graduated last year?" he asked dubiously, raising a brow as if he refused to believe such a thing. "Why would Austin Galloway expose my sister?"

"Because he—" I stopped immediately, almost spilling Carter's secret. Just weeks ago she'd made me swear not to tell Dylan that they'd once dated, and even now, I was sure she was still depending on me not to tell him.

"AJ told me," I told him honestly. "The night of the party, right after you left to go look for Carter, AJ confessed to me."

Dylan sat back in his chair with his arms crossed and a deep scowl, listening intently. And so, as he sat quietly, I told him everything, leaving out the part about Carter once dating Austin. I knew Dylan would ask why Austin would do such a thing, so I told him it was to expose our relationship, which was also true.

"Why would—?"

"Don't ask me why, I really don't know. Austin's an asshole; that's my only answer." I huffed. "I mean, come on. It's Galloway. He graduated and still goes to high school parties and stuff. It shouldn't be that surprising that he decided to start drama."

Dylan rolled his eyes again but remained silent.

"So, really, your reason to hate me, though it's understandable... It's not actually true," I finished, leaving an expressionless Dylan sitting completely still in his desk chair.

It was quiet for a while, and my anxiety started skyrocketing as Dylan just stared at me.

"Look, you're not entirely forgiven. I'm just glad you weren't behind it."

"Seriously? And how come you're not going after Austin now after what he did to your sister, yet when you thought *I* did it, you wanted to murder me right then and there?"

Dylan sat back again. "Don't get me wrong, I wanna fucking kill him. However, I only attacked you right then because first, for one obvious reason, you were right there. And second...well, because, you know, you were my best friend. I didn't expect my best friend to do that to my little sister, even though you didn't really do it... if that even makes sense. I'm just mad that you both went behind my back about it," Dylan said, picking on a loose thread hanging off the hem of his shirt. "But anyway, she's my little sister, you know? I got defensive. I know Carter and I fight more than half the time you're here, and even more when you're not, but I'm her big brother. And... You know, I—" Dylan lowered his head, looking away from me before mumbling, "*I love her.*"

"I'm sorry, what?" I asked, a grin spreading across my lips as I tried to maintain a serious face. "Did you just say you love your sister—?"

"Harry, I swear to god, if you tell her I said that, I'll deny it—"

"I won't," I told him, biting back my grin.

Dylan's face suddenly went sour, as though he'd bitten into something awful. "Ugh, god. You guys are *dating* now." He started to pretend to gag at the thought of us together. "Don't invite me to the wedding, I beg of you."

"Calm down." I chuckled. "We've only been dating for like a month. Which reminds me, I have to get her flowers or something."

I looked at Dylan, who was shaking his head at me in disapproval. "You're such a girl, man." I flipped him off and opened the door to his bedroom.

"Wait, Harry?"

"Yeah?"

Dylan looked at me, embarrassed, and said, "Are we good now?"

I smiled gratefully as I nodded. "We're good."

"Harry, you don't have to stress yourself out about this." Carter laughed as she ran her fingers through my hair.

"I'm not stressing, I just want to do something special for you,"

I said, pressing a kiss to her forehead.

"Well, even though you don't have to, I'm really grateful for it. You really are the sweetest, you know that?" she told me, snuggling closer onto my side and hugging my waist. We were sat in her backyard, sharing one of those lounging lawn chairs, trying to avoid talking about Carter finally going back to school tomorrow.

"What do you want to do tomorrow, baby? We can do anything you want right after—you know."

"Up to you, honestly. We can eat loads of junk food and watch loads of movies. That would make the best anniversary for me."

"You sure? You know we can go out and actually do something, right?" I asked, and Carter nodded with a lazy smile. "All right. If that's what you really want. But if you change your mind, say the word, and we'll go wherever you want."

"Well..." Carter pondered for a moment. "Joe's Pizza & Pasta sounds good. You know where that is, right?"

"Sure. Consider it done."

Carter held onto me tighter before she went quiet. Then suddenly she whined, "*Ugh*, I don't want to go to school tomorrow."

"I know, baby." I sighed into her hair, hoping that leaving multiple pecks on her head would help her ease up. I couldn't imagine how she was feeling. But the most I felt I could do was be there for her.

"I was humiliated. I've been absent for most of the week, and I highly doubt they've forgotten about it. I really don't want to go, Harry, I'm scared—"

"Hey, don't worry about them. Just keep your head up and don't give them the time of day."

"It's easier said than done. What happens when—?"

"Baby, relax. They're nothing but stupid people who feed off of other people's lives. If they're going to waste their time gawking at you, let them. Just pay them no mind."

"And if they say something to me?"

"Well, that's when I'll step in and say something back." I shrugged and smiled reassuringly at her. She tried to smile but instead buried her face into my chest.

High school can be a flat-out cruel place, but I'd be damned if anyone would dare to try and harass Carter for a simple mistake that was never even meant for anyone's eyes but mine.

"Look, I'll be there for you, okay?" I reassured her, tilting her chin to look up at me. "I'm gonna go. But I'll see you tomorrow. I'll pick you up." I smiled and watched her force one in return; her eyes were screaming in fear.

"Great."

I bent down and kissed her once more before saying, "I love you." I left through the backyard gate after that.

FIFTY-TWO

[CARTER]

"You know, I could have easily walked to school," I grumbled as I got into Harry's car. I clutched my queasy stomach as he drove us both to school.

"Carter, you know full well you'd have to wake up at least twice as early to get ready and walk half an hour to school." He glanced at me with a smirk as he thankfully cruised at a slow pace.

"I could have woken up early," I retorted with a scowl, feeling combative.

"Yeah, okay," he scoffed. "So, you're telling me you would've woken up at six *every* morning to walk to school at seven *every* day?"

"I...I could have tried," I mumbled, crossing my arms and staring out the window in agony as we crept closer to school.

Harry rolled his eyes, drumming his fingers along with the

faint song playing from the radio. Whatever song was playing, Harry was completely offbeat with his finger-drumming. Perhaps he was just as nervous as I was?

When we parked, I immediately felt my chest tighten. I didn't want to even think about how everyone would view me. And when they saw me with Harry? *She's so dumb to take him back after what he's done to her,* they'd say. And as much as I didn't want to care about what people thought about me, I wasn't ready to hear all the side comments and whispers from those who knew nothing yet had seen a little too much of me.

No one had really known who I was. I mean, people knew of me, but it was as Dylan's little sister, or that girl Mitchell dragged to parties. And now, those who'd seen the picture and the aftermath of it would know exactly who I was.

Harry grabbed my hand as we walked in through the back gates of the school, and one at a time, a few heads turned, noticing us with wide eyes.

Harry's thumb traced circles on my hand as we walked. Though he looked completely chill, I could read the subtle tension on his face. And in a way, it calmed me down a little. Knowing Harry was nervous, though he probably wouldn't admit it, helped ease my tension. My eyes glued to my feet as we continued walking. Then, I could feel the pressure increase, and the second I looked up, my heart dropped immediately.

"Well, what a massive surprise." Mitchell's voice sounded venomous. "Honestly, I would've thought you'd moved across the country to avoid ever coming back."

"Nice to see you, too," I mumbled.

"Easy there, Mitch." Harry patted Mitchell's shoulder before he could make another snide comment. "It was all a massive misunderstanding. She knows the truth now so there shouldn't be any bad blood between you two anymore." Harry turned towards me. "Anyway... Carter? Anything you wanna say?"

I glanced from Harry to Mitchell, who had that impatient, snarky look on his face.

"I'm sorry I didn't listen to you, Mitch. You were right."

"I was a little surprised when you blocked me but, hey. It's whatever. You were bound to realize I was right, anyway."

As Mitchell turned to walk away from us, Harry cleared his throat to catch his attention and turn him back. Harry nodded his head towards me.

"What?"

"Oh, come on." Harry narrowed his eyes. "You know you wanna hug her. You've talked about her nonstop this whole—"

"Uh, no, sweetie. That was your obsessed ass, so don't even—"

"Just shut up and hug her!" he yelled, laughing at his reluctance.

Mitchell rolled his eyes, holding back a smile with his arms wide open for me.

I smiled in embarrassment as I shook my head before walking over and engulfing him in an embrace. "I missed you," I mumbled against him. He pulled away with a genuine smile.

"Well, who wouldn't?" And I laughed.

FIFTY-THREE

The week was only half-done, and I already wanted to just sleep in for the rest of the year. I'd only missed about a week of school yet I felt like my summer had been cut short.

Harry and I didn't go to Joe's after school. Instead, we wound up doing exactly what I'd first suggested at his house. We talked endlessly, eating loads of junk food and watching '80s movies that the Sundance channel was playing nonstop.

"See, I wish I could wear outfits like that," I commented, continuing to stuff my face with sour Life Savers.

"I can see you wearing that type of stuff. The mom jeans, windbreakers, grandma sneakers, and big hair." Harry nodded. "Then again, you rock that big hair every morning until it goes flat again."

I shoved Harry as he laughed at his own joke.

"I'm serious. That style is so iconic. My parents were so lucky. I could never pull off anything like that." I watched the current movie in awe.

"I highly doubt that." He smiled. "You could look like Quasimodo and you'd probably still be gorgeous."

"*Probably?*" I raised a brow with a smirk.

"*Okay*," Harry stammered, "not probably. Definitely. You definitely would. Honestly."

"I see. Nice reference, by the way."

"It's true. I mean, Esmeralda fell in love with him despite his looks." He shrugged with a smug look, looking like a know-it-all.

"Well, I hate to burst your bubble, but...Esmeralda didn't fall in love with Quasimodo." I crossed my arms as Harry instantly frowned. "In fact, she didn't end up with anybody in the book. But in the movie, she ended up with Phoebus."

"Who?" he asked.

"Phoebus."

"Phoebe?"

"Phoebus."

"Phoebo?"

"*Harry.*"

"Yes, baby?" He smiled teasingly.

"*Ugh*," I groaned. "You're so annoying."

"Isn't that one of the reasons why you love me?"

"More like one of the reasons why I shouldn't," I said, smiling and laughing right after.

"That was cruel, Carter." He shook his head before laughing to himself as well.

Harry knew my humor well enough by then to know that I was joking. And he knew *me* well enough to know that I would never stop loving him.

EPILOGUE

One year later

[HARRY]

With every eager push and shove, I grew more desperate. I went up on my tiptoes to try and see, but only became more and more frustrated. Why was everyone here so damn tall?

"Excuse me." I huffed. I was done trying to be patient and letting others pass in front of me. The crowd was insane, and it was blazing hot outside the theater that had served as the graduation venue. I ripped off my jacket, my white silk shirt sticking to me.

I checked my phone to see if anyone had responded, but there was nothing. They were all too busy. And my phone was nearly dead from taking so many pictures and videos, not to mention how shitty the cell reception was here.

"Come on!" I yelled in frustration as I raised my phone higher for a better signal.

This was getting ridiculous. I knew there'd be a lot of people attending, but geez, did they all have to be in the same spot?

I turned around and bumped into someone, hearing an exclamation in a familiar voice.

"Ouch!"

I sighed in relief. "Elizabeth."

"Damn, Harry." She shook her head with a small smile. "At least say sorry."

"I apologize, Liz. I'm infuriated right now."

"I can imagine. I can't find either of my parents, my stepdad, or my own stepbrother."

I shook my head, annoyed. "This is ridiculous. Why can't people clear out already?"

"Because they're each taking a million pictures."

Finally, I spotted someone—Mitchell, somehow looking sweat-free and at ease in his long robes. I took Elizabeth's arm and began pushing and shoving through the crowd.

"What happened? Where are we going?" she asked, but I was too irritated to reply.

When she realized who we were battling towards, she shook me off and ran towards Mitchell. He stumbled as she practically tackled him, and AJ had to hop out of the way, laughing.

AJ had decided to come out about eight months into dating

Mitchell—I was smug that I'd been the second person he'd come out to. It had been a secret I'd had no idea he was struggling with, but I, Ryan, and everyone else had overwhelmed him with support and love. Even his parents, whom he'd most feared talking to, had been encouraging.

"Finally!" Mitchell exclaimed, removing his honor roll cords. "Jesus, that was hell."

"I can't find my parents or your dad. Have you seen them?" Elizabeth asked.

"If I had, then I'd be with them, Lizzie."

I didn't even pay attention to their banter as I continued looking around the place. People were finally starting to head to the parking lot, but the whole scenario felt like we were an ant colony under a magnifying glass. My anxiety was getting the best of me. Where the hell—?

"Harry?" Mitchell said, tapping my shoulder. "Are you all right?"

"No, I'm not. It's still so fucking crowded, even with the people leaving. I'm getting pissed," I told him, my heart beating like mad. *I don't get it. It wasn't like this last year.* "Mitch, have you seen—?"

"Harry!"

I spun around and saw the most beautiful girl running towards me with a smile so big it could make the whole world stop.

I opened my arms wide just before Carter crashed into me. Her arms wrapped around my neck as her lips pressed onto mine, giggling against my mouth.

"I'm so proud of you. You look gorgeous."

"Thank you, babe," she mumbled against my lips. When she pulled back, her smile made me melt. "I'm so glad you came."

"What?" I said with a grin. "Why wouldn't I come? It's your graduation, this is a big moment for you!"

Carter blushed like mad and reached up once again for another kiss I didn't mind having.

"Eww," said AJ, wrinkling his nose. I finally let her go, deciding that was enough PDA.

"Where's your family?" I asked Carter.

"They were right behind me, actually." We spotted them just a couple feet away from where we were, making their way towards us.

Once we were all together, and Mitchell and Elizabeth had tracked down their parents, we all decided to go out to eat.

The families rode separately to IHOP, knowing that most restaurants would be packed. Carter, Mitchell, and Elizabeth rode with me. It felt like old times as we laughed, joked, and teased one another.

At dinner, I was sat in-between Dylan and Carter. Carter was deep in conversation with Mitchell and Elizabeth, which left me to talk with Dylan.

"So, how's your summer?" Dylan asked, taking a sip of his lemonade.

"Pretty good," I answered, though it'd been way better than just "pretty good." Dylan and I had remained friends, but it had taken time for us to be neutral again. We weren't as close as before, but things were going pretty well. "My family and I had a lot of barbeques and stuff, a lot of beach days. It was great having Carter there for most of them. Just a regular summer, I guess. How about you, though? How have you been since...you know?"

"Since Lindsay?" he asked, and I only awkwardly nodded in response.

"Honestly..." Dylan sighed before giving me a smile, something I hadn't been expecting. "Pretty fucking great. I didn't realize just how much of a dead weight she was. She was great and everything at first, but after a while, it was like all the signs of how terrible she was were hitting me all at once."

"We'd been trying to tell you," I mumbled, holding my glass of water up against my lips before taking a sip.

"You know she actually admitted to kissing you that night at Melissa's party?" he stated, surprising me even more. But before I could ask how that had come about, he beat me to it by answering, "She was actually drunk when she told me. We were kind of fighting, and she did it to get under my skin. That's actually why we broke up."

"Seriously? Ah, dude. I mean, I wanted to ask what had happened, but we weren't talking that much yet," I told him, which was true. "I'm sorry."

"Are you, though?"

I snorted. "Well, no. I hated her. We all did; we just didn't have the heart to tell you. We thought she made you happy."

"Are you kidding?" Dylan said, giving me a look of

embarrassment. "She made my life hell." I laughed in response, Dylan breaking out into a grin as he shook his head to himself. "I actually quit drinking and smoking, too."

"Oh, yeah. Carter told me, dude. That's great. I heard you've been doing pretty well. You started working at a music production place, yeah?" He just nodded, grinning. "Congrats, Dylan. I'm proud of you."

I could have sworn he almost blushed. "Thanks, but I don't want to make it into a big thing."

"Why not? This is huge!"

"Well, what about you?" he asked, turning it around on me. "What are you doing?"

"I'm studying literature and psychology over at Broward College—a double major as promised, per my parents. I'm also working as a mechanic, which I'm sure Carter already told you. Nothing big. But, seriously, man, why aren't you excited?"

"I don't know." He shrugged, his expression shifting to worry. "I guess I don't want to jinx it, you know? I've got a lot of good things going right now. Last thing I need is me blowing my chances and ruining it for myself."

"Well, just know that we're all proud of you, Dyl," I reassured him, earning a smile in return.

"So, anyway, you and Carter spent most of the summer with your family," Dylan said, clearly trying to change the subject. "Is that all?"

"Yeah, pretty much. Carter finally met my sister, actually."

"Really?" Dylan asked, now very interested. "How *is* Emma, anyway?"

"Mm-mm." I shook my head at Dylan who had that smug look on his face that I knew all too well. "Don't even think about it."

Eventually we went back to eating, listening to the parents quiz each other's children about all the big life choices they'd have to make.

"You know," Elizabeth said, the first victim, "when I was a little girl, I wanted to be like, a ballerina or something. But now, I think I want to tackle motivational speaking and possibly nursing, given my *acceptance at Nova*." The table erupted with cheers and congratulations from all of us.

Then came Mitchell, dramatically standing up with his glass of water in hand. "Well, when I was little, I wanted to be famous. Don't get me wrong, I still do; the dream lives on. Except I'm going to start out small, obviously. I'll work my way up to entrepreneur status in no time while I make some side cash working at Publix, which, by the way, just hired me for the summer."

We congratulated Mitchell, as well.

Then it was Carter's turn. "Well, I hate to be a copycat, but, like most of my high school says, I'll just reword it a bit," she said, earning a laugh from most of us. "Anyway, so when I was a little girl, I couldn't wait to grow up and become a singer or an actress. But after middle school, I realized my off-key pipes weren't exactly helping that. I've always really loved reading, but not enough to be able to bear studying it for four years. Something told me that maybe those plans just weren't in the cards for me, so I decided to really find myself this past year. As cheesy as that sounds, I feel like my senior year helped me realize who and what I wanted to become. So I've come to the conclusion that I want to study psychology."

I knew her parents were happy that she was pursuing a major that would allow her to help others with their mental health, and they couldn't help but feel their medical careers had had some influence in that decision.

When dinner was over, I decided to take Carter on a one-on-one date. It was unplanned and last minute, but she deserved a good grad night. No one could possibly be as proud of her as I was.

Well, her parents were probably prouder, but I admired her and how strong she was. She was one of the three strongest, most important women I knew, right next to my mother and my sister.

When we got in the car, I had no idea what to do or where to take her. With one hand on the wheel and the other on her thigh, I looked over at her. She stared out the road with a small smile, her hand over mine as she sat back and hummed along to the music playing on the radio.

"Carter," I said, and she looked at me with those big blue eyes. "Where to?"

She smiled as bright as the sun, a smile that had come to be my sunrise and my sunset, and she said, "Anywhere, as long as I'm with you. I love you."

I pressed my lips to hers and replied, "And I love you."

THE END

ACKNOWLEDGEMENTS

Here we are, at the end of something that's only just beginning. I'm going to try to get through this without being a blubbering mess. I'm not much of an emotional person, but this experience has definitely made me shed a tear or two. More tears than I can admit when I'm alone, though.

I just want to start off by saying a massive thank you to Di Angelo Publications for this amazing opportunity of publishing my very own first novel. Thank you to Sequoia for finding me and offering me the biggest opportunity I only ever thought I'd see in my dreams. Thank you to Ashley, Stephanie, and of course Elizabeth, the awesome editors who were super helpful and made this experience easy and enjoyable for someone who was just starting out in all this. All three lovely ladies made sure to stay true to my vision and I couldn't be more thankful to work with such a wonderful team.

A huge thank you to Wattpad; my forever home. I have no idea where I'd be in life if I hadn't found the platform and poured my heart out into the stories that people seemed to enjoy reading and relating to. When I first started this book on Wattpad, it was a complete joke. I had only written it for fun. The dialogue was crap on purpose and there was no plot, whatsoever. I got very few notifications such as little reads and very few votes (like 3 or 4 per chapter) with my 27 followers. Then, seven months go by and I start getting a thousand notifications daily, my book hit a million views, I got ranked #1 in the fanfiction category, (This was a huge honor at the time), I started getting messages and multiple posts on my page. And all that came to mind when all this was happening was, *woah, I only blinked!* I never expected any of this, and to say I was thankful would be an understatement. It's unbelievable! Truly blows me away and I could never put into words how grateful I am.

I also wanted to say thank you to those who inspired me to write these awesome characters. Thank you to my dear friend Miguel who inspired Mitchell with his witty comebacks, fierce attitude, sharp tongue, confidence and unique persona. Thank you to Rosie, Sarah and Naomi and many other close friends of mine who, all combined, inspired Elizabeth's kindness, love, loyalty and her headstrong personality. I grew and learned a lot from these friendships that I just had to write about for you all. I fell in love with them and watched them grow the way I wrote them out to. Carter carried most of my personality and traits (not all) so I inspired myself to make her the way she is and how I wanted her to be. And then also a huge thank you to Harry Styles for being the dreamboat he is. I dedicated over a decade of my life to someone that kept me going and yet has no idea. I'm forever thankful for him.

The biggest thank you of all, though, goes to my readers. To those who stuck to this book and made it to the very end. To those who were here from the beginning (I could name quite a few!) and remained loyal and patient with me since the very start of this adventure. This book wouldn't be what it is today without you guys. I grew a bond and playful relationship with all of you. From the way you guys made me laugh, cry and smile with all of your comments and sweet messages that I receive to this day. There's no amount of thank you's in the world to let you guys know just how much this means to me.

Lastly, I want to thank myself for being my own supporter and pushing myself to continue to write a story I didn't have faith in at one point. Not many people in my personal life really knew about my life on Wattpad. In fact, I was a little embarrassed of the idea of people finding out that I wrote fanfiction about a celebrity that had no idea that I existed. But now with this opportunity I am forever grateful for, I couldn't care less.

So, with all that being said, that's the end of that. I can't believe how far we've come with this story. All I can say now is thank you, yet again. And that I love you all with every inch of my heart.

ABOUT THE AUTHOR

First time writer, Karla De La Rosa, residing in the suburbs of Northern Jersey, spends her days writing on Wattpad when not working her full-time retail job. Never really knowing what she wanted to do as a career in the future, she found her calling at just the age of 17 when a simple story she solemnly decided to write for fun slowly became a hit on the writing platform. Having been diagnosed with depression at a young age, Karla was able to heal and find comfort and stability by writing out parts of her life and pouring her heart out into her stories.